SIRENS UNBOUND

Book One of the Fifth Mage War

LAURA ENGELHARDT

ISBN: 9781071259191

Cover design by: Hampton Lamoureux of TS95 Studios
Editing by: Lottie Clemens and Floyd Largent
Print Layout by: Booknook.Biz

Special thanks to my beta readers, Jannie and Carol, and to the critters.org workshop.

Published in the United States of America
July 2019

Blest be the tie that binds
our souls in magical love;
the fellowship of kindred minds
is like to that above.

Together we face our foes,
united our burdens bear,
and often for each other know
a true and committed care.

When we are forced apart,
the inward pain resounds;
but we shall stay a-joined in heart,
and hope to be re-bound.

From terror, hate, and pain,
united we shall be saved;
and perfect love and friendship reign
safely bound in enclaves.

– Rite of Binding for Children 10th ed. (2002),
by Theodore Fawcett, p. 7.

In the wake of the Iron Age, Aphrodite created sirens for the primary purpose of preventing fae extinction. Sirens are self-replicating constructs who serve as a kind of magical battery: they harvest human fertility and desire, store that power internally, then transmit it to the fae. It is only through siren intervention that the fae are able to reproduce in our iron-poisoned world. Indeed, siren intervention is sometimes the only thing that will prevent a faerie from fading.

– Sirens: An Overview for the Newly-Transitioned, 3rd ed. (2015), *by Mira Bant de Atlantic, p. 4.*

Prologue
Thirty Years Before

Marisol's perennial lightness seemed somewhat forced when she pulled Cordelia aside as the group alighted on Yorkshire's drab shoreline. "Now Cordelia, this will be but a brief visit. Just remember: once you've attended the Aos Sí this time, no one will be able to gainsay you on the basis of immaturity. They'll be forced to acknowledge you as precocious, and within the next decade, you'll have a place beside me at Court. All you have to do is to get through the next few days."

Marisol's encouragement actually made Cordelia even more anxious. Her progenitor had known about the junior expedition for months, but had never mentioned the possibility that Cordelia might be included. Had she known, she would have accepted Marisol's offer to shepherd her through her first attempt at fertility transfer at one of the smaller fae preserves in the States. But Cordelia had been enjoying her freedom in Atlantis too much to risk encountering her mother in the U.S.

Her mother always said it was useless to look back, so Cordelia plastered on a bright smile and nodded. Marisol's eyes twinkled, and the faint lines of tension on her forehead smoothed out. She squeezed Cordelia's hand. "You'll be perfect!" Marisol promised.

Courtier Vincent led the dozen young sirens off the narrow sandy beach up the trail that led to the plateau marking the entrance to the North York Moors fae preserve. Sirens had a natural resistance to fae magicks, so whatever spells had been cast to encourage humans to keep their distance didn't hinder the group's progress.

Nevertheless as Cordelia crossed the grassy plain into the forest beyond, she felt a slight stickiness on her arms and face, almost as if she had walked through a cobweb. The others seemed to be feeling the same thing because they brushed at their faces and arms as well, though they didn't seem bothered by the sensation. Cordelia heard laughter, but when she turned, there was no one there. While the fae, and the seelie in particular, were known to enjoy games and mischief with humans, she wondered how much truth there was to the stories of the Aos Sí's dark humor.

All fae were dependent on sirens to combat their iron-sickness, but the Aos Sí especially. After the Third Mage War, almost two hundred thousand fae had been imprisoned in North Yorkshire. When the mage cabal abandoned England in the nineteenth century, they had called iron to the surface of the soil, ensuring the Aos Sí would remain confined by the constant drain on their strength. Now, this group of fae needed the sirens for their daily survival.

How the Aos Sí must hate us, Cordelia thought, and shivered. It was summer, so it wasn't cold, but somehow the dim light of the forest reminded Cordelia of the winter sun, bland and dull. You couldn't even see the sky beyond the thick canopy of foliage. At least the iron didn't sicken the trees.

"I think we will find a dryad for you, Cordelia," Marisol remarked from behind. She huffed a little as she tried to keep up with the faster pace Vincent had set. Cordelia slowed so she could walk next to Marisol. "Dryads are fairly gentle, and totally attached to their trees. They don't play like the seelie, but I'm not sure you're ready to play games with the fae just yet."

Marisol sounded anxious again. *A little late to be worrying now,* Cordelia thought. She consciously strove to recall the lessons from her mother's textbook: "The fae need sirens. No fae has ever hurt a siren." But her mother had also cautioned her that what the fae viewed as hurtful was quite different from what sirens considered hurtful. The fae were immortal, after all.

Cordelia was grateful that Marisol was at least considering what kind of fae should be her first. "A dryad, rather than one of the moss folk or a brownie?" she asked hesitantly.

"Yes, I think a dryad would be a good choice. They're sweet and somewhat single-minded. There's a rowan I like quite a lot. He's attached to Titania's tree, so is rather a special dryad, after all."

Cordelia's mother had always hated Marisol's fixation on status, but Cordelia was grateful for her attention to such details. Contrary to her mother's determined obliviousness, status mattered on Atlantis. And in the States, too. Everywhere, really.

"Of course, Marisol," Cordelia said. "Whatever you think best."

"Nanna, remember," Marisol corrected, squeezing Cordelia's arm gently. "I *am* your progenitor, after all."

"Nanna," Cordelia obediently replied, and Marisol smiled.

"I think you should go today. Get it over with, don't you think? Then you won't be fretting about it."

Cordelia's heart pounded, and she thought she'd rather watch a few of the more experienced sirens first. But she said nothing, not knowing how to admit to Marisol that she was scared.

"You know, I'll show you first. I'm full to the brim, and it does get rather uncomfortable feeling so stuffed. Of course, it's important when coming to the Moors that you're as full as possible. The Aos Sí need so much. It's impossible, really..." Marisol's cheer faded and her voice trailed off.

Perhaps the Reconcilers were right, Cordelia mused. This continued imprisonment of the Aos Sí wasn't good for the Atlantics either. All the sirens who cycled through the Moors seemed to return in a very bad mood. Even her progenitor's air of carefree *bonhomie* evaporated for a time after she returned from one of her trips to England.

Marisol had been asked to serve as a courtier because of her prodigious capacity for fertility transfer. It was said she could hold the full fertility of more than a dozen humans, and such a power was obviously greatly needed here. While Marisol relished the status her power gave her, she never seemed quite herself after traveling to Yorkshire.

"Marisol! You have returned!" a deep voice echoed through the small clearing, and an enormous silver-white falcon flew down from the trees to cross their path before soaring back to its perch above. Its wingspan stretched at least six feet across, and Cordelia wondered if the bird might in fact be a glamoured fae.

The trees shook a little as the leaves of the large hawthorn on their left slowly bloomed into a dense fog of small white flowers with pink speckles. The whiteness of the blossoms glowed in the dim light of the forest. The rest of the group were a bit farther ahead, but at the sound of the faerie's greeting, paused to look back.

The juniors had welcomed Cordelia on the expedition, despite the fact that she'd been a last-minute addition and was far less prepared than they were. She knew that but for Marisol's influence, she wouldn't have been included, but then Marisol probably wouldn't have agreed to chaperone had it not been for her. Perhaps the juniors were only being nice to her because of that; everyone knew how beloved Marisol was by the fae. Having her shepherd them through this obligatory visit to the Aos Sí would definitely reduce their risk ... if it was, in fact, risky. One moment, the juniors would speak as if visiting the Aos Sí were no big deal, but in the next, they'd remind each other of the various atrocities committed by the Aos Sí during the Third Mage War.

As the heavy odor of wet, rotting leaves overcame the smell of honeysuckle that had originally welcomed them into the forest, Cordelia moved closer to Marisol, who seemed delighted by the hawthorn's transformation. Cordelia now understood why the others were so grateful for her presence, and tried to find some comfort in Marisol's enjoyment of the fae magick.

The white flowers slowly shrank back into the tree's branches, and gradually a white face emerged from the greenery. The seelie's pale skin glowed like the surface of the moon, and only the scattering of pink freckles across his cheeks broke up the luminosity of his face. He had grass-green eyes, and a full mouth that smiled a welcome at Marisol. He was easily the largest person Cordelia had ever seen; standing more than seven feet tall, he towered over Vincent, who had come back into the clearing with the group.

"Boyaryshnik, you always know me, no matter what face I wear." Marisol giggled and extended her hand in a limp wave.

Boyaryshnik bowed over Marisol's hand, his massive torso folding in a perfect ninety-degree angle. He was so close, Cordelia could see the lace trim on his gray shirt twist suddenly into bark and then back again. So this was a seelie. She had never met one of the fae elite before. Her mother had warned that because the seelie aped human ways, they were even more dangerous than the fae who appeared less human: Their mannerisms made it too easy to forget that the fae thought so differently than humans or even sirens. At least living with sirens for the past four years enabled Cordelia to ignore Boyaryshnik's shocking handsomeness.

His cheekbones and chin seemed almost chiseled into perfection, and the thin, close-cut fabric of his gray shirt and old-fashioned breeches were designed to show off his musculature. Unlike the sirens, who often draped their magical beauty beneath loose-cut fabrics, the fae were known to enjoy accentuating their glamoured figures with their clothing.

"Marisol, I did not expect you for months! This is a real treat." Boyaryshnik's voice rumbled in a deep bass that Cordelia found unexpectedly appealing.

"And who is this delight beside you?" Boyaryshnik focused his attention on Cordelia, who felt her face grow hot as she looked away from the faerie's glowing eyes. She wasn't affected by him, not like a human would have been, but nevertheless she felt uncomfortable with his attention.

"This is my offspring, and I am pleased to accompany her on her first trip to visit the Aos Sí." Marisol didn't offer her name, and Cordelia was frankly relieved when Boyaryshnik glanced about at the others who had formed a semicircle around them.

"Ah, these are the young Atlantics Titania promised were coming to play."

Cordelia saw a flicker of light around the edge of the clearing and realized that there were probably several fae hiding in the undergrowth.

"We shan't be staying long enough to play many games this time. But come, I'm full to bursting, and you seem even paler than usual after your elaborate display."

"Marisol, really? Can't this wait until we get to the old-growth forest?" Vincent complained.

"We're here, and you said we ought to do a demonstration before the group splits up. So why not get started now? Never say I'm anything but diligent at my work." Even Cordelia caught the barbs in Marisol's tone. Clearly, Vincent's offhand put-downs of Marisol as too flighty to serve as a courtier had reached her ears. Perhaps she had come on this trip to prove her worth to the High Court, and not merely to ensure that Cordelia succeeded at this rite of passage.

"I had better start us off. After all, my capacity is double yours, is it not?" Marisol spoke sweetly, and didn't bother waiting for Vincent's acknowledgment before moving even closer to Boyaryshnik.

"Ah, so I'm to be a demonstration? Is that all I am to you, love?" Boyaryshnik seemed impossibly flirtatious, but Cordelia thought his face looked tense.

Marisol ignored his comment as she looked at the junior sirens. "The Aos Sí are simply fae, just like all the others you have met. There is no difference, really. Watch." Marisol gestured, and Boyaryshnik obligingly knelt down, so that his face was within Marisol's reach. "Just a gentle kiss to restore what you lost when you loosed your gyrfalcon," Marisol said softly.

"You noticed," Boyaryshnik rumbled.

Marisol patted his shoulder. "I love your falcons. And you called my favorite for me. Such a welcome deserves a guesting-gift in return." Marisol clasped her hands on the sides of his face and kissed him gently on the mouth. Cordelia could see his eyes flutter, then close. The sound of rain enveloped them, and as Cordelia looked around to see where it was falling, suddenly Boyaryshnik stood up and Marisol stepped back, practically into Cordelia.

It seemed that Boyaryshnik's whole demeanor had changed. Cordelia couldn't pinpoint exactly why she thought so. Perhaps it was the languid grin that had changed his visage. His prior smile had an edge to it that she hadn't noticed until it was replaced by this new expression. It was almost as if he had been starving before, but now had finally had a feast.

"Ah, Marisol, for that, I will let you *fly* my birds. Come, let me lead the way." And with that, Boyaryshnik swept Marisol to the front of the group.

Cordelia's gaze was caught by the flash of a firefly, and she paused, wondering whether it were truly a firefly, or perhaps a will o' the wisp. Suddenly, she realized that she was in danger of being left behind, and hurried to catch up. A tree root rose in her path, and Cordelia stumbled. Out of nowhere, a rail-thin woman appeared, taking her arm to steady her.

"Take care," she said, so softly that Cordelia wasn't sure she had actually heard her. Her eyes and skin were a pale blue, and her touch was as cold as she looked. Perhaps she was a vila, though her long hair was more colorless than blond. It seemed to float behind her as if blown by a nonexistent wind.

"Thank you," Cordelia responded politely, then remembered that gratitude was not an emotion understood by the fae. She waited nervously as the faerie considered her.

"You are younger than the others," the faerie finally said.

"Yes."

"I am much older than those who remain. Older than Ares, older than Taara, older than Titania, older even than Num and Nga, whose greed cast us out," the faerie whispered in almost a sing-song soprano.

"Oh?" Cordelia looked around urgently, hoping Marisol would realize that she had been left behind.

"Do not fear, child. I mean you no harm. I have sent a look-alike ahead to mask our little conversation."

Cordelia gulped. Sirens were generally immune to all but the most powerful of fae magicks. For this slender faerie to have cast such a spell meant she was quite powerful indeed. "Why did you want to speak with me?" Cordelia was honestly surprised at being singled out, and didn't feel at all relieved by the faerie's assertion that she didn't intend Cordelia harm.

"I want to give you a welcome-gift. A gift that only one such as I can give. A gift freely given."

"'Beware the gifts of the fae,'" Cordelia quoted without thinking, then gasped.

But the faerie only smiled. "Fairly said. But this is a gift of truth. You value true-telling, no?"

"I thought the fae couldn't lie," Cordelia said.

"We can't, but truth is more than just the absence of lies, is it not? Truth is pure and brilliant and hard like a diamond. Real truth shines like a jewel and pulses from your heart. I think that you are one who would value truth." The faerie tapped Cordelia's chest gently, and she felt the ice of the vila's hand sink deeply to circulate through her body, like frozen blood. The sound of her own pulse throbbed in her ears.

"Diamonds are also sharp," Cordelia murmured.

"Absolute truth is sharp, but would you rather live in a fog of unknowing? Of deception woven out of misdirection and obfuscation? Would you remain *ignorant*?"

And here the faerie touched upon her weakness. Indeed, Cordelia hated feeling so stupid. So unqualified. Having to pretend to understand what she didn't.

Knowing she didn't even know the right questions to ask to gain the understanding that might make her less of a fraud. "What *truth* do you have to share?" she asked hesitantly.

"The truth of our existence here. I will let you feel what we feel, amplified perhaps, like sunlight refracted through diamonds. But only for a brief spell, instead of an eternity." Suddenly, the thin faerie disappeared into an explosion of icy wind that whipped through the trees, surrounding Cordelia in a shroud of freezing mist.

A soft keening began at the edge of the clearing, growing in volume and intensity until Cordelia had to cover her ears against the sound. It was so painful that Cordelia didn't even realize she was crying until she felt herself gasping for air, then noticed the hot wetness of her tears dripping onto her knees. She didn't know when she had dropped to the ground, or how long she had huddled there.

While her heart should have been pounding under the strain, it seemed to beat in an ever-slower tempo. Cordelia felt the clenching of her heart-muscle as it tried to contract, and each second was an agony of fiery cold as her chest tried to rise. *This must be what humans feel when they drown*, she thought. Cordelia panted, but still couldn't get enough air.

The oppressive weight that had knocked her down and compressed her into herself gradually dissipated, until only the shocking memory of pain lingered. It was an odd feeling: Not relief or euphoria, but an absolute ennui. Cordelia had never *not* cared about anything before. But in that moment, Cordelia didn't care if she died or if the pain started again or if she just stayed frozen on the wet ground forever. She just didn't care.

Then she felt a touch of ice on her forehead, breaking the spell. A soft voice whispered in her ear: "Truth."

Part One

The Ties That Bind

It is estimated that almost ten percent of the mundane human population are latent sirens. Most will never transition to active status, and the current survival rate for those who do transition is less than one in four for females and less than one in ten for males. Congratulations on surviving your transition! That you have arrived in a safe location and are reading this book is a testament to your own skills, the quick actions of your progenitor, and God's own grace.

– Sirens: An Overview for the Newly-Transitioned, 3rd ed. (2015), *by Mira Bant de Atlantic, p. i.*

Chapter 1

The lights in Amy's office clicked off again. She waved her arms so that they'd come back on, and glanced at the time on her computer monitor. It was almost four in the afternoon, and she'd been sitting at her desk since before seven trying to figure out what had gone wrong. Her head was throbbing with a bilateral frontal lobe headache.

Eyestrain: she had been reviewing fMRIs non-stop for hours. Perhaps the annoying motion-activated lights had some benefit besides ostensibly saving energy. At least they signaled that she had been sitting for far too long. She stood up, flexing her back, and looked out the window to the left of her desk.

She wished she could see the harbor, but the building was too far from the waterfront. The city seemed dark for mid-afternoon, with the dull cloud cover and steel-gray sky making it feel more like evening. She rubbed her eyes and looked across the rooftops. Shifting her focus to use her distance vision would help her headache. That, and perhaps eating something.

Before she could sit back down to continue her third review of the day, Amy's attention was captured by the teetering stack of print-outs on the corner of her desk. She glanced around the room. Clutters of papers were piled on every surface. Her desk was covered with

charts, anatomy scans, research journals, and miscella-
neous paperwork; a maze of haphazardly stacked medical journals blocked the way to the door. Although her
walls still showcased her various diplomas and awards
in a fairly orderly fashion, Amy had to admit that her
office had become a non-functioning space. While she
didn't consider herself to be neurotically neat, there
was a point where the mess overwhelmed her to the
point of dysfunction.

Amy spent the next two hours in a flurry of cleaning. She had Gillian bring in a recycling bin from the
printer room, and filled it almost to the brim with paperwork that wasn't helping her solve the problem. At one
point, her cellphone buzzed and Amy knew without
looking at it that it was Cordelia; her other siblings
always called her work line. Well, Mary did; Thomas
never called. Amy decided she'd call Cordy back later.
She really wanted to finish this small project at least.

At last, she looked around, and her desk was clear.
She had even borrowed some of Gillian's Clorex wipes
and cleaned off her desk and credenza. Now only a few
reports remained. Amy felt infinitely better. She might
not be accomplishing much in terms of curing Patient
B's vision loss, but at least she had accomplished something today. Paring down the clutter had definitely
helped her regain her equilibrium. Surveying her
orderly office ushered in a burst of optimism, and Amy
felt newly confident that she would figure out what
had gone wrong with the operation.

With her desk so clean, Amy decided not to spoil it
by ordering dinner and eating it in her office, as was her
norm. She'd go out for a change. Staring at her computer

screens for the past week hadn't brought her any closer to a diagnosis, and she needed to clear her head.

"Good night, Gillian," she called out as she shut her office door. Gillian was their lab administrator and office assistant. Amy had hired her four years ago due more to her vivaciousness than any particular expertise. Their previous administrator had been a no-nonsense, older woman, who had worked with Eli forever and was rather set in her ways. Dealing with her had always required just a little extra care. So Amy had been happy to find someone easier to deal with, if less efficient. Gillian wasn't what you'd call a self-starter, but she was cheerful and willing to do whatever Amy asked.

"Good night, Amy," Gillian replied, but Amy was already halfway down the hall. She knew she walked fast and had a reputation for always being in a hurry. "Can't-Catch Bant," her colleagues used to call after her when she'd been a resident. A fairly lame nickname, but then they had all been rather sleep-deprived back then.

Amy liked feeling that she moved with purpose, but knew the sense of accomplishment it gave her was illusory. Rushing around wasn't conducive to methodical thinking. Other people went to the gym to get a work-out, but she went to the gym to slow down. Literally. Tonight, Amy was determined to head to the gym, set the treadmill at a mild 2.0 pace, then swim some laps. After all, that was how she'd managed to think through her dissertation.

She hadn't really left the hospital since Patient B had awakened from surgery last week, and was starting to think that her intense focus on the case was counterproductive. She needed a break.

Amy walked swiftly past Eli's office. He was in D.C. today, trying to assure Commander Thompson that despite the minor setbacks in the operation, they were nevertheless making progress. Eli Eisner had been her mentor since she came to Harvard Medical School post-residency, and had been the department chair when she invented the optic nerve-graft procedure that surgically cured amblyopia about ten years ago.

It had been a surprise when Eli insisted that she take full credit for the procedure, and Amy still felt a thrill when she heard someone refer to it as the "Bant Procedure." Most senior surgeons didn't hesitate to claim their juniors' successes as their own. But Eli was either unusually fair or extraordinarily arrogant — perhaps both. He puffed himself out as the "invisible" guiding force behind his department's success, saying it so often that his role was far from invisible. But Eli was magnanimous. While claiming their successes as his own, he nevertheless let his doctors publish with their own names on the bylines.

And his style worked: Eli was now the acknowledged genius who had transformed Harvard's neurology department into the premier facility of its kind. The best neurosurgeons in the country competed for a spot in their lab; Amy herself had been here for more than fifteen years.

It was a shame Eli wasn't in town; it had been a while since they had gone out for dinner. As Amy strode down the corridor, she noticed that Ted's light was still on, though he wasn't in his office. Ted Riccie was a new addition to their lab. A via-enchanter from the Danjou Enclave, Ted had joined their team as the

Danjou's delegate for their joint research project on mage sight.

Amy thought that they had developed a fairly good rapport since Ted had come to the lab last year. Still, some of his notions were extremely foreign, even disturbing. The culture shock had run both ways; Ted found her sense of medical ethics "quaint," as he put it. Before now, Amy had never been interested in the politics of the U.S. enclaves that operated as semi-autonomous regions within the country. She vaguely knew they weren't democracies in the same way the broader mundane U.S. was, but issues like that were things her sisters liked to debate.

Ted was the first mage she had ever really known. Working with him was like being back in boarding school, when she'd been surrounded by ultra-wealthy kids with such a different understanding of how the world worked. At that point in her life, the experience had been more intimidating than bracing; but now, she found the challenge of Ted's perspective interesting, if somewhat shocking.

Amy knew that Ted was one of the pre-eminent via-enchanters in the country, so she took for granted that his perspective was mainstream for mages. Before meeting him, Amy had never questioned her responsibility to ensure that her patients made informed choices. But Ted laughed disparagingly at the very notion of consent protocols. Apparently, when the enclave decided one of their mages would undergo experimental surgery, the mage had surgery. End of story; patient consent was irrelevant. Amy was very glad she wasn't a mage.

Rounding the corner, Amy almost plowed into Ted. "Oh, excuse me!" she said, backing away.

"Such a hurry!" Ted exclaimed with a smile. "Got a hot date?"

No one dared flirt with Amy in the lab anymore — at least, not until Ted arrived. Somehow, his mild interest felt more welcome than the previous attempts by men even more handsome than Ted. Maybe she was getting old. "Well, I'm starving and was going out to get something to eat. Want to join me?" Amy asked.

Ted appeared to be in his early thirties, though with mages, you could never be sure of their exact age. Skilled mages mastered the art of maintaining constant cell regeneration, and could live for centuries before dementia set in, eroding their ability to cast spells. At just over six feet tall, with a solid physique and dark hair highlighted by a few gray sparkles, Ted was quite attractive. He had a charisma that pulled Amy in, more from his projection of self-confidence than from his navy-blue eyes and firm jaw.

"Sure," Ted replied. "Just let me pack up." He walked into his office, and Amy leaned against his doorframe, watching as he picked among the clutter on his own desk to stuff his briefcase with a few print-outs and sealed test tubes.

Ted's office wasn't nearly as clean as Amy's was now, but it wasn't in bad shape. Unlike Amy's paper-filled office, all of Ted's available surface area was covered with racks of neatly labeled test tubes and Erlenmeyer beakers. Oversized flip-boards displaying multi-colored schematics stood where the credenza should have been, and she recognized their comparative diagrams of brain anatomy tacked on his wall. Looking at the ring stands with open vials pushed up behind his computer monitors, Amy wondered how Ted didn't worry about spilling liquid on the electronics.

"I was thinking lobster rolls," Amy suggested.

"Sounds good. I love all the seafood in Boston. It's been one of the perks of working here," Ted said as he zipped up his bag. "Let's go."

Amy led the way down the hall, moderating her typical fast pace. By tacit agreement, they didn't discuss Patient B's case, though Amy knew that they had both been obsessing over what had gone wrong since Barry Riccie had woken up unable to see the world with his previously perfect mundane vision. She tried to console herself that no one else could have done any better. The operation had gone exactly as planned, so they must have missed something when they designed the procedure. Amy supposed she shouldn't have expected to immediately replicate her last success.

Ten years ago, amblyopia (commonly called "lazy eye") had been a relatively minor visual impairment in the U.S. that was typically diagnosed in early childhood when it could be treated with patching and visual therapy. But before the development of the Bant Procedure, all doctors could do for adults with untreated amblyopia was cosmetic surgery to limit the walleyed drift in one eye that was characteristic of the disorder. The revolutionary grafts into the optic nerve that Amy and her team developed in the Bant Procedure actually enabled the optic nerve to regenerate. Now, with surgery and visual therapy, patients whose nerves had atrophied were able to see with 20/20 vision.

This project was exactly what she'd been looking for ever since. It was thrilling to be in charge of Project Hathor, even if there were some geopolitical strings attached. While Eli was still the department chair and nominal lead, everyone knew that this was Amy's baby. Sure, she consulted with Eli regarding their approach, but Eli hadn't really practiced medicine in years. This was her project. And her failure.

Amy knew she was being hard on herself; it was too soon to tell if the operation were truly a failure. In fact, it was a clear success in many ways. Barry Riccie's parents were mages, but he was a mundane. Born without magical vision, he was incapable of controlling magick. While proclaiming that he didn't personally think mages were superior to mundanes, Ted had made it clear that having a mundane born into a mage family was seen as somewhat shameful in the enclaves.

Before the operation, Barry saw the world clearly with 20/20 mundane vision, but lacked the ability to perceive magick … and he felt that lack as sincerely as a mundanely blind man would in a world full of sighted individuals. Amy reminded herself that while the inability to perceive magick was normal for any other mundane, for Barry, it represented a serious disability.

"I've been through the fMRIs twice today," Amy said as they walked out of the hospital, unable to help herself from bringing up the project. "I still can't understand exactly why the operation eliminated Barry's mundane vision."

"You'll figure it out," Ted said with a shrug that Amy found immensely irritating. It was great that he had confidence in her, but his apparent lack of concern was irksome.

"This was not a side-effect that we predicted or even seriously discussed with the patient," Amy noted.

Ted must have sensed her irritation, because he turned to look at her. "Relax, Amy. Barry would have undergone the operation even if you'd told him that he'd definitely lose his mundane sight. You've seen him; he's thrilled with the results. For him, the operation was a success. He sees magick; he's a mage. That's all he's ever wanted. Sacrificing his mundane vision is a minor setback in what was otherwise an unmitigated success."

"But he can't control magick. He *sees* it, but what good is seeing magick if he can't manipulate it?" Amy asked.

"It's only been ten days. The grafts are new, and you said yourself he's still healing. Our children aren't born casting spells — it takes years for mage children to develop physically, not to mention learning all the necessary skills to cast. It's too soon to tell whether Barry will eventually be able to."

Ted never seemed to get excited about anything. His perfect composure was one of the things that irritated Amy the most, but she nevertheless found herself seeking him out. Ted wasn't one of her junior doctors, but was part of the program and understood their work. With him, she could let down her guard a little. His incessant optimism was frustrating, but it was worth it to have someone around to confide in.

His different point of view could also be invigorating, and often made her think in different ways.

They'd barely started talking about the operation, and she already felt less guilty that her cure for Patient B's blindness had destroyed his mundane sight. Nevertheless, she was determined to fix it.

Neptune Oyster was an upscale seafood place that was a bit of a hike from the hospital. While Amy had planned to go to the local dive around the corner, she had changed her mind when she ran into Ted. Tonight, she would reorient her thinking and get back on track. Clearing out her office, having a decent meal for once, and heading to the gym would give her the necessary perspective.

There was a bit of a wait for a table, so they headed to the bar for a drink. The bar was at the front of the restaurant, and had a shiny, dark wood top. The back wall behind the bartender was decorated with lit glass shelves holding what looked like a hundred bottles of different liquors. Even the top-shelf bottles were half-empty. This was a high-end restaurant, and people actually ordered the really expensive stuff.

It was fairly crowded, but they snagged two seats near the large bay window. Amy had never seen Ted order anything stronger than beer or wine, so when he ordered a scotch and soda, she had to wonder if he was feeling more strain than his unflappable attitude revealed. Amy ordered a dirty martini and ate the olives off the toothpick. Since she hadn't eaten at all today, she felt the impact of the gin almost immediately.

"Do *you* think the operation was a success?" Amy asked Ted, with a directness that she attributed to the mild buzz she was feeling. *Never ask a question if you're afraid to hear an honest answer*, her mother used to warn. But Amy was asking, despite her fear of Ted's response.

"It doesn't matter what I think," Ted replied tersely. "The only thing that matters is what the elders think."

"Your tone tells me they *don't* think it was a success," Amy responded.

"Nothing short of perfect would ever be a success for Elder Simon. But others are calling it a qualified success," Ted said before he sucked down the last of his drink. He looked like he was considering chewing the ice. Amy sipped her martini.

"Elder Simon was the man who brought Barry to the hospital, right?" Amy asked, though she knew he was.

"Yeah. Simon is Barry's father. He's been an elder for centuries, and acts like he owns the Danjou. He makes everyone's life a living hell. Barry probably volunteered for the operation just to get out from under Simon's roof." Ted waved the bartender over and gestured for a refill.

It was hard to believe they'd been working together for over a year now. The first time they went out for drinks, Ted expressed surprise at the presence of wait staff. Apparently, at enclave establishments you ordered via bespelled menus, and the drinks arrived by auto-piloted, miniature flying carpets.

"Are you happy to be out of the enclave, Ted?" Amy asked. "It's been an adjustment." It occurred to her that Ted might view her in the same way she did him: a safe confidante. He certainly seemed a lot more forthcoming tonight than he typically did at the hospital.

"It's been interesting. You mundanes have such a different approach. I know you all think we have no freedom, that we're in some kind of cult. But I had a lot of independence in the enclave. I'm a Riccie, but my clan has pretty much left me to my own pursuits. Project Hathor is the only time they've actually ordered me to do anything. I've never spent so much time outside the enclave, but I can't say I've been unhappy with the assignment. The way you and the other doctors work is fascinating." Ted chuckled.

"What?" Amy asked.

"You just worry about such different things. It makes me think there's something to living without magick."

Ted wasn't slurring his words, but their conversation seemed to be veering into the kind of late-night intimacies typically only shared when you're drunk. "What do you mean?" she asked.

"You care so much about your patients. You worry about them. And not just you — even Commander Thompson and the rest of the DoD. You mundanes were so horrified by what the Djinn Dictator did to Gerhard Hass, we didn't even suggest repeating it to get a subject for this project." Ted had lowered his voice, and Amy had to lean closer to hear him over the noise of the crowded bar.

Despite herself, Amy was shocked. "The enclave would have eliminated a mage's sight just to have a subject for this project?" Gerhard Hass was a mage spy who had been caught by Amir Khalid a few years back. The Arabian dictator had surgically eliminated his ability to perceive and use magick, but his mundane eyesight was not affected. He eventually escaped, but died during the operation to repair his mage sight.

The Danjou claimed that the Amir's treatment of Hass was the impetus behind their participation in the project, but Amy had her doubts; something about her partners' reasons for participating in such a novel joint venture didn't ring true to her. Amy herself had jumped at the opportunity to lead such groundbreaking research, and tried to avoid dwelling on everyone else's motivations.

"Surgically blinding someone isn't that different, really, from our normal method of handling criminals. We don't have the kind of massive prison system you mundanes do. We just blind our criminals magically so they can't cast spells, and send them back into the care of their clans. Until our preliminary meetings with you, we honestly didn't see performing a surgery to blind one of them as such a big difference from our normal process."

"Haven't you heard of the Tuscaloosa experiments? Or what the Nazis did to prisoners in the concentration camps? No ethical doctor would ever be willing to perform such an operation!" Amy couldn't keep the shock from her voice.

"See?" Ted raised his glass to her. "You mundanes care so much. No mage would think anything of operating on a prisoner to reverse-engineer the magical lobotomy the Dictator's doctors invented. You fret endlessly about consent, but even Elder Simon would be confused if you asked for his consent. Mundanes care about everyone."

"Well, not *all* mundanes," Amy had to admit. "That's why we have medical ethics in the first place. But even though we're all Americans, you mages don't seem to value individuals the same way we do."

"We're all Americans, all right, but different," Ted agreed. "You mundanes talk about your 'rights' as citizens and such. It's a marvelous philosophy to see such value in each person. To actually care what a person might want, and think they have any right to object to what your leaders demand 'for the good of the many.'" Ted sighed. "Regardless, I wouldn't give up my magick just for that. Not for anything."

"I wouldn't give up my independence, let alone my safety, just to get magick. It seems like way too high a price to pay. The elders order you to go somewhere, you go. They tell you to submit to an operation, you submit. It's worse than being in the army," Amy said. She gestured to the bartender for a second cocktail.

"Amy, you can't understand what you're missing," Ted's pitch had risen. This was the first time Amy had really heard any strong emotion from him. "A man blind from birth doesn't know the beauty of a rainbow. Mundanes are handicapped. You just don't realize it." Ted's face flushed, and he looked at her with trepidation.

Was he a closet mage supremacist? Well, Amy had more or less assumed all mages were, and was honestly amused by the idea that she — and almost ninety-nine percent of the human population — were handicapped.

"Seriously, Ted? You consider mundanes disabled because we can't see magick? I mean, my brother is fluent in four languages — does that mean I'm disabled because I only speak one? Or what about my older sister, who has perfect pitch? You know, my younger sister can hold her breath underwater for almost five minutes. By your way of thinking, I'm the black sheep of my family."

"Those are just different levels of ability. I'm talking about a whole sense that you mundanes lack. You're literally *lacking a sense*. You can see, but you don't see the full spectrum." Ted spoke earnestly, and focused with a drunken intent on picking his words.

But Amy scoffed. "Butterflies have ultraviolet perception. Snakes see infrared. Are humans handicapped in comparison? Do we need to figure out a procedure to get us those senses?"

Amy wondered whether Ted really thought he was better than her because of his magical ability. Mages were rumored to believe they *were* better than mundanes, and a lot of mundanes treated them like they were. When a mage condescended to speak to you or seek your advice, you were supposed to feel flattered. What bothered Amy, if she were being truly honest with herself, was that she did feel flattered by Ted's attention.

"I don't know. But I wish you could see what I do." As Amy heard the sincerity in Ted's voice, her flare of resentment faded, and she stopped to look into his earnest face for a moment. Amy propped her head on her hand and gazed deeply into Ted's eyes.

"What do you see? What is it like?" she asked with sincere curiosity.

"It's so hard to explain; I'm not even sure where to start." Ted paused, thinking. "Well, there's this old poem. So few mages create any art; but there was this French mage who wrote poetry, and one of her poems captured it. At least for me. Let me find it." Ted fumbled with his phone and started typing and scrolling.

"Ah, here it is. It's translated, but I think the original was in verse. 'A glow that erupts from the sun and slides off the moon / Hovering around the candle, linking life in love / All colors and none. Sound mixed with taste and touch and smell / Blended into an overload of purity to cleanse the soul / But what is light? Merely chains that tether spirit to flesh.'"

Amy was struck by the oddity of the moment. The romance of poetry in a noisy bar was so twenties, and she was almost fifty. Still, she felt a pulse in her middle.

Ted paused. "That was Jehanne Mahoult. I don't know how to explain it better. I don't know how to describe the way light becomes patterns. Sometimes with a feeling; sometimes with a sound. Some mundanes have been diagnosed with synesthesia, where they hear a chord, then see colors, or taste a food and feel an impression on their skin. Mage sight is like that, and not like that." Ted sighed. "It's so hard. What is a rainbow to a blind man? And why try to explain it, when he can never experience its beauty?"

"Is that what mage sight reveals?" Amy asked, "Beauty?"

"Oh, yes," Ted breathed, and Amy felt the hair on her arms rise at his beatific expression. "Even when put to an utterly evil purpose. How can a spell so cruel, so evil, be so very beautiful? But it is. The world is beautiful when seen through mage eyes. We see every link, every pulse of life—"

"But what about death and the dying?" Amy was fascinated, despite her best effort to maintain a professional distance.

"The soul radiates through. You won't find an atheist among the mages, much as we've been reviled by most world religions."

If Ted was telling the truth, that was ironic. There were more atheists than believers among mundanes in Europe and North America now. After being hunted down by mundanes for centuries based on flawed interpretation of scripture, how peculiar that mages were now the most faithful of humans.

"Well, I'm Catholic, Ted. And we believe that magick performed in furtherance of God's will is moral. We're a lot more liberal on magick than sex, though." Amy had to laugh a little. *The Boston Globe* had just splashed yet another front-page story about a Boston priest who had been defrocked for an affair with a parishioner.

"Excuse me." The hostess arrived with two menus. "Amy? Table for two?"

Amy nodded.

"Your table is ready. If you'll follow me," the hostess said, gesturing back towards the restaurant area. As they walked to the back of the room, Amy took in the candlelit atmosphere, where each table was set with low vases of fresh flowers on white tablecloths. She started to wonder if she'd perhaps misled Ted with her choice of restaurant.

Amy liked Ted as a friend and colleague. Until his unexpected foray into poetry recitation, she had never thought of him in any kind of romantic capacity. Time to nip the vibe in the bud, before it could lead to something they might regret. Amy was determined to spend the rest of the evening talking about Patient B. She needed Ted too much to risk losing his focus on something as ridiculous as romance.

While the first mage wars predated the creation of sirens, the Atlantics were active combatants in the Third Mage War, and the Pacifics' transport of Asian mages to South America in the thirteenth century is widely believed to have precipitated the Fourth. However, siren actions have also averted war. For example, by protecting the silica-salt trade during the Middle Ages, the Mediterraneans prevented several mage battles for the Sahara. Most recently, war was averted in the mid-nineteenth century when the Indians acquiesced to the Cabal's Australian exodus, while the Pacifics refused to grant the Asian enclaves safe passage.

– Sirens: An Overview for the Newly-Transitioned, 3rd ed. (2015), *by Mira Bant de Atlantic, p. 148.*

Chapter 2

Amy swiftly led her surgical team into the conference room where Eli waited with their DoD partners for their first post-op briefing. While she knew their team was still the best for the project, she had to wonder whether the DoD wanted to make any changes, or whether, like the Danjou, they viewed the operation on Patient B to be a "qualified success."

Dr. Graham Litner was her protégé. He had gotten his medical degree and doctorate at Harvard before turning thirty, and she considered him among the best neurosurgeons she had ever worked with. His dexterity and stamina were remarkable. At this point, Amy had to admit, he was probably a better surgeon than she was. Instead of feeling threatened by that knowledge, Amy actually felt proud.

This must be something of what Eli felt when he looked at his department. She had trained Graham as a resident, ensuring he had gotten the right kind of experience to develop his skills. While Graham was as arrogant and ambitious as they came, he respected her. More importantly, he needed her: for all his skill on the table, he lacked the creativity that would truly make him a world-renowned doctor. Amy could get him there.

The third member of their team, Dr. Arnold Tucker, was older than Graham. He had already started losing his hair, which he disguised under a deep comb-over. Arnie had been part of the Gerhard Hass surgical team, and it was through his connections that they had gotten so much information about that botched surgery.

"Amy, I'd like to introduce you to Dr. Stephen Villar, Director of DARPA." Eli rounded the corner of the board table when Amy walked in, flanked by Graham and Arnie.

The two men accompanying Eli practically reeked of the military. Commander Thompson was in uniform, as usual; a solidly-built white man in his mid-fifties, Thompson seemed more relaxed than Amy would have thought, given the fact that Dr. Villar was here. Villar was taller and older than Thompson, with blue eyes and a rounded chin. He looked like an aging football player, but his soft facial features made him seem less intimidating than his bulk would otherwise suggest.

"Dr. Villar, this is Dr. Amy Bant, our lead surgeon on Project Hathor."

"I'm so pleased to meet you in person," Stephen Villar said, shaking Amy's hand.

"Likewise," she replied. At least his handshake wasn't too competitive. Amy could never remember exactly what DARPA stood for, but it was a big deal for the Agency Director to come to their lab. Most of their interactions were with Commander Thompson, the program manager overseeing their research for the Joint Chiefs.

Since they had begun actively preparing for the operation, Eli had been spending a lot of time in D.C. Actually, he was the one who managed all their contacts with Washington — it had been months since Amy had spoken to any of them. The problem was that everyone who worked at DARPA, the agency co-sponsoring the project, had an engineering or physics background, and the nuances of a magical medical research project were almost impossible for them to understand

"And of course, you remember Commander Thompson," Eli continued as the program manager reached out to shake Amy's hand. Thompson was fairly new to the R&E division of the Department of Defense. He was a Navy surgeon who had been seconded, or "reassigned" as he put it, due to the DoD's serious concerns about the Arabian threat. Thompson actually visited the lab at least once a quarter, and had enough of a medical background to understand their terminology. It would have been better had he been a neurologist or ophthalmologist, but he was a lot easier to work with than the rest of the DoD.

Villar was a retired Army captain, but unlike Thomson, his doctor title came from a Ph.D. in mechanical engineering. His whole DoD experience had been in the Air Force Research Laboratory working with airplanes. He tried to analogize the procedure they had developed with his past work on airplane exhaust systems, but it was a poor fit, and Amy worried that Villar still didn't understand what they were doing.

Project Hathor was new for everyone, really. The mages had never partnered with mundane doctors before, so they didn't understand medical practice, and neither Amy nor anyone else on the team understood how magick was actually perceived or manipulated. The DoD's contribution had mainly been in the form of financing, as well as the project's name. In addition to confusing enemies and allies alike with endless acronyms, the DoD seemed to like fanciful project designations and had named the project after the mythical Egyptian goddess who had restored Horus' sight after Set destroyed it.

Before proceeding with the operation on Patient B, Ted and Amy had spent almost a year developing the detailed anatomical analysis that mapped differences between mundane and mage brains. As highly educated as the DoD team was, they just didn't have enough background to understand how truly experimental and cutting-edge their research was. Even the preliminary anatomical work they'd done would advance the field exponentially.

Amy completed the introductions for the rest of her team, and hoped Ted would get there soon so they could start. She wanted to leave enough time for Eli to take Villar on a tour of their facilities before his planned visit with Patient B.

"Congratulations, Dr. Bant. Eli came down in person to report on your remarkable success," Villar said with a smile.

Eli was so relentlessly positive, Amy worried for a moment that he'd misled the DoD. *But surely he would have explained the side-effects*, she thought. Maybe Dr. Villar was simply flattering them.

"We believe Project Hathor is vital to our efforts to secure lasting peace with Arabia," Villar continued, looking at her team. "So we are extremely grateful for all of your dedication. From what I gather, the operation has been an amazing success, and I'm glad to finally meet you all in person."

"Thank you so much, Dr. Villar," Amy said. "We've made significant progress since the project started. It's a real honor that you made the trip up here."

"Of course. Eli has been phenomenal about keeping us all apprised of your work, but at this stage of the endeavor, I felt it was important to meet the team in person, and to see Patient B before he was discharged back to his family."

Amy was taken aback, but kept her expression neutral. She wasn't aware that Barry Riccie was being discharged any time soon. Certainly, he had healed enough that he could have left the hospital last week, but having him here in Boston instead of out in Hesperia, where the Riccies' estate was located, definitely made it easier to continue her observations.

Ted walked into the boardroom just in time to catch Dr. Villar's statement. "Yes, Elder Simon has requested that his son return to the enclave, so arrangements are being made for his flight. I just found out yesterday." Ted's voice rumbled with a hint of apology.

"Theodore Riccie, Via-Enchanter of the Danjou," Ted said, holding out his hand to shake Dr. Villar's.

"Dr. Michael Villar, Director of DARPA," Villar responded, shaking Ted's hand.

"It's an honor to finally meet you, sir," Ted said with a smile that didn't reach his eyes. His tone had shifted to a level of polite formality she hadn't heard since he had first arrived in Boston. Amy found herself second-guessing the briefing she'd prepared. She was far more used to working with doctors than she was with such senior laypeople. But Amy was experienced in plastering a confident expression on her face.

Dr. Villar's announcement that Patient B was going home rattled her. The project had been inches from termination at least twice before; both times, Ted and the Danjou elders had been able to reframe their research in a way that kept the DoD interested. Now that it seemed like the Danjou were backing away, and somehow she needed to make sure the DoD felt like the project was still on track. Eli used to be so good at managing their sponsors, but this project seemed beyond even his abilities.

The six men sat down on either side of the long conference table, as Amy walked to the lectern at the front of the room and dimmed the lights. She picked up the laser pointer with the ease of long practice. As the room faded into the glow of the large screen behind her, the familiarity of presenting took over. Amy clicked onto the first slide, which displayed the project name and the classic image of the Eye of Horus.

"The focus of today's presentation will be an overview of our status on Phase Two of Project Hathor. In Phase One, as you recall, we conducted extensive research into the perception of magick. Due to security concerns," Amy nodded in Dr. Villar's direction, "our live subjects were drawn exclusively from the U.S. enclaves. However, we were able to cross-compare some of our anatomical findings with Gerhard Hass' surgical reports and autopsy records, as well as autopsy records from a handful of mages in Europe and South America.

"By reviewing functional magnetic resonance imaging, or fMRIs, and MRIs of more than fifty mages, we were able to isolate the regions of the brain involved in the processing of magical sensation. We were also able to identify certain physical differences in the structure of mundane and mage optic nerves."

Amy flipped rapidly through the slides, which all of the people in the room should have seen in prior presentations. Their detailed work in the first phase of the project would be heralded as groundbreaking when she was finally able to publish their findings. Due to security concerns, they were precluded from publishing any results until the DoD gave its approval. While the DoD and, to a lesser extent, the Danjou Enclave couldn't truly appreciate how important their findings were to the entire field of magical medical research, Amy knew they were seminal.

Other studies had focused on genetic differences between mages and mundanes, seeking to isolate the genes that caused a human to be able to perceive and manipulate magical energy. This was the first research that had ever been done to compare human neurological structures. They now knew what parts of the brain were involved with mage sight and the manipulation of magical energy. The only physical difference between mages and mundanes was one extra nerve connected just below the optic nerve. The team had named it the "sub-optic nerve." Based on their analysis of Patient B and the Hass autopsy results, they had determined that the sub-optic nerve was integral to magical perception.

Once they were free to publish, their findings on how mages oscillated their perception of white light between magical and mundane sight would make Graham and Arnie's careers, as well as cement hers as perhaps the foremost neurosurgeon in the world.

"Of course, our research into magical perception is only the first part of the project, but is nevertheless a crucial first step. As the Djinn Dictator's experimentations proved, understanding the physical components of mage vision is valuable in its own right. Blind a mage, and they cannot cast: magical vision is a necessary precursor to magical manipulation.

"The key physical difference between mages and mundanes is the existence of the sub-optic nerve. A very small percentage of the population — less than two percent of all the mundanes we analyzed — have sub-optic nerves. And in those mundanes, the sub-optic nerve does not connect to the occipital lobe in the same way it does in mages."

Amy flipped through the slides to the one with Patient B's pre-op MRI, comparing it with Ted's MRI. Before this project, no mundane scientist or doctor had ever been able to study mages like this. When they'd asked Ted to participate as a control, he'd been indignant at first. Then he insisted that Amy and the other doctors on the team submit to the scans as well. *What was good for the gander was good for the goose*, he'd said with a whiff of humor. One of the oddities of reviewing her own scan was the realization that she fell into the tiny percentage of the mundane population with an unconnected sub-optic nerve. Perhaps there was a mage somewhere in her family history; Amy wished Mom were alive to ask.

"Three weeks ago, we operated on Patient B, a twenty-two-year-old male whose magical perception did not develop. We have termed his condition *sub-optic nerve hypoplasia*. Magical intervention has not been able to correct this kind of visual impairment to the sub-optic nerve itself. While Gerhard Hass' sub-optic nerve became non-functional due to damage inflicted through surgery—"

"The Amir's surgeons cut his sub-optic nerve," Eli murmured in an aside to Dr. Villar, who nodded.

"—Patient B's sub-optic nerve simply failed to fully develop. Through a series of nerve cell grafts, we connected Patient B's sub-optic nerves below his optic nerves in the occipital lobe." Amy moved her pointer to identify the new connections on his post-op MRI.

"And he can perceive magical energy now?" Dr. Villar asked.

"Yes. Almost immediately after the surgery, the operation to connect his sub-optic nerve was successful. Via-Enchanter, would you care to elaborate further?" Amy moved from the podium to hand the laser pointer to Ted.

"Thank you, Dr. Bant." Ted stood and began to explain his part of this morning's presentation.

"A mage's perception of magical energy is essential to their ability to manipulate magick. While there are a few reported cases of magical synesthesia — notably among great mages such as Aphrodite and Chía — magical perception is otherwise always visual. Mages oscillate their view of white light between their optic and sub-optic nerves, thus sensing an overlay of magical energy atop mundane sight.

"It isn't quite like infrared or night vision goggles, gentlemen. Toggling between images from the optic or sub-optic nerve is a learned skill, typically developed by the age of ten. But unless their vision is particularly acute, mages perceive the world through both senses simultaneously. In order to prevent an overload of sensation for Patient B, before he awakened from surgery, we reduced the amount of white light in his room. Then we gradually increased the volume or 'brightness' as you would call it, while monitoring the patient's tolerance. As you may be aware, the level of ambient magical force differs greatly depending on the environment.

"In a magick-poor city like Boston, most ambient energy is derived from the sun or moon itself, and settles in various reservoirs. Since Boston is not a high-energy location, it was an ideal setting for this particular operation. Keeping the patient here for a period of time was also sensible, as the Danjou Enclave is located in the Mojave Desert, which has the highest concentration of magical force in North America."

Ted was not interrupted, although they had all heard this before. Amy allowed her mind to wander. Perhaps Eli had already explained to Villar that the "reservoirs" of which Ted spoke were actually people, and to a lesser extent plants, animals, and objects. The fact that the mages pulled magick out of people to cast their spells had been a disconcerting revelation.

While Ted had assured her that she would never notice the difference one way or another, it was unsettling. All the magical devices they relied on — from air conditioners and refrigerators to electric plants and garbage disintegrators — supposedly used silica salt to maintain their spells. With the price of silica salt so high, Amy wondered if the mages were researching how to power them with energy stored in mundanes.

Amy glanced at the men from the DoD. Both appeared to be focusing intently on Ted's explanation, but Amy suspected that the real reason they were here was to meet Patient B before he was whisked back to the enclave. She wouldn't be allowed access to him there — mundanes weren't allowed into the gated mage communities. If the DoD had further doubts about continuing to fund the project, seeing the results could sway them.

Perhaps bringing Patient B home was more about their subject as a person, as opposed to a signal that the Danjou were pulling out. Both of Barry's parents were Danjou elders, and while he had spoken with them since the operation, neither had come to visit. Amy hoped that was all it was.

"Gentlemen," Amy stood up after Ted finished explaining the Barry's magical perception test scores. "Before we visit the patient, please remember that his mundane vision was compromised by the operation. While we are still working to understand and correct that problem, at this point the patient is unable to see details such as facial expressions, although he can perceive the outline of most people and objects. Are there any questions?"

"Good morning, Barry," Amy said as she and Ted walked into his room. Eli was taking Villar and Thompson on a brief tour, and Graham and Arnie had gone back to work reviewing the fMRIs.

"Hey Doc," Barry replied, turning away from the window at the far end of his room to stare at her. Barry shared many of the same facial features that his cousin Ted had, but Barry's navy-blue eyes gave him a guileless expression that made him seem even younger than twenty-two.

His incisions had healed, and apart from losing his mundane sight, he had no further complications. He had also proven to be a remarkably easy-going patient. While most others of his age would have become antsy to leave their room, Barry had spent the past few weeks either standing at his window and staring out into the Boston streets below, or teaching himself to juggle with the three bean bags filled with silica-salt that Ted had given him.

"How are you feeling?" Ted asked.

"Great," Barry replied. "No changes from yesterday."

Amy walked over to check his head. They had removed the staples ten days ago, and the incision site was a faint line just above the base of his head. He'd have a white scar about seven centimeters long just behind his ear, but it would soon be undetectable unless someone were looking for it. Amy looked at his chart. There was really no physical reason why he couldn't be discharged.

"Barry, Dr. Villar and Commander Thompson from the Defense Department are here visiting us and wanted to speak with you this morning if you're up for it," Amy said.

"Sure," Barry replied. "That's no problem." They had told Barry earlier in the week that the DoD would like to visit, and Barry had been remarkably easy-going about that as well.

"Any change in your vision, Barry?" Ted asked.

"No. No change. It's really amazing. You're covered in glitter again, Doc," Barry replied, turning to look out the window again.

"What do you see, Barry?" Amy asked. She'd asked the same question daily ever since he had begun standing at the window after the operation.

"It's just so *beautiful*," he replied. Like he always did; Barry wasn't especially descriptive.

Amy looked at Ted, who just shrugged. She remembered his comments at dinner last week: *like describing a rainbow to a blind man.*

"Are the colors still swirling? Have you been able to detect any patterns?" Amy wondered, watching Barry's profile as he stood transfixed by the window.

"They change so frequently. It's better than any movie I've ever seen. Little sparks of color." Barry had an almost rhapsodic expression on his face. If she hadn't seen his affect before surgery, Amy would have been concerned that the surgery had impacted his emotional state to a clinical degree. But even before the surgery, Barry had been almost simple in his demeanor.

"I'm going to see if Jonah Eris can come help you learn how to interpret your vision once you're back at the enclave," Ted said.

Barry turned away from the window to face Ted. "Back at the enclave?" he repeated, his face suddenly wiped of all expression.

Amy was concerned by the sudden change and shifted nervously. "Other than the loss of your mundane sight, you've made a fantastic recovery. Honestly, it's been unfair of us to have kept you away so long," Amy said.

"Your father requested your return," Ted said without expression.

"I see," Barry said.

There was an awkward moment of silence before Ted pulled a glasses case from his jacket pocket, and took out a wire-rimmed pair of old-fashioned spectacles. "Barry, I got these from a friend of a friend. I want you to have them."

"Wow, they sparkle like crazy!" Barry said.

"You're seeing the spell embedded in the glass," Ted replied. "It's a complex spell that our best silica enchanters haven't been able to replicate."

"What do they do?" Amy asked.

"They allow the mundane blind to see," Ted replied, handing the glasses to Barry, who put them on immediately.

"You have a cure for blindness?" Amy asked, shocked.

"They are ... hard to come by," Ted said, then dropped his voice to whisper for Amy's ears only, "They were made in Arabia." That explained why they were so hard to come by. Arabia had been interdicted for almost a decade, and relations were only getting worse. The U.S. had no trading relationship with them whatsoever anymore, and had been pressuring its NATO allies to cut them off completely.

It made sense that Arabian mages would have created something like this. Blindness ran in Amir Khalid's family — his mother was said to have been both magically and mundanely blind, and now his younger sister had been stricken with magical blindness. In fact, it was the Dictator's ongoing and quite personal quest to cure blindness that kept the DoD's interest in Project Hathor alive.

Barry lifted the glasses off, then let them settle down on his nose again. He peered outside with them, then took them off altogether, shaking his head. "No thanks," he said, handing them back to Ted. "I never want to see the world through my old eyes again."

"But they can help if you want to read or look at the computer—" Ted started.

"No way," Barry said flatly. "I can't see magick with them on. I never want to see the world so plain again."

"I know they only permit you to see in black and white, but they would enable you to have almost a full range of mundane vision," Ted said, sounding somewhat insulted.

"I never want to have mundane sight again," Barry declared. "This surgery was the best thing that ever happened to me. I don't know how I was able to exist before! When I see now, I taste the vision. I hear music in my eyes. This is beyond anything so dull and lifeless as the sight I had before. I don't know how mundanes live with themselves. No offense, Doc." Barry ended his passionate tirade by falling back into the bland, superficial charm he had exuded before.

Ted folded up the glasses silently and put them back into the case. "We're flying commercial. Our flight leaves at ten tonight. Make sure you're ready to go by seven," he said without expression. Amy watched, nonplussed, as Ted walked out of the room without waiting for a reply. Meanwhile, Barry picked up one of the bean bags Ted had given him and began rolling it in his hand, his face a blank mask. Beyond her worry that she was losing access to her only research subject, Amy was growing increasingly concerned at his reaction to what should have been welcome news.

"Barry, while you're physically able to travel, you don't *have* to leave if you don't want to," Amy told him.

"My father wants me to come home. I have to go," Barry's voice was emotionless.

"It would definitely be easier for us to continue our research if you remained in Boston. I can arrange for you to have an apartment through campus housing."

"You don't get it. This project is my father's project. If I don't go home, there *is* no project anymore." Amy thought she saw him struggle to plaster the carefree expression back onto his face. "I'm a mage now," Barry said. "My mom told me when we talked last week that she was organizing a binding ceremony."

"Binding ceremony?" Amy repeated.

"It hasn't been done on a grown-up in over a hundred years. But of course there are mages around who remember attending them back then. My mom has been picking their brains. I just didn't expect her to get it together this fast."

"What's a binding ceremony?" Amy asked.

"The geas binding to the Danjou. All mages have it. It's a … a status symbol," Barry replied. His lie was obvious.

"You undergo a ritual binding to your enclave? What does that do?"

"It's a loyalty pledge of sorts. Unbreakable. Bound in ties to all the Danjou. Like a marine's tattoo: *Semper Fi*. A ceremony kind of like a bris — you know, the covenant of Abraham? I don't know. It's special. Sets you apart. An unbreakable bond for all your life. Like that book, *Unbound*."

Barry was mixing so many metaphors he made no sense. Amy had heard of the book he referenced, but had never really been interested in literature.

"Look, Doc," Barry continued. "I'm kind of tired now. There's a lot I gotta do before I leave, I guess. And those Defense guys are coming around. I kinda want to get my act together, if you know what I mean."

Barry looked so lost, Amy felt sorry for him. She had never been known for having a particularly good bedside manner. She was a surgeon, not a psychiatrist, for Christsake. But listening to Barry, watching as his energy seemed to shrink inward and his whole demeanor shifted from happy to resigned, she wondered if she shouldn't keep him at the hospital a little longer. But there was no medical reason not to sign his discharge.

By fueling her last spell, also known as the "Atlantic Curse," with her own death, Morgan le Fay bound all sirens, latent and active, in a permanent blood-geas. Cursed with confoundment, latent sirens cannot even comprehend the word "siren," which is why you never heard of sirens before your transition, and why your latent relatives cannot understand what has happened to you now. Morgan le Fay is widely respected as a great mage, but her greatest, most insidious spell is not described in mundane histories. The Atlantics may have defeated her on the battlefield, but with her final spell, Morgan le Fay caused far greater devastation to her vanquishers, and indeed, to all sirens.

– Sirens: An Overview for the Newly-Transitioned, 3rd ed. (2015), *by Mira Bant de Atlantic, p. 34.*

Chapter 3

By the time Eli had finished the tour, Barry had regained enough of his equilibrium to exhibit the same careless *bonhomie* that reminded Amy a little of her brother, except Barry had none of her brother's charisma. Barry did seem to charm the men from the DoD, though, and they were definitely impressed with his ability to see, while not seeing. If they had any doubts that the operation had restored Barry's mage sight, their visit with him erased them. His lack of concern with his lost mundane sight did surprise them, but his obvious belief that gaining mage sight more than made up for that loss helped persuade them that the operation had truly been a success.

Her patient's obvious discomfort with returning home nagged at Amy. It wasn't mere annoyance at losing her proximity to her only subject; his continued inability to articulate any specifics about his new sense of sight wasn't likely to change even if she had more time to question him.

Before lunch, she'd looked up the book he'd mentioned on the internet. It was one of the few mage-written literary works in the Western Lit cannon, and revolved around a mage whose enclave bindings had been dissolved by the binder's death, and his decision to be re-bound. This geas-binding seemed to be a lot more permanent, significant, and painful than just getting a tattoo, so Amy could understand Barry's trepidation. Still, it didn't appear life-threatening, and according to Wikipedia, all enclaves required it. So who was she to interfere?

"Dr. Bant, do you believe you could replicate your surgery on another patient?" Villar asked.

Amy pulled herself back into the meeting; this was the senior strategy session, and not a good time to zone out. Eli, Ted, Commander Thompson and Dr. Villar were all waiting on her response. Fortunately, it was a question she had anticipated.

"I believe we can repeat the operation with the same or better outcome. But there *is* the question of finding another subject. When we discovered the physical differences between mages and mundanes in Phase One, our pool of potential subjects became much more limited than we originally expected. Our research has only identified two mundanes with sub-optic nerves on which we could operate."

When they had started the project, they initially thought they would be able to operate on any mundane soldier, and thus limit the disadvantage that came with not being able to perceive magical workings and spells. Given the extensiveness of Arabian magical technology, that disadvantage would apparently be a significant problem in any military engagement with Arabia.

The discovery of the physical differences between mundane and mage humans put that goal out of reach with their current level of knowledge. Eventually, someone might be able to perform a sub-optic nerve transplant — but that wasn't possible now. Ted had actually been the one to save their project from the trash heap. It was Ted who had located Patient B, and it was the Danjou who had persuaded the DoD that their joint venture still had value from a military perspective.

"A recent CIA report indicates that the Djinn Dictator has operated on another mage — this one was not able to return to her people, however. And it isn't clear whether she is still alive," Thompson said.

"Where was the mage from?" Ted asked.

"Australia. Central Intelligence believes their source to be reliable, but they were unable to verify the report with anyone Down Under. Notably, however, the Cabal did announce new restrictions on travel to and from Arabia, so we have a high degree of confidence in the intel."

"Does this new report change anything on our end?" Eli asked, with a kind of narrow perspective that was unlike him.

"Our timeframe has accelerated," Villar replied. "We may need to make an announcement sooner than we had anticipated."

"Given the complications with Patient B's surgery," Amy said, "I think we should wait on any announcement until we're able to discover why the operation eliminated the patient's mundane vision. We need to complete a second operation that restores mage sight without that side effect."

"Or, we could operate on Patient B again and see if we can repair it," Thompson suggested.

"I'm not sure that will be feasible," Ted said. "Elder Simon has recalled his son, and the patient himself is not overly eager to undergo additional surgery to regain his mundane sight at the risk of losing his new-found magical vision."

"You said you had already identified another possible subject?" Villar asked Amy.

She held back a sigh. "During our Phase One MRI reviews, we identified two mundanes with undeveloped sub-optic nerves, but only Patient B was suitable. However, we only reviewed around a hundred samples. If we performed more MRI screenings, we could potentially identify a new subject. The initial project scope called for us to operate on a military volunteer. If we could obtain MRIs from more potential subjects, we might identify one with atrophied sub-optic nerves."

Amy was already mentally dividing the work. Graham would need to review the scans. Arnie could continue his review of Patient B's fMRIs to see if there had been any neuron disruption in the optic nerves as a result of the operation.

"The situation in Arabia is growing worse," Villar cautioned, shaking his head.

"Also, I'm not sure why we need to delay," Thompson added. "The surgery was a success: your patient couldn't perceive magical energy before, and now he can. The Djinn Dictator will view that as the outcome he's been trying to achieve all along."

"I don't think the Dictator will want to blind his sister in his pursuit of a cure," Eli countered.

"I disagree," Ted said. "His sister's life is at stake. The Dictator and his sister were born in the early 1700s. Without mage sight, his sister can't cast the daily spells needed to regenerate her cells. There's only so much even a great mage like Khalid can do for another person. We're mages, not fae."

"Do we know when Loujain lost her sight?" Amy asked.

"Not definitively, but the earliest evidence we have is that in 1997, the Dictator began seeking out visual specialists, beginning his," Thompson paused, "*experimentation* shortly afterwards. So we believe it must have happened sometime before that."

"She's running out of time," Ted said confidently. "She's already into her third century. Even if they were able to slow her aging with daily external spells, it's almost impossible to hold for long. At best, they have another decade. But I'd say the Dictator is getting anxious."

Amy considered Ted's assessment. If anyone would know, it was him. The Danjou had made it clear that he was the best via-enchanter in their enclave.

"Well he must be anxious if he's willing to risk straining his relationship with the Cabal," Eli opined.

"That's our opinion as well," said Villar.

"We're scientists, not soldiers or spies," Amy said. "We won't have nearly the same insight on this as you have."

"You'd be surprised, Dr. Bant," he replied. "But in truth, we didn't come up to Boston solely to observe the success of your operation — which is undeniable, even if you believe improvements can be made. Just as we have spies in Arabia and Australia, the Dictator and the Cabal have spies in America as well. Sometimes a meeting off-site can be more secure."

"I have ensured that there are no magical listening devices in our lab," Ted stated.

"Of that, I have no doubt, Via-Enchanter," Villar said, inclining his head. "The DoD has also taken steps to prevent any mundane spying. In fact, this location is probably more secure than the Pentagon, if only because Project Hathor is currently less well-known. The very selection of DARPA to manage it was a strategic choice to bury its significance."

"I get the sense that I may lack a full understanding of the DoD's objectives in this project, Dr. Villar," Amy said. Villar seemed to be hinting at something, and his smile seemed more predatory than friendly.

"I agree," added Eli. "Commander Thompson, just yesterday you repeated your claim that the government's goal in Project Hathor was to secure an information advantage, and restart the failed silica-salt negotiations with Arabia."

When their Phase One anatomical analysis proved that the DoD's original objective would be unachievable, the Danjou had resuscitated the government's interest in Project Hathor by suggesting that the U.S. could use their research to entice the Amir back into the talks he had abandoned over a decade before.

"Dr. Bant, Dr. Eisner, after meeting Patient B, I'm confident we have that information advantage now. Because of your brilliant and outstanding work, we have an even greater opportunity than we initially sought," Villar said, leaning across the table for emphasis.

"The Dictator is still seeking a cure for Loujain," Ted interjected. He didn't seem at all surprised by Villar's air of suppressed excitement, but then nothing seemed to faze him.

"The Amira's time is running out," Thompson emphasized.

"Dr. Villar, if the Amir is still attempting to surgically blind subjects for his experiments, we absolutely have an information advantage. But we can't rely on one operation as sufficient evidence that our procedure will be effective. Indeed, our first experiment resulted in serious damage to the patient, which we need to better understand." Amy was very concerned that the DoD seemed about to hail their one operation as a success and move on.

"It would obviously be better if the operation didn't eliminate mundane sight," Villar conceded. "But I think we have enough."

"Enough for what?" Eli asked the question before Amy could.

"Enough to let the Djinn Dictator become aware of your findings and invite your team to visit Arabia on a humanitarian mission," Villar said, sitting back in his chair.

No one spoke for a long moment. Eli sat as if frozen, and Ted simply looked at Villar and Thompson from behind his calm mask. Finally, Amy broke the silence. "Arabia is under interdict."

"We can waive that for a humanitarian mission," Villar responded promptly. He had clearly been thinking about this long enough to come up with counters for any objections they might make.

"Is the President aware of this?" Eli asked. Amy thought it a rather presumptuous question, but Villar took it in stride.

"Both the President and Congress are concerned about the growing Arabian threat. While the President hasn't been specifically briefed about this project, he has authorized the Joint Chiefs to undertake a number of projects designed to prepare us to address that threat. The Arabian Interdict specifically permits humanitarian efforts that have been authorized by the DoD."

"You want us to operate on the Amir's sister?" Amy asked, appalled.

"Yes — or at least to receive an invitation to come to Arabia to examine Amira Loujain," Villar replied calmly.

"But why does the U.S. Government want to do that?" Eli asked.

"Arabia is a closed country. Some view this as an ideal opportunity to normalize relations and win concessions. Others see the potential to gain additional information about conditions in the country," Villar responded.

"You plan to insert spies into the medical team," Ted speculated.

"I wouldn't use that word," Villar demurred.

"Nevertheless," Ted countered.

"You would certainly be included in the mission." Dr. Villar looked at Ted. "The Danjou Enclave has been critical to Project Hathor's success."

"I wouldn't be able to get past the djinns. I'm geas-bound."

Amy and Eli both looked at Ted in askance.

"The Dictator has laid a protective spell across his empire to prevent anyone geas-bound from crossing his border. Anyone magically bound will draw his djinn, and be torn apart by their winds. From a siren to an enclave mage, none can pass," Ted explained.

"I'm sorry," Amy asked. "A scion?"

"A siren," Ted responded. At Amy's quizzical look, a flash of enlightenment seemed to run across Ted's face. "Pardon me. I'm using technical terminology. Anyone who is bound by a geas cannot cross into Arabia. Khalid set up the boundary in the 1920s when he solidified his hold on the Sahara. He wanted to keep the Europeans out. Of course, that keeps us out as well."

"The enclave could unbind you," Dr. Villar offered.

"It's a blood-geas." Ted smiled tightly. "It cannot be broken except by the death of the binder. My aunt bound me, and she is married to Elder Simon. I don't think I will be participating in any expedition to Arabia. Though it is certain that the enclave will indeed seek to send someone. I'll speak with Elder Simon when I return."

"*That's* why you came to the lab," Eli accused. "Not to observe Patient B, but to observe my doctors. We're scientists, Dr. Villar, not soldiers and certainly not spies!"

"Please, Dr. Eisner. No one is asking you to be anything other than what you are!" Villar did seem taken aback by the vehemence in Eli's voice. "It's true that I wanted to come here myself to meet the surgical team as well as to see Patient B."

Villar looked at Amy and continued, this time with a greater tone of sincerity. "Dr. Bant, no one would force you or anyone on your team to travel to Arabia. Even if it represents the best chance we've had in fifty years to resolve our problems with the Amir."

"You would be expecting us to travel to an interdicted country that no American has visited in over a decade," Amy said quietly.

"You'd have our full support," Thompson leaned onto the table. "Dr. Bant—"

Villar cut Thompson off. "You don't need to make any decisions now. Dr. Eisner, at this point I don't even know that we would need any civilian volunteers.

Dr. Bant is right, finding another subject and performing a second operation is eminently sensible. Commander Thompson is a highly skilled surgeon. We've decided that he should join the project team on a more day-to-day basis. Then he could gain the experience he would need to perform the operation and act as the lead surgeon on any Arabian visit."

Amy could only look at Villar, wide-eyed. She couldn't believe he would actually be that stupid; or perhaps he was simply playing the fool. There was no way Thompson could perform the kind of experimental neurosurgical procedure they had just developed. It was like asking a Pan Am pilot to fly a space shuttle.

"Any humanitarian exhibition to Arabia would be under U.N. auspices. You would be treated with kid gloves. The Amir needs you," Thompson persuaded.

"And if his sister dies on the table? Or your spies are discovered?" Amy challenged.

"The Dictator will expect spies to be embedded into the surgical team. The issue for him will be identifying the spies. As the Commander said, this trip would be a high-profile U.N. humanitarian mission, and the Amir can't risk the kind of world sanction he would receive were he to act precipitously. In any event, given your background and world-renown status, you would never even hit his radar as a likely spy. As you know, he needs you quite desperately." Villar projected confidence as he flattered her, but Amy didn't trust him one bit.

"You've given us a lot to think about. I'm sure we'll be discussing this further," Eli said. Amy took his hint, though she would have liked to have ferreted out more information from the slippery Dr. Villar.

"Regardless. Our immediate objectives have not changed, have they, gentlemen?" Amy asked. "If you intend to have anyone perform an operation on the Djinn Dictator's sister, we had better ensure that we can perform it as safely and effectively as possible. One successful operation is not nearly enough. Especially when that operation did not result in perfect vision."

Amy smiled. She too could feign complete confidence. At least now she finally believed she knew the real reason the DoD was sponsoring her research; but this new directive was almost as impossible as their original desire to augment soldiers with mage sight.

"Agreed, but our time is limited. Information has a way of leaking, and it's imperative that we maintain our advantage," said Villar.

The room was quiet for a moment. Amy felt trapped by their expectations. Now that she had heard Dr. Villar's explanation, the DoD's goals seemed so obvious.

Villar continued briskly, as if this were no more monumental than planning a conference, looking around the table at each of them in turn. "As you suggested, Dr. Bant, we will need another subject. You and Commander Thompson should decide on the parameters for a screening program before we go back to Washington. Once a candidate is found, the surgical team, including Commander Thompson, will perform another operation, which I have no doubt will be another brilliant success. Whereupon Harvard will make a televised announcement regarding your work, and we will see if the Djinn Dictator bites."

Aphrodite's magical virtuosity alone is not the basis for her acknowledged place as the greatest mage who ever lived. Indeed, she is revered as much for her humanitarian response to the devastation of the Iron Age as for her magical prowess. Never forget that it was Aphrodite's self-sacrifice that ensured the fae's survival. By constructing the sirens, and binding her spells into perpetuity with the power of her own death, she prevented the extinction of the oldest sentient species on Earth. As a newly transitioned siren, you are a child of Aphrodite, with the responsibility to preserve and protect the fae; to fulfill the purpose for which Aphrodite gave her life.

– Sirens: An Overview for the Newly-Transitioned, 3rd ed. (2015), *by Mira Bant de Atlantic, p. vi.*

Chapter 4

Cordelia stood up, her skin tingling with the thrill of finally getting her challenge underway. The other courtiers looked up from their paperwork with bored expressions. *This time it will be different,* she thought. Though only eighteen of the twenty-seven courtiers were at Court today, and all had heard the Reconcilers' arguments from her before, this time she had Isioma and Daan on her side. She had spent six years working behind the scenes to orchestrate this moment, and now the High Court would hear a call to arms, instead of the bland recitation of facts and statistics they were used to.

"The continued imprisonment of the Aos Sí in England is a crime against our very nature!" Cordelia's voice rang through Tiven Hall. "Louisa, I know you disagree. I know you think it a kindness that we even allow the remnants of Morgan le Fay's army to rot on that iron-studded island. But it is *wrong.* Indeed, it is an affront to our very creation that we are party to this torture."

She had planned the moment carefully, waiting for the right time to push Atlantea into making a decision. Louisa, called out by name, had to respond to Cordelia's opening challenge. She shifted almost as often as

Cordelia's mother did, and was now wearing the shape of a busty woman with pale blue eyes and a high forehead, her dirty-blond hair pinned back in an unforgiving bun.

Cordelia's mother had told her that it was disorienting to physically transform so often; keeping a standard style of dress or hairstyle could help you maintain your sense of self. But Cordelia suspected that Louisa consistently chose this hairdo more to remind people of her position than to keep grounded in an unfamiliar body. Louisa had commanded Atlantea's army since the War of Succession more than a hundred and fifty years ago.

Louisa stood to address Cordelia, planting her hands squarely atop the heavy oak table. "I do disagree. We are not the cause of the Aos Sí's suffering."

Louisa may have thought that her pose gave her an air of command, but Cordelia thought she just looked hunched over and weak. She glanced around the room, trying to get a sense of the undecided courtiers, but had a hard time reading their expressions.

"It was the Cabal who salted the ground with iron and steel," Louisa continued in a strident tone. "I will not stand for this constant misattribution of blame. We sirens are not mages, able to call metal to the surface." She pointed at the empty seats around the table, her finger jabbing the air fiercely. "Moreover, we have continued to be their saviors! Many of the most powerful among us are not at this table tonight because they are in England, aiding our imprisoned enemies. Yes, enemies! These are not mere descendants of those who fought with Morgan le Fay; these are the very same fae who empowered her to rise up against the very ocean itself!

"The Aoi Sí never renounced Morgan le Fay. Freeing them would simply revive the Third Mage War, which, as we all know, only ended when the fae were imprisoned. Do *you* want to go back to the horrors of that war, Cordelia? Because I certainly don't."

Louisa was in rare form tonight. Her voice rose and fell like an angry sea stirred by a nor'easter. She practically spit poison when she mentioned Morgan le Fay's name. Louisa was an avowed opponent to the reconciliation movement, and much of the old guard followed her lead. Fortunately for Cordelia, the Reconcilers were on the rise on Atlantis. There had even been demonstrations last year — something that hadn't happened previously during all of Atlantea's reign. The Atlantics were beginning to think that their part in the war hadn't been as benign as their historians had led them to believe. There was also the undeniable fact that the rest of the oceans treated them like pariahs.

Isioma rose, and Cordelia looked around the table to see how her entry into this tired fight would be received; the undecideds definitely seemed intrigued. Isioma was even older than Atlantea, her strength second only to the queen's, and was widely viewed as cautious and shrewd. Winning Isioma's support for reconciliation was probably the greatest success of Cordelia's political career thus far.

"You are right when you say that we did not poison the earth with iron and steel," Isioma began in a rich contralto. She had changed her form since their last meeting, and now wore a Mediterranean look, with dark curly hair and wide-set, dark eyes.

"That was the work of the Cabal, who made sure the Aos Sí were safely confined before they abandoned England for Australia. But our hands are not clean. They can never be clean. England is fully within our domain; it is an island surrounded by *our* ocean. It has been *our* choice to let the fae remain on that island. Inaction can be as great a sin as action, Louisa. And we have failed to act." Isioma sat down amidst the slow murmur that was growing among the courtiers.

Before now, Isioma had allowed the other courtiers to think she stood with the old guard and their unwavering support for the status quo — irrespective of the increasingly dire reports on the Aos Sí's health, or last year's protests on Atlantis. Like Louisa and most of the older Atlantics, Isioma believed that the mages had made a mistake by leaving Morgan's army alive at all.

Certainly, it would have made all of their lives simpler had the mages simply executed the Aos Sí in 522. Their deaths would then have been but one more atrocity perpetrated during that horrific war by long-dead sirens and mages. Instead of dealing with fading prisoners-of-war, the modern Atlantics could then have merely denounced their forefathers' misdeeds as a horror never again to be repeated. But that hadn't happened, and the remnants of Morgan's losing fae army remained trapped in the North Yorkshire moors.

If Isioma's support was critical to convincing Atlantea that reconciliation wasn't merely a fad for the younger generation, Daan's support was critical to persuading the more mercenary courtiers that reconciliation made political sense.

Daan stood, pausing to look around at the undecideds. "For years, we had thought that the Pacific and Indian sirens were simply unhappy with the outcome of our War of Succession." Daan's voice was a strong tenor that cut through the surprised murmuring regarding Isioma's change in view. He continued to survey the room, looking down the horseshoe-shaped table at the assembled court, before inclining his head towards Atlantea, who sat expressionless in her heavy, mother-of-pearl inlaid chair. Cordelia longed to know whether their arguments were making any headway with her. At the end of the day, the High Court served Atlantea; it would be her decision alone.

"We believed that their refusal to allow intermarriage, their territorial bans, their snubs, all stemmed from their misguided support of the usurper. But as we now know, while we were fighting for Atlantis, the Cabal was salting England with iron in preparation for their own exodus to Australia. It is our failure to stop the Cabal that made us pariahs. The other oceans view us as war criminals. This has gone on long enough. Had we known what the Cabal was planning, we would have acted! That they chose to commit this atrocity while we were in the midst of a civil war is telling. We must relocate the Aos Sí."

Daan appeared to compose himself, though Cordelia knew most of his speech to be more performative than heart-felt.

"Isioma is correct," Daan continued. "England and the imprisoned fae are within our territory. It is not the place of the other oceans to free them. This is *our* responsibility." Daan sat down, smoothing his dark hair back and turning to his neighbor, who nodded vigorously in agreement.

Daan had been relatively easy to win over. He was a born siren like her, but unlike her, had been named courtier more because of his intellectual ability and financial skills than any great intrinsic power. Siren power was fueled by fertility, and the only way for a siren to increase their power was through increasing the number of their living, active siren progeny. Yet Daan's attempt to arrange a marriage last year between his latent daughter and an Indian's latent son had been rebuffed. Cordelia wondered if this had been the first time anyone had turned him down, because Daan still fumed over that insult, as if it had been the worst thing to ever happen to him.

Another member of the old guard began to drone on with more of the same arguments against the dastardly Aos Sí, who were apparently so different from the rest of the fae. While she pontificated, Cordelia watched the seven undecideds, whose support could sway Atlantea. They seemed more embarrassed than entranced by her opponent's tired rehashing of Third Mage War atrocities committed almost fifteen hundred years ago.

When the old guard courtier finally sat down, Cordelia stood and addressed Atlantea directly. "Atlantea, the pressure on you to act has been growing at a grassroots level since before I moved to Atlantis thirty-four years ago. That pressure will only grow in strength as the anniversary of the Third Mage War armistice approaches."

Cordelia held up her hand, as if to preclude interruption, even though none of the old guard would ever be so impolite as to interrupt. "None of your courtiers have incited this fervor, but many of us have witnessed it. You asked us to serve on your High Court to provide you with our best advice and counsel. We are sworn to be your hands when the need arises. As your sworn courtier, I tell you: you *must* relocate the Aos Sí. And I hereby pledge to be your hands in this matter. You cannot afford to allow them to remain in England any longer."

Cordelia had been deliberately provocative. By directing her argument at Atlantea before consensus had been achieved, she was sidelining the old guard. By referencing her arguments as being made in fulfillment of her courtier oath, she was implying that her opponents were failing to do the same, impugning their honor. Louisa rose to the bait.

"You impudent upstart! What do *you* know of service? You weren't even alive during the War of Succession! What have you done for Atlantea? You know nothing! Are nothing! *You* be Atlantea's hand in this? Absurd! I will be her hand and wipe this problem from the face of the Earth as our ancestors should have done!

Their mistake is one *I* will correct by drowning the lot of them. Let the Atlantic rise up and swallow that misbegotten corner of England, and we will be free of this once and for all!"

Vincent, Louisa's closest ally, sat next to Louisa. His eyes fixed on her with growing alarm as she spat out her rage-filled tirade. He stood quickly and took her arm, squeezing slightly. "Louisa is overwrought," Vincent told the shocked and now silent room. "She does not mean that."

"Oh, but she does," Cordelia said quietly from her seat. "Many of us will *never* forgive the perceived betrayal of the Aos Sí. None of us were even alive during the Third Mage War, but somehow the pain and hatred of that time has been passed down as some kind of loathsome inheritance. But mass murder is not, and can never be, the answer."

Cordelia stood now to tell the Court what they didn't want to hear. Because of Louisa's outburst, she had this one chance that they might actually listen. "We have no legitimate cause to destroy those we were sworn to protect, even if they sided with Morgan le Fay. Even if they roiled the ocean with their power during that ill-fated war. And even if you agree with Louisa that our ancestors should have slaughtered the Aos Sí, doing so now would not only be a crime, but would cause the relatively minor problems we have with the Pacifics and Indians to erupt into a full-fledged war. We are disdained by the other oceans because we allowed our sometime ally to harm the fae. Were we to destroy a fae nation ourselves, all the oceans would have no choice but to rise against us!

"Courtiers, I am not calling upon you to forgive the Aos Sí. I am calling upon you to allow us to forgive ourselves. We cannot be whole while we allow this atrocity to continue."

Cordelia played her next card; she was bluffing, but didn't think they would call her on it. "I have spoken with Jarl Georg. The Aos Sí will not be welcomed back in Europe. The Third Mage War erupted over control of the Taiga, and the winning fae faction will not permit their return."

Cordelia noted the looks of interest when they heard that Cordelia had spoken with the Jarl. While her many-times-removed-great-grandfather had neither supported nor opposed her plan, she knew that the courtiers would interpret the mere fact that he had stirred himself to investigate the issue as evidence of support for Cordelia.

"There is one place where they can be relocated. One place where they will no longer need our continuous aid just to survive." Cordelia paused a beat as Atlantea's eyebrow quirked up. This was her strongest card, and her best hope to win Atlantea over. "The Congolese rainforests."

The room erupted in chatter. "Africa!" one of Louisa's supporters shouted in disbelief. Some courtiers were nodding their heads. She had previewed the idea with Daan and Isioma, as well as a few select supporters, who were ready with their arguments in favor. Vincent and Louisa whispered furiously, and Cordelia wondered if her public exposure of the old guard's murderous intent would be enough to sway Atlantea into action. Vincent rose again.

"You make valid points, Cordelia." Vincent inclined his head towards her, the very picture of urbane politeness. "But your vision of this problem is far too broad. Do we only narrow our focus, and this thorny problem becomes much smaller. Our immediate problems have nothing to do with questions of exile or imprisonment, but simply with the iron in the soil. Remove the iron and steel, and the fae will recover. The Aos Sí only suffer because of this poison spread by the Cabal upon their own exodus. Remove the iron, and we remove the fae's suffering. There is no need to look beyond that."

Cordelia watched, stone-faced, as the old guard and many of the undecideds nodded in agreement. The problem was not the imprisonment of the Aos Sí, but the iron in the soil.

Daan tried to insert a note of reason, but the old guard did not seem interested in his thoughts. "Vincent, this is a fair point, but one that we have previously considered, and rejected as infeasible. The Cabal is not open to reason on this point. Our delegates approached them a mere half-century ago, and their response was to send an envoy back to salt the soil with steel, lest the iron rust too quickly. The Cabal will brook no interference with their judgment, and any mage to go against them will soon face their displeasure. None of the mage enclaves will risk war with the Cabal over the fae. There are no lone powers strong enough—"

Daan's speech was drowned out. "What of the dwarves?" Vincent challenged, and the murmuring started again.

"It doesn't matter who takes the iron from the soil, the risk of Cabal retaliation is real, and why this was not pursued before. We have been over this many times." Cordelia's voice rose, and she stopped speaking when she realized she was as much at risk of losing her temper as Louisa. It didn't matter, because she had lost momentum. The old guard was excited to put their weight behind this "exploration," which would only delay the issue of fae freedom yet again. Delay meant continuation of the status quo.

Zale, who had been at Atlantea's right hand since she took the crown, finally rose to speak, and Cordelia's heart skipped a beat. His face was inscrutable as always. Courtier factions courted him on all issues, but only very rarely did he grant his support. Of all the undecideds, Cordelia knew, his opinion would have the most weight with Atlantea. And of all the courtiers, he was the one she most admired.

"Sirens." Zale's baritone resonated around the room, and the side conversations quieted. Cordelia suppressed the frisson of pleasure she felt at the sound of his voice. Zale had not previously weighed in on the reconciliation movement, but unlike Daan and Isioma, Cordelia had hesitated to approach him.

"It is not meet that we should allow the fae within our domain to suffer and fade from iron poisoning. The Pacifics and Indians are right to shun us: our tolerance of fae mistreatment is a betrayal of our very creation. We must act, and not because of the pragmatic arguments put forth by Daan, though those are compelling, nor because of the mass demonstrations of which you advise, Cordelia. Truly I say, Isioma, your assessment is correct: our failure to right this wrong is a grave sin."

Zale was ever the consummate politician. Cordelia's heart pounded. She honestly didn't know whether he would sway this her way or not. Zale looked at each courtier in turn, as he addressed the heart of their concerns. "But while all of you who plead for action are right, Louisa's concerns are sensible, and must be truly considered. We cannot forget the bloodthirstiness of the Aos Sí; indeed, any failure to exercise caution could prove disastrous. Iron removal without agreement from the Cabal could result in another war. We sway from one extreme to the next in our quest to remove this festering thorn."

The courtiers rumbled again. Zale was only summarizing what they already knew, and so he lost the room to their side arguments. Cordelia looked around the table, identifying those who did not appear moved either way. These were the pliable courtiers: the ones who felt no passion for either side. Their support could perhaps be bought, and might ultimately change the tide if Atlantea still remained unpersuaded.

Atlantea rose, but her movement did not spark any immediate response from her courtiers. She actually had to strike the tintinnabulum on her left. The melancholy sound of the bronze bells ringing in a pentatonic scale cut through the din in a way that made Atlantea's admonition of their discourtesy feel more sad than angry.

"My courtiers, you continue to provide me with the best advice and counsel. I have heard your thoughts, and must ponder their import to determine the safest course of action for all of the Atlantic." Atlantea met each of their eyes in succession. Cordelia's heart sank with the queen's word choice. They had been making the "safe" choice — inaction — ever since the end of the Third Mage War.

"While many of the same arguments made over the course of the last century have been made again in this session, we must all acknowledge that the world today has changed. Our analysis of the value of these arguments must likewise change to reflect the difference in our position. Since the Cabal salted the earth, we have had to ever increase our resources designated to preserve the Aos Sí. You have all seen the grim reports on their situation from our sirens stationed in Yorkshire as support. It is likewise true that modern mundane notions of reconciliation have influenced our own people, who clamor for justice."

Atlantea took a breath, then continued. "But all of these truths must be put aside for the moment. I am in need of your counsel on a pressing matter." Atlantea paused a moment. "Know you all that I am in possession of a true prophesy."

There was a collective moment of shock around the table. Not merely because of Atlantea's startling change in topic, but because of the topic itself: prophesies were rare beyond measure. There were many mages with the talent for prognostication: predictions about potential futures most likely to result based on existing reality. But a prophesy was different; in a prophesy, the oracle's prediction of the absolute future was inescapable.

Because the future seen in a prophetic vision was unavoidable, Cordelia often thought there was no real purpose in seeking one out. And prophesies were dangerous; history was filled with tales of leaders who sought to outmaneuver a prophesy, only to precipitate the inevitable. At a minimum, Atlantea's announcement had effectively put on hold any discussion about the Aos Sí until whatever was prophesied came to fruition. Cordelia was so frustrated by the truth of that, she had a hard time focusing on Atlantea's words.

"The Oracle has prophesied the start of another desert-based mage war. The Danjou Enclave sent one of their mages to obtain a prophesy of the next mage war almost three decades ago. I have been monitoring the situation, and it now appears likely that this war will begin during my reign."

Atlantea's staccato deluge of information was unusually direct, and there was a moment of silence as the courtiers processed her speech. Everyone hoped that the era of mage wars was behind them, or at least that a mage war wouldn't be fought during their lifetime. When mages battled, the world burned. Even the last mundane world war, when the U.S. dropped an atomic bomb, didn't come close to replicating the world-wide devastation of the previous mage wars.

"A war fought in a desert is unlikely to have any impact on us, Atlantea," a courtier finally opined.

"Perhaps. But just because the Oracle saw an image of battle on desert sands doesn't mean that the conflict will be primarily based in a desert. Their vision may simply be of a pivotal battle." Atlantea replied calmly.

"What did the Oracle see, specifically?" Zale asked. Cordelia was somewhat surprised to see furrows on Zale's forehead. He had been Atlantea's closest confidant since before the War of Succession; if Atlantea had not told him about the prophesy, then she had truly kept this information secret. Her abrupt decision to disclose it to the High Court now worried Cordelia almost more than the substance of the prophesy itself.

"There is not much that we know; prophesies are tricky to interpret. Queen Sophia of the Mediterranean obtained a personal audience with the Oracle to verify what our spies reported: When asked to predict the next mage war, Delphi saw a scene of battle in a desert shimmering with heat. Humans primarily, with battle mages swirling in color amidst the clashing mundane armies. Weres ranged the field, while aircraft fell from the sky. The Danjou have come to believe that the types of tanks and aircraft described by the Oracle are similar in design to those in use now." Atlantea had a distant look in her eye.

Cordelia wondered how accurate the Oracle's description of mundane weaponry was. Military gear seemed to change every few years. The Oracle, who was always embodied in a trinity, was barely able to communicate clearly with questioners. They were so high on the chemical fumes swirling through the

Delphi cavern to enable their visions that the information they provided was really quite limited.

"What are the other prophesies?" asked Isioma.

"We don't know. The Oracle refused to provide any further details to Queen Sophia, refusing even to acknowledge that they did produce other prophesies of the same events for other suppliants. Yet all great magicks run in threes. Queen Sophia was able to confirm with the Pacifics that a prophesy was given to the Cabal, but they declined to share more information. The Mediterraneans told me that Amir Khalid personally visited the Oracle. But no one has been able to break through his barriers to ascertain anything about what he was told."

Many courtiers asked questions, and one foolish individual had the nerve to challenge Atlantea outright on keeping this prophesy to herself for so long, but no one had any other insights. The meeting dragged on, with talk going in circles until finally Louisa stood up.

"War is not to be feared," Louisa challenged and the room grew silent. Louisa looked around the table, her eyes lingering on those whose questions had hinted at a lack of courage. "We have seen war before. We have fought before. We are ready. We *will* be ready, whatever comes."

"And if the Earth burns, Louisa?" Zale began quietly, but his voice rose in volume and pitch as he pinned her with the sincerity of his concern. "What will we do when battle mages ally with mundane armies with their bombs and drones and tanks? How will any of our powers matter if the humans nuke the Arabian desert into glass? If they flatten the Great Western

Desert into radioactive dust that coats the planet in magical ash? How will all of our *experience* waging war help us then?"

"It's a *prophesy*, Zale. What the Oracle proclaims will happen. That is the nature of prophesy. All of our talk here will not change that," Louisa said quietly, but her eyes shone with a fierceness that Cordelia had not seen in her before. Suddenly, Cordelia could see Louisa as the great leader she was said to have been during the War of Succession.

"Louisa is correct. Our talk will not change what will come. But Zale, I will need your help. There is much to consider. Preparations must be made," Atlantea said.

"I have always been yours to call," Zale proclaimed, and others around the table murmured their assent.

"We will be ready," Louisa stated with a firm promise.

Cordelia sat quietly, thinking. This prophesy changed everything … and nothing.

Unlike mages, who train for decades to manipulate magical energy, mage constructs use their more limited magick instinctually. While additional training can help sirens gain greater control over their powers of fertility transfer and opposite-sex influencing, no amount of training can reduce a siren's deleterious effect on fertile members of their same sex. Moreover, no one has discovered any means by which a siren can increase or decrease the amount of the ocean's particular favor, which remains stable from birth or transition. It isn't clear why the ocean bonds more closely with some sirens than with others, but all sirens are beloved by the sea to some extent.

– Sirens: An Overview for the Newly-Transitioned, 3rd ed. (2015), *by Mira Bant de Atlantic, p. 27.*

Chapter 5

Cordelia floated in the sea, but didn't feel at all peaceful. She had come down early that morning after a restless sleep to regain her equilibrium. She knew the Atlantic loved her; even more than most sirens, the Atlantic adored her, and she could usually depend on her daily swim to recharge her optimism. But today, the ocean was agitated. *Something is wrong*, Cordelia thought, and it probably went beyond the bombshell Atlantea had dropped upon her courtiers last night.

Cordelia spent at least a few hours a day in the sea, and since other members of the High Court did as well, no one interfered with her communion. It was almost a mark of being a powerful siren, to *need* the sea. For the sea to need you. But Cordelia admitted privately that it was also a massive self-indulgence. She didn't need more than a few minutes in the Atlantic to know how it felt. She didn't need much more than that to know what it knew and cared to share with her. But it was such a relief to be alone with the Atlantic that she always stayed longer, buoyed by its affection and freed from the double-speak and petty deceptions that plagued the rest of her life.

Today the Atlantic was uneasy, and Cordelia wondered how much of that was a reflection of the courtiers' own unease. She hoped that her own tension wasn't leaching out to trouble the water. The Atlantic often reflected and refracted her feelings to such a degree that sometimes she didn't know if she was instigating the emotions she felt, or if they were pouring into her from the sea itself.

She had gone over the sequence of events repeatedly last night. So close. She had been so close! But Atlantea's shocking revelation had removed any possibility of prevailing now. At this point, no courtier would be able to focus on anything but the possibility of a mage war in their lifetime.

Cordelia sank down to the ocean floor to lie upon the sand. *The reconciliation movement is dead,* she thought. She had two choices, really. She could abandon the cause to which she had devoted the last two decades of her life and move on; or she could try to resurrect it. To somehow persuade people that the looming prospect of a catastrophic war not only didn't change the necessity of reconciling with the Aos Sí, but somehow made it a more critical imperative.

Cordelia pondered as she let the currents take her further from shore, propelled by the ocean's desire to pull her into deeper water. She drifted deeper, untroubled by the change in pressure, and let the Atlantic breathe for her. Cordelia admired the multi-hued colors of the water as she glided through the different temperature bands, hoping that if she sank far enough, the Atlantic would provide her with better insight.

But enlightenment was not forthcoming. Perhaps she was too consumed by her own turbulent thoughts to open fully to the water. The ocean simply provided no peace today, and Cordelia shot back to the surface, propelled by the nervous agita that bled through the Atlantic and multiplied her unease. She simply didn't know what to do.

Cordelia started floating slowly back to shore, watching the streaks of clouds surround the dim glow of the sun, and tried to clear her thoughts. Despite her best efforts, she was unable to calm herself, and her slow return only amplified her feeling of being penned in. *I shouldn't have spent so long worrying in the water*, she thought as she drew closer to Atlantis and saw how the ocean churned around her in reflected agitation.

Unlike her brother Thomas, Cordelia would never be content merely attending court events and visiting the fae preserves from time to time. Long before campaigning for a spot on the High Court, Cordelia had come to accept that she would not be happy living that kind of life — even if many thought she was moving too quickly into a role that most sirens only sought after their own offspring had transitioned.

Maybe it was her mother's influence. Mira seemed so impervious to her own success. Cordelia fantasized about doing something as important to the sirens as writing a textbook, but her mother sloughed it off as if it had been nothing, that it was no big deal; all she had done was to write down what the experts told her.

But of course it *was* a big deal, and her obsession with making transition safer had saved so many sirens in all the oceans; the transition survival rate had almost doubled since publication of her first edition! Then there were her older mundane sisters, who had also achieved remarkable success in the mundane world. Look at Amy, about to accomplish another once-in-a-lifetime achievement. What had Cordelia to show for her efforts? Her latest attempt to accomplish anything real was floundering on the back of an oddly timed announcement.

Atlantis' beaches were not meant for relaxing, and Cordelia picked her way carefully up the stony shore, drying off instantly as she emerged. The limestone had been polished into smooth round rocks, but would never be pulverized into sand by an angry sea. Storms didn't destroy a siren's home, and there were almost 250,000 sirens living on Atlantis. Their island was situated roughly halfway between Paraiba in Brazil and Sierra Leone in Africa. While supply ships came regularly, Atlantis remained unknown to most humans. The ships' crews didn't want word of their lucrative trade route to reach competitors, and in any event, were compelled to silence by the port officials.

One of Atlantea's guards appeared on the walkway surrounding the beach, and started down towards Cordelia. While she had expected to be observed, she hadn't expected to be greeted. Cordelia gathered up her discarded clothes, pulling on her robe and bending down to put her on shoes.

How quickly things can change, Cordelia thought, tying her sneakers. Perhaps she was being overly optimistic, but she couldn't really see how a mage war fought in or over a desert would impact them. Only the barest edge of the Sahara, on Arabia's African frontier, even drew close to the Atlantic coastline. But her own lack of imagination wouldn't stop other courtiers from developing all sorts of plans to keep them out or pull them more deeply in, depending on their ambitions.

Cordelia had generally floated above the fray by virtue of her relatively low profile. She didn't maintain her own court, but was always welcomed at — even actively solicited to attend — other courtiers' events. She supported their pet projects, at most offering what she thought were well-thought out improvements or mild criticisms that didn't block them. She had spent years acting as the supporting player. A valued supporting player, she had thought. Yet all her efforts to build a foundation to challenge the status quo and finally break the Aos Sí free had been a waste of time.

Cordelia had barely gotten her shoes on by the time the swiftly walking guard was close enough to greet her. The only official uniform worn by Atlantis' guards was their visible weaponry, though most generally wore red, a color rumored to provide some disguise from mage sight. This guard followed the typical pattern, wearing a red shirt over loose red pants, with an M4 carbine in a shoulder sling and a silver-and-steel *mokume-gane* sword holstered at her waist. The mixed-metal blades were only really used by the Atlantics, who worried about both were and fae attacks.

"Welcome back, Courtier," the guard said in a high voice. She would be a coloratura, Cordelia thought.

"Thank you," Cordelia replied.

"Atlantea has requested that you attend her this afternoon. Word was also left in your rooms, but I thought you might appreciate more advance notice."

Cordelia looked more closely at the guard. This was an unexpected kindness. "I'm sorry; I'm sure we've met before, but I can't remember your name." Cordelia started picking her way across the stones.

"I'm Helen," the guard replied. "We sat at the same table at one of the Reconciliation Group year-end dinners a while back. I wouldn't expect you to remember me."

Cordelia felt a flash of embarrassment that she couldn't even master the basic skill of remembering her supporters' names. Some politician she was! But she shook off the feeling: seeing a fellow Reconciler in person helped her regain some of her lost equilibrium. While she knew objectively that reconciliation was significantly more popular among the broader Atlantic population than among the courtiers, it was still uplifting to see a supporter in person. Cordelia used that mild boost to suppress her gnawing worry over Atlantea's summons.

"I'm grateful for the early warning. Has there been any talk about last night's Court session?" Information disclosed in high court meetings was supposed to be kept in confidence by the courtiers, but something always leaked. Cordelia wondered if there had been enough time for rumors of the prophesy to make the rounds among the guards. If anyone should be made aware of a possible war, the guards should be first in line.

Helen stopped, looking directly at Cordelia in a way that made Cordelia certain she must know. "No one has said anything, but it isn't only the Atlantic that is troubled."

Cordelia glanced back at the sea. Despite the lack of wind, white-capped waves pulled at the stone shore. Ugly gray foam was left among the rocks as each wave receded. "I can't thank you enough for meeting me like this. I've spent the night and most of this morning trying to decide whether my priorities should really change. I wonder what you make of it." Cordelia continued walking back up the rocky shore towards the path that wound its way up to Atlantis House.

Helen walked next to her in silence for a moment. Finally, she said, "I've been guarding Atlantis since I came of age," looking straight ahead. "I focus on the enemies I see, and not on those who haven't yet materialized."

While Helen's sentiment was practical, it was also somewhat short-sighted. If no one was on the look-out for possible dangers, they could all be blindsided when new enemies emerged. While that was the role of Atlantea and her High Court, not the guards, Cordelia agreed with Helen in this particular case. There were too many unknowns with the Oracle's prophesy — they only knew that another mage war was coming. They didn't know who, where, why, when, or how. There were too many possibilities obfuscating the real problem that remained directly in front of them: the imprisoned and dying fae.

Cordelia shook Helen's hand American-style as they parted on the path that led up to the castle entrance. Helen's perspective had been more clarifying than Cordelia's swim, and she continued to ponder the matter as she moved through the courtyard. A coming mage war only made it more imperative that they resolve the Aos Sí issue! Their continued imprisonment remained an obstacle to the Atlantics' relationship with the powerful Pacific and Indian communities. Perhaps the need to repair those relationships before a mage war started would be sufficient incentive for the High Court to take action now.

Cordelia acknowledged the gate guard with a vague nod as she entered the private wing. All courtiers had rooms in Atlantis House, which had been built after old castle was destroyed during the War of Succession. Those who'd known the old castle claimed that the new structure's modern conveniences more than made up for its lack of old-world charm.

While Cordelia didn't have any basis to make the comparison, she thought the current castle was rather charming in its own right. It had been fashioned in a style similar to medieval castles, with walls of bleached limestone topped by turrets and walkways. The main difference between Atlantis House and a medieval castle (and in Cordelia's mind, the main improvement) were the large glass windows that enabled you to see the Atlantic from almost every room.

Despite the ocean's unease, the swim had at least been good for Cordelia physically. Her tension headache was gone, and she finally felt awake, despite her restless sleep. Now she had the energy to wonder why she was being summoned. Atlantea almost never met with her privately; certainly, far less frequently than she did with other courtiers. She tried to tamp down the eager hopefulness that this summons signaled Atlantea's favor.

Her mother had been one of Atlantea's favorites for as long as Cordelia could remember. But so far, the only favoritism that had trickled down to Cordelia had been her own placement on the High Court — and that, Cordelia suspected, had been mainly due to Mira's refusal to serve, and Atlantea's desire to keep her close.

Her mother tried to spend as little time on Atlantis as possible. Mira was now in an almost self-imposed exile in Brazil, where she claimed to be developing key relationships with the Brazilian fae and the were-jaguar clans for the Atlantics. Since the Brazilian fae had emigrated from Europe before the Iron Age had truly taken hold in South America, the rainforests provided a rich source of power for them. Although they still needed siren intervention to reproduce, Cordelia doubted that her mother really needed to spend so much time in the Amazon for the fae.

She'd tried to understand why her mother kept Atlantea and Atlantis at such a distance, but had finally given up. Marisol opined that it was depression, that Mira couldn't let go of her past life as a human, and all she had lost. While it was true that transitioned sirens struggled with the biological and cultural changes, her mother had been a siren for longer than she had been human, and Cordelia wished she would just accept it.

While Cordelia had been born a siren, had grown up knowing who and what she was, Mira only transitioned at the moment of Cordelia's birth. Cordelia's older siblings were born human, and her mother refused to give any of them up. But at some point, a siren with a human family had to make hard choices. Her mother had made them. Enough.

Atlantea wanted Mira to return to Atlantis, but Mira always had a seemingly reasonable excuse. The thought that her own placement on the High Court was some kind of tacit agreement between Atlantea and her mother undermined any feeling of success her courtier status should have conferred. By asking for Cordelia's service, it was almost as if Atlantea had sealed a kind of bond with her mother, without forcing Mira to make any oaths directly. It rankled Cordelia that her political success was probably more due to her mother's stubbornness than her own intrinsic strength.

And Cordelia *was* strong. The Atlantic adored her, desiring to please her almost as much as it sought to please Atlantea. Even if her powers of compulsion and fertility were relatively weak, those powers were more commonplace, and would be naturally enhanced when her own offspring transitioned. Only a siren beloved by the sea could be a contender for the throne.

So while Atlantea may have wanted to bind Mira to Atlantis through Cordelia, perhaps that wasn't her only rationale. Maybe Atlantea had requested Cordelia's service at such a young age to solidify her own loyalty. After all, the queen had more than a century left in her lifespan, and the only thing that worried Atlantea more than a mage war was the prospect of another civil war. Cordelia's own oath prevented anyone from attempting to seat her as a puppet on Atlantea's throne.

Cordelia reached the door of her apartment at Atlantis House and walked into her sanctuary. It was small, as befitted her junior status at Court, but Cordelia loved it. The far wall of the front room was covered in a thick tapestry that had been one of the gifts given by Queen Sophia upon Atlantea's ascendance.

She loved the design, which depicted Aphrodite's construction of the first sirens, sacrificing herself to give them life. Every time she walked into her room, Cordelia felt a renewed sense of purpose just from looking at her ancient ancestor. Her desk was positioned to face the windows overlooking the sea, and she noted that the ocean's agitation had only grown since she'd left the shore. For the ocean to be this disturbed, Atlantea herself must be distressed. The rough seas would radiate out from Atlantis all the way to Argentina and Denmark.

Cordelia picked her outfit with care. If Atlantea was this upset, she didn't want to make any missteps. Her summons had to be related to yesterday's session, and she was not ready to give up on the Aos Sí. She looked past her red dresses and suits, which might signal her readiness for a mage war, and pulled out a green, kimono-styled wrap suit. The weight of the layered silk jacket felt like armor to her, and she felt prepared to argue that if anything, a looming mage war only increased the urgency of gaining a rapprochement with the Indians at least.

Atlantea had chosen the silver receiving room for their meeting, which was unusual, and Cordelia struggled to make sense of it. The silver receiving room was on the north side of Atlantis House, connected to the ballrooms, meeting rooms and other public spaces of the castle. Because of its distance from the private wing, it was generally used for small audiences with foreign envoys and others not connected to the High Court. Cordelia tried not to read too much into the location.

She considered the worst case: Atlantea could be summoning her to tell her privately that the Reconcilers had to stand down in face of the imminent threat of war. That was the likely reason, but would also be highly unfortunate: Cordelia had sworn personal loyalty to Atlantea, and as wrong as such a decision would be, Cordelia couldn't really imagine disobeying her. But hope fluttered in Cordelia's chest. As much as she tried to prepare for the worst, she was truly hoping that this meeting signaled Atlantea's favor towards her proposal. She had thought through everything. It could still be done, and there were so many reasons why they should try to resolve the Aos Sí situation before any mage war began.

Cordelia's musings preoccupied her all the way through the long corridors until she reached the central anteroom. The silver receiving room was one of several chambers connected to it. Its high arched ceilings and richly carved moldings added architectural interest to what was, in essence, a glorified waiting room.

This space was often used for music, and could be a rather boisterous venue on those afternoons when Atlantea and the courtiers held open audiences, no appointment necessary. Impromptu concerts on those days were the norm, as various courtiers showcased their latest collection of musical talents. Entering now, when it was so silent, felt almost ominous. In any event, Cordelia preferred to see the ocean. The anteroom was an interior space, and despite its rich décor, Cordelia thought that the lack of a view of the sea made it an uncomfortable place to wait.

Fortunately, Cordelia didn't have to struggle without the ocean's comfort, as the guards ushered her in immediately. Atlantea was seated near the windows at the far end of the room, and rose to greet Cordelia: a sign of high favor that caused her heart to lift. Cordelia bowed perhaps more deeply than required, so great was her relief at Atlantea's warm greeting. At Atlantea's gesture, she took the seat across from the queen's.

While Atlantea did not face the sea, the view from the windows seemed to surround her in a mantle of strength. Cordelia wasn't simply facing Atlantea, she was facing the symbolic embodiment of the Atlantic itself. For a few moments, Atlantea simply looked at Cordelia.

Atlantea rarely left Atlantis, so did not transform her appearance often. For the past two or three years, she had worn an Icelandic visage: blond and lanky, with bright green, almond-shaped eyes and cheekbones that

Laura Engelhardt

were practically carved into her face. It was a strong look, suited to a queen, Cordelia thought.

"Last month you marked eleven years of service on the High Court," Atlantea stated.

"Yes, Atlantea. I swore my oaths as courtier when you asked for my service eleven years ago," Cordelia responded. It was not unusual for Atlantea to begin an audience with a recitation of her subject's pledges (or lack thereof). The War of Succession had left scars on all participants that would be unlikely to fade anytime soon.

"I have been very happy with your service, Cordelia," Atlantea said. "You have been able to move the High Court in the proper direction, without making too many enemies."

"Thank you, Atlantea," Cordelia responded, unable to keep the flush of pleasure from rising in her face. She *had* tried to avoid making enemies, though some, like Louisa and Vincent, would be her enemies merely because of their disparate politics. Atlantea's words may have been flattery, but it was so rare to hear any praise, Cordelia couldn't help but feel pleased at the compliment.

"There is a mage war on the horizon. I had hoped it would not come to pass during my reign, but that appears now to be the reality we must accept. How will you serve me in wartime, Cordelia?" Atlantea's eyes narrowed on Cordelia and she felt almost pinned under the weight of Atlantea's stare.

"I serve, Atlantea. In war or in peace, I serve. I admit I don't have any special skills at battle or intrigue. But

I can provide you with advice and manage logistics. My queen, the prospect of all-out war makes it even more necessary that we resolve our residual issues with the fae to achieve a rapprochement with the other oceans. We can't afford to remain isolated. If the deserts are at play in this war, we'll want an alliance with the Indian and Pacific sirens.

"Or at a minimum, clean relations with them," Cordelia added hastily as Atlantea's eyebrow raised at the word "alliance." Alliances had a way of backfiring. The perennial entanglement of non-mages in mage wars seemed to stem from alliances, and Atlantea had been an avid isolationist since before she took the throne.

"A desert war is most likely to affect the Indians. The deserts of Arabia and Australia border their domain." Atlantea stood up, turning her back to Cordelia to look out at the Atlantic. "I have not spoken to the Raj since before I took power, but Queen Sophia has passed along the Oracle's pronouncement and reports that he is troubled. Kōkai-Heika appears less concerned. But then, the Pacifics appear to be repeating our mistake in getting involved with the Cabal."

The Cabal was unabashedly magophilic, but their reverence for the great mages of history didn't extend to mage constructs. The Atlantics had learned the hard way that the Cabal saw them as nothing more than useful tools to exploit — a lesson, it seemed, that the Pacifics would have to learn afresh. "Are you worried about the Cabal?" Cordelia asked.

"I'm *always* worried about the Cabal," Atlantea answered, sitting back down with a sigh. "I don't like how cozy Kōkai-Heika has been with them. Even as he spurns our overtures, he sends ambassadors to the Cabal. Who salted England with iron to poison the Aos Sí? It certainly wasn't us. Yet he flatters and ingratiates himself with those *mages*."

The way Atlantea spit out the word "mages" seemed to roil the ocean even further. The hair on the back of Cordelia's neck rose. Everyone knew how much Atlantea disliked mages, but until this moment, Cordelia hadn't realized how deep-seated her dislike ran. A toxic combination of hatred and fear, she thought.

"The Raj still hasn't responded to our overtures?" Cordelia asked.

"No. He refuses to recognize any of our envoys. Our only communication with the Indians has been through back channels."

"If you worry about the Pacifics and their relationship with the Cabal, wouldn't it be sensible to finally resolve the issue that divides us from the Indians?" Cordelia asked.

"It seems the prospect of a mage war has not changed your mind on the Aos Sí. And yet your solution is … complicated."

"Atlantea, truly it is *not* complicated," Cordelia said earnestly.

"Your proposal requires a multi-year undertaking," Atlantea said.

"True. But it will not be as resource-intensive as you might think."

Atlantea stood again and looked out the window at the pounding sea. "War is coming," she said, with her back still to Cordelia.

"Yes," was all that Cordelia could think to say, as her sense of unease grew. In any normal private audience, Atlantea should have ordered refreshments. And why was this meeting taking place in the silver receiving room?

"Louisa, Zale, and Georg are my most battle-proven courtiers," Atlantea said, and Cordelia felt her heart sink. Louisa was her most fervent opponent and neither Zale nor the Jarl were her allies. Atlantea turned back and looked at Cordelia. "You aren't pregnant, are you?" Atlantea asked.

"No, Atlantea," Cordelia said, somewhat startled by the apparent non-sequitur.

"Pity," Atlantea sighed. "By the time I was forty-five, I had borne seven human children. How else do you think I could have more than two dozen living siren descendants now? You're the only courtier with no active offspring."

"That's true, but I am sure that eventually one of my latents will transition; with the benefit of modern technology, I'm better able to monitor and prepare for such an event. But Atlantea, I'm not sure how this is at all relevant."

"I know I'm rumored to be opaque in my speech, so I will try to be especially clear now. We're running out of time, Cordelia. Now, I haven't shared all the details of the Oracle's prophesy with you or the rest of my courtiers, but I can tell you that we don't have three years to prepare for a large-scale migration of the Aos Sí. And while I truly wish I could have given you more time to prepare, you don't have the luxury of remaining cocooned in Atlantis any longer. There's a mage war on the horizon, and I can't be sure that I will survive it. Your relocation plan for the Aos Sí is a good one and might have worked. You can still make it work later."

"Atlantea—" Cordelia began, but Atlantea held up her hand.

"You are mine to call. Whether you serve on the High Court or not, you swore a personal oath to me."

This was worse than Cordelia had imagined. Gaining Atlantea's support for her relocation plan in the face of a mage war had been a long shot, she knew. But being in this cold, formal room, where strangers to Atlantis were met, Atlantea's strange focus on her lack of offspring, her apparent belief that Cordelia was "cocooned" in Atlantis — all coalesced into the beginnings of a disaster for which Cordelia had not prepared.

"I'm yours to call, Atlantea. Always. But hear me out—"

"As you remain true to me, I will remain true to you. I have thought about this, Cordelia. You don't have many progeny. If you are to be in a position to succeed me, you must have siren issue. Two latent children aren't nearly enough to ensure that in a century at least some of your offspring will transition. Mayhap you ought to compel your son to follow your brother's ill-advised example, and ensure his transition."

Cordelia's eyes widened and she had to still her features into impassivity. Her brother, Thomas, had surprised the entire siren community when he transitioned after donating sperm in college. No one had paid sufficient attention to the advances in mundane fertility science, and certainly no one had anticipated that a siren could be born through such means. But for her mother's swift action to locate and protect Thomas and his genetic children, all or most of them would have perished. Atlantea had been quick to forbid her people from deliberately using such "unnatural" means to produce siren offspring. For Atlantea to suggest she actually seek out her son and orchestrate his transition was beyond shocking.

"Atlantea, I can't imagine my need for siren offspring is so great that I should attempt to engineer such an event. But I can certainly seek to carry another child if you think that wise." While Cordelia certainly hadn't been thinking about having another child — a pregnancy would restrict her ability to visit the fae, after all — if this was what Atlantea wanted her to do, she could still carry out the initial phase of migration planning from Atlantis.

Atlantea continued as if Cordelia hadn't said anything. "You've also made a great study of Europe in your quest to aid the Aos Sí. It's time I had someone I could trust pay a call on Queen Sophia."

"Atlantea, I would of course be pleased to visit the Mediterranean for you. And your warning about ensuring I've laid sufficient foundation for the future is well-taken. However, I'm yours to call. If you want me to focus on war preparations, I can absolutely do that."

Cordelia knew she was scrambling, and worried that her desperation was showing.

Atlantea stood up and reached out her hands. Cordelia's mind blanked as she stood up to mirror the queen's stance. "Cordelia," Atlantea said formally, taking Cordelia's wrists and squeezing them gently. "I thank you for your service on the High Court. It is with a heavy heart that I hereby accept your resignation. Taking the time now to bear another child is a wise decision on your part.

"Obviously, the stress of serving as a courtier would be counterproductive to bearing a child, and your sacrifice in stepping down at this juncture is eminently prudent — though I could not bear to have you depart entirely from my service, and would be most pleased if you would visit Europe as my envoy. I have already spoken to Queen Sophia, and she is delighted to extend you an invitation to visit Kasos."

Atlantea squeezed Cordelia's wrists again, then let her go. Cordelia stood motionless for a moment. She wasn't quite sure what had just happened; it was almost as if she were floating outside her body, watching the scene unfold. Atlantea had just removed her from the Court? Why? Perhaps Atlantea realized that Cordelia was frozen, so she continued speaking, giving Cordelia's mind a chance to catch up.

"I know you prefer to travel by ocean, as do I. I will therefore have your things packed and sent ahead for you. I would also like to send a few gifts with you for Queen Sophia. One of the pieces I commissioned isn't ready yet, so if you could delay your departure until it arrives, that would be ideal."

Cordelia simply blinked. Not only was she being fired, she was being sent into exile. What had she done wrong? Atlantea smiled for the first time since Cordelia had entered the room, and she knew that she was missing something. Some clue about what this all meant. But she had been dismissed. So clearly, so cleanly. The only coherent thought Cordelia could muster as she left was gratitude that she had at least been fired in private.

Many newly-transitioned sirens have a hard time redirecting their focus from what they have lost to what they have gained.

– Sirens: An Overview for the Newly-Transitioned, 3rd ed. (2015), *by Mira Bant de Atlantic, p. 60.*

Chapter 6

Mira hated being summoned to Atlantis. Fortunately, Atlantea knew that and only rarely ordered her to appear. This time, Atlantea had summoned her to help explain the prophesy to the courtiers. What possible "developments" at the High Court session yesterday could have necessitated that she disclose it so abruptly? Atlantea had chosen to keep the Oracle's prophesy a secret for decades. Why had she suddenly decided that now was the time for a revelation? Cordelia might believe Atlantea was an inspired leader, but Mira didn't have that kind of faith.

The currents altered around Mira to propel her swiftly through the deepest part of the ocean. Every time she entered the sea, she reminded herself that no siren had ever drowned. The first time she actually sank underwater, it had been a shock not to feel the strain of remaining without air. Mira still needed to consciously let out her breath and tell herself to inhale.

And even after all these years, it was still astonishing that drawing sea water into her nose and throat felt exactly like breathing air. Despite the fact she had been siren longer than she had been human, Mira would sometimes suddenly sputter and cough underwater, as her mind rejected the possibility. Her instinct of needing air would probably never go away; she was like an amputee trying to scratch a phantom itch on a missing limb.

After recovering from her recent coughing fit, Mira spent several moments marveling at the perfection of Aphrodite's creation. She never felt the pressure of the ocean above, although she knew she was at a killing depth. The magnitude of the sea was usually enough to help her find perspective.

Her son Thomas might wish that traveling through the sea were as exhilarating as a drop from a plane or as thrilling as a ride on a roller coaster, but being propelled underwater at over a hundred and fifty miles an hour didn't actually feel all that much different from traveling in a high-speed train or airplane. You simply didn't feel the speed. And while immersion in the sea usually more soothing than exciting, it was taking Mira longer than usual to relax into the ocean. She supposed that was due to the unusual nature of her recall.

Her relationship with Atlantea had always been somewhat strained, even after Thomas' transition when she gave up the pretense of being human. They just had very different hopes for Cordelia. While Atlantea had never said it outright, Mira knew she saw Cordelia as a likely successor.

But the last thing Mira wanted for her youngest daughter was the burden of being Atlantea ... and the last thing Mira wanted for herself or Thomas was the burden of supporting Cordelia as Atlantea. None of them was ruthless enough to crush the opposition that would undoubtedly form. But the Atlantic's favor for Cordelia was unmistakable: it adored her. Unless a less-beloved siren killed Cordelia before Atlantea died, Cordelia would likely succeed her.

The magnificence of the ocean and the luxury of her long-distance swim eventually quelled her worrying. Swimming was like praying the rosary for Mira: it centered her in the present, and filled her with a feeling of purpose and inner peace. Finally arriving at Atlantis' rocky shore, Mira picked her way carefully up the beach. It was twilight, and the moon had already risen low over the horizon to share the sky with the setting sun. While it had been a long trip, she hadn't really appreciated the passage of time.

Mira stubbed her toe and cursed as the calm of her day dissolved amidst the harsh reality of being back in Atlantis. She really should have worn shoes. Her reluctance to return must have bled through her subconscious, because yet again, she had forgotten. Every single time she walked barefoot onto Atlantis' shore, she felt like she was undergoing an unnecessary penance.

By the time Mira got to their apartment, she had lost every ounce of peace she had gained on her sixteen-hundred-mile trip. But she didn't have time to settle in, because when she opened the apartment door, she was surprised to find Cordelia sitting on the couch.

"Cordelia?" Mira asked. Cordelia almost always stayed in her own rooms at Atlantis House instead of their family apartment. Unless she or Thomas were visiting, Cordelia preferred to be in the palace, and Atlantea's summons had been so urgent, Mira hadn't taken the time to tell Cordelia that she was coming.

"Mom, what are you doing here?" Cordelia responded, without standing up.

"Atlantea called. I suppose you know about the prophesy now?" Mira flipped on the light switch. Cordelia had been sitting practically in the dark.

"*You* know about the prophesy?" Cordelia asked.

"That's why Atlantea summoned me," Mira replied briskly. "You remember Jonah, of the Danjou Enclave? Well, we actually met when I took Mary to boarding school for the first time. He had been on his way to visit the Oracle when I ran into him. It was by mere chance that we discovered the existence of the prophesy."

Mira went into the kitchen and flipped on the lights in that room too. She hated sitting in the dark.

"You've known about this since Mary went to boarding school?" Cordelia asked, surprised that it had been that long. Mom was always going on and on about her chance encounter with Jonah "at a rest stop on the New York Thruway" as if that had been the strangest thing that had ever happened to her.

"Yes. Imagine meeting an enclave mage at a rest stop on the New York Thruway," Mira replied as she pulled a soda out from the fridge. She was still proud that she had been resourceful enough to seize upon their unusual meeting, gaining an information source with the Danjou.

Mom can be so predictable sometimes, Cordelia thought. She repeated the same old stories over and over, while leaving out all the important things. "I can't believe you never told me about the prophesy," Cordelia replied dully.

Mira looked over at her. Cordelia's reaction wasn't nearly as heated as she would have expected. Cordelia could play the outraged victim almost as well as her oldest daughter, Mary. Thomas and Amy were more easy-going. "What's wrong?" Mira asked sharply.

"Nothing," Cordelia lied.

"*Something* is wrong. Is it the prophesy? Does Atlantea think war is imminent?" Mira came back into the living room, firing questions like a machine gun, and Cordelia wilted under the barrage.

She waited, but when Cordelia failed to answer, Mira wondered if her daughter were troubled by something other than the prospect of a mage war. She took a deep breath and tried to soften her approach. Cordelia's face was oddly blank, and Mira thought she looked pale. Ignoring Cordelia for a moment, Mira sat down on the chair next to the couch, where she could see the ocean out the window, and listen to muffled pounding of the surf. The fading daylight hid the water's surface, except where undulating flashes of light reflected off the wave crests.

"When I first told Atlantea about the prophesy," Mira began again, "I thought for sure she would tell the High Court. She was so upset. Neither you nor I have experienced war, so I suppose we just don't have the same points of reference as do the sirens who lived through the War of Succession. And Atlantea has an almost pathological aversion to mages. As terrified as any rational person would be at the prospect of a mage war, given Atlantea's hang-ups, I'm surprised she's been able to handle the information alone for so long." Mira watched Cordelia out of the corner of her eye. Something was very wrong.

"She spoke to Queen Sophia about it," Cordelia remarked flatly. There was something in her voice that Mira couldn't quite make out.

"But she only just told the High Court now. And I *swore* that I would tell no one." Mira hoped Cordelia would forgive her for keeping the secret. It seemed that she was cursed to keep secrets from all her children. Neither of her latent children knew she was still alive, and until now, neither Thomas nor Cordy knew about this prophesy. At least one set of her lies of omission had been remedied. Oddly, she didn't feel as unburdened as she thought she would.

"I suppose Atlantea didn't want her courtiers to know about the prophesy until she knew its fulfillment was imminent," Cordelia mused.

"I think you're right," Mira responded. "She worried that with too much advance knowledge, certain courtiers might disguise preparations for another civil war in any broader mobilization effort."

There had been three contenders for the Atlantic kingship when Atlantea's predecessor died unexpectedly in the mid-nineteenth century. Ama, the usurper, had tried to take the crown by force, instead of allowing the Atlantic to choose its favorite. She had waged a particularly bloody campaign of assassinations, eliminating most of the "undecided" sirens with any degree of power before the rest of the Atlantics even knew that a war had begun. If the third contender, Georg, hadn't allied himself with Sisi, now Atlantea, Ama might have been queen — legitimate or not.

Little wonder that the Atlantics were treated like pariahs: they were soaked in blood. And little wonder also that Atlantea feared another bloody transition. The way she managed her High Court was as much about containing potential usurpers as it was a way to actually govern.

Cordelia was probably right: the queen's decision to share the prophesy with her High Court now indicated that she had received some indication that the mage war was more imminent than Mira had supposed. She imagined at least some of the courtiers would use her visit to Atlantis to invite themselves to Mira's compound in Brazil, hoping to avoid the fray. Others would see a mage war as an opportunity to gain advantage. But really, Louisa was probably the only person on the Court who would embrace the idea of a war. *Louisa would relish spending her final years on the battlefield,* Mira thought.

"Atlantea does worry about certain courtiers," Cordelia remarked without much enthusiasm.

"Cordy, what did Atlantea say yesterday?" Mira asked directly. As Cordelia recounted yesterday's Court session, Mira noticed that she barely mentioned the reconciliation debate. After months of hearing about Cordelia's endless preparations, Mira knew this was the meeting where she had planned to pitch her reconciliation plan. Atlantea's pronouncement about the prophesy obviously threw a wrench in the works, and it was notable that Cordelia was glossing over it now.

"And then Atlantea asked to meet with me privately," Cordelia concluded, looking down at her hands as if examining her nails for breaks.

"She asked you to meet with her privately?" Mira parroted back. "Today?"

"Yes." Cordelia sighed and looked directly at her mother for the first time since Mira had walked into the apartment. "I'm not being cagey. I'm just having a difficult time understanding what just happened. To be honest, I feel even more unsettled now than I was when I first joined the High Court."

With a little more prompting, Cordelia explained the broad outline of her meeting with Atlantea that morning. When she finished, Cordelia wasn't the only one perplexed, and they both sat in silence for a moment as Mira collected her thoughts, and Cordelia slumped back on the couch.

"Maybe it isn't what you think it is," Mira finally said, rubbing her chin as she always did when she was thinking hard about something. Cordelia told her that it was annoying — it made her look like a storybook villain, no matter which pin-up star she resembled — but she didn't stop.

"And what do I think it is?" Cordelia challenged, standing up. "Do I just *think* she kicked me off the High Court? Because I know she did. She said so. Do I just *think* she exiled me to Europe? No, I don't just think it; I know she did. Because she arranged it with Queen Sophia before she even told me. What I don't know is *why*! Why she wants me out of the way. Why she went to so much trouble to throw me out in this convoluted fashion." Cordelia stalked into the kitchen; she moved like a cat, all liquid grace and elegant outrage.

"Tell me again what happened at the High Court meeting last night," Mira said when Cordelia's pacing eventually brought her back into the living room. "And this time, don't gloss over the Court's discussion on reconciliation."

Cordelia shook her head in exasperation.

Even though Mira understood that her daughter needed an outlet for her anger and hurt, it didn't feel great to serve as her punching bag. Now, at least, she thought she understood the pattern of events. Cordelia just couldn't see things clearly. Despite Mira's best efforts, she couldn't convince Cordy that Atlantea was mortal just like them. She didn't walk on water. Well, actually, she *could*, but that was beside the point.

"Look, Cordelia," Mira began, and despite Cordelia's attitude, Mira could tell that she was paying close attention to what she was saying. "Louisa has always been a risk to Atlantea. She only became a reluctant supporter when it became clear that powerful sirens would have to pick sides. She's been managing our military since Atlantea came into power. And she hates you and your ideas. The fact that at least half the guards support reconciliation drives her crazy. The only reason she hasn't been someone you needed to worry about is because she's almost a hundred years older than Atlantea and will soon be dead.

"If Atlantea is sending you off the island, my guess is that it relates to her concerns about Louisa. Zale knows where Atlantea's heart is better than anyone, even if he rarely shares that information publicly. What does he think?"

"I haven't spoken to anyone about this," Cordelia said. This wasn't something she wanted to think about, let alone share with Zale! Dropping back onto the sofa, she opened the can of soda she had taken from the kitchen. If she ever needed a jolt of caffeine and sugar, it was now. She still hadn't caught her balance since her meeting with Atlantea, and her mother's hopping from idea to idea wasn't helping.

"It would help to get Zale's perspective. Although," Mira paused, rubbing her chin again. "Atlantea's inane talk about your lack of progeny is hard to follow."

"That made no sense to me," Cordelia stated, carefully neutral. This was a difficult topic for them. She knew her mother had been unhappy with her decision to follow siren childbearing customs. Since they had moved to Atlantis when she was twelve, her mother had called pregnant sirens "cuckoos," a double-entendre of sorts that disparaged them as crazy, while judging them for "abandoning" their children to be raised by others. Never mind that the Atlantics placed their children with amazing parents, desperate to have children of their own.

But Cordelia thought her mother's aversion to adoption was probably more due to her unresolved transition trauma. Writing her book had definitely helped her mother come to terms with her own change, but that hadn't been enough after Thomas' unusual transition. She wondered if her mother had only delayed her despair at losing her mundane life with her obsessive quest to find her brother's test-tube babies. It had been thirty years, and she still wasn't over it. But her mother's issues weren't relevant to Cordelia's current problems.

"It sounded like Atlantea approved of your relocation strategy," Mira continued, "except that by telling you to get pregnant, she is effectively trying to prevent you from visiting the fae. And yet, she's sending you to Europe. It's a mixed message, for sure."

"What do you mean, a 'mixed message?'" Cordelia demanded.

"Perhaps Atlantea wants the fae problem solved. But there are bigger concerns at play now, and she needs her High Court focused on the prospect of a mage war. She needs at least some of them to help prepare. You always said the biggest problem with relocation as a means of reconciling with the Aos Sí was the time it would take to actually build the ships to transport them. I guess she could be telling you to take a year to do it — I don't know. Atlantea should stop playing these guessing games. It's so counter-productive." Mira let her frustration show.

"You think she wants me to move forward on the project? Even though the High Court didn't approve it?" Cordelia was scandalized.

Mira snorted. "What, you think everything happens because the High Court approves it?" Mira shook her head. "How many times have I told you that the High Court is an affectation? Atlantea keeps all her powerful sirens close — and uses the High Court as a tool for that purpose. But the Court has no real power. You know that."

Cordelia bit her tongue. They'd been having this argument since Cordelia was a teenager and Mira insisted that Marisol's stories of the High Court were made-up fantasies and wishful thinking. Cordelia knew the High Court wasn't the pinnacle of purity she had believed it to be when she was new to Atlantis, but it also wasn't the non-entity Mira tried to make it out to be either.

"Mother, let's agree to disagree on the power of the High Court. In any event, it's no longer really relevant for me," Cordelia said crisply.

"Oh, Cordy," Mira said. "I'm so sorry. It doesn't matter that being a courtier wasn't what I wanted for myself — or for you, for that matter. It's what *you* wanted."

"You know, I didn't go back to my rooms after that meeting. I walked out of the silver receiving room and into the public chamber, and I felt like I didn't belong anymore. I can't believe Atlantea met me in the damned silver receiving room like I was nothing to her. A stranger. Everything is just changing so suddenly. She knew all of this for years, and said nothing. *You* said nothing."

The worst part of being a mother was watching your children suffer and not being able to fix it. Little children, little problems; big children, big problems. And even the obvious truth that this change wasn't the end of the world, that there was some purpose behind it that they just needed to uncover, didn't change the fact that Cordelia was hurting.

"Things will look better in the morning," Mira said, and knew the platitude sounded weak almost before she completed the sentence. But Cordelia didn't even make a face. She was usually so high-strung; watching her shrink into herself like this was killing Mira.

"I guess. Maybe I should just go to bed," Cordelia said. It wasn't even eight o'clock.

"Tomorrow you should meet with Zale," Mira encouraged.

"I don't want to sit down with anyone on the High Court after they hear I'm no longer on it," Cordelia countered. "I don't want to be around to see them gloat."

"Zale likes you," Mira encouraged. "It won't matter to him anyway. He's always been closest to Atlantea — if anyone could help you understand her meaning, it's Zale. And if you're worried about running into someone who's heard about your new status, head over early before the news has a chance to spread."

Mira deliberately refused to use the heightened language Cordelia did. Cordy hadn't been fired, not really.

Roles ebb and flow. This change in responsibility and status wasn't even a setback, though Cordelia, so fixated on it, wouldn't be able to see that now.

"Zale is a night owl. He ends his days with an evening swim, and never gets up before noon." Cordelia stood up, putting her soda down. "I'm going to see him now."

"Now?" Mira repeated. "How do you know he'll be around? And in any event, I don't think you're in the proper frame of mind—"

"No, now is perfect. I saw his face when Atlantea told us all about the prophesy. She kept it a secret even from him. That's got to hurt. I'm going to see what this all means to him," Cordelia announced, and strode off into her childhood bedroom in a frenetic burst of energy. Waiting until the morning wouldn't do anything except leave her to agonize over everything all night long.

Mira was nonplussed by the speed with which Cordelia sailed through the apartment, changing out of the rather conservative green suit she was wearing and into a more relaxed silk pareo. *Not a look Cordelia typically favors,* Mira thought. But if Cordelia were choosing her clothes as a kind of symbol, the insouciance of the yellow wrap shouted that she didn't care what anyone thought. The boldness of that choice was all Cordelia, and Mira felt a sharp sense of pride at Cordelia's resilience. Cordy would be fine.

Transition occurs when a latent siren sires an active siren child. As with all other great spells, the axiom 'Magick Likes Threes' holds true with Aphrodite's. Rarely will a latent siren's first child be born active; typically, it is only the birth of the latent's third child or even their third child of the same gender that will activate Aphrodite's spell. As a parent, you are naturally concerned about making the best decisions for all of your children, active and latent alike. Transition teams have been established in all siren communities since 2000, and you should contact your local team if you need any assistance with this aspect of your transition.

– Sirens: An Overview for the Newly-Transitioned, 3rd ed. (2015), *by Mira Bant de Atlantic, p. 107.*

Chapter 7

The swirl of energy that Cordelia brought into a room was gone in less than a heartbeat as she charged off to Atlantis House. Mira took a moment to reflect in the sudden quiet after Cordy strode out. Mira wasn't sure that seeing Zale would actually clarify anything, but it was certainly better for Cordelia's peace of mind than wallowing in her room all night. At least she would feel like she was making some progress.

What had Atlantea done? Cordy was so loyal, so convinced of Atlantea's leadership, she'd walk through water for her ... and Atlantea had just stripped her of everything that mattered to her. Could this really be about placating Louisa, or was something else going on? Mira was honestly surprised that Atlantea hadn't at least given her some warning that she was going to disclose the prophesy. She worried at the abruptness of all these changes.

God, she *hated* Atlantis, with its bitter pool of hidden motives and poisonous politics! Transitioning into an active siren was only the first of the many shocks she had endured since stumbling into this odd world. Mira tried to be mindful of all the blessings that came with her new self, but got caught up again in cursing her change.

Of course, her pre-transition life wasn't perfect, but it had certainly been less complicated. Back then, her sole ambition had been to be a wife and mother, and all that had come abruptly to an end with Cordelia's birth.

At first, Mira hadn't even realized what had happened. Any difference in physical sensation was overwhelmed by the effort of childbirth: the pain, the exhaustion, the exultation, all had led to a blurring of reason. So in the delivery room, Mira didn't actively process the hospital staff's responses as abnormal.

First the nurse, who loudly announced that other patients needed their help while roughly shoving Cordelia into her arms and stomping to the door. Then Dr. Rogers, who bubbled over with compliments for her, taking Cordelia into his arms to rock, and lingering until the nurses paged him multiple times.

Later that day, she did wonder over the nurses' failure to respond to her requests for water, their reluctance to give her pain medication until scolded by the resident (who hovered insistently), and the way they all looked at Jack. Jack Bant was good-looking: at thirty-four years of age, her husband had been fit, tall, and blond, with bright blue eyes. Women always noticed her husband.

But the nurses' noticing had been different. While other women admired, even flirted with, Jack, these women seemed caught in a tropism. At the time, she had been too tired to say anything, and could only stare, bemused, at the soap opera-worthy scene. The nurses brought blankets (after scolding Mira for requesting a blanket in August), and cooed over Cordelia (after remarking audibly to each other that Cordelia was the ugliest infant they had ever seen). One nurse literally batted her eyes at Jack (something Mira had only seen in B-movies).

Another nurse rushed into her room, just to drop her pen in front of Jack. She bent down so close to him that when she picked it up, that her bottom practically grazed his legs. Jack seemed shocked at their behavior, blushing bright red in embarrassment.

It seemed like every nurse on the floor had come into her room, after ignoring or insulting Mira only moments before. Finally, Jack asked them to step out to give them some privacy. Mira couldn't believe it when one actually winked at Jack, while offering to babysit their older children. Then Dr. Rogers had come in, and there was another abrupt reversal. He smiled at Mira and asked her if she liked the room. Puffing out his chest, he explained that he had moved another mother out to ensure that Mira received the best room in the maternity ward.

Then he looked at Jack with such anger that Jack actually took a step back. For a moment, it seemed like Dr. Rogers was going to punch him. But instead, he coldly told Jack to wait outside so he could perform his examination. Mira's gentle protest quickly changed his mind: of course Jack could stay if that's what Mira wanted! The doctor praised Mira's silent stoicism during her sixteen-hour labor (Mira didn't recall being particularly stoic, or silent for that matter), smiled at Cordelia, and cuddled her like she was his very own baby.

Given the oddities at the hospital, Jack and Mira didn't wait for the usual discharge date, and despite the doctor's pleading, they left that afternoon. But the odd behavior of those around them continued, even after they got home. The ladies from their parish came every day bringing food, and even wine! As long as Jack opened the door, they were all smiles. But if Mira opened the door, they practically spit in her face. All were openly flirtatious with Jack; such abnormal behavior from women who considered themselves keepers of the faith.

Strangest of all was Mira's mother's refusal to drive down to see her newest grandchild. Mary claimed she had spoken with a fortune teller a few days before Cordelia was born to find out if Mira was going to have a boy or girl. The charlatan terrified Mary by making dire threats that if she visited, the newborn baby girl would die.

Since the "mage" had correctly guessed the sex of the child, her mother was convinced the prophesy was true. Mira had tried to persuade her that it was nonsense. Even if the woman *were* a mage, only a small percentage of mages studied prognostication — and there was no way Mary could afford a true reading. Any real fortune teller would be sequestered in an enclave, not living in Newark, New Jersey! But Mary was adamant; neither Jack nor Mira could change her mind.

Jack's parents had died before they were married, so if it hadn't been for their neighbor, Mrs. Tellman,

Mira would have been lost. Frannie Tellman was the only person, it seemed, whose attitude hadn't changed. Before and after Cordelia was born, the older woman had treated Mira and her family like the daughter and grandchildren she had never had. Mira missed her still.

A week after Cordelia was born, Mira slipped down to the beach around dawn. Jack had gone to work earlier that morning for the first time since Cordelia's birth. They owned a boat rental and filling station, and Labor Day weekend was a busy time for rentals. Mrs. Tellman was staying over at their house, and Mira felt the need to touch the water. She brought Cordelia with her; it was only a few blocks to the sea, and Mira decided it could never be too early for a beach baby to feel the ocean on her feet.

After all, she had introduced their other children to the ocean when they were infants. First had been Mary, named for her mother, then Thomas and Amy. Even though Mary had been born in January, Mira had bundled her up on a bright February morning and taken her down to the gray winter ocean. The sand was frozen tight, so it had been easy to walk. And Mira sat with Mary just at the edge of the shore at high tide and watched the waves slowly recede down the beach until tiny treasures were revealed.

That's how Mary got her first medal. As more sand was exposed, a glint of gold caught Mira's eye; and when she reached into the frigid water to see what kind of shell it was, she pulled up a heavy gold chain upon which a miraculous medal hung. It felt like a gift from the sea to Mary, as if the ocean knew her name and rejoiced.

While Mira always found treasures when she walked the beach, her first visits with her children brought extra-special objects. She had found an ancient-looking gold and ruby ring when she brought Thomas to meet the sea, and a slightly tarnished emerald and silver necklace for Amy, her May baby. Jack marveled at her finds, but since he also discovered treasures during his own beach walks, it didn't seem as unusual to them then as Mira now knew it to be.

This time, when Mira sat with Cordelia at the shore, letting the surf roll over her feet and ankles, she was astonished to see a woman walk out of the sea. The sun gleamed behind her, framing her in a golden haze.

Mira shifted Cordelia into one arm, and shaded her eyes, blinking, sure that it must be a trick of the light. But it was indeed a woman, dressed in what appeared to be a blue nightgown that dried as she emerged from the water. As she came to the shore, the light foam at the edge of the surf congealed on her dress, covering it in a grayish-white lace. The woman sat down next to Mira on the sand.

Mira's mouth fell open in surprise as she stared at her. The sound of the waves rolling, the birds calling, and the ever-present wind seemed to stop altogether as Mira stared at the woman and the woman gazed over the water. It crossed Mira's mind that the woman might be a mage. But that was unlikely. While she had never personally met a mage, Mira recalled that Morgan le Fay had been the last of them with any power over the sea.

The woman's silence didn't feel hostile, and Mira didn't feel unacknowledged even though the woman hadn't said a word to her. Mira had the strong impression that the woman had come to meet them … if the person sitting next to her was even a real woman. She was so beautiful: buxom and pale, with dark brown hair curling in gentle waves to her hips, and gray eyes that glowed like moonlight. Mira wondered if she were fae. She had heard of selkies who could transform from seal to person. With an effort, Mira closed her mouth. Cordelia woke up at that moment and started twisting her head back and forth.

"Cordelia is hungry," said the woman.

While Mira wanted to ask how the woman knew her baby's name, she was afraid to engage with her at all. But she was also afraid to try to leave, in case she were a faerie, and this a trap. So many *Mission: Impossible* episodes featured rescues of mundanes held captive by fae glamours. And there was that famous case in California where a faerie had been caught trying to steal a human baby to substitute his infant changeling in its place.

"Will you leave my daughter and me unharmed and unchanged?" Mira tried to phrase her question as tightly as possible. She knew that the fae couldn't outright lie, but skirting the truth was a well-honed art form with them.

Now the woman smiled and looked at Mira. "I am certainly *not* fae. But that was a well-formed question," she praised. Hints of her smile played around her eyes as her face grew more serious. "And while I'm not geas-bound to tell the truth, I don't mean you or your daughter any harm. In fact, I came here to claim and protect you. Even though we haven't met, I'm your father's grandmother's great-grandmother — so, your many-times-removed grandmother. And while I don't intend to harm you, I very much doubt our meeting will leave you unchanged."

"What are you?" Mira finally asked, giving Cordelia her finger to suckle.

"I'm a child of Aphrodite, but I transitioned centuries ago, while you are but newly active. We're sirens — me, you, Cordelia, your man. Constructed from Aphrodite's own genes, merged with those of the sea nymphs, and made whole by Aphrodite's magick. I tracked you down when I felt the uptick in power that came with Cordelia's birth. My name is Marisol. I came because I want to make sure you survive."

Cordelia had begun to mewl and cry softly. Mira had been so frightened; she remembered clutching Cordy even closer to conceal her trembling hands. This insane encounter felt too real for a dream, but so unreal at the same time. The woman's name was Marisol. Mira recalled that her mother had suggested Marisol as a family name when she was pregnant with Mary.

"Perhaps let Cordelia touch the water and she'll calm down," suggested Marisol, turning her gaze from Mira to watch the sea.

Mira hesitated to follow the instruction, unsure of whether it would be more dangerous to listen to Marisol or ignore her. But Cordelia's continued fussing made up Mira's mind. She hoped a monster from the sea wouldn't charge out as she shifted further down into the surf to let her right hand wet itself in the waves, before tracing Cordelia's face gently with it.

Cordelia's whimpering stopped abruptly, and Mira marveled for a moment at her daughter's sudden expression of pure joy. Cordelia seemed so delighted with the sensation that Mira unwrapped her from the light blanket to free her arm and let her feel the sea. The moment Cordelia's hand met the water, a wave lurched up and swallowed them. Mira's heart stopped as she experienced true terror for the first time in her life.

But the water immediately solidified beneath her, pushing Mira and Cordelia up after a second so that it was like she was reclining in an easy chair, with a thin line of unusually warm water covering them in a gentle blanket. Cordelia began cooing and blowing bubbles, patting the top of the water with her tiny hands. Mira looked to where Marisol had been and didn't see her. Then she turned and saw Marisol pop her head out of the water a few feet away on the other side.

"Oh my, but the Atlantic loves Cordelia," Marisol said. "The ocean practically drove me to you. I've never been pulled so fast through the waves before."

"This is so strange," Mira finally said.

Marisol leaned back to recline on the waves. "I know," she said. "But it's real, I assure you. Transitions are not easy. I almost died when I was reborn, and you're only the first of my progeny I've found in time." Marisol's face became briefly shadowed in pain before relaxing into that self-satisfied expression Mira soon came to associate with her.

"You should know that your lineage is a powerful one. You're descended from Atlantea herself. While that probably doesn't mean anything to you now, it will one day. A very powerful line indeed. And I can see that Cordelia will be a force to be reckoned with!" Marisol's pleasure in her conjecture sounded almost threatening.

Perhaps she doesn't intend us any harm, but she's not here solely out of the kindness of her heart, Mira thought, pulling Cordelia even closer.

"Sirens are magical constructs," Marisol continued, her voice rising and falling in inflection to mirror the water undulating around them. "Like the weres, we were created by one of the most powerful enchanters ever. Aphrodite had the strength of the sea running in her veins, and she died to give us her power."

Mira could hear Marisol's voice, but she wasn't really listening. She was distracted by the sound of the ocean. It was as if it were humming to her, singing a lullaby that she could just pick out if she listened closely.

"Pay attention!" Marisol scolded, and Mira startled. Marisol huffed. "You're overwhelmed. Too much change, too quickly. Listen to me. You must understand the following things, or you and Cordelia will certainly die." The flatness in Marisol's tone, more than the words themselves, focused Mira abruptly. Mira wished to sit up, and to her surprise, the ocean obliged, pushing her upright.

"What you must understand—I mean, really, truly understand — is the depth of hatred female sirens inspire in fertile women," Marisol's voice had an odd tone to it. "They can't abide us. Some instinct drives them to seek our destruction. They can't help it, and they can't be reasoned with. Women who were your best friends yesterday will seek to undermine and even hurt you today."

Mira started to ask a question, but Marisol raised her arm imperiously. "Do *not* let a woman babysit Cordelia! That's how most siren girls are lost in infancy: killed by their female caregivers. Now, the upside is that fertile males will adore you — they can't help that, either. Men will do anything you ask them to do. Your voice has a power of compulsion over fertile men that, with time, you'll learn to use."

Mira's mind flashed through the abnormal responses of the hospital staff and church ladies. "That's female sirens. What about Jack?" Mira asked.

Marisol shrugged. "It's the reverse for him. Fertile men will hate him, and women love him. His progenitor had better come soon. We lose more males than females during transition because of how violent human men are."

Marisol's utter lack of concern for Jack was chilling. Jack was at work, and most of the people who rented boats were men. She remembered her panic, and how she had struggled to get back to shore. She remembered the sound of police sirens, and the ambulance that raced past her as she hurried to the marina.

Mira didn't want to remember anymore.

She poured a large glass of wine and stared at the dark water visible through the window. It had been forty-five years since Cordelia was born and Jack had been killed.

Jarl Georg had been late. Mira didn't remember him coming to New Jersey at all, though perhaps he had started out and turned back when he felt Jack's passing. She and Cordelia first met him when Cordelia was about four.

Mira didn't feel old, really, and knew she didn't look her age, but so much time had passed. The fae had encouraged Mira to hone and shape her memories through reflection, so they couldn't control her present self. But her brief recollection of Cordelia's birth had left her so unsettled, she supposed she had spent too little time reflecting. The fae could be right; putting those memories into perspective might be the only way to avoid being captured by her past. Though perhaps so much reflection was better suited to fae than sirens. Her ruminations tonight had only made her feel trapped by memories, mistakes, and might-have-beens.

Despite the beauty of the night skyline, Mira felt morose. She needed to press on. Nothing she could do now would change what had happened then. Mira had met mundane Nigerians who believed in the curative powers of bright sunlight and joy to fade bad memories. They didn't reflect on a constant parade of the past, but danced in the sun to heal. Maybe she needed less reflecting and more sunlit dancing. Things would look better in the morning.

But there would be no time for dancing or even swimming tomorrow. Atlantea had summoned her — ostensibly to help soothe the courtiers' anxiety over the Oracle's prophesy — but now Mira suspected her summons had been more to do with Cordelia than anything else. Perhaps Atlantea wanted to ensure Cordelia didn't make a fuss. But Atlantea owed Cordelia answers. Frankly, Atlantea owed her answers as well. Tomorrow, she would force her to speak plainly for once.

An active siren's normal lifespan exactly equals that of Aphrodite, who was five hundred and thirty-three years, four months and twenty-four days old when she died to complete the siren spell. Almost half of all sirens who survive their transition year ("T1") will die of natural causes at the age of 533 years, 4 months and 24 days. More than 90% of T1 fatalities result from murder by fertile humans. While this remains the largest cause of premature death post-T1, the rate drops significantly post-T1 to 34%. Other post-T1 causes of premature death include: suicide (28%), accidents (14%), disease (9%), other murder (8%), and unknown (7%).

– Sirens: An Overview for the Newly-Transitioned, 3rd ed. (2015), *by Mira Bant de Atlantic, p. 61.*

Chapter 8

Cordelia knew she was being impulsive, but somehow it didn't really matter anymore. She had been the dutiful plodder for years, and what had she accomplished? Nothing. If her mother, ever the reasonable and measured one, thought Zale had answers, then she would see Zale. Enough time wasted! She paused in front of his apartment, then knocked before she lost her courage.

"Cordelia, I'm so glad you called," Zale said when he opened the door. Even though Cordelia had never visited him before, he seemed oddly unsurprised to see her there. For a moment she wondered if Atlantea had already told him about her dismissal, but then she noticed that Zale seemed quite unlike himself overall.

Tonight, his feet were bare and his shirt hung over his pants. His hair was mussed and flopped to one side to frame his face. Zale was one of the more buttoned-up of the courtiers, and she had never pictured him so informal, even in the privacy of his own rooms.

"Can I get you anything? Water? Wine? I have a bottle of red open. It's very good," Zale kept up the patter as he ushered Cordelia into his parlor. Zale's apartment at the castle was larger than most, consisting of three rooms instead of the usual two, so he was able to maintain an actual sitting room instead of a receiving area-cum-office.

Cordelia accepted a glass of wine and sat down on one of the settees. Zale sat across on the other and refilled his cup. While dinner at the palace would have officially ended only a little while ago, the scattered plates indicated that Zale had probably skipped the communal meal in favor of solitude.

His failure to join the Court at dinner made it more likely that Zale hadn't heard about her changed status. Cordelia wondered for a moment at how to phrase it. She wasn't sure she was quite ready to characterize it as a voluntary event, but she had spent the walk back to Atlantis House trying to convince herself that "European Envoy" constituted some kind of special status.

"You're kind to see me like this." Cordelia sipped the wine, using the distraction of drinking to cover her nervousness. She had decided to come here so impetuously that she lacked any clear plan for their conversation.

"It's not kindness at all," Zale said, his voice rougher than usual, his face tired. "Call it self-interest. The idea of a mage war in our lifetime came as a bit of a shock. You must have realized yesterday that no one on the High Court was aware of the prophesy — at least no one who was at last night's session. Atlantea has spent the day seeing various courtiers individually, but I haven't spoken with her about it yet. I don't know what to think right now."

Zale looked expectantly at Cordelia, and despite herself, she felt flattered that he would seek her opinion. "I'm not sure I've had enough time to really reach any conclusions at this point." She hesitated. "And I know I'm not as experienced as you are. But I do wonder how we might be drawn into this war."

Zale's unusual dishevelment was probably a sign of stress, and Cordelia chose her words with care, hoping that by approaching the problem logically, she could help him regain his typical equilibrium. "I agree with the consensus that Arabia or maybe western Australia is the most likely location for the battle in the Oracle's vision. But a desert war isn't a natural fit for us. It's not like when Morgan le Fay commandeered the Atlantic."

Cordelia paused, considering. She appreciated the fact that Zale didn't interrupt or jump in with his thoughts. Even before joining the High Court, she had idolized Zale. If Marisol was her earliest and most visible ally, Zale had been the ally she aspired most to have. It was irrational to hope for his support, but she did anyway. Her mother had told her more than once that Zale liked her; now Cordelia was trying to believe her.

"I don't know. While Atlantea has kept us out of any official alliances, my mother isn't the only Atlantic who collects favors. So perhaps a stupid promise made by one of our own will drag us all into it. But most likely, if there's a threat to the fae, we'd have to respond." Cordelia looked at Zale to gauge his reaction.

"Yes, if the mages threaten the fae again, I think we would have to intercede." Zale ran his hand through his hair. Usually slicked-back like a banker's, his hair was now tousled to match his guise of a sun-touched, teenaged Adonis, though his face looked old as he considered the prophesy.

"Another desert war. The first mage wars are remembered only in legends. It's hard to imagine another such as those. Now, I'm not terrified of mages like Atlantea; I've seen their value. They're only mortals like us — with typical mortal failings and mortal virtues. Mages and mundanes fighting, though…" Zale shook his head. "Among all the peoples, human ingenuity is unmatched. For humans to turn their greatest virtue towards such evil is unfathomable."

Zale drained his glass. He looked more troubled than Cordelia had ever seen him before. Suddenly, the gravity of the situation they were facing became much more real to her.

"Perhaps it won't be as bad as the First Mage War. I mean, mages are said to be less powerful now than they were before the Asian deserts were destroyed. It could be that this mage war will be more …" Cordelia paused, searching for the right word. "… minor. I mean, consider the American Conflict. That was isolated among the mages on just one continent. Historians only call it the Fourth Mage War because of the famines after Quiletoa erupted."

"You don't consider the Fourth Mage War a catastrophe?" Zale gestured wildly with his hands. Cordelia had never seen him this unfiltered. "More people died during Chía's misbegotten attempt to conquer the continent than during all the prior mage wars combined! When a fifth of the world's population is killed, does it really matter that they didn't take part in any battles? Didn't even know it was happening? When mages fight, the devastation is borderless!"

"Zale, I'm not trying to discount the horror of war — especially a mage war. And if the Oracle predicted it, it *will* happen. But knowing it's coming can help us perhaps avoid some of the damage. Times are different now. Human ingenuity, fae strength, our own power to compel — there are so many ways we can contain any crisis. I don't understand why Atlantea even told us about the prophesy; there's too much we don't know. We're going insane with worry because we can't make any real plans yet. It's honestly a distraction from the Aos Sí crisis, which *is* ripe for action."

Cordelia reached out and took Zale's hand. The despair in his face overcame any shyness she had previously felt about getting so close to her idol. "Zale, you seem like you've given up before we even know what kind of crisis it will be. You can't give up before anything even begins." Cordelia almost whispered her last words.

Zale sighed. "You're right. We don't know enough and all of my worrying over this is doing nothing but sending me into a dark place. Atlantea refused to see me today. I think she knew I'd be too upset to be of any use to anyone right now." Zale squeezed Cordelia's hand, and looked down.

"I'm not a coward," Zale said, looking directly at Cordelia, who flushed under the weight of his gaze. "I fought for Atlantea during the War of Succession, and I'll fight again now if that's what's necessary. I just can't wrap mind around the insanity of mages. Maybe you're right. It's fear of the unknown driving me in circles. Too many questions and too little direction."

"But we can make a difference. We'll find ways to ring-fence the crisis. I don't know, even stave off the worst of the destruction." Cordelia flushed. She'd been accused of being a Pollyanna before. But this time, she thought her optimism was justified. More than one human battle had been prevented before it could begin because a siren laid a compulsion on a key player. Crisis averted.

Zale continued to look at her, and Cordelia felt the full force of his attention atop the heat of his hand on hers. Sirens might be immune to their own magick, but they could still feel the appeal of a handsome man who appeared to concentrate on their every word. He didn't seem to be dismissing her words as inanities spoken by a naïve dreamer.

"The Oracle didn't see the fae in their vision. Maybe this war will be contained amongst the humans," Cordelia speculated, distracted somewhat by Zale's intensity.

"Mages tend to drag their allies in when they scorch the earth. I can't imagine this conflict would be an exception." Zale let go of her hand and leaned back, rubbing his temples.

"I hadn't thought the fae allied themselves with mages," Cordelia remarked.

"I've always thought it's our half-fae ancestry that leads us to seek out favors and make bargains. Mark my words: individual faeries have alliances with individual mages. Favors asked and granted. Worse even than we sirens. You can never predict how the entanglements will pull." Zale picked up the carafe. "Did you really come here to ask me about the mage war?" he asked, coming around to sit next to her on the settee as he refilled her glass.

Cordelia's mind blanked. She had come here to get his perspective on why Atlantea had exiled her, but somehow the moment didn't feel right. *Never ask a question for which you don't want an honest answer*, she reminded herself. If Zale told her Atlantea was done with her, she didn't think she could maintain her calm façade. Cordelia buried her pain under a raw burst of anger: how dare Atlantea treat her this way!

"Would you think me so shallow that I'm not concerned about the prophesy?" she asked, her tone rougher than normal.

Zale startled, clearly taken aback. "Honestly, it's such a horror to even think about another war, I wanted to focus on something else." His face tightened in a grimace, and while Cordelia realized she had misspoken, she didn't know what to say. She took the carafe to top up Zale's glass, then sipped her own.

"I didn't mean for you to think I oppose your proposal to relocate the European Fae," he finally said, breaking the somewhat awkward silence.

"You don't?" Cordelia asked cautiously. Her pain at Atlantea's rejection was still so raw, she grasped at a chance to talk about the cause that had been her sole focus for so long.

"Cordelia, I've never been your enemy. But I've not been your ally either," Zale's voice was back to that usual urbane baritone that stroked Cordelia's skin. No matter what form he wore, his voice always seemed to resonate with something deep inside her. Zale put down his drink and shifted closer.

"I made my alliance with Atlantea years ago and I don't plan to make any others." The bluntness of Zale's words was softened by his earnest demeanor. He seemed so anxious to tell her this, it was like he truly cared what she thought.

Zale continued, "Atlantea and I are roughly of age. Unless fate interferes, she'll predecease me only by about twenty years. I don't want to get involved in another siren succession. You've been looking for allies for the long-term, and it's clear that unless something dramatic changes with one of your age-peers, you will be the ocean's choice when Atlantea passes."

Zale's voice softened into a plea for understanding. "I can't take part in another regime. I've served for long enough."

"All right, then," Cordelia said, disappointed but unsurprised. Gaining Zale as an ally had always been unlikely. Somehow, she didn't even care what he said, as long as he kept talking. It seemed like all his energy was focused exclusively on her. She looked down for a moment, then back at him. His gaze hadn't left her face. "Zale, you can't think that only reason I've been part of the reconciliation movement has been because I want to be the next Atlantea—"

"I never said that. I don't believe that," Zale interjected hastily.

"But then why are you supporting more delay? Delay simply extends the status quo, which you know cannot and should not last."

Zale sighed. "You visited England once, right?"

Cordelia nodded.

"I lived there as support for a decade. Oh yeah, I spent ten solid years there." Zale's eyebrow arched sardonically at Cordelia's surprised expression, and he relaxed into his story. "Just after the War of Succession, Atlantea sent me away to supposedly 'investigate the Aos Sí situation.' Really, she just needed me off the island. The losing faction needed someone to hate after Ama was killed. Letting them blame Zale, 'the Kingmaker,' was easier than putting down further rebellion."

Cordelia shook her head.

"But it was a good thing that I was there. We were so caught up in our own struggles that we didn't even know what the Cabal had done to the Aos Sí. I mean, the Raj had refused to recognize Atlantea, citing atrocities we had allegedly committed. And we even didn't know what the Indians were talking about! When I got there, we finally discovered that the Cabal had salted the entire isle of England with iron before sailing off to claim Australia."

Zale shivered, and Cordelia felt the hair on her arms rise at the tone in Zale's voice: he was hypnotic in his recitation. "Slivers of iron throughout every last patch of earth to ensure the fae's compliance. And would you believe that after I left, the damn Cabal sent the Tudor mages to sow *steel* into the moors?" Zale shook his head.

"I know what happened," Cordelia said gently, though she hadn't known that Atlantea had exiled Zale before. It sounded like Atlantea had a habit of tossing aside her closest allies. But maybe it was because they *were* her closest allies, and the queen knew she could depend on them. Cordelia mentally kicked herself; only she could be so wildly optimistic as to spin a dismissal into a mark of favor. Zale was so loyal, so strong. But then, he'd had a hundred and fifty years to get over the anger and pain of his own exile.

"Just because you know the story doesn't mean you really understand it." His voice dropped with suppressed emotion, and she shivered at the sound. "I've walked every part of that land next to the fae imprisoned within. That iron doesn't just keep them weak, it's the most potent poison I've ever seen. In the thousand years between the Armistice and the mage exodus, there'd been no serious decrease in the Aos Sí population; they only started fading in earnest after the mages scattered iron and steel.

"And we allowed this, or at least didn't stop them. We neglected to watch over the second-largest fae nation in our domain because we were too busy killing ourselves. You're right; the Reconcilers are right. We wronged those we were created to protect. But now what? What happens when the Aos Sí demand reparations?"

"Reparations? What could possibly make up for that?" Cordelia asked, "If they demand ... what? Our service, our death? Our suffering? What does that get them?"

"You're assuming they're still sane. They've been tortured for centuries."

"My plan was to start small. To relocate a small community. Just a small group—"

Now Zale interrupted, "Do you think they wouldn't wait? Wouldn't simmer and wait another three hundred years to extract vengeance? The fae are immortal, Cordelia. They wouldn't do anything more than hail us as saviors until their strength was at its zenith."

"Fine. I get it. I don't agree, but that's a valid concern. So what next? We just uphold the status quo until they all fade away?" Cordelia demanded.

"No. You're right. Despite the risk, despite the consequences, you're right. You're *right*," Zale looked at her earnestly. "And I didn't raise these concerns at the Court session because I know we can't continue on this way forever. The Aos Sí are suffering, fading, dying. All because of decisions *we* made. If freeing them means we get slaughtered, maybe that's the right outcome. I don't know; I'll be dead by then anyway."

"Awfully fatalistic," Cordelia murmured. "The fae can't lie. Titania herself swore to me that they had no desire for revenge."

"Revenge for what? The war or their imprisonment? No desire for revenge doesn't mean they won't take it anyway. But Daan's right: we can't continue to be the pariahs among the oceans. The Pacifics and Indians have refused all intermarriages since the Cabal's exodus. We don't even have envoys at their courts."

"Zale, the fifteen-hundredth anniversary of the Armistice is only a few years away. It resonates with people. It's the opportunity we've been looking for to move forward." Cordelia leaned forward.

"I get the hook of the anniversary. But you need to have a better plan than just spiriting them away to the Congo. It's too risky to give them such a power source. Look at the Brazilian fae. They claimed the rainforests, and their power in that domain is near as strong as it was before the Iron Age sapped them."

"You think the Aos Sí are too crazy to be trusted with a jungle." Cordelia's voice was flat.

Zale ran his hand through his hair. "Maybe," he spoke more slowly. Cordelia was surprised that he seemed so unsure about his own views on the issue. "It may not seem rational to worry about them regaining a pittance of their strength, but these are not merely the descendants of the fae who fought in the war — they are the *actual* fae who fought and suffered and watched their lovers and friends fade away."

"But if they are consumed with vengeance, it's the Cabal, not us, who should be worried. *We* didn't salt the earth. Even if they do regain all their former power, they have no real reason to attack anyone but the Cabal." Cordelia felt her face flush, whether from the wine or pleasure at the sense she was winning him over, she wasn't sure, but she pressed her advantage.

"And when have you ever heard of a faerie, let alone a whole fae nation, succumbing to insanity?" Cordelia continued. "They suffer from obsessions and sometimes inexplicable passions, but the only people who've ever really destroyed the Earth have been mages."

"And what if freeing the Aos Sí throws fuel on the fire of this coming war?" Zale demanded.

"You didn't even know about it until after you opined that we needed to be cautious," Cordelia insisted.

"And that only means we need to be even *more* cautious. You underestimate them, Cordelia. Fae power isn't just illusions and healing. They tap the power of the forests' life force. They can change the weather. If they wanted to, they could destroy the Earth—"

"I have *never* underestimated the fae," Cordelia cut Zale off. "Do you think the other fae will just sit around and let them destroy the planet we all share? What do you think the Brazilians would do if the Aos Sí tried such a thing? Or Nga and Num, who drove them out of the Taiga in the first place? If a mage war is coming, having the Aos Sí's favor, even if it were only to last a hundred years, might prove to be the advantage we need."

Zale waved her off. "Your voice spins dross into gold. Save your crazy speculations for the other courtiers." His eyes held hers, his voice resonant. Perhaps it was the wine, or the stress of the past day, but their heated discussion had invigorated her ... and Zale too. Until now, Cordelia hadn't supposed that perhaps she affected Zale as much as he affected her.

"I misjudged you," Cordelia offered, looking down. "I'm sorry."

"I'm sorry too," Zale murmured. "Atlantea reminded me last night that I could have handled my concerns with your plan more privately than by posturing in Court." He sighed. "I suppose I worried at our speaking in private like this."

Cordelia wondered for a moment whether Zale was *really* Atlantea's lover. They had never acknowledged such a relationship, but rumors had them in each other's beds since before the war. Cordelia decided she didn't care, or perhaps she did: the chance to indirectly hurt Atlantea added a sinful spice to the moment.

"You worried about meeting with me?" she asked, reaching out to smooth a lock of Zale's slightly disheveled hair back. Cordelia had always admired him, and unlike the besotted humans who adored her merely because she was a siren, his eyes burned with a real passion.

"I shouldn't have," Zale whispered, reaching out to pull her closer to him. "But I've wanted to do this since you first joined the High Court."

"And I have wanted to do this since I first saw you," Cordelia said, taking Zale's face into her hands.

This was the escape they both needed. It was like slipping into the ocean, and Cordelia let go of everything outside of the moment. Her pain at Atlantea's dismissal, the prospect of war — all were immaterial now. Zale's desire for her was real, and the visceral pull of his passion was enough to anchor her in the present.

All of their fretting about the future faded into irrelevance beneath their slick intimacy. Just like the fae, a siren's lust affects the very landscape. The ocean outside the castle relaxed into a dance that night of rollicking swells and deep undertows. Cordelia felt her flesh bind with her spirit in a glow that enlightened the contours of Zale's body for her to savor, and the Atlantic's earlier agitation was swept away in its reflected delight.

There are five sirenic oceans, each with their own siren communities: the Pacific (168.7 million square kilometers), the Atlantic (85.1 million square kilometers), the Indian (70 million square kilometers), the Arctic/Baltic (15.6 million square kilometers) and the Mediterranean (2.5 million square kilometers). There are no records of any siren with an affinity for the Southern Ocean. Each sirenic community has their own unique culture and customs, and I am deeply indebted to my co-authors on each of the following chapters regarding the Pacific, Indian, Arctic, and Mediterranean communities. Despite our differences in culture and custom, we all share a deep and abiding love for all oceans, as well as our shared mission of preventing fae extinction.

– Sirens: An Overview for the Newly-Transitioned, 3rd ed. (2015), *by Mira Bant de Atlantic, p. 197.*

Chapter 9

"Mira, you look wonderful," Atlantea said, gesturing for her to approach.

Atlantea had chosen to meet Mira in one of her private salons at the south end of Atlantis House. An elaborate breakfast had been set for two in the round turret area of the room, where floor-to-ceiling windows displayed a full view of the surrounding ocean. This was one of Mira's favorite rooms in the castle because of how the nook seemed to float above the sea. The Atlantic was calm today, almost bucolic in its bouncing waves that undulated out to the horizon.

At least the tone of her meeting with Atlantea was poised to be quite different from that of her daughter's yesterday, she thought, sitting down and admiring the sparkle of mid-morning sunlight on the crystal and silver. What a change in circumstance from the chaotic and bare breakfasts of her youth! While last night she had felt inordinately saddened by the odd twist of genetics that had caused her to transition into an active siren, Mira felt quite differently sitting in this luxurious setting, with the breathtaking vista to her right and the nutty smell of Kona coffee surrounding her. But then, she usually felt happier in the morning. She said a silent prayer of gratitude at her good fortune, and accepted Atlantea's offer of coffee with cream and sugar.

Atlantea quite obviously did not want to discuss business right away. But then, they never did. Unless she invited others to their meetings, Atlantea liked the illusion of an intimate meal amongst friends. Their talks had begun shortly after the success of Mira's book, when she had declined the queen's offer to join the High Court. At first, Atlantea had been suspicious of her motives, but after a few decades, they had settled into a closer kind of relationship than Mira suspected the queen had with any of her actual courtiers.

How lonely it must be for Atlantea, Mira thought. Her tumultuous succession had forever changed her relationship with all the sirens who had once been her friends and lovers. Atlantea claimed to be unhappy with Mira's "obstinate" refusal to join the Court, but Mira thought her stubbornness actually pleased Atlantea. It was a rare someone who didn't ask for favors from Atlantea. Perhaps she thought she owed Mira for the transition textbook, but since Atlantea had enabled her to stay in the mundane world for years, Mira considered that bargain met. It wasn't Atlantea's fault that she'd lost her mundane life prematurely.

"How is Thomas doing?" Atlantea asked, almost as if she could read Mira's thoughts, which, as usual, had wandered towards the impossibility of his transition.

"Very well. He finished that fortress of a house last year, and now has an Amazon army guarding him," Mira replied, coming back into the present.

"I'm glad. I know you worry over him," Atlantea said as she buttered her toast.

"To be honest, I'm simply happy that he's finally left the Jarl's court. Thomas would never have been happy with the life of a hanger-on."

"You mean, *you* would never be happy with Thomas leading the life of a hanger-on," Atlantea said, pointing her butter knife at Mira. Mira inclined her head in acknowledgement of Atlantea's point.

"Perhaps. But I hated seeing him waste his life up north. I don't think he really did anything at court, except attend parties and make up odd new sports. At least now he's conquering his fear of being out in the human world. But I can't imagine he'll stay in Brazil forever. He's too restless for that."

Mira considered how far Thomas had come. He was much happier now that he was outside his progenitor's influence. Perhaps it had been Jarl Georg's remarkable indifference to Jack's death, but she had never liked him. She certainly didn't trust him.

"Well, I do like that he's made such inroads with the were-jaguar clans. That played out better than I had expected." Atlantea was referring to her decision several years ago to ask Mira to mediate a conflict amongst the jaguars. The weres tolerated Mira, but had never quite embraced her. Thomas, with his love of sports and careless *joie de vivre*, was quite popular with the clans.

For Mira, letting go of her mundane daughters had been the hardest part of her transition. Thomas seemed to mourn his loss of male companionship in a similar way. Male friendship was so different; it had taken her a long time to really understand that Thomas was truly stricken by losing his teammates. She had just never seen that kind of connection as anywhere near as important as family ties.

"The jaguars love Thomas. They admire his willingness to play with them, even though they are so much stronger and faster. But somehow Thomas holds his own. I can see why he was so popular in the satellite courts. People like to be around him."

"We may wind up needing to use the friendships he's forged sooner than we had thought," Atlantea said sadly.

"You said you'd finally decided to share the prophesy with the High Court," Mira stated. "What's changed?"

"I didn't tell them everything," Atlantea cautioned. "So be careful what you tell them when they ask. I only told them what the Oracle saw, not the words they spoke."

"That was wise; too often, words are subject to misunderstanding. The images are clear, and the words often misinterpreted." Mira considered how she and Atlantea had struggled with the meaning of the Oracle's pronouncement for so long. She shuddered to think of how many different interpretations the courtiers would have for such a cryptic response to the Danjou Enclave's question: "How will the war be won?" The Oracle had responded, "Siren surgeon's sight."

The enclave never should have asked such a question in the first place, Mira thought. They were doomed to receive a cryptic response; though she knew from Jonah that the mages believed they had perfectly phrased the question so as to receive the most useful information.

Atlantea looked out at the calm sea. "I still haven't been able to uncover the prophesy given to the Cabal, but now I'm sure that Kōkai-Heika knows it. He has more information than we do, but will not share with us, or any of the other oceans for that matter."

"But that's not new; we've talked about his reaction and his close relationship with the Cabal before. Has something changed with the Pacifics?" Mira tried to nudge Atlantea back to her original question: why had she disclosed the prophesy to the High Court now?

"Kōkai-Heika's desire to appease the Cabal makes it more likely the Pacifics will be drawn into any war in which they are involved. Sadly, that hasn't changed. But others are working on that problem for me," Atlantea said, looking at Mira intently. This was perhaps Atlantea's way of reminding her that she wasn't the only agent Atlantea had in the world, nor her only confidante. Not that Mira wanted to be, or even thought she was.

"You're not one to ignore any possible threat," Mira said truthfully. While she didn't revere Atlantea the way Cordelia did, she did respect her deep need to protect the Atlantic.

"No," Atlantea agreed. "We can't afford to ignore any of the Oracle's guidance. Through the enclave prophesy, we know that one of the pivots on which the war will turn is connected to the sirens."

The Oracle's response to the enclave mages had, of course, been of deep interest to Atlantea. There were few doctors, but even fewer specialists, among the sirens. It was simply too difficult for them to interact with humans long enough to gain the requisite training. At latest count, there were only eight siren surgeons world-wide. "Have you identified the pivot?" Mira asked.

"Perhaps. Did you know that the U.S. enclaves began partnering with mundane scientists on various mage-related research projects?"

"Vaguely, I guess. I think I read about some genetics research. A few years ago, maybe?" Mira tried to recall.

"Yes, that's right. Initially they started researching genetics — and indeed the bulk of their joint projects focus on why some mages have mundane children and vice versa—"

"I expect that interest was driven by the Amir's birth," Mira murmured.

"Certainly. It *is* uncommonly strange that the most powerful mage to emerge since Chía had mundane parents," Atlantea agreed.

"And his sisters are rumored to be quite powerful as well," Mira added.

"Yes, well. Arabia is such a closed society, it's nigh impossible to gain any real intelligence from them." Atlantea was impatient with Mira's digression, and swiftly moved the conversation back on track. "Lately, their research interests seem to have shifted. The Danjou have partnered with Harvard University and the U.S. Department of Defense to set up a research facility."

Mira's heart skipped a beat. Amy was at Harvard. She saw the expectant look on Atlantea's face, and knew in that instant that Amy was involved. Her fears were confirmed when Atlantea continued speaking.

"Your daughter, Amy, is a neurosurgeon at Harvard. Do you know anything about her latest project?"

"Amy developed a cure for amblyopia almost a decade ago. Her whole career has been devoted to *mundane* research. She would have nothing to do with magick." But Mira didn't know that for sure, and despite her rapid denial, she knew at some level that Atlantea wouldn't be telling her this without a degree of certainty.

"Ask your Jonah, but I understand she is at the center of a project to restore mage sight," Atlantea said in a gentler tone than Mira's rough defensiveness should have warranted.

"Amy is not a siren. She's a mundane who doesn't even have children," Mira stated firmly.

"Amy is a latent siren; she is a surgeon and she is working on a cure for magical blindness." Atlantea's tone may have been gentle, but her logic was relentless.

"Cordelia speaks with Amy often. She never mentioned any such project." Mira did not want this to be real, but in her heart, knew that it was.

"Cordelia actually mentioned it last week when I asked about her mundane sisters. She told me that Amy had just completed an experimental optic-nerve operation. She seemed quite proud that her sister was on her way to developing a second 'Bant Procedure.' And I received confirmation that indeed, the Danjou had sent a Class 5 via-enchanter to Boston to partner with Harvard and the U.S. government on a project to restore mage sight. A man named Eli Eisner was appointed to head the first magical neurology research lab. That is the same lab where Amy works."

Mira didn't say anything for a moment. Amy had worked with Eli since her second post-doc. She had intervened with Eli back then to ensure that Amy would be treated fairly, but had otherwise not directly interfered with her life; it was too painful to be so close, yet remain invisible.

How could Cordelia neglect to tell her about this? She knew how much Mira relished any news about how her lost daughters were doing — especially something that would be as important to Amy as a new project like this. But Cordy had clearly been so caught up in her own struggles that she'd forgotten. And of course, Mira hadn't told Cordelia about the Oracle's prophesy, so Cordelia couldn't be expected to have understood the broader implications.

"Amy is obsessed with her work. She has no time or interest in global politics," Mira declared.

"Amy's interests or inclinations don't really matter," Atlantea responded bluntly. "We always thought that the only way the Atlantic would be drawn into a mage war would be through alliances. And given how carefully I've avoided forming any official alliances, it is perhaps through blood ties that we might be bound into the coming conflict. Your daughter may well be the pivot on which the war's outcome will turn."

"I highly doubt Amy could be the fulcrum that changes the course of any war. She is completely fixated on her work. Always has been." Mira's heart pounded as she tried to persuade herself that this was a mistake.

Atlantea smiled sadly. "The Danjou must think it possible, else they wouldn't have sent their best via-enchanter to work with her. I'm not sure which is worse for her, really: if she *is* the pivot, or if the Danjou merely believe she is."

Atlantea was right. If the enclave believed Amy were the pivot, they would stop at nothing to ensure she swung their way. Even when an outcome was pre-destined, mages always believed they could change it. "Have you thought about what we should do about this?" Mira asked.

"I've thought about what we shouldn't do," Atlantea smiled grimly. "Louisa commands my armies because she eliminates threats. A pivot in the hands of the Danjou would be an uncontrollable risk."

"Telling Louisa about the Oracle's words would be a death sentence for Amy." Mira swallowed.

"And unlikely to change the outcome in any event," Atlantea agreed. Mira kept her face quiet as she reminded herself again that Atlantea didn't care about any of them as individuals. She was so totally focused on the survival of the Atlantic as a whole that they were all expendable pawns. If Atlantea thought assassinating Amy would reduce the risk of them being drawn into a mage war, she wouldn't hesitate — despite her quasi-friendship with Mira.

"I suppose we need more information about what is happening in Amy's lab," Mira admitted. She was so worried now that it was hard to think clearly. Losing her daughters was a wound that had never healed. *Damn Morgan le Fay to hell!* She couldn't even warn Amy about the risk she was facing. Thomas' singular transition had changed everything; no siren her age should have to transform with every fertility harvest!

"We need more information," Atlantea agreed. "But I'm not ready to share the Oracle's verbal prophesy yet."

"You didn't bring me here to talk to the courtiers or even to soothe Cordelia," Mira accused, as she finally realized what Atlantea was about. "You want me in Boston."

"Can you think of anyone better suited? This is too important for both of us." Atlantea's gaze shifted over Mira's shoulder, as she focused on a point out in the distance.

"Someone *trained* to be your spy," Mira suggested.

"We are the only two sirens who know about the pivot. I doubt the Danjou elders shared the prophesy broadly, and the Oracle will only state their words once. Prophetic speech isn't even written down any-more — not after what happened to Oedipus. Attempts to avoid one's fate have always rebounded in a worse way. You have always kept my secrets, Mira. This is too important."

"Don't ask me to do this," Mira pleaded. Lying to her children had been hard, but cutting Amy and Mary out of her life had been even harder. Of course, on spe-cific occasions she had briefly intervened, as if she were their guardian angel. But all of her brief interludes in their lives had been to help *them*; to keep them safe. Atlantea was asking her to help the Atlantics. She had to know that if asked to choose between her children and the Atlantics, Mira would choose her children.

"There is no one else I can trust," Atlantea said bluntly.

"I won't choose you over her," Mira declared.

"I know," Atlantea said simply. And indeed, Atlantea knew. That had always been the condition of Mira's service.

Neither of them said anything for a moment. The tension that had built in the room slowly faded, now that Mira had accepted Atlantea's demand and Atlantea had acknowledged the terms under which Mira would fulfill it.

"Withholding knowledge of the Oracle's words is prudent," Mira finally said. "But withholding your reasoning for dismissing Cordelia is not." There. She had tossed down the gauntlet. If Atlantea wanted her in Boston, she could at least explain why she asked Cordelia to resign.

"You never wanted Cordelia on the High Court," Atlantea temporized.

"But you put her on it anyway, and she has exceeded your expectations many times over."

"I have my reasons," Atlantea said.

"Close-lipped as ever," Mira remarked. "Don't you think Cordelia is entitled to a better rationale than a lack of siren progeny? Even as ignorant as I am of politics, that sounds weak."

Atlantea snorted at the idea that Mira was ignorant of politics. "The old guard will find that a perfectly adequate explanation, Mira. Many will take it as a sign that Cordelia finally has her priorities in order — that she has given up her relentless campaign on behalf of the Reconcilers, and is accepting reality and the status quo."

"And why is that important? All of your obfuscations simply make matters worse," Mira declared.

"It's time Cordelia grew up," Atlantea stood up and started pacing. It was a sign of how open she was being with Mira that Atlantea would allow her to witness her at anything less than her usual self-contained demeanor.

"Being a courtier was good for her. I don't regret asking for her service, though Zale insisted she was too young. Zale was an old man even when we were both in our first century." Mira noted that Atlantea strode with the same cat-like grace that Cordelia had. Perhaps Cordelia resembled her much-removed grandmother more than she had previously realized.

"Zale doesn't understand that experience can only hone the natural ability you have to begin with. Our Cordelia is blessed with an abundance of natural ability," Atlantea continued. Atlantea had always claimed Cordelia as hers. While barely acknowledging other sirens in her line, Atlantea had claimed Cordelia practically from the moment of her birth. Somehow, Cordelia seemed oblivious to that fact, though it hadn't been lost on the rest of the High Court.

Everyone knew that Cordelia had Atlantea's favor, and that knowledge had eased her entry into the cliquey and polarized Court. With Atlantea's tacit backing, Cordelia had built alliances and showcased her clear thinking and sincere service. Her innocence had somehow become part of her charm, as opposed to a source of aggravation to those courtiers who had been less privileged.

"Cordelia has benefited from her work on the High Court, but so have you. No one else would have been able to act as your lightening rod for the reconciliation movement without being crushed by the old guard," Mira said.

"She went too far the other day. I can't lose the old guard while we're on the verge of a mage war. And I don't want to lose her, either."

Mira was a little alarmed by Atlantea's view that Cordelia was putting her life at risk by advocating for the Aos Sí. Perhaps it wasn't just Cordelia who was naïve; Mira never would have expected a siren to face assassination over what seemed to her, in the grand scheme of things, a relatively minor disagreement.

"And telling the old guard that she's having another baby to leave on someone's doorstep will somehow calm their concerns?" Mira asked.

"She should have had at least four children by now," Atlantea snapped, annoyed by Mira's constant harping over one of the basic aspects of siren society. Sirens didn't really abandon their mundane babies; they made sure their children were well cared for and deeply wanted by their adoptive parents. Active sirens had no choice, really: it was cruel to separate from the child at puberty, when they began to feel the impact of sirenic magick.

"And yes, it will satisfy Vincent at least, and Vincent will persuade Louisa to stay her hand, convince her that Cordelia is no longer a threat. Perhaps Cordelia will use this as an opportunity to *do* what she thinks is right, instead of wasting decades talking to people." Atlantea sat back heavily in her chair.

"You think she's too cautious?" Mira asked. "Too bound up in the trappings of politics?"

"She's too *American*," Atlantea said flatly. "She spent too much time in civics class learning about your style of democracy to be effective. I wish you had come to Atlantis when she was born."

Mira didn't bother replying to that. They'd been through this argument before. "If you would simply tell Cordelia what you expected, she would do it. You know she would."

"Telling her would defeat the point of her standing on her own feet. Her instincts are wrong, and I won't be around forever to tell her what to do. As important as the Reconcilers and old guard seem to think the Aos Sí problem is, ensuring the next Atlantea is strong enough to protect the ocean is the single most important thing there will ever be."

Mira secretly thought Atlantea's ego had run amok a bit, but she would never let her know that. "So you've set her up to either act on her own, without the Atlantics' support, or to hide away for a while, schmoozing with the Mediterranean as if she were Thomas, while the rest of the High Court prepares for war."

"You are not to tell her any of this," Atlantea commanded.

"I'll tell her that you were concerned about her safety from the old guard, and stress that you can't afford to lose anyone with a mage war on the horizon," Mira countered.

"Fine, fine," Atlantea waved her off. "When will you head to Boston?"

"I'll leave soon." Mira leaned back in her chair, looking out over the perfect day outside. She would need the calm of an ocean swim. Atlantea was right; she had to find out what the mages wanted from Amy. Mira watched Atlantea sip her coffee, resolutely pushing aside tomorrow's problems. Atlantea seemed somehow frail, despite the impossible perfection of her appearance. It showed in the way she held her coffee cup: all of her motions seemed more deliberate than usual.

Mira hadn't been on Atlantis in almost a year, but Atlantea was wearing the same visage she had the last time she had been there.

"When was the last time you left Atlantis?" Mira asked.

Atlantea snorted. "I don't remember. It's been a while."

There was a wistful tone in Atlantea's voice. If Thomas' transition had ultimately cost Mira her ability to carry on the pretext of being human with her mundane daughters, Cordelia's birth had cost Atlantea the ability to travel among humans generally. The power surge that had come with it had turned Atlantea's voice into a compulsive force, whether or not she intended any coercion. Her mere presence in a room with a fertile male was enough to drain him; and any fertile woman who saw her was driven to violence. Mira might have lost her daughters, but Atlantea had lost her freedom.

"You need a vacation," Mira said. Atlantea laughed at that. A genuine laugh that quickly faded. Mira reached out and clasped Atlantea's hand. "You need more friends," she said. "You're completely isolated here. I don't know how you do it."

Atlantea took a deep breath. "I have the sea," she said.

"Yes. But as much as it talks to you or cradles you or even comforts you, it isn't your friend or lover. Seriously, this can't be good for your mental health. At least you used to get out from time to time. You haven't left Atlantis — even to visit the fae — in over a year. I'm going to Boston for you. I'll get more information. Let your courtiers take some time to digest the news and present you with some plans for once. You go and traipse through the Taiga, visit Jarl Georg, I don't know. But get off this rock for a while."

"I tell everyone we're facing a mage war and then head off on a vacation?" Atlantea asked incredulously.

"I'd hardly view visiting the Siberian fae as a vacation. Ninety percent of your High Court would rather visit the Aos Sí than set foot in the Taiga. Anyway, your courtiers would just think it's related to war preparations. I know you like Num, and Thomas still raves that no faerie throws a party like Nga."

It had been Nga's disagreement with the Aos Sí that had erupted into the Third Mage War so long ago. Double the size of the U.S., and yet somehow the Taiga's massive expanse of boreal conifers *still* wasn't big enough for a few million fae. Mira may have embraced her duty to preserve the fae, but she found their penchant for self-destruction absurd.

"You remember the oddest things," Atlantea said, but she looked out the window into the distance, and Mira could tell she was seriously considering it. "I haven't thought about Num in decades."

Mira thought Atlantea was lying. Atlantea liked Num; over the years, she had told Mira more about him than any other faerie. Num, like Atlantea, rarely made contact with humans. Since Atlantea couldn't seem to let down her guard amongst her own people, and couldn't be around humans for long, that really only left the fae and the weres.

"Think about it," Mira suggested. It couldn't benefit anyone to have Atlantea isolated, alone, and stewing in a mixture of her two greatest fears: mages and warfare. "Maybe they'll tell you something you don't know. At the least, you'll have a change of scenery. And perhaps coming back with a strong new look will remind everyone that you are still the Atlantic's protector."

Born sirens differ from transitioned sirens in several key ways, including a more gradual maturation process that extends through childhood and adolescence. Siren 'puberty' occurs around the ages of twelve or thirteen, when a born siren first develops the ability to take and bestow fertility. This is a dangerous age, the time when the siren's effect on fertile members of the opposite sex changes from one of almost paternal adoration to unbridled lust. It is highly discouraged to bring adolescent sirens into mundane communities. Born sirens need time to adjust to their changing powers, and in this modern age, affected humans often struggle against any feelings of desire for a child. Such humans may even seek to harm the object of their desire, rather than experience what they consider to be an 'unnatural' sensation.

     – Sirens: An Overview for the Newly-Transitioned, 3rd ed. (2015), *by Mira Bant de Atlantic, p. 79.*

Chapter 10

"I hope you drained him," Devin spat in disgust when he saw Mira's new appearance.

"Of course," she said, scowling. She looked like an underfed twelve-year-old girl now, with long, white-blond hair and enormous blue eyes that were almost cartoonish in their size. Mira reminded herself to be grateful for finding this mark. Perhaps it was divine intervention.

At least after encountering her, he would never be troubled with the urge to have sex again. In this instance, perhaps, Aphrodite's spell was a blessing for more than just the fae. Ever since Thomas had transitioned, Mira had become powerful enough to consume more than her mark's fertility: with some effort, she could also completely suck all sexual desire and drive from him. This was not the first time she had been grateful for that added ability.

"I need to change again before we leave." Mira felt incredibly vulnerable. Arousing men in the guise of a twelve-year-old, while simultaneously stoking violent hatred in women, was perhaps the most dangerous situation she could be in. Transformations were always shocking to one degree or another, but this was the worst transformation she had had in a while. No siren could control what form they took, and she didn't yet have the knack for predicting what kind of deep-seated fantasy a man might have. She didn't know whether a mark dreamed of the girl next door, a porn star, or a child. Hence this debacle.

Devin had transformed first. They had arisen from the water, to the shock of a middle-aged woman seated not five yards away. She had been perched on a foldable stool in front of an easel, painting the sunrise, when they emerged. She froze, her brush mid-stroke, her mouth gaping like a fish.

Unlike Mira, Devin didn't have any compunction about taking fertility. Humans had stolen the Earth from the fae; the least they could do was to give back such a small thing. Mundane fertility was legendary: while all other sentient species struggled to reproduce, mundanes flourished to the extent that they risked overpopulating the planet. In any event, Mira assuaged her guilt by reminding herself that the woman was nearly forty and unmarried. It was possible, but unlikely, that she would have wanted a child anyway.

But Mira's new form, more than her need to aid the fae, necessitated that she change again, and quickly. Devin took her hand in an effort to seem more fatherly than predatory to any passersby. Despite being one of Louisa's warrior-spies for over fifty years, he seemed anxious. Cautious, perhaps. They were effectively behind the lines, in enemy territory, and Devin was well-aware of the risks.

Mira adjusted her wool shawl while she hiked up her loose (and now extremely oversized) wrap dress she so she could walk. After most transformations, this dress style typically hit her new figure anywhere from an inch above to three inches below her knee. This time it was floor-length, and she was tripping over the hem in her far-too-large flip-flops.

They were in Pope John Paul II Park in the Dorchester neighborhood. It was a weekday, around six-thirty in the morning, and the park was sparsely populated; only a handful of joggers and cyclists had crossed their path so far. Last night they had crossed the Atlantic, arriving in southern Boston via the Neponset River. Given the amount of time Atlantea expected them to spend here, they needed to exchange favors with the local fae to help them build their identities. It was too difficult nowadays to breeze into a Western city without identification, credit cards, or any form of electronic paper trail, and get a decent hotel room, let alone an apartment. Fae glamours were ideal for passports, driver's licenses, credit cards, and even cash.

The sun glinted off the river to their right. It was a cooler morning than they were used to in Atlantis, but unseasonably warm for early November in New England. A male jogger in a color-blocked gray and yellow windbreaker and leggings finally emerged from around the bend in front of them and started to slow down as he approached. When he drew closer, Mira could see that he was middle-aged and wearing a wedding ring. Perfect.

"Hello," Mira said as he came closer. "This is my friend, Devin. You won't hurt my friends," she said, infusing her voice with a mild compulsion before the man could say or do anything.

"Of course not," the man said, bemused. This man was no pedophile, and his struggle against the impulses her siren pheromones triggered was apparent in his pained expression.

"Don't worry about how you feel," Mira suggested gently. "This isn't real. You know that this park contains a fae preserve deep within. The fae wear many different glamours."

The man calmed somewhat, but Mira could tell he was still unhappy. He seemed like just another middle-aged man with too many worries and too little ambition. But Mira's compulsions sometimes affected people more strongly than she intended, and they could occasionally appear addled or high. So perhaps it was her own bad influence that made him seem so unappealingly blank. "What's your name?" Mira asked.

"I'm Pete. Peter O'Hara. What's your name?" Pete asked.

"My name is Mira. Do you have any children?"

Devin was wisely silent while Mira screened her mark. While Mira's compulsion would prevent Pete from attacking Devin, it was better for him to try to fade into the background. Devin was keeping one eye on Pete, while looking to see if there were any other passersby who might become a threat. They needed to get off the trail, but given the amount of mass she expected to need for her next transformation, Mira didn't want to stray too far from the river's support.

"I have three. Two boys and a girl," Pete said. "What are you doing here? Are you lost?"

"I'm looking for something. Would you help me? We were going to look just over there." Mira gestured towards the split-rail fence that lined the path. It was an odd place for a fence, given that it only ran twenty feet or so, and didn't actually fence anything in or out. But tall marsh grasses were clumped in front of it, providing a small amount of cover in what was otherwise an overly exposed area.

Devin stayed where he was, but Pete followed as Mira shuffled towards the fence in her ridiculous outfit. She would have taken off her flip-flops, but the ground was too cold. "Do you want any more children?" Mira asked, turning back to look at Pete.

"Children?" Pete answered hazily. "No, three is enough for us." He frowned.

"Don't worry," Mira assured him. "Sometimes the fae can bestow blessings. Wouldn't it be nice to make sure you didn't have more children than you could care for? And make sure someone who truly, truly wants a child can have one?" Mira didn't feel guilty for misleading Pete on her identity. He could be a latent siren, and any talk of sirens would simply sound like gibberish.

Pete nodded his assent to her suggestion as she reached out to take his hand. She hadn't been this small since she herself was a girl, and felt a flash of vertigo as she saw his hand close around what was obviously hers, but seemed too small to really belong to her. Mira led Pete behind the brush, then took his other hand, pulling him down to his knees.

Mira's heart was beating faster and she felt Pete's pulse racing under her hands to match hers. She leaned forward to kiss him, stroking her hands up to grip his forearms, and pressing her arms and cheek against his. She needed physical contact to draw out the power of possibility that was his fertility. Not his actual life-force, but the potential to engender life. Was fertility transfer theft to feed the starving, or a kind of pre-murder? As always, Mira prayed God saw it as the former, and thus forgivable; noble, even. Pete's body was pliable in her hands; she pressed against him, and willed it. Her sex quivered and she grew damp. She felt a salty mist on her face, heard the sound of distant bells tinkling in waves of minor chords.

Pete gasped. It was a sharp pain, she had been told. A pain mixed with pleasure like an orgasm, but not. Something that overpowered the senses. Your nerves knew that something was happening, but something so strange and strong it couldn't be categorized as either pleasure or pain. And then it was over. Her heart was pounding, Pete's heart was pounding, and she slowly released him, inching several feet away, still on her knees and hidden by the marsh grass.

She was glad to be wearing the shawl as Pete stared at her, his eyes glazed over, too shocked to move or speak. Mira panted slightly with the effort of just staying upright, but she was too unbalanced. Pete made no effort to move towards her as she slid bonelessly to the half-frozen ground.

The change always hit Mira hard, and while it wasn't a violent shift, as werewolf changes were portrayed in the movies, with breaking bones and general ick, it was more physical than the instantaneous transformation of a fae through glamour. Changes in mass were a difficult kind of magick to sustain, which was probably why Chía stuck with jaguars and wolves when constructing the weres. Ra's sphinxes would probably have died out on their own in a few centuries if they hadn't been exterminated first; to gain and loose hundreds of pounds in a change was simply too much to sustain.

Typically, Mira's own transformations required only a little more or a little less mass. This time was different. Instead of gaining five to ten pounds, now she needed significantly more. Such a massive change so close in time to her last transformation was making her nauseous. The air around Mira became as dry as the desert; this change might have killed her mark had they not been so close to the river. Pulling more than fifty pounds of water from the air alone would have been impossible, but the river's proximity prevented her change from draining Pete of his water-weight, as well as his fertility.

Mira's dress had been loose before, which was a good thing. Her arms, legs and torso lengthened. Mira grimaced with the pain, though her expression was lost as her face and jaw blurred. She closed her eyes, and tried to keep her lips loose as she breathed through the moments until she felt her body become her own again. Reforming this time had taken more than a minute, and most of her shifts were complete in less than fifteen seconds. When she could breathe normally again, Mira extended her hand to Pete.

"Help me up, I think I tripped. Stupid flip-flops. I should have worn more sensible shoes." Mira's voice had deepened to an alto, and her hand into the tan bronze of a white girl on summer vacation, instead of the translucent pallor and breathy coloratura of the pedophile's fantasy.

Pete helped her up. He was dazed by his own alteration and didn't really recognize her. She picked up her shawl, now flecked with dirt and grass, and walked back to the pathway where Devin waited. Looking down, Mira was grateful that her chest had only grown only to about a 34E. She pulled a strand of hair forward: more a true blond than a dirty blond.

Given Pete's age, she was guessing a Christie Brinkley-kind of look, though she'd been surprised before. Sometimes boys had spent their formative years looking through their fathers' naughty drawers, and she'd become a spitting image of Betty Grable and Patti Boyd on more than one occasion. She was relieved Pete hadn't been fixated on porn. Sometimes the back-punishing weight of those breasts drove her to harvest fertility in an attempt to transform into a more practical body.

"Is he still watching?" Mira asked as she reached Devin, who looked relieved when he saw her new appearance.

"No. He's checking his pockets."

"Maybe he thinks we were robbers. Well, I didn't take anything tangible. He'll have a crazy story to tell his wife when he gets home. Another legend of the fae won't hurt. Let's get out of here before he tries to talk to us."

Devin hoisted the scuba duffle they had brought with them and they walked rapidly back up the path, towards the bend from which Pete had emerged. The trail would lead further into the park, to the salt marshes where Cordelia had told her a nõiamoor lived.

Cordelia visited Mary and Amy at least once a year. Whenever she visited the States, Cordy always made time for at least one trip out to the local fae preserves. Mira felt a sharp pang of pride in her daughter's sense of duty. Mira didn't even have to remind her to do it; it had become as normal for Cordelia as attending church was for Mary. Such a small act to command such a sense of achievement, but regardless, Mira felt she had done at least one thing right as a mother.

While Cordelia's fertility powers weren't as developed as Mira's, her visits were nevertheless eagerly received by the fae. When she wasn't able to fully assist a faerie, Cordelia would often make arrangements for another siren to visit. Her extensive notes and recommendations about the various fae communities in and around Boston almost made up for the fact that she had stolen Thomas away to help her on her European sojourn. Typically, Mira would have cajoled Thomas into partnering with her on any extended trip to mundane society, but she had to admit that Devin was a good substitute.

Devin hadn't fought in the War of Succession, but Mira thought he would have been quite the hero had he been alive back then. He was suspicious where Mira was too trusting, and had somehow managed to maintain his weaponry skills through every transformation. No new body had any muscle-memory, and each had its own peculiar strengths and weaknesses. While it seemed to take Mira months to adapt (if she even did before her next transformation), Devin seemed to instantly find himself within his new skin.

Massachusetts, and indeed most of North America, had scattered pockets of "wild spaces" inhabited by the second-wave of fae immigrants. Long after the Aos Sí lost their battle over the Taiga, and the Brazilian fae made their dramatic cross-Atlantic voyage, the second wave of European fae came to the New World. Indeed, many of the more solitary or anti-social fae had relocated to the nascent United States, trading their fading magick for their preserves.

But sirens were always welcome.

Mira knew when they had crossed the boundary separating the mundane park from the fae preserve when the morning sunlight faded into shadow, and the scent of loam filled the air. The salt marsh should have been bright in the early light; there were no trees to shade it. This was a rich land, but a land that would bear no fruit without them. They had barely entered the faerie's domain when the half-consumed tree standing in the middle of the brackish water shimmered into a lavender lady.

"Cordelia said her dam might come one day, and look you now! Mira Bant de Atlantic, as I live and breathe," the nõiamoor sang out in a raspy voice. Her features were sharp, with a beak-like nose and deep-set gray eyes within her lavender face. Her arms resembled birch branches, with peels of lavender bark rolls curling like ruffles on sleeves that didn't exist. The nõiamoor flexed her multi-jointed hand in greeting; her fingers were so long and thin they looked like spines affixed to her palms. Sirens had a natural resistance to fae magick; while that could be useful, sometimes Mira wished she only saw the same glory of their glamours that humans did.

"We have indeed," Mira said. "We keep our promises."

"As do I," the nõiamoor said. "As do I." But her tone rendered her assertion into an ominous threat, instead of a guarantee of good faith.

"What do you seek, fae maid?" Devin asked formally.

"Power, pleasure, pain," the nõiamoor replied. "Not necessarily in that order."

"You are a hunter," Mira accused. "Cordelia may have promised that I might one day visit, but not that I would aid you."

"Ahhhhh," cried the nõiamoor in a sound that pierced the mist and sent a flock of starlings into a scattered flight.

"You do not seek what we have to offer," Devin said.

"I do not seek a child, true," said the nõiamoor. "But I need you still. I am but a shadow of my former self, unable to cross the marshes to visit the wood wives on the other side of the park."

"Perhaps that is for the best," Mira said flatly, turning as if to leave.

"NO, no," the nõiamoor cried. "I do not hunt them!"

"Is that a promise?" asked Devin.

"I shall not hunt the wood wives do you grant me the strength to leave this marsh," declared the nõiamoor.

"What will you hunt?" asked Mira.

"Animals. Only animals," promised the nõiamoor slyly.

"We are all animals. I will not help you hunt sentient beings," Mira said.

"What of trespassers? I must protect my home." The nõiamoor sounded reasonable, but Mira suspected she would find a way around any promise. It was too bad nõiamoors were so skilled at glamours. Mira generally only visited fae seeking children. She and Marisol were gifted with a relatively strong power over fertility. It felt wasteful to squander it on a faerie who wanted nothing more than to venture further from her power center.

"Trespassers to your current domain within its current borders are fair to hunt. But no others." Devin's new form spoke in a higher tenor than his last apparition, and Mira missed the harder resonance his last body would have given to his warning. Still, the compulsion coiled around his words whipped across the marsh to lash at the nõiamoor. While she wasn't fertile, and thus immune to his power, Devin's strength nonetheless echoed across the wetlands.

"Trespassers to my current domain only," the nõiamoor nodded.

"We also need papers. Passports, driver's licenses, and credit cards," Mira said.

"Done," agreed the nõiamoor.

With their bargain struck, the nõiamoor waded, or perhaps floated, out of the grassy water. She was smaller than Mira had expected — only tall enough to reach Mira's chest. Mira reached out to lightly clasp her shoulders, which shone with a soft, pulsing glow. The faerie's lavender skin was surprisingly soft, almost like rabbit fur, though it was hairless. The nõiamoor leaned in, and Mira kissed her full on the lips.

The giving of power was less intoxicating than the taking of power, and Mira was better able to check her sensations. In less than a few seconds, she pulled back. Though Mira's midsection still pulsed with stored power, the nõiamoor had no need of so much. It wouldn't do to overpay this hunter for such a minor favor.

This principle of magical symmetry also applies to constructs: no inherent power comes without a corresponding vulnerability. Sirenic influence on fertile persons is counterbalanced by the infertile's immunity to their power. Sirenic strength over members of the opposite sex is balanced by the extreme hatred they engender in members of their same sex, and so forth. Sirens have no special physical powers, and you are as much at risk from disease and accidental death as you were before your transition. That said, sirens whose taking of fertility results in a transformation can self-heal otherwise mortal wounds through their bodily change.

– Sirens: An Overview for the Newly-Transitioned, 3rd ed. (2015), *by Mira Bant de Atlantic, p. 28.*

Chapter 11

"Dr. Eisner?" Mira called out.

Eli Eisner was trying unsuccessfully to hail a cab outside the Tosteson Medical Education Center. It was just after four in the afternoon, and since many cabbies switched shifts at four, there were few to be found. At Mira's call, he dropped his hand and turned to find the source of the sound.

Despite the fact that Mira stood against one of the pillars flanking the entrance and was almost hidden by the bustle of people going in and out of the center, Eli located her almost immediately. Mira may not have had Devin's gift of compulsion, but her voice was strong enough to attract the attention of any man she wanted. Eisner hurried back to where Mira was standing.

"Dr. Eisner," Mira said, "I knew that must be you! It's been a while since we spoke, but I'm so glad I ran into you."

"I-I am sure I would have remembered meeting you, miss," Eli stammered, enraptured by the song he could feel running through her words.

"I'm sure you meet so many people," Mira said. "I can understand why you don't remember me. We met in London at the World Congress for Neurology back in oh, maybe 2000 or 2001, I think. You've done such impressive work since then! I would love to hear more about what you're working on now."

"I'm free right now," Eli replied eagerly. "I don't imagine you have time to sit down?"

"Actually, I'm waiting for a friend of mine. But I *am* free for dinner if you don't have plans." Mira wove a mild compulsion through her speech, but it was almost unnecessary. Eli was already entranced by the artificial pheromones sparkling in her blood. He had been just as susceptible before when Mira had briefly engaged him to ensure he treated Amy fairly.

"I would love to have dinner tonight," Eli exclaimed. "I can get us into Menton; I know the owner. It's a fabulous restaurant on the waterfront."

"Ah, but a quieter setting might be better for conversation. Perhaps something more intimate? I hope you won't find me forward if I invite you to my apartment. It's close by, and that way we can learn more about each other."

Out of the corner of her eye, Mira saw Devin deftly catch the hand of a woman about to accost her. She would have to wrap up this meet-cute quickly.

She barely focused on Eli's stammered assent to her suggestion that he come by around seven. Mira whisked her business card from her coat pocket, freshly printed with her new address for just this purpose, handed it to the bemused Eli, and hurried off. She could feel the aging doctor staring after her, still caught in her lure. He was so besotted he hadn't even asked her name or spared a moment to wonder how someone as seemingly young as she was could have met him before.

She had almost reached the corner when Devin caught up with her. "Well that went well," he murmured.

"Thanks for stopping that woman."

"Thanks for getting us off the street so quickly." Devin opened the door of their town car, which waited for them at the end of the block. While Eli's assistant hadn't been susceptible to Devin's formidable power, he'd nonetheless been able to use his not inconsiderable amount of natural charm to wheedle the doctor's schedule from her. Birth control was a double-edged sword; its elimination of fertility made it easier for Mira to get around solo, but harder for them as a siren team.

"Take us back to the apartment," Mira told the driver after they had both gotten in. "And do not hear or remember our conversation," she commanded. Mira hadn't been lying when she told Eli her apartment was close by. With their new documents, it had been fairly easy to arrange for a short-term lease in a furnished apartment building that catered to physicians and patients visiting Harvard Medical Center for extended stays. It was a bit further from the seaport than Mira would have liked, but convenient for their purposes.

"Did you keep in contact with your mundane children after transition, Devin?" Mira asked while they idled in the traffic that seemed to plague every city Mira had been forced to visit.

"No," Devin replied. "Not really. I did check in on them from time to time. I went to my girls' funerals, met my grandchildren. But it felt quite foreign. I was no longer really a part of their world."

"It's difficult to slip in and out of your children's lives," Mira said.

"I think it's harder for a mother," Devin replied. "My wife died when our active son was born. It's hard to say now whether it was from natural causes or the midwife's intervention. Lots of women didn't survive childbirth back then. My sister lived in the same village. It was natural for her to take the girls in when my progenitor arrived, and I told them I'd found new work abroad."

"What about your son?" Mira asked.

"There's an empty grave next to my wife's with his name on it. I didn't raise him, of course. But when my grandson transitioned, I took his girl in. It was almost like a second chance."

"Your grandson didn't make it?" Mira surmised.

"No. I wasn't swift enough. You might have thought I'd learned better after I lost my Catherine, but I was too far away. Boys are hard to keep safe."

"Yes," Mira agreed.

"Thomas is lucky." Devin peered out the window of the car. They were inching along past orange construction cones, as the flagman waved their side of the street through.

"Boys *are* hard to save." Mira thought back to that terrible time. She'd had the benefit of having studied transition intently for years, so had recognized the signs of her power uptick almost immediately. Unlike many sirens, she was also able to accurately guess which of her descendants had made the change and knew where he was. "But finding his children was also hard. We lost one," Mira said.

"I hadn't realized." Devin looked at her. "Like a punch in the gut," he said. "A loss that you never seem to get over."

Mira nodded. "I heard that the Indian Court is encouraging their latents to use mundane *in vitro* technology."

"That's what I heard too," Devin agreed, shaking his head. "Risky. Very risky."

"I guess they don't think they have much to lose. Even with a mundane culture that supports arranged marriages, their population has shrunk more than ours has. Encouraging latents to donate sperm and eggs is fine, as long as they keep track of the recipients." Mira tried to look on the bright side. But for all their worry about their declining population, the Indians had still not employed sufficient resources for the continuous monitoring of so many potential transitions. Their death rate was frankly appalling, but so far had not dissuaded the Indians from using *in vitro* fertilization technology.

"They'd be better off trying to fix their population issue rather than pointing fingers at us. They're worse even than the Pacifics when it comes to casting blame for Morgan le Fay's spell." Devin sounded aggrieved.

Mira grimaced. "That's only because the Pacific Court seems to have embraced the Cabal. You'd have thought they'd learn from our mistakes. But instead, they seem to have jumped right in where we left off."

"With another mage war brewing, Louisa is especially troubled at their closeness."

"I know," Mira replied. "We need to repair our relationship with the Indian Court."

"If that's even possible," Devin said darkly.

"Does Louisa feel the same way about mages as Atlantea does?" Mira wondered, thinking about the dangers the Cabal posed to the foolhardy Pacifics.

"No one feels as strongly about mages as Atlantea does," Devin snorted. Mira liked his sense of humor.

"True. But you're avoiding my question." Ever since they had arrived in Boston, Mira had been trying to get a sense of Devin's loyalties. While the Atlantics would need Louisa's leadership if they did wind up fighting a war, her uncompromising protectiveness posed a risk to both Amy and Cordelia.

"Louisa sees mages for what they are: weapons. But she's bound to obey Atlantea, who won't have anything to do with them." Devin paused for a moment, as if sensing what Mira really wanted to know. "Mira, you know that *Atlantea* chose me for this task, much as she chose you? I wasn't sent here by Louisa."

She hadn't known that, and it did make a difference. But she still wasn't sure how much she could trust him. Taking people at face value had cost her dearly on Atlantis, and Mira was resolved not to make that mistake again, not when its reverberations could put Amy at risk.

"Atlantea often sends those she trusts to perform tasks that she doesn't want to admit must be done." Mira felt him out.

Devin smiled, shaking his head in frustrated agreement. It could well be that, like Mira, Devin was one of those sirens Atlantea tapped for her odd jobs, giving vague guidelines and leaving you to intuit what she wanted. Even the transition textbook Mira had written came from Atlantea's gentle admonition that if she was so unhappy with her own transition, she ought to make it better for others. Mundanes complained about their micro-managers, but Atlantea was impossibly hands-off. There had to be a happy medium.

The car finally pulled up in front of their building, and their doorman ushered them into the lobby. While

Mira had already compelled Matt to treat Devin with courtesy, he nevertheless glared darkly at him; Mira's compulsions were nowhere near as strong as Devin's. Matt did smile broadly at Mira, though, and without any prompting, hurried into the backroom to gather the packages that had been delivered for them today.

As far as Mira was concerned, the only benefit to being in a city was the fact that *anything* could be delivered here. So much safer. But she had been glad to get out today. The two of them had been holed up in Boston for almost a week, and their forced idleness while they laid the groundwork for their assignment had been more draining than she'd expected. Mira was glad that tonight she would finally meet with Eli, and hear for herself what Amy was actually doing.

As Mira again wondered how she could possibly protect Amy if she were indeed the pivot, a woman in a dark coat came through the revolving door. Since the doorman was in the backroom, it didn't strike Mira as out of the ordinary until she dropped her purse and its contents spilled onto the floor.

"You whore! You devil-spawned whore!" the woman hissed, pulling a pistol from her pocket.

Mira's reflexes weren't nearly fast enough, and Devin was too far from them both. But just as the woman took aim, Devin jumped between them. The bullet meant for Mira ricocheted off Devin's chest and drilled a hole right through the modernist painting hanging on the lobby wall. Belatedly, Mira dropped to the floor. But Devin hadn't stopped moving. After blocking the bullet, he grabbed the gun from the woman's hand, pulling her into his arms in one liquid motion. The woman's eyes fluttered closed, and an expression of pure bliss came over her as the doorman ran back into the lobby.

"What's going on here!" he demanded. "Miss Mira, are you all right?" The doorman moved swiftly around the counter to kneel down next to Mira. Devin was whispering softly, words Mira couldn't quite make out. The smell of beach roses bloomed, overpowering the acrid scent of gunpowder.

"Yes, yes," she stammered, allowing the doorman to help her to her feet. "I'm fine. Thank you. Devin, are you all right?" Mira was astonished that Devin was still standing. Mira had never seen a bulletproof vest that could not only stop a bullet, but cause it to ricochet.

"I'm fine," Devin replied, releasing the woman and handing her back her gun, which she placed back into her coat pocket. "This is Ellen Prine," he announced in a falsely cheerful voice. "She thought we were those talent scouts from California. She's some actress!"

"I'll say," Mira murmured.

The doorman continued to fire off questions, which Devin answered in a calm voice. Ellen Prine appeared shell-shocked, staring at Devin as if he were the only person in the room.

"Shh. Matt, it's fine. It's fine," Mira's voice shook, and she cleared her throat, hoping to be able to project the same soothing sound that Devin was casting. "I'm fine. Just a silly stunt gone wrong." Mira laughed, and her voice sounded far away to her. She needed to sit down in a safe place again. "Matt, I truly am fine. Let's let Mrs. Prine head out to find the talent scouts. She got the wrong couple, and the wrong building. She'll never come back here again. Right, Devin?"

"Mrs. Prine is leaving," Devin agreed. "Ellen, you will never threaten Mira or me or anyone else ever again." The sound of waves crashed in the distance, and Matt frowned.

"Matt, you won't report this to anyone," Mira commanded. "Just a silly stunt. In fact, isn't there security footage?" Matt nodded. "Why don't you get us our packages, then go and erase it. It wouldn't do for people to think something happened that didn't really."

Once Ellen left and Matt had handed Devin their packages, they were finally able to get into the elevator. As the doors closed, Mira exhaled sharply. "I'm shaking. No one has ever gotten this close to me before."

"Never?" Devin sounded surprised.

"I usually avoid cities. But being in Boston is a lot more dangerous than I expected," Mira said, swallowing. "I could use a drink."

"Me too."

Their apartment was decorated in a bland modernist take on corporate chic. The white walls, white chairs, and white sofa seemed far colder and less friendly now than when they had first arrived. There wasn't even a colorful throw pillow or modernist painting to soften the starkness.

Mira went straight to the window in the living room, yanking the blinds open. This was the main reason they had chosen this particular apartment. Even though the building was in the middle of the city, they could see the harbor and ocean beyond from every window. The floor-to-ceiling glass may have presented a challenge to mundane furniture placement, but it made Mira feel like she could step out into the sea.

It was too dark to see more than a glimmer of light on its moving surface, but Mira watched the lights move with a numb intentness as Devin opened the packages in the kitchen, then poured their drinks. Mira turned around and tried to smile, though it she knew it was weak. Some agent she was; well, she had warned Atlantea that she wasn't right for this. While she had lived for almost two decades in mundane society, she had never actually been attacked before. Not like this. Either the world had changed, or Atlantea's protection all those years ago had been far stronger and better hidden than she had realized.

"Irish whisky," Devin said as he came around the counter with two glasses. "It's a long pour, but I think we both need it."

"*I* certainly do," Mira agreed, taking a long sip. The liquor burned in her throat. She could tell that this body had not yet built up any tolerance to alcohol. "How were you able to stop that bullet?" Mira asked, feeling more centered now that they were in a safe location, and she could at least see a glimmer of ocean.

"I brought some of the guards' toys with me. Just in case. A good thing, right?"

"Right. So, what kind of toy?" Mira asked, a rueful smile on her lips, "And do you have one for me?"

Devin laughed then, and Mira joined in, feeling a sudden giddiness as the adrenalin from their near-death escape drained away and the buzz of the whiskey took hold. "I brought three," he said.

Mira raised her eyebrows quizzically.

"In case we need to do an extraction," Devin answered her unspoken question.

Mira felt her eyes begin to tear up at his thoughtfulness, and she pressed her tongue against the roof of her mouth to stop them from flowing. While it was highly unlikely she would even need to meet with Amy, let alone extricate her from some kind of danger, Mira was nonetheless touched. "So, is it something you're wearing? It's some kind of magick, certainly," she speculated.

Devin spun in a circle. Without his overcoat on, Mira could see that what she had originally thought was a priest's cassock only resembled one. While the mandarin collar had a white underlay, the cut of the black, vestment-like robe was actually quite different. It was straight on top, with loose, but not voluminous sleeves. When Devin turned, she could see the inserts of fabric that made the skirt full; a priest's robes were typically not so voluminous.

"This is bullet-proof. No, there isn't any metal woven into the fibers, so it's safe to wear around the fae. The Möngke who live north of the Gobi ruins make them. From what we hear, their spell-weaving techniques are unique. These robes can stop most but not all bullets — an M4 at close range will shred it — but they are the best modern armor we have."

"And here I thought you were smart to wear a priest's collar, since it might cause a man to pause for a moment before attacking." Mira moved closer to get a better look.

"Well, certainly that's why I stuck in this white insert." Devin smiled tightly. "It wasn't part of the original design."

"How do they work?" Mira asked, reaching out her hand. Devin obligingly raised his arm so she could feel his sleeve. The fabric didn't feel any heavier than it appeared. It seemed slicker than pure cotton, but didn't have the sheen of silk.

"They're the same as bullet-proof vests. Just put one on and pray that the Möngke weaver mage is still alive if a bullet heads your way. I hadn't anticipated the ricochet effect, though. Going forward, we should both wear them in case a deflected bullet bounces like it did downstairs."

Mira winced at the thought of another attack, and worried at potentially injuring a bystander by trying to protect herself. She hid her discomfort by focusing on the design. "Why robes?" she asked, and Devin shrugged.

"It's wasteful to buy anything tailored for those of us who transform. The ones I brought are the kind typically sold to the Arabians. The Australians prefer fussier styles. But fashion aside, I think these are better than the Aussie ones. The Arabs insist on multi-mage spells, so these robes probably won't totally fail if one of the casters dies."

"I'm surprised I haven't heard of them before. Shouldn't all our people be wearing them?"

Devin drained his glass and set it down before responding. It suddenly occurred to Mira that he was paying very close attention to her; sizing her up, perhaps. But she had endured transition; an attempted murder was *nothing* compared to that.

"Louisa has been stockpiling for the apocalypse, and most sirens never venture into a mundane city.

Look at you — after Cordelia was born, you high-tailed it out of New Jersey and into that tiny island town in the Carolinas. Now you're holed up in an isolated fortress on the Brazilian coast when you aren't running errands for Atlantea."

"You seem to know a lot about me," Mira said.

Devin looked at her scornfully. "I'm a professional; I do my research."

Mira looked at Devin levelly. He was standing directly between her and the door at parade rest. It wasn't just his preternatural agility, no matter what form he took on, that made him a soldier. More than just a soldier, certainly. While there was no official rank in Louisa's cadre of warrior-spies, Devin was a leader, to be sure.

Whatever his loyalties, Mira was suddenly spectacularly grateful that he was here. She downed her drink and smiled broadly at him, the alcohol making her a little unsteady on her feet. "Could I have one of them now? After all the incidents today, I don't even want to open the door to this apartment without wearing it."

It was nearly six, and they only had an hour before Dr. Eisner showed up. Mira was betting that he'd be able to tell her all the details of Amy's research. Maybe he'd even know something about her life. She sat down on the couch while Devin went to get the robe. Looking out at the dark sky, Mira felt a wave of homesickness so strong, a sob caught in her throat. Of course, she had left the home she missed so desperately a lifetime ago. But she didn't want to think about that; get the info and get out. That had to be her priority.

Part Two

Siren Surgeon's Sight

Genetically, sirens are more mage than fae, but as with all constructs, they are limited by the confines of their constructing spell. Sirens cannot perceive magick, and active sirens are only able to cast the spells bequeathed to them as part of their original design. Similar to all other mage-constructs, mages cannot counter-spell the effects of sirenic magick. However, sirens are unique in that their fae heritage renders the fae unable to counter the effects of their magick also.

– Sirens: An Overview for the Newly-Transitioned, 3rd ed. (2015), *by Mira Bant de Atlantic, p. 34.*

Chapter 12

A knock on her office door startled Amy out of her deep concentration on the monitors in front of her. She rubbed her eyes, which blurred as she changed her focus from the MRI images on her screens to the doorway ten feet away. "Come in," she called out, and was extremely glad when Ted Riccie opened the door. "You're back!"

"I am indeed. Elder Simon finally let me leave." Ted made a face.

It was the Monday before Thanksgiving, and Ted had left well before Halloween. Amy had started to wonder if he were ever coming back. She was gratified that Ted seemed to be almost as frustrated with his absence as she was.

"How's our patient?" Amy asked, standing up to clear the papers off her guest chair so Ted could sit.

"He's doing well," Ted said, sitting down. But his blank expression made Amy wonder how truthful he was being.

"When did that ceremony take place, I don't remember what you called it—"

"The Binding Ritual? That was a few weeks ago. It went well. Everything as planned. Rachael, Barry's mother, was thrilled at having hosted the event of the year. No adult has been first-bound since the Danjou Enclave was formed back in the 1700s."

"And Barry is adjusting to being back home all right?"

"As well as can be expected," Ted replied cryptically.

"You're full of non-answers," Amy accused.

"Amy, I just got back." Ted wiped his hand over his face, and she could see signs of strain that matched her own. "Give me a chance to get my head back in this game, and we can start jousting again."

"Sorry. It does seem like you've been gone a long time." Amy sat back down in her chair. Leaning forward, she gestured at the stack of print-outs, and Ted dutifully looked over at them.

"You wouldn't believe how quickly these military folks can move once they have their marching orders. Within a week after you left, the DoD had rolled out the screening program. We're getting dozens of new MRIs to review every day now. The goal is to have every member of some elite unit scanned by March. Well, everyone who isn't geas-bound. One of your elders made that a condition. But we've already reviewed more than a thousand different scans, and it's all we can do to keep up with the volume. In any event, I'm glad you're back."

"Well, I can at least help review the MRIs," Ted said.

"Thank God for that! And even though you weren't here these last months, it was worth it that you stayed in Hesperia. With the follow-up fMRI you were able to send, we were finally able to rule out Arnie's theory that the nerve grafts somehow impacted the flow of electrical impulses. Now at least he can stop fixating on neuron disruption as the probable cause."

They shared a smile at Arnie's single-mindedness. He could be brilliant at times, and was like a dog with a bone when convinced of something.

"I'm glad they arrived okay," Ted said, still smiling.

"So while I'm glad you stayed with our patient, it's been hard trying to move forward without talking to you. Why didn't you answer your phone?"

Ted sighed. "Let's just say it's complicated. The less Elder Simon was aware I wanted to return, the easier it was to actually get back here. In his mind, I think being outside the enclave is more punishment than reward. Keeping you and the team at a distance made it easier for him to decide I needed to go back."

"I thought you said he considered the operation a 'qualified success.'"

"No, the other elders do. Nothing short of perfect will ever satisfy Elder Simon. He's still angry that his son can't cast — though it's way too soon, in my opinion. And for good or ill, I'm being held responsible."

"And I thought academics were cutthroat," Amy murmured. "Well, we're both glad you're back. Maybe all your experience with crazy politics will help us figure out what's going on with the DoD."

Ted arched his eyebrows. "Oh?"

"They want a progress update almost every day now. 'Did we find anyone? Are we ready to do a second operation?' The same questions, but they're really putting on the pressure. Something has changed, but they won't say what. Eli flies to D.C. constantly now. But his view is that nothing has really changed — just that more senior people at the DoD have gotten wind of the project."

"That's possible," Ted opined. "If the Joint Chiefs have taken an interest, that could explain the extra pressure — and their own alacrity in carrying out their end of the project."

"Commander Thompson has actually begun calling me directly, would you believe it?" Amy complained. "And to think I used to be a little peeved that he would only talk to Eli. I owe Eli a debt of gratitude that he spared me from all that before."

"I thought Thompson was supposed to be here with you? *'Training,'*" Ted intoned sarcastically, making air-quotes as he repeated Villar's directive.

"That didn't last long," Amy replied. "Thompson was quick to bow out. Villar has to know his suggestion that Thompson perform this surgery is ludicrous. Thompson at least knows there's no way in hell he could perform this kind of operation. But I'm glad he's managing the scanning program. He's got his team working hard. They're very good, too."

"Have you been thinking about the DoD's grand scheme?"

"How could I not?" Amy answered rhetorically. "Thompson's anxious. I think that's why he's started reaching out to me directly. Trying to build up some kind of rapport so he can convince me to go. Or to send Graham or Arnie."

"You can still get out," Ted said. "If the DoD can mount this kind of search for another patient, they can find a military or ex-military neurosurgeon to come train with your team."

"It's not that simple, Ted. I wish it were," Amy sighed, leaning back in her chair. "Or maybe I don't. I can't say that I've ever truly been indispensable before."

"No one is indispensable," Ted said flatly.

"No, but some people are easier to replace than others. This is not an easy surgery to learn or perform.

Graham can do it. I'd even let him operate on me for that matter, he's that good. But I wouldn't trust Arnie to do it solo, and I can't imagine any military neurosurgeon has had the specialized training, let alone the experience, that we've had.

"That said, I'm sure the DoD is working on contingency plans. When Thompson first started calling me, I thought he was going to tell me that they had found another doctor to join the team. But so far, nothing."

"Graham's that good, huh?" Ted asked.

"He's perhaps the best surgeon I've ever worked with — let alone trained. But I'd never ask one of my doctors to go somewhere I'm not willing to go."

"A true leader," Ted said, without a hint of teasing in his voice.

Amy blushed. "It's not that. It's just wrong. Besides, Graham has a wife and two kids. He's got a lot more to lose than I do."

"Just because you don't have a family doesn't mean you don't have a lot to lose."

"You aren't married, are you?" Amy asked.

"No. I've avoided that commitment fairly adroitly."

Amy's intercom beeped. "Amy, your sister is on line one. Do you want me to tell her you'll call her back?" Gillian asked.

"Speaking of family ..." Ted said, standing up. "I just stopped by to let you know I was back. We can catch up later."

"Okay," Amy said, waiting until Ted walked out, shutting the door softly behind him, before picking up the phone. "Put her through," she told Gillian. It had to be Mary. Even though she had two sisters, only Mary called her office line. Despite asking Cordelia numerous times to call her work number, Cordy always called her cell. She loved her sisters, but birth order was inescapable: Mary would always be dictatorial, and Cordy the spoiled baby.

"Hi, Mary," Amy said.

"Amy, I'm glad I got you. You've been so busy, it seems." Mary's voice had a warm undercurrent to it. She'd been a fairly successful singer before leaving the performance circuit to marry Mike.

"I know. It never seems to stop."

"Well, that's why I'm calling. I spoke to Cordy earlier today. She and Thomas are both coming for Thanksgiving this year. If you can drag yourself away, we'd be able to spend the holiday together."

That was a surprise. Cordelia and Thomas rarely both made the trip in for Christmas, let alone Thanksgiving. Even before Thomas had started his Brazilian tourism business, he'd been a bit of a global playboy, using his inheritance from Mom's death to fund exotic trips. It seemed a bit of an empty life to Amy, so she'd been happy (and Thomas had seemed a lot happier) after he started his business. She always meant to visit him and try it out, but never seemed to find the time. When this project was finished, Amy decided, she would finally go to Salvador.

"I don't know if I can get away this year, Mary. Will the kids be there?" Amy adored her niece and nephew. She was Alicia's godmother, but loved spoiling both of Mary's children outrageously. Cordelia was John's godmother, and while Amy knew she loved being an aunt, she almost never came on the holidays or graduations or any significant event — too many people.

Cordy had been diagnosed with agoraphobia as a child, and they'd spent much of their childhood catering to her fear of crowds. But she'd adapted. Underwater photography was the perfect thing for Cordelia: isolated and in the sea. They'd grown up on the coast, and while they all loved the water, Cordelia had been half-dolphin from birth. Mary jokingly called Cordy their 'Jacques Cordelia,' after the famous French explorer, Jacques Cousteau.

"John just started his new job, so he won't be able to come for such a short visit, but Alicia will be there. She could use your advice on which semester-abroad program to pick for next term. The deadline is coming up." Mary always knew the best way to cajole Amy into a visit.

Amy wavered. She knew that after Alicia graduated, she might not be able to spend the holidays with them so easily. And it was only a few days, really. She could come back on Saturday, so she wouldn't miss too much time in the lab. "Okay, okay, you've convinced me. I'll come. But don't expect me to cook."

"Don't threaten to cook!" Mary responded with mock horror.

"It's late to book a flight, but maybe I'll splurge this year."

"The thing is, we're doing it at Mom's house."

Now that Mary had hooked her into agreeing to come down, she dropped *that* bomb. After Dad's death, Mom had avoided all the publicity by taking them to a distant relative's house on a remote island; then they moved to a tiny village on the outer banks. They kept the house after Mom died so that she and Cordy would have a home to come back to when they weren't at school. But now, Mary was really the only one of them who ever used it. She'd actually just finished a huge renovation, so Amy supposed she shouldn't be too surprised that Mary would want to show it off.

"Mary, it's just so hard to get there." Amy knew she was whining, but didn't care.

Mary was unsympathetic. "Use some of the millions you never spend to charter a plane."

Like her siblings, Amy had received sizable insurance settlements from her father's death. But Mary was right: Amy never spent money on anything. Probably because her circle didn't include anyone who lived that kind of lifestyle. No one she knew carried Prada bags, or wore red-soled shoes, or flew first class. They were academics, flaunting their own peculiar form of status symbols: titles, accolades, awards and citations. Amy actually went out of her way to avoid ostentatious displays of wealth. It was hard enough quieting the whispers that she'd slept her way to tenure, or flirted her way to a book deal, without adding *independently wealthy* to the checklist of reasons why Amy Bant didn't deserve to be where she was.

But traveling at Thanksgiving was a nightmare even under the best of circumstances. It was the off-season in Ocracoke, and since Cordelia was coming, it would probably be better for them to convene at the beach house anyway. Honestly, chartering a plane probably wouldn't be that much more expensive than finding a commercial ticket this close to Thanksgiving, and she'd be able to get back to the lab a lot quicker.

"I was planning to charter a flight anyway," Amy replied archly. While Mary probably knew she hadn't been planning any such thing, it wouldn't do to give her older sister the satisfaction of knowing that she'd yet again organized Amy's life for her.

"I'm glad that's settled," Mary said. "What's up with you? Why are you still working 'round the clock?"

"How do you know I'm working 'round the clock?" Amy countered.

"Because this is the first time you've picked up, and I've been leaving messages with your assistant since Halloween. I knew you must be obsessed with something — you usually at least call me back."

Amy sighed. "It's a long story. We can talk about it at Thanksgiving."

"You have to go; I get it."

Amy felt a pang of guilt, even though there was no hint of reproach in Mary's tone. Perhaps that was it: Mary *did* understand. She always forgave, and she asked for so little. Mary was so much like a saint that Amy hated her sometimes. But she turned away from her monitors and looked out the window, the coils of the phone cord kinking in protest. "I just don't want to talk about work. It seems like all I do is talk about MRIs and occipital lobe anatomy. Tell me what's going on with you. Aren't you planning the big Christmas concert at the cathedral this year?"

"That's right. It's been crazy. You'd think conducting a children's choir would be easier than working with adults, but it's not. At least with adult choirs, you don't have parents to deal with."

"You need to be tougher. The National Children's Choir is one of the most prestigious children's choirs in the country. Be a little more of a maestro and a little less of a mattress," Amy suggested, and Mary laughed.

"It's not that easy. But I *have* gotten a lot less tolerant of the parents' shenanigans over the years. I'm just not a tyrannical person."

"Even when you were a diva, you weren't a diva," Amy smiled.

"True. Anyway, it's good to finally talk to you. Mike has been obsessed with this case that's finally wrapping up — it's been a nasty piece of work, and I'll be glad when it's completely finished. But I know he'll want to talk to you about it at Thanksgiving. Now that you've been working with mages, he thinks you're the expert on them too."

"Mike's working on a case with mages?" Mary's husband, Mike, was a truth-teller, one of those rare changelings whose fae gifts were limited to serving as a living lie-detector. Although Amy was generally a truthful person, she was very glad she wasn't married to Mike. He could have made a killing in the private sector, but instead chose to work for the government. Maybe this Thanksgiving, she could pick his brain for tips on getting along with military types.

"The case involves spells, not mages directly," Mary replied. "After all, they police their own. But a key witness in his case was apparently bespelled, and Mike has been up in arms over it."

Mike was an upright guy and Amy had always liked him. They were kindred spirits: the family considered her overly-serious, and Mike was so stiff he oozed honor out of every pore. "I'm not sure I actually know all that much about mages, but it'll be interesting to hear about his case, for sure," Amy said.

"That's great. I won't keep you much longer. But you should definitely plan on coming for Christmas too. Cordy and Thomas have both bowed out — maybe that's why they're making such an effort to come next week." Mary was relentless.

Amy smiled. No matter how busy she was, she never wanted to spend another Christmas alone again. When she was younger, she occasionally drew the short straw and had to cover Christmas at the hospital. Now she could set her own schedule, more or less. "You know I wouldn't dream of skipping Christmas. I don't even own any decorations — I'm always with you. But why can't they make it?"

"Well, Cordy has a new project in the Mediterranean. You should ask her about it. She didn't sound all that excited, really. But *I* thought it sounded amazing. Thomas is apparently launching some new thing for skydivers, so he can't get away this year. But at least we'll all be together for Thanksgiving. I can't wait to show you how great everything came out!"

Amy felt a sudden wave of gratitude for Mary's persistence in keeping their family together. But for her efforts, Amy suspected that she would have completely lost touch with her siblings; she often forgot to call Cordelia and Thomas. It was such a shame; she and Cordy had been so close growing up. She should call her. Thomas too. But first, Amy was determined to show her gratitude by feigning intense interest in Mary's remodeling choices.

The Mediterranean is often compared with Switzerland, as a result of their long history of neutrality during intra-siren conflicts. Home to the birthplace of sirens, the Mediterraneans permit sirens of all oceans to visit, with the proviso that any conflicts be left outside their water's borders. In part due to their policy of extreme welcome, the Mediterranean has become the most popular siren tourist destination. The festival of Aphrodite in April is perhaps their most famous festival, with parties held almost daily throughout the month. However, their New Year's celebrations are also quite popular, and the total siren population during these times can swell to more than triple its usual size.

– Sirens: An Overview for the Newly-Transitioned, 3rd ed. (2015), *by Mira Bant de Atlantic, p. 203.*

Chapter 13

Thomas danced among the hundreds of guests crowding the floor below with a looseness that Cordelia envied. Even when she wasn't as anxious as she was now, she had never been as able to be as in the moment as her older brother. She leaned on the balcony rail, sipping her watered-down wine as she let her gaze slip from person to person.

There were almost five hundred guests at Queen Sophia's New Year's Eve celebration in the famed Grotto of Aphrodite. The term "Grotto" was a serious misnomer in Cordelia's opinion, because the room was anything but intimate. This grotto was the largest, most modern ballroom Cordelia had ever seen, inserted into the shell of an ancient Byzantine temple. A balcony ran around the perimeter of the upper story, where guests could get a better view of both the dancers below, as well as the ornate tilework on the surrounding sandstone walls.

The elaborate murals of Aphrodite's life that ran across the ceiling were carefully illuminated by glittering pin lights that made the images seem almost alive. Instead of a chandelier, the centerpiece of the room was a massive gilt dome that opened to the sky. The circumference of the opening was perhaps twenty feet in diameter, and the oddly intense moonlight shone down like a spotlight on the dancers below.

But as stunning as these elements were, the most striking architectural detail of the grotto was its glass floor. The entire building sat suspended a mere foot above the sea, and the undulating ocean could be seen beneath the dancers' undulating bodies. Cordelia was determined to stay until sunrise, imagining that as the number of guests petered out, the morning light through the open dome would illuminate the ocean's floor and render it even more splendid than it was right now.

When they arrived on the island of Kasos, they'd been met by one of Queen Sophia's guards, who escorted them to the Atlantic suite at the palace. The warmth and richness of their rooms thrilled Thomas; though almost anything would be more luxurious than the suites at the Jarl's cold court. Cordelia merely noted that the ornate style provided plenty of places to hide listening devices, and doubted that she had found them all. It was well known that the Mediterraneans considered knowledge of their guests' secrets a fair trade for hosting them in Aphrodite's home country.

The entire layout of the Mediterranean guest quarters had been designed to permit representatives of the different oceans to mingle informally. The Pacific, Atlantic, Indian, and Arctic suites opened into a shared set of common rooms where meals were served, and a constant stream of musical entertainment was offered. Kasos wasn't merely a neutral locale, it was the place where the oceans went to negotiate when they didn't want word of their discussions to leak back home. As the shock of her meeting with Atlantea faded, Cordelia had gradually come to believe that her "exile" wouldn't really be an exile after all. But she had no idea what kind of deal Atlantea might want her to strike here.

Rahul and Shravya were dancing near Thomas, and Cordelia thought she might join the Indian envoys on the floor. She had spent the last few weeks quietly gathering information about them and the Pacific delegates, and now felt prepared enough to orchestrate a private meeting with them.

Cordelia was glad Thomas had agreed to come with her; while she suspected Louisa had slipped at least two of her warrior-spies onto the island, at least they weren't staying with her in the Atlantic suite. Just before flowing into the Mediterranean, she had asked the Atlantic to tell her if any other Atlantics had recently preceded her through the Strait of Gibraltar. The sea had acquiesced, sharing the sounds of the two sirens' hearts with her. Perhaps they were tourists, but Cordelia had to assume they were not.

She supposed she was glad for whatever extra protection they offered, and thought perhaps she could take advantage of their presence by ensuring the image of herself she presented was curated for Louisa's consumption. The one thing they couldn't know was that Cordelia was *not* giving up on the Aos Sí. Zale was right: she needed to obtain more first-hand information from Yorkshire, but Zale had inadvertently complicated her plans to do just that.

Cordelia swayed lightly with the music, her face set with an artificial smile that hid her inner maelstrom of thoughts. Ever since her last Court session, her life had become a series of unexpected shocks. As soon as she thought she had found her footing, the rug got yanked out from under her. Cordelia snorted: at least she'd obeyed Atlantea with greater alacrity than perhaps even Atlantea would have expected. She tried to find the humor in the situation.

While sirens served as fertility batteries, it wasn't all that easy for active sirens to conceive. Their fecundity had always been a gift for others. So Cordelia's unexpected pregnancy was in equal parts a true gift and a true frustration. She had left for Kasos expecting to use her time in Europe to meet again with Titania in England. That was off the table — at least until the baby was born.

While Louisa and the old guard would perhaps be mollified by Cordelia's adherence to traditional values (and Cordelia intended to make sure Louisa's spies got wind of her pregnancy very soon), Atlantea might not be as pleased. Why send her to the Mediterranean if not to further their court's unofficial relationships with the Pacifics or Indians? If Atlantea's desire had been for her to sire a cross-oceanic child, that was now off the table.

That said, Thomas was here, and as Cordelia watched him dance, she could tell that he was as popular with this group as he had been reputed to be when he served at the Jarl's satellite court. Thomas had a kind of insouciant charm that predated his transition.

He could inhabit a moment like no one else, pulling you into the joy of existence, tomorrow be damned. It could be intoxicating. Just as Cordelia turned to head back to the dance floor with him, she almost bumped into Marisol.

"Cordelia! I've been looking everywhere for you," her progenitor cried, embracing Cordelia tightly.

Despite her frequent form changes, Cordelia always knew it was Marisol. She wasn't entirely sure why or how she knew; her mother had told her that the ability to discern sirens despite their physical bodies came from a siren's connection to the sea. Mira had waxed on endlessly about a complicated-sounding theory, but Cordelia hadn't paid too much attention. The upshot was that no siren — at least no Atlantic siren — could easily deceive her with a transformation.

"Marisol, I should have known you'd be here! You usually come for Queen Sophia's New Year's party, don't you?"

Marisol released her, then patted Cordelia's stomach; she must have felt her slight bump. "You're increasing!" Marisol exclaimed with delight, and Cordelia nodded. "That is wonderful news! I'll have to tell everyone."

At least Marisol's appearance had solved her issue of how to get word back to Louisa. "I can't believe I was this fortunate," Cordelia replied, leading Marisol off the balcony through the arched entry that led to a quieter hall. "But don't let my mother know. Atlantea has her doing something in the States, and I don't want her to think she has to rush over here."

"It will be our secret, just like the old days," Marisol promised, sounding like the giddy teen she appeared to be, as opposed to the centuries-old great-grandmother she actually was. Marisol's form was a nice change from her usual northern European look. Long, straight black hair cascaded around her tawny face, while thick eyebrows arched over gray eyes.

"Where have you been?" Cordelia gestured at Marisol's body. "This is a new look for you."

"Turkey. I've been all around the Mediterranean this past week, regaining my energy for the celebration."

"Why were you so drained?" Cordelia asked.

"Atlantea asked me to stop by England on my way out here. My fertility powers are unmatched, you know," Marisol tossed her hair back.

Cordelia did know; Marisol never stopped reminding her, and everyone else, of that fact at every occasion. How Marisol loved being on the High Court! Cordelia felt a pang of jealousy, which she quickly suppressed. "England? To visit the Aos Sí?"

"Yes. Atlantea often sends me there because of my unusual strength."

"Really? You never mentioned that," Cordelia replied, without letting even a trace of sarcasm into her tone. For once, she was grateful for Marisol's endless braggadocio. She needed information, and here it was for her. Cordelia linked arms with Marisol and they strolled down the hall to the back stairs.

"Well, I don't like to brag," Marisol said. "But it seems like they can't get on without me anymore. It used to be that Atlantea would ask me to visit Yorkshire once a year or so — especially after Thomas transitioned and my powers grew so much. But now, I'm over there so often, I'm thinking of buying a little house on the edge of the Moors to keep my things in. It's so annoying to replace everything all the time."

"That's certainly inconvenient," Cordelia murmured sympathetically. "Why do you think she wants you there so often?"

"Well, Atlantea can't go herself, you know. She never leaves the island. Except, did you hear? She's off to the Taiga next month! Alone, for that matter. I suppose the Arktisa won't mind her brief passage through the Arctic to get there."

This was a choice bit of gossip, and Cordelia tried to ignore Marisol's fluttering tone, and all the implications of Atlantea's departure to keep Marisol on the subject that was most important: the state of the Aos Sí. "You must be so honored that Atlantea relies on you so much," Cordelia flattered.

"Well, it's a huge bother, I must say. So much work. I have to drain almost twenty men before I even head over there. And that's depleted the day I arrive. So then I have to head out and start over again. It's really too much, you know."

Marisol's bragging aside, she was truly powerful to be able to hold the fertility and sex drive of twenty people. The most Cordelia had been able to hold was three, but then her powers were on the weaker end of the spectrum. Even Thomas could hold more than she could. How shocking though, that Marisol could expend so much power in just one day! How fragile *were* the Aos Sí?

"But Nanna Marisol, don't you always say, 'the sooner drawn, the sooner gone?' Seems like more prep work than actual time spent in England."

"True, true. But one draw is never enough anymore." Marisol actually looked troubled by that fact. Her thick eyebrows drew close as wrinkles formed on her brow. "Nowadays I need to spend at least a week, harvesting and bestowing, harvesting and bestowing. It's exhausting. And they never ever have any children!"

The troubled look on Marisol's face surprised Cordelia. Marisol was usually so focused on her own desires, she rarely saw others except as extensions of herself. Perhaps she saw the fae's lack of progeny as an indictment of her own power. But it would be unlike Marisol to blame herself for something so obviously not her fault; no child had been born to the Aos Sí since the Cabal's exodus. Cordelia hoped, as unlikely as it was, that her progenitor's seeming concern was driven by newfound empathy for the Aos Sí's plight.

"But here you are, pregnant at last! I'm so glad. Your other children should be of child-bearing age any time now, and soon perhaps you'll have a transition to manage. It's so much better now that your mother wrote that book; so much easier for your generation. I can't wait to see how your power expands!"

Marisol was determinedly changing the subject. But Cordelia had heard enough anyway. The Aos Sí situation seemed to be even worse than she had expected. And here she was, pregnant, and therefore unable to visit the fae without risking her child. "How long will you be staying in Kasos?" she asked, as they strolled back towards the balcony.

"Well, I thought perhaps a week or two. But since you're pregnant, I'll have to stay with you! There are so many people who will want to meet you. I'm going to introduce you all over."

"That would be wonderful, Nanna Marisol! But do you have to go back to England? Or Atlantis?"

"Oh, well. I suppose. Perhaps I can just splash back and do another quick circuit with the Aos Sí, pop over to Atlantis to give them the update, and then come back here. I really am just so delighted. Will it be a cross-oceanic babe?"

"No, de Atlantic like my others," Cordelia sighed. "I'm too strongly bound to the Atlantic anyway."

"Well, I'm so glad!" Mira glanced out at the dance floor below. "Though it's a shame that you won't have a chance to snag Rahul for an interlude. He is quite the lover, and even if his Raj isn't interested in alliances, Rahul certainly wouldn't mind siring a cross-oceanic child."

Cordelia looked over the floor as well. She didn't see Rahul, but knowing he was willing to risk conflict with his king was good information to tuck away for the future. "I saw Shravya dancing near Thomas. Do you want to go out on the floor?" Cordelia asked.

"Oh no, dear. I wish, but this body is still too new for me; I'm two left feet right now. But you go ahead. I'll send some of the boys from the Arctic by; they are totally adorable."

"I'm exhausted," Cordelia sighed, rubbing her bare feet. She had pulled off the suede-soled dance shoes all the partiers wore, and was half-sitting, half-reclining on the glass floor. After midnight, the partiers started pairing off, slowly drifting away until there were only perhaps fifty left.

As customary, the Queen herself departed after the stroke of midnight. The various musicians had finally stopped playing dance music around four in the morning, and now there was only a string quartet left playing softly on the dais, as the few remaining revelers waited for the morning light. Thomas tossed her a couple of pillows he had kindly fetched off the settees and settled down next to her with a grunt. They stared up at the ceiling, waiting for the sun to bring the Grotto to its full magnificence. "I can't believe it's another new year, already," Thomas whispered.

"That's a rather trite sentiment," Cordelia snarked.

"You don't keep me around for my scintillating repartee," Thomas countered.

"Wow, that's a lot of vocab words to cram into one sentence."

Someone abruptly turned off the aimlessly roving spotlights and pin lights in the ceiling murals. With the room lit only by the wall sconces, the Grotto suddenly felt much more intimate than it had before. The remaining revelers quieted, most seeking places on the floor beneath the open dome, like she and Thomas had. The early light grew stronger, and the soft haze made the gilt dome seem to glow from within.

"I really appreciate you coming with me," Cordelia said, turning to look at her brother's profile.

He snorted. "What else are big brothers for? But honestly, I wish we were in Brazil. You know, it's eighty-five and sunny in Bahia right now."

"Is it still okay that you're away?" Cordelia fretted.

"Don't worry about it. It's fine. Kadu said he and the other jaguars were enjoying the new kites we brought in for kitesurfing. They can only go in the water when I'm not around, so it's cool. We'll just wait to try out the wingsuits until I get back."

"What are wingsuits?" Cordelia asked.

"We just got them. They're suits you wear parachuting to help you glide farther and with greater control. Marcia thinks we can get skydiving clubs interested with this new offering."

"So you need to get back, right? I know I cut into your schedule by asking you to come out here."

"If it weren't you, I'd have been in Boston with Mom, and this is a lot better."

"You don't always have to drop everything when we call," Cordelia said.

"You always do for me," he replied. Though in fairness, he hadn't really ever asked Cordelia to do anything for him.

"I have a big favor to ask," Cordelia said after a pause.

"Uh-oh," Thomas replied.

"Marisol brought back some news, and while I'd like to check it out myself, I'm kind of stuck here until the baby's born."

"Sounds ominous." Thomas replied flippantly; Marisol's gossip was generally benign.

Cordelia lowered her voice even further. "She's been going back and forth to England a lot, and even she seems worried. Her fertility powers are incredibly strong, but she made it sound like it was more than even she could handle."

"You know how she likes to brag," Thomas said.

"I know. That's why I would have gone out to see for myself. But in my condition, I can't go."

"You want me to go," Thomas said unhappily.

"The North York Moors are practically on the ocean. You wouldn't have to set foot in human territory," Cordelia wheedled.

"I'm nowhere near the siren Marisol is when it comes to the fae."

"Who is?" Cordelia replied. "And anyway, I'm not asking you to do what she does. I'm just asking you to visit them for a little while until I can get out there. Just see how they act."

"Until you can get out there? What, you mean stay until after your baby is born?" Thomas was genuinely surprised. This was a big ask.

"Shh. Keep your voice down. Listen, this may be the only time we're able to talk privately," Cordelia said. "Louisa's spies aren't lurking close enough for me to hear their hearts, and I highly doubt Queen Sophia has devices here after the ear-splitting blowout she just hosted."

"What's going on that you need such secrecy?" Thomas wondered.

"I don't think Atlantea wants us to give up on the Aos Sí. I just think she doesn't want to be involved with it at all. I think she sent me out here because I'm still pledged to her, and she doesn't want her courtiers' focus split by this issue."

"That sounds like wishful thinking to me," Thomas countered.

"No, it's not—"

"It sounds like exactly what you want to believe."

"Whether it is or isn't, I'm not giving up on them," Cordelia snapped.

"Shh. Keep it down, or you won't be keeping anything secret for long."

"I won't give up on them. It's wrong. You know it's wrong. We've talked about it."

"Yes, but it's not worth your life — or mine for that matter — to fix this. I don't know why you act like this is your responsibility, Cordy. We didn't get the Atlantic into this mess. You've already done what you could at Court, and got sent here for it. Maybe you need to let this one go. You can't save everyone."

"Look, there isn't anyone else. How can I not feel some responsibility when I can maybe fix it? You think I want this?"

"Yeah, I kind of think you do. You've always wanted to be a martyr, and here's your big chance." Thomas started to stand up, but Cordelia sat up, grabbing his hand before he could leave.

"Don't storm out. Please. I need you. More than ever, I need you. Come on," Cordelia pleaded, looking up at him much as she had when they were children.

The early morning light was starting to penetrate the gloom of the water beneath the glass. Even the Mediterranean seemed to swirl around her.

"I'm such a sucker. You're a real pain, you know." But Thomas sat back down anyway.

They were silent for a moment. Cordelia lay back down to stare at the sky and Thomas eventually settled back next to her. They watched as the clouds visible through the dome lost their pinkish tinge to flow like white streaks across the canvas of the sky.

"You want me to, what, hang out in North York Moors? For like six months?" It had taken some effort, but Thomas' voice was even again.

"Not hang out. And not right away. Marisol said she had to go back in a few weeks. I was thinking maybe you'd offer to go with her — you know, learn from her vast experience or something. Then she'd come back here, and you'd stay to practice your skills or I don't know, maybe you develop a crush on one of the sirens stationed there. I just need someone I can trust to let me know what's really going on. Maybe talk to Titania if you can. Just to let me know what you think of the whole situation."

"I don't think you need me for that. The whole situation is a disaster. We all know it. I don't need six months for that."

"It's more about getting a sense of how ..." Cordelia paused, searching for the right word. "... how *angry* the fae seem."

"They're beyond pissed," Thomas said.

"And how would you know? You·haven't been there since your junior trip."

"It's how any rational person would feel."

"What I mean is, do you think they're still sane? You know, after being practically immersed in iron for so long? If you interact with them regularly, over a few months, maybe you'll get a better sense of whether their need for us is tinged with resentment or hate or something like that."

"You know the fae are way too skilled at hiding their true feelings for me to really know anything," Thomas said.

"It's a long shot, I know. But isn't it better that we try?"

"You're crazy, you know that? This is crazy."

"I can't just do nothing," Cordelia insisted.

"You could. But you won't."

"I won't," Cordelia agreed.

"All right."

"Just like that?" Cordelia asked.

Thomas reached his arm over and ruffled her hair like he used to when they were children. "Just like that. Now be quiet and let me watch this famous light show."

Sirens were created to preserve the fae. While this does not mean you need to spend every waking moment harvesting fertility and bestowing it on the fae, you should expect to devote significant time with them. Consider this a form of community or military service. The fae are very different culturally, as well as biologically from us, and numerous books have been written by and for humans regarding their cultural norms and conventions. You will find recommendations for further reading in Appendix B. Before venturing onto a fae preserve, you are strongly encouraged to review these resources. The main thing to remember is that the fae need sirens. Outside of the mage wars, no fae is known to have murdered a siren.

– Sirens: An Overview for the Newly-Transitioned, 3rd ed. (2015), *by Mira Bant de Atlantic, p. 103.*

Chapter 14

The old abbess watched Thomas walk out to the surf, and he gave her a brief wave before allowing the Atlantic to pull him out to sea. Hers had been a small order of Carmelites in Le Havre. A small order, but with a substantially younger population than he had expected. Since coming to England, Thomas had been all up and down the coast of France. From Valognes to Morlaix to Bayeux, Vannes, Valmont, and Plouharnel. He had lost track of how many small towns he had visited to harvest enough power to keep the fae from fading.

This trip had reminded him of his life before Dad died. Being surrounded by women in penguin garb had brought him back forty years, to when he'd attended St. Peter School in Point Pleasant. He still remembered the sound of Sister Mary Joseph's habit brushing against the desks as she sought the perpetrator of whatever nonsense they had orchestrated. And of course, it had been him; and of course, she'd found him out.

Traveling through the ocean like this, Thomas couldn't regret his transformation. The exhilaration and simultaneous peace of being at one with the water momentarily erased his feeling of dread at the thought of returning to the Aos Sí preserve. It was only the pleasure of traveling beneath the sea that could get him to even attempt to go back. The Atlantic must have known he needed more support than usual, because Thomas was swept down deeper than necessary to avoid the shipping lanes and ocean trawlers. The ocean shared her treasures with him: glowing fish, a fissure in the ocean floor where giant purple lobsters crawled, and best of all, a half-broken World War II vintage submarine.

Maybe it was just an illusion, but he felt like the ocean slowed him even more as he passed, just to enable him to have a full view. The ocean loved him. This certainty was only possible for Thomas when he traveled like this. It was like the Atlantic knew Thomas was coming to play, and made an extra effort just for him. Despite knowing that when he emerged from the water, his certainty would drain from him almost as quickly as the water dried on his skin, Thomas nevertheless relished this moment. Thomas willed the Atlantic to slow his pace; he was not eager to return. It had been almost five weeks since he'd arrived with Marisol, and each trip back across the channel was harder to endure. The day of the party, he'd thought visiting the Aos Sí would be the lesser of two evils. Now, he knew he'd made a huge mistake.

At the time, he had been struggling to act the playboy, a role he felt ill-suited for now. It was like he'd burned that part of himself out when he left Jarl Georg's court. Now, fitting himself back into that mold for the Mediterraneans was like putting on pants two sizes too small. But the minor discomfort of playing the careless partier with Cordy paled beneath his helpless agony of bearing witness to the fae's suffering.

The ocean slowed his pace to a crawl, and he was grateful for the respite. It took all his will, and all the treasures of the sea, to keep him moving towards northern England, as opposed to back to Brazil. While France was just a brief trip south across the channel, his decision to harvest here had been driven less by his need for the ocean to wash away the hideousness of the moors, as by the excuse it gave him to use his French. Kyoko had taught him French in a magical instant, and speaking it made him feel closer to her. Before arriving in Yorkshire, he had dreamed of her, but now his dreams of their brief meeting were so vivid, she was always on his mind. In the Moors, it seemed like his memories of Kyoko were the only beautiful truth left.

He couldn't wait to go to bed now, because sleep was such an exquisite escape from the fading fae with their failing glamours. Cordelia couldn't have known what a horror the Aos Sí preserve was. He was sure she never would have asked him to come to this Godforsaken place had she actually known.

An image of Kyoko, the small indentured mage from Rio, flashed through Thomas' mind. He had never had a good memory for faces, but hers was practically engraved on his brain. She must be a via-enchanter of sorts, given her ability to take and give knowledge of languages. Her skin had been a translucent white, and the contrast between the pallor of her skin and her black hair and eyes had been jarring. She looked more like a vampire than her master, Gerel, whose skin had glowed like the fae when she had let go of his hand.

No one had actually introduced them, but as Kyoko had held his head, he felt a whispering like the wind bending trees, *My name is Kyoko.* He heard her in Japanese, where she gave him an honorific he had certainly not earned, as if he were her lord. Her hands were soft and cool. Thomas' pulse quickened. In that moment, he felt, he knew her more intimately than was possible. *"Kyoko-sama,"* Thomas had breathed, worshiping her. The hair on the back of his neck raised, and he sensed the vampire who pulled Kyoko's leash. Kyoko let go: *"Eu terminei. Está feito,"* she had said. But Thomas knew for certain that she wasn't finished, and it wasn't done. They had yet to begin.

Angus mac Og was waiting for Thomas near the edge of the moors. It was a cold spring, and the damp chill permeated the air and seemed to settle in Thomas' bones. The sand of the North Atlantic shores always seemed to be a dirty color. While the Bahian beaches weren't the pristine Caribbean white, they were nonetheless of a finer texture than the coarse silica endemic to this area. Thomas waded to the shore, the ocean conveniently taking back the droplets that clung to him, till even his clothes were fully dry. Angus held out his hand in greeting, that perpetual smile on his face.

"Well met, siren!" Angus clasped his forearm and pumped it, Thomas reciprocating, charmed once again by the fae's seeming delight to see him. Angus' visage flickered a bit between glamours, his eyes changing from green to gray and back again. But his tousled wheat-colored hair and sharp cheekbones remained the same. Angus was about Thomas' height, but his hands seemed almost too big for his frame. Fae proportions were just different from humans'.

"How did you know I'd be here now?" Thomas asked.

"Ah, that's a mystery to be sure." Thomas just looked at him, and Angus sighed. "Ah, well, if you're going to be like that. I asked a favor of the selkies, of course. They always watch for siren comings and goings." The selkies were a race of fae who had given up their ability to transform from seal to human millennia ago in order to escape the worst effects of iron proliferation.

"You always seem so happy to see me," Thomas remarked as they walked up the short beach to the tree-lined path that led to the heart of the North York Moors Preserve.

"I'm happy to see everyone," Angus replied drily.

"Who would you like me to visit today?" Thomas asked, steeling himself.

Angus' face fell. "I had wanted you to visit Lachlally … but sadly, she faded away last night."

Thomas felt a pang of guilt. If he hadn't been so massively self-indulgent in extending his stay in France, she might still be around. As if knowing his thoughts, Angus gripped Thomas' shoulders in a quick hug, never breaking stride. "Not your fault, lad! Never your fault. We fail and fade, but that's as much on us and our failure to keep the hope of joy alive as anything. Even under the best of circumstances, we fae do fade away when our feelings fail. Lachlally gave up on joy years before you arrived, Thomas."

Angus' statement only made Thomas feel worse. God, he hated being here. "You must hate us," he remarked.

"No, no, you hate yourselves. We simply endure. One day things will change. They always do. We can outwait you." While still sounding blithe and cheery, Angus' comments seemed to have a layer of steel beneath.

"I'd be angry. We have so much and do so little."

Angus shrugged. "It is what it is. You are who you are. My hating you or not hating you won't change that."

Thomas didn't know what to say to that. So instead, changed the subject. "Want to race?" he asked. Thomas and Angus had begun playing challenge games since Thomas' arrival and Angus' informal adoption of him. Angus served as kind of guide to rest of the Aos Sí, and Thomas enjoyed their races. They'd run through the dormant fields, jumping sudden obstacles as various fae appeared in their path to impede or aid their progress. Thomas suspected that Angus let him win every once in a while, but Angus insisted that would ruin the sport for the other fae who were betting on the outcome.

"Are you sure you're up for it, lad? Meriweather is betting against you this time, and he's a sly one for sure."

Thomas felt the thrill of challenge and nodded. "To the rowan tree in the deep woods?"

"Aye, then. Count it."

"Three, two, one. Off!" Thomas and Angus said in unison.

A flock of goldeneyes veered overhead, their distinctive white bellies and black feathers blurring. The first of the fae obstacles were probably glamoured into their flight. Thomas noted, then ignored them, utterly focused on the trail ahead. Angus certainly didn't hold back, and he was fast. Thomas had never been a distance runner, but even before his transition, he'd been an athlete. His record in the 800m butterfly might even still hold at Loyala.

The first half-mile was the tricky part. It always took Thomas at least a mile to find his pace. As Angus sprinted ahead, a gnarled tree stump appeared suddenly in his path, and he had to leap over, barely clearing it. A hand emerged from the middle of the wood, waving encouragingly as Thomas gained a bit of ground to Angus' early lead.

As if the wood sprite's intervention called for a counter, a snarling, red-bearded lion leapt out ahead of Thomas. But even as it appeared, the glamoured image flickered and shrunk back down into its true, tiny form. The now-small will o' the wisp fluttered to one side as Thomas continued running at top speed. Siren resistance to fae magick made it an almost competitive race.

Angus may have been faster at the start, but Thomas always had a reserve of energy to help him with a strong finish. As they came off the coastal forest path and onto the rolling hills of open meadow that marked the midpoint of the course, a trio of reddish-gray roe deer startled at their pace and bounded away. A ring of greenish fire erupted on the path before him: the will o' the wisp was trying again. But the fields were damp, and a flock of seabirds swiftly descended, spraying water and disrupting the wisp's concentration. Their honking seemed like laughter to Thomas.

As they came upon the old growth forest that marked the center of the fae domain, Thomas' heart began beating with more than merely his effort. This was the ultimate test: could he discern fact from fiction, glamour from reality, to find the true path? Which was tree and which was foe? Thomas deftly dodged around one faerie's leg, which was masquerading as a birch branch, dropping to roll swiftly below another faerie's disguised arm. Angus was not so lucky, having fumbled into a spider web, and had to pause to cast a counter-spell to negate his opponent's trap.

The dark canopy of the evergreens almost blotted out the dim March sunlight, but Thomas could just make out the bright red berries of the rowan tree perhaps another three hundred yards ahead. The tree bore fruit year-round, a signifier, he had been told, of Titania's hold on the land, despite the iron and steel sown throughout. The fae were rightly proud of their rowan's flourishing.

Just as Thomas was about to reach the tree, his foot plunged deep through a hole in the forest floor. He hit the ground hard, bracing his fall with his left arm. He hadn't been watching carefully enough where he put his feet, and had stumbled through a tar-circle. The bog faerie, who must be betting on Angus, laughed loudly as Thomas pulled himself up and tried to unstick his foot. At least he hadn't broken anything, Thomas thought. Angus freed himself from the spell and passed Thomas on their final sprint just as Thomas yanked himself clear.

They ran the final yards of their sprint neck-and-neck. Thomas glanced at Angus. His face was flushed with effort and his eyes glinted with a swirl of sparks. Thomas tried to outpace Angus with a burst of speed at the end, but it wasn't enough. With only ten feet to go, Angus suddenly jumped with both feet, and was flung ahead, as if he had catapulted off a trampoline — which of course, he had: a trampoline of moss, laid in his path by one of the buschgroßmutters, who were cheering for Angus.

Thomas was only a few seconds behind, and as he cleared the course and slapped his hand on the trunk, he could hear a mixture of cheering, booing and chortling behind them. At least they had provided the assembled Aos Sí an afternoon of entertainment.

Breathing heavily, Angus shook Thomas' hand.

"Good race! Thomas. You almost had me this time."

"Close, but no cigar," Thomas huffed.

"Ah, but you won last week. It was my turn."

The two of them sat, leaning against the rowan tree. The assembled fae who had emerged at the conclusion of the race seemed to glide off, though Thomas knew some of them were still likely lurking about. Now that the exhilaration of the race was over, Thomas knew there was only unpleasantness left ahead.

"All right," Thomas said after he recovered, standing and offering Angus his hand. "Let's get this over with."

The pixie's home was near a stand of oak trees, not far from the old growth forest they had just raced through. Pixies were some of the smallest of the fae, standing only three feet tall, with nut-brown complexions and hair the color of the flowers in the gardens they frequented during the summer months. Angus and Thomas had to crawl through the door to the cottage, and practically consumed the room with their bulk. The pixie sat motionless in a wooden rocking chair; it seemed like she hadn't even the energy to set it rocking. The faerie was a faint ghost of her former self, with a blank expression and an absolute stillness that made Thomas worry whether she was even still alive. Her hair had faded to a dull tan, and her face was almost translucent in its pallor.

"Derryth," Angus called the pixie's name gently.

Derryth seemed to come into herself. It was frightening, as if a doll suddenly came to life, instantly switching from no expression to one of intent focus. "You've come back," she said in a high-pitched voice that scratched like shells mangled together in a raging tide. The hair on the back of Thomas' neck stood up.

"I have indeed, just as I said I would. And look you, I have Thomas Bant de Atlantic with me. Come to breathe some life into you."

Derryth's focus shifted from Angus to Thomas, but slipped off again quickly. "Ah, Angus. Save your sirens for those who still want to care."

"Derryth, come now. Things will look better in the morning. A bit of strength and you'll be able to see things more clearly."

"Angus, my darling boy. You take the offering for me and let me go. I've had enough. Enough pain, enough marking time. My gardens have faded, and I am ready to go too."

"You can't mean that," Angus said, sounding shaken. "You've always said that if you will go, you'll go surrounded by flowers. It's only just March. Take some strength and wait for full summer."

Derryth twitched her fingers in a weak scold. "Tut, tut. You'll try to keep me with the lure of summer gardens. It's harder to let go in the summer sun. But I've had enough, Angus mac Og. My light has gone. I am just ready to let go."

Thomas looked at Angus, whose face had twisted in pain. Angus shook his head.

"My last wish, Angus mac Og. Enjoy my garden. I've waited to give you a taste of early summer." With that, the pixie seemed to fold in on herself. She dropped back into the almost comatose expression she had had when they entered her home, dissolving into a white mist that suddenly erupted in a burst of scent. The room filled with the heat of July, the smell of honeysuckle and peonies almost overwhelming in their conflicting perfume. Thomas could taste summer ... and then all he tasted was ash.

They backed out of the small house in silence. Thomas was in shock. He'd never actually seen a faerie fade before. He had never met her before, but felt an immense sadness nonetheless. The two walked in silence back towards the small village that had been built for the sirens stationed in the moors. Angus finally broke the silence. "You're troubled."

"I'm so sorry, Angus."

"It was her choice, Thomas. We always have a choice. She was done. I had hoped she would at least try for one more summer."

"How do you *do* this?" Thomas asked in despair.

"What do you mean?"

"How can you stand to see such suffering? This can't be the first time one of your friends has died in your arms. I didn't even know her, and it's terrible."

Angus stopped walking and looked at Thomas. "You don't belong here," he said flatly.

"I'm sorry. I—"

"It's nothing you've said. You just don't belong here. Those others—" Angus gestured towards the village, "— are either true believers: children of Aphrodite, intent on saving the fae from imminent destruction; or sadists, who secretly enjoy the suffering, while disguising the fulfillment of their innermost desires from the fanatics. You are neither of those types."

"I'm here to help," Thomas said.

"Perhaps. But at what expense? You never said who sent you here. It has been nigh on three decades since Marisol brought anyone here, and that was a novelty in and of itself. Why are you really here?"

"I thought I could help," Thomas said wanly, a sense of inadequacy suddenly welling up from a deep place within his soul.

"Go home, Thomas. You are too good for this place." Angus sounded defeated.

"I can't leave you like this."

"You have my permission to go. Go back. Haven't you learned enough? Seen enough? You are not the type to volunteer for this. You are one who is meant to run races, and share joy, and laugh in the sunlight. You are what I used to be. We are not meant to be corpsmen, serving as medics to living corpses. If I could, I'd go with you. But I'm stuck here. Go home. Get out of this place while your spirit is still intact."

Siren resistance to fae magick is not absolute immunity. Depending on the strength of the fae, you can still be bespelled. That can be beneficial, where, for example, you have need of their healing powers. But bear in mind before visiting a preserve, that with the more gifted fae, you will succumb to their magick if you do not actively fight against it.

– Sirens: An Overview for the Newly-Transitioned, 3rd ed. (2015*), by Mira Bant de Atlantic, p. 106.*

Chapter 15

Angus must have sent an aisling to haunt his dreams and send him fleeing back to Brazil, because that night, Thomas dreamed a true memory of his meeting with Kyoko. A dream of the pure past, unfiltered and unedited by the passage of time and his own wishful fantasies.

Dreaming-Thomas saw himself as if from above, watching as Then-Thomas plunged through the waters of the Southern Atlantic for his first trip to Brazil. He could feel the slickness of the water, while seeing himself below as if he were in a movie. Though he knew he dreamed, he relished the chance to see Kyoko again.

Thomas experienced again the shocking difference between the Southern Atlantic and the Northern Atlantic. He had spent too much time in the cold north, trying to make it love him. While the ocean didn't call to him the way it did to his mother and sister, in Brazil, Then-Thomas could almost hear the Atlantic's song: a soft swaying murmur, whose exact words were just out of earshot, but whose bubbling joy made him smile. A real smile, a real lightening of heart. It was like when Excedrin kicked in on an insistent headache: the absence of pain, a shocking delight in its suddenness.

Then-Thomas hadn't realized he had been actually feeling anything — especially pain — until the feeling was suddenly swept away by the unexpected euphoria.

Dreaming-Thomas saw his mother waiting for him as he emerged from the rough surf at Praihna beach in Rio de Janiero. At the time, he had never even noticed the surfers behind him. Two had wiped out quite spectacularly when the Atlantic bounced him onto the shore. Mira drove up in an armored car, and again he felt the struggle he'd had to pull the heavy door closed.

Thomas had come when Mira called; he always came when his mother asked for help. "Who are we meeting?" Then-Thomas asked, and Dreaming-Thomas remembered his irritation at being summoned to Rio. "Why did you want me to come to Rio? You said we needed to be in Salvador tomorrow afternoon for the preliminary mediation session."

"You're not going to like it," Mira warned, and Then-Thomas felt his heart pause a beat in concern. She took a deep breath, then paused. "Just give me a chance to explain."

Dreaming-Thomas thought that was a stupid way to start an explanation. If he wasn't going to like it, warning him of that fact wasn't going to help.

"I called in a favor owed me by Gerel, who won last year's vampire fight for control of Rio. Her indentured mage is going to grant you fluency in Portuguese in exchange for one-half of one day of your life."

Mira had spoken quickly, her tone cajoling. He liked the apparition she wore back then. It had been a beautifully different look for her: skin the color of toasted coconut, hair a wavy caramel blond, and brilliant green eyes. Dreaming-Thomas wondered if his mother missed any of her bodies after she changed.

"It's such a small price to pay to be able to speak and understand the language like a native — you'd spend years of your life trying to learn it anyway, and you'd never have a proper accent."

"Mom, that's totally unnecessary for such a short trip: I memorized all the standard phrases in Portuguese for emergency compulsions. It's not like I'm moving down here or anything."

Then-Thomas felt smothered by his mother's incessant fretting over his safety. But Dreaming-Thomas noticed how her face tightened when he said he wasn't moving to Brazil. Of course! That had been her intent all along; her summons had been another attempt to lure him away from Jarl Georg's cold court. This time, Dreaming-Thomas acknowledged, his mother's gambit had worked.

"I overpaid for the skill myself before the war, and Gerel acknowledged her debt. There's no way she could have won against Meng Tian without the boost I gave her. She agreed to these terms for use of her mage if she won. Of course, if she'd lost, there'd be no way I could have collected, so I'm not sure why that was a condition. But whatever." Mira's voice faded.

His mother took too many risks. She always had.

But Then-Thomas experienced only a wash of relief. Perhaps her trigger warning had been a good idea, because he had been primed for her to ask him to accompany her on a visit to an army barracks or some other Godawful place with a bunch of aggressive men. Visiting a vampire seemed relatively innocuous in comparison.

As if sensing he was wavering, Mira looked at him. "If you want to know Japanese as well, you can get that for another half-day. That was my deal — Gerel's mage gave me fluency in the two languages she spoke: Portuguese and Japanese. She took English from me, and I overpaid because Gerel was preparing to oust the vamp who ran Rio. Until her mage's indenture runs out, I can have any of the mage's languages in exchange for a half-day."

Then-Thomas thought this request was somehow less frightening that most of her requests: this time she only wanted him to meet some vampire slave and lose a day of his life. Knowing Japanese at least could be useful if he ever got a chance to visit the Pacifics. "You bargained with a vampire? You take too many risks," Then-Thomas said, letting Mira know without saying so that he'd do it.

Dreaming-Thomas could see the relief on his mother's face. At least he could recognize a gift, even if it wasn't one he'd have chosen, and accept it graciously. Then-Thomas felt a sense of pride that he could handle his mother's offer, knowing that she could not have expected such a calm response from Cordelia. Atlantea despised mages, and Cordy idolized Atlantea to the point of adopting the queen's prejudices as her own. Then-Thomas imagined her views on vampires would likely be much worse than her feelings towards living mages. Dreaming-Thomas wanted to tell his old self that Cordy wasn't so superficial. Certainly naïve, but not as racist as he used to think.

And then, his mother's relief led her to take on her professorial persona which irked him as much now as it did then. Then-Thomas tuned her out, but Dreaming-Thomas couldn't escape so readily.

"In his quest to build the perfect weapon," Mira lectured, "Chía left hundreds of his mage-enemies as the walking dead. But given the amount of infighting amongst them now, I'm surprised there are any vampires left. No one likes to talk about them, but every major city has at least one vampire hunting in it. Saõ Paulo has at least two, and according to the Pacifics, Shanghai has four! The Shanghai territorial war has been going on for decades."

"What did you mean anyway, 'losing a half-day of my life?' I thought vampires sucked blood or something like that?" Then-Thomas asked.

"Only in the movies," his mother replied. "Vampires consume life-force. Similar, I guess, to how some mage healing spells work. Vampires need one day of a person's life to sustain themselves, and more to gain any extras like glamours or strength, etcetera. They take it by touch. And yes, it hurts — but only in correlation to the amount of life they drain. So I doubt you'll feel anything worse than some muscle aches."

Dreaming-Thomas was grateful he had rashly decided to take all the languages she offered, if only because it had extended their encounter. Kyoko had given him French as well as Portuguese and Japanese. At some point between when she had enchanted his mother and their meeting, she had somehow acquired French too. Dreaming-Thomas felt a pang of jealousy that Kyoko had stroked someone else's thoughts the way she had his.

The memory of their drive faded, and Dreaming-Thomas felt vertigo as time blurred to the evening he met the woman he couldn't forget. He dreaded seeing her, anticipating the pain of losing her yet again; at the same time, he yearned to feel her touch. It was as if their brief meeting had linked them, and he was only fully himself when she was in his mind.

Thankfully, his dream sped Dreaming-Thomas through his terrifying encounter with Gerel. The intense, split-second agony of her taking a day-and-a-half of his life was softened into an indistinct haze. Though Dreaming-Thomas knew that her gnarled hands with their sharp nails had been unbearably cold, he did not again feel the icy burning that had caused Then-Thomas to recoil. The dream fast-forwarded him away from Gerel's frightening presence into the small room, where he had awaited her indentured mage. Dreaming-Thomas watched his mother walk back into the vampire's larger parlor, half-closing the door behind her, when another door slowly opened.

And then the dream slowed to show him Kyoko's entrance in lavish detail. She entered through that other door in a gliding gait that entranced him now even as it had then. All the colors were amplified in his dream: somehow the utterly straight blackness of Kyoko's hair was glossier and more brilliant than he had remembered, her skin even more radiant. Dreaming-Thomas absorbed the perfection of her oval face, feeling his body stir as he was entranced by the crystal intelligence in her gaze. Her upturned eyes were so dark he couldn't look away. He savored the glory that was his Kyoko all over again.

Then-Thomas felt the softness in her voice as she asked, "Are you ready?"

Dreaming-Thomas watched himself nod, as she sat down next to him. She seemed so slight in his dream, but Then-Thomas had seen her as unimaginably strong. Then-Thomas looked bewitched, and she hadn't even begun her spelling.

Kyoko looked at him intently, then reached her hands up to gently cup the sides of his head. Then-Thomas experienced her mind in his as a whisper of sunlight caressing his exposed nerves; the lightest of touches across his very soul. There was no pain, no awareness of change, yet he was *changed*.

"*Watashinonamaeha Kyokodesu*," she said.

"Kyoko-*sama*," Then-Thomas breathed, worshiping her. What a magick this was! She had picked apart his thoughts, ever so gently and ever so precisely. Dreaming-Thomas thought he saw pulses of colors swirling around them as if in orbit; multi-colored threads of light dancing in intricate precision as she gifted him with comprehension. Then she released him, and the world was bland and dull again.

"*Eu terminei. Está feito,*" Kyoko said coldly to his mother, who had poked her head back through the door.

"Thomas, I'll only be another few minutes. Are you okay here?" Mira looked warily at Kyoko.

Then-Thomas nodded, and his mother shut the door behind her, with one long last look at Kyoko.

Dreaming-Thomas wondered what additional business she needed to conduct with Gerel. His mother was always collecting favors, which she banked against a rainy day. Perhaps his mother was more fae-like than all of them that way.

"Is this feeling a side effect of your spell?" Then-Thomas asked Kyoko in English. He couldn't regain his equilibrium. This fixation on her was not the expected outcome.

"Do you feel something?" Kyoko asked hesitantly. She glanced over at him without moving her head, somehow making that conservation of movement teasing, as opposed to shy.

"I haven't felt like this since my first crush in middle school. I don't know why, but I want to know you."

"It isn't a side-effect of my spell. At least, I have never known anyone to have such a reaction. But my feeling for you is a spell. You're a siren. I have never felt this attraction before," Kyoko spoke warily and both Dreaming- and Then-Thomas felt the punch of self-directed hatred.

"You must be the siren of sirens, then," Then-Thomas spoke earnestly, his voice humming with a magnetic resonance that Dreaming-Thomas could still feel in his bones. "Because I have never felt such a desire for anyone in my life. My heart is beating so fast, it's like I'm running a marathon! And if you feel even half what I do, then I am a terrible creation for forcing you. You must not be affected by me!" Then-Thomas felt the resonance of his compulsion as his hands shook with effort, and his voice, normally a warm baritone, resonated with the power of the sea.

There was a silence, then Kyoko reached out and took Thomas' hand. "I don't think your magick works that way," she said gently. "But I love you more for trying. Sirenic magick is so strong. And I don't mind *your* spell, it doesn't press on me like your mother's. Thomas, I don't like your mother; I feel the need to slap her in the face, to scratch out her eyes, to—" Kyoko broke off, inhaling sharply, then speaking with more control.

"The only thing that prevents me from harming her is the leash of my indenture to Gerel. But yet, even as I want to rip her apart, I also love her somehow because she's *your* mother. We're speaking the language we both learned from her; it's the first thing we share," Kyoko's eyes reflected the light. They were so dark and luminous that, looking at her, Thomas felt like he was gazing into an eclipse.

"You have bewitched me as surely as I have bewitched you," Thomas whispered, tracing his finger gently across her cheek. "But I would free you if I could." Dreaming Thomas felt the truth of Then-Thomas' statement. He had a burst of insane confidence that even if he lacked the instinctual allure of a siren, he would still win her through the unbearable force of his own admiration for her, if nothing else.

"I am not sure why you feel anything for me," Kyoko said. "But I would not set *you* free, even if I could." There was steel in her voice. Dreaming-Thomas knew she was telling the truth, and he grew hard. He wanted nothing more than to be possessed by her.

"Are you a witch?" Then-Thomas asked. "I don't care if you are. I don't care about anything except you. Say the word, and I'll kill the vampire-bitch for you!"

Then-Thomas meant it; Dreaming-Thomas regretted that he had *not* attempted to kill her. He had never felt such reckless courage, despite the terror that Gerel's mere presence inspired. He had no skill to fight a vampire — let alone a vampire who had destroyed other vampires — but for Kyoko, he would try.

"I couldn't bear it if you were hurt. If you *died*, Thomas! Swear you won't do anything!" Kyoko gripped his other hand, and her warmth radiated around him.

"No, not unless you swear you will free yourself and come to me," Then-Thomas felt rash. He had never met a mage as powerful as Kyoko. She was so precise and so strong. She was the needle that pierced efficiently. She was the guillotine that killed instantly. She was a song in his blood. He wanted her then, he wanted her now, he wanted her always.

"I will come to you when I'm free," Kyoko promised.

"Be ready when she calls," whispered the aisling. And Thomas woke up.

"I'm done," Thomas told Cordelia from the safe distance of Salvador. He was grateful that the faerie mound in North Yorkshire interfered with satellite and radio waves, so he had a slim excuse for having not told her he was leaving until after it had become a fait accompli.

"What do you mean, you're done?" Cordelia asked, her voice crackling over the line. It was a bad connection.

"I'm back in Brazil, Cordy. I wasn't useful — they didn't need me — I ... I couldn't take it anymore." Thomas struggled to find the right words.

"How could they not need you? This line is not secure, Thomas. Why didn't you come back here? It would have been helpful if we could have discussed this in person."

He couldn't explain to Cordelia why he didn't go back. It seemed crazy even to him. It was inexplicable, yet felt too real. Perhaps that's what he deserved for allowing an aisling into his dreams at night. "Listen, Cordy. It's bad. Much worse than I thought. Worse than you even imagine. Do I think there's a danger that a faerie could turn on us? There's always a danger." Thomas swallowed. "When you can, go and see for yourself. But be prepared."

"I have so many questions! Can't you just come back here? I guess I could come to Brazil for a short while. Maybe we should meet in Atlantis; it's practically midway, but honestly, I really shouldn't leave right now. I've made significant progress with the Indians. There's so much going on—"

Thomas cut her off. "I can't leave Brazil right now; I'm needed here. But it would be absurd for you to come to me for such a tiny amount of information. I don't have any definitive answers for you. All I can tell you is that you shouldn't give up. Don't give up, Cordy. *Do not.*"

"Okay, Thomas," Cordelia said, sounding troubled. "I have to go."

"Thomas, thank you for doing this."

Thomas stumbled over his words. He reflexively wanted to say, "No problem," but of course, it had been a huge problem. "Love you," he finally rumbled.

"Love you too," Cordelia said, and hung up.

Thomas pulled a Coke out of his refrigerator. Something about the caffeine combined with sugar made it more of a stimulant for him than coffee. He hated feeling this way. Feeling like he'd let Cordy down. Let Angus down. Let everyone down again. He hadn't spoken to Mary almost since Thanksgiving. Perhaps he'd give her a call.

A memory flickered through his head, and he smiled. She had been eight to his six when Dad died. After the funeral, one of the cops was telling him that he was the man of the house now and had to take care of his mother and sisters. Thomas remembered nodding solemnly, scared of the man in the blue uniform, with his gun and dark mustache.

His mother had been standing in the back, away from the crowd, holding Cordelia, while Amy rolled on the ground in front of her, throwing a tantrum as only a three-year-old could. Thomas had been adrift. Then Mary had swooped in, telling the cop that *they* would take care of each other, thank you very much, and took his hand to lead him back to Mom.

Mary had leaned down, jerking Amy off the floor, and telling her to stop it right this instant. Miraculously, or perhaps because of the novelty of the situation, Amy had stopped. Then the five of them had simply stood there for the rest of the awful thing: Mary holding him and Amy in either hand, with Mom holding Cordy in one arm and hugging Mary with the other.

Mary always made him feel better. But he'd wait to call her. He didn't deserve to feel better just yet.

It's unclear why active sirens struggle to conceive. Some speculate that this was a deliberate design decision intended to limit the siren population, but others believe it to be an unfortunate consequence of the siren spell's complexity. Once pregnant, however, sirens are more likely than other magical beings to carry their babies to term. While other magical constructs (as well as mages) suffer a high rate of miscarriage, Aphrodite's spell design ensures that the siren mother and her growing fetus are not both magical, thereby limiting the amount of magick confined in one body. For latent sirens, the siren spell is activated at the moment of birth, and an active siren can only conceive latent children.

– Sirens: An Overview for the Newly-Transitioned, 3rd ed. (2015), by Mira Bant de Atlantic, p. 73.

Chapter 16

Cordelia was late for breakfast this morning, and her stomach growled with hunger. She was supposed to have met Shravya a half-hour ago, but overslept. At least Queen Sophia made sure there was plenty of food at the buffet, so even if she did miss the Indian envoy, she could at least look forward to a hearty meal.

While she didn't much care what she ate (she'd hardly consider herself a gourmand), even Cordelia appreciated the Mediterraneans' hospitality. The breakfast buffet typically included everything from the fish and rice dishes common at the Pacific court, to the cheese and rolls of the Arctic, to Indian chutneys. Though since her first trimester, she had learned to avoid adventurous eating, and began loading her plate with more conventional fare. As she looked at the steaming stack of naan, wondering if that would be plain enough, she hoped Shravya had waited for her.

Cordelia had started courting Shravya and Rahul because they were Raj Varuna's envoys, but had been pleasantly surprised to find that she and Shravya had struck up a genuine friendship. At least it was genuine on her end.

Cordelia pondered the novelty of that. Thinking about all her relationships since she moved to Atlantis when she was twelve, it occurred to her that she wouldn't call any of the people she knew friends. She had her family, of course, but her last real *friend* had been Jennifer Crawley in the fifth grade. She supposed her lack of friendships wasn't too surprising. There were few sirens who were the same age, and while a twenty- or even hundred-year age difference doesn't make that much of a difference when you're forty, it's a huge divide when you're seventeen. And when she reached her majority, she'd immediately joined the High Court, so she hadn't had much of an opportunity to get to know people before politics interfered. But she'd always had her family, and until now, hadn't really thought she was missing anything.

Cordelia finished loading her plate and walked into the dining room to look for Shravya. "Mother!" she exclaimed, genuinely shocked to see Mira sitting next to Shravya near the head of the large dining table.

At Cordelia's entrance, Mira stood and walked over to her. Her mother was wearing the guise of another busty blond with carved cheekbones. A common look, but one that probably let her blend in better in Boston than the more dramatic raven-hair and ebony-skin she had worn at their last meeting.

"You always recognize me," Mira said joyfully, before pulling Cordelia into a hug. "*I* almost didn't recognize *you*," Mira whispered in Cordelia's ear, before squeezing her tightly, then releasing her.

Cordelia was almost full-term now, and her obvious pregnancy had drawn envious stares from many of the sirens at Queen Sophia's court. "Who told you?" Cordelia asked.

"The question isn't who told me, but why *you* didn't tell me." Mira shook her head. "But we'll talk about that later." Mira drew Cordelia to the empty seat at the head of the table, next to where she was sitting with the Indian envoy. "Shravya has been filling me in on all the adventures you've been having."

"Oh yes," Shravya replied. "We've become quite close these past months. Cordelia, I can't believe you didn't tell me that Mira Bant de Atlantic was your mother! I mean, I suppose I should have realized, but I didn't make the connection. I wouldn't be here except for her."

Cordelia struggled to get her balance back. Why was her mother here? Was it possible that Atlantea had sent her to Kasos to check up on her?

Mira smiled. "You aren't the youngest siren at the Mediterranean Court, Cordelia. I think Shravya here is a decade younger, at least."

"And I'm not the youngest one here, for that matter. It's amazing, Cordelia, that this is your first visit," Shravya exclaimed.

"It seems like Kasos attracts a lot of the younger sirens. What did you think of the Arctic twins?" Cordelia was proud that her light tone betrayed none of her inner turmoil.

Shravya laughed. "The twins are too wild even for me! Did you hear about what they got up to with the girls from the Pacific? I hear that the Pacifics are headed home after that debacle."

"Queen Sophia herself doesn't seem to engage in much of this partying, though," Mira observed.

"True. But she invites me for coffee at least one afternoon a week, so I feel that I've gotten to know her a little bit." The gold beads at the ends of Shravya's braids clinked together as she tossed her hair back.

"Cordelia told me that Raj Varuna is your progenitor," Mira said. While their conversations had been brief since Cordelia arrived in Kasos, Cordy had mentioned her new friend more than once, and Mira was curious.

"That's right. But it was my grandfather, Luciano, who found and claimed me. He had read your book, you see, and knew the signs. He came right away and took us to Agalega."

"Both your parents also?" Cordelia asked.

"Yes, but my mother went back, and I never met her. My grandfather actually raised me, but I still see my father from time-to-time. He was the one who persuaded the Raj to send me here as his envoy."

"It seems to be a common tactic across the Oceans to send young sirens as envoys to Queen Sophia's court," Cordelia remarked in a wry tone. Her early rise as a courtier had prevented such a sojourn.

"It's been quite interesting," Shravya said, turning back to Mira. "And I'll have to tell Luciano that I met you! He'll be most impressed."

"You make me feel like a celebrity," Mira laughed. "You said you were planning to be here through the end of summer. Are you headed anywhere else afterwards?"

"Well, it depends, I guess, on whether I get pregnant, too," Shravya gestured at Cordelia. "If I do, I'll probably go back to Agalega. If not, I'm not sure where the Raj will send me."

"Are you excited? Do you have parents picked out?" Mira asked.

"Mom, I don't think Shravya wants to talk about all of that."

"How about you? Will you place this baby with a family here, or back in the States?" Mira's voice was relatively even, but Cordelia felt accused nevertheless.

"I have it all worked out," Cordelia said tightly.

As if sensing the tension, Shravya rose. "So, we will have dinner tomorrow, right?" Shravya asked, and Mira nodded. "Cordelia, why don't you come too? I told your mother about Peskesi."

"I don't remember that restaurant being here the last time I was on Kasos," Mira said.

"It's very good," Cordelia agreed. They firmed up plans to meet the next day at eight for dinner, and Shravya left, waving to the other sirens who had entered the dining room.

"Mom, you've been in the Atlantic Suite here, right?"

"Yes, many times. It's enormous. Do you like it?"

"Let's go there. I need to eat, and it's too crowded to talk." While it was generally deemed poor manners for the guests to take food to their rooms, the other sirens simply smiled at Cordelia as she walked out with her full plate — one of the few benefits of being so obviously pregnant.

"Queen Sophia redecorated," her mother remarked when they walked in. "I don't remember this much gilding before."

Cordelia glanced around. "It does have the look of Marisol's house to it. Perhaps she advised on the change in décor." While Marisol's house was over-the-top, Cordelia thought this room was more tastefully done, even if was too ornate for her mother's taste. The gold leaf inlay on the coffered ceiling was particularly nice, in her opinion. The furniture floated in the over-sized parlor, almost too small for the scale of the room. While Cordelia sat on the dull yellow velvet couch, her mother glanced around the room.

Cordelia struggled for a moment to reach her plate on the glass coffee table, which was too low and far from the couch. Instead of moving, she picked her plate back up to balance it atop her ball of a belly, then cut into the thick *croque madame* sandwich with a gusto. Mira stared at Cordelia for a moment, then smiled and shook her head at how adroitly Cordelia managed to use her body as a table. She walked around the room as her daughter finished her meal. "When are you due?" Mira asked.

"The midwife thinks the end of July."

"That's only a month away. I'll have to go back to Boston for a week or so, but I can be back by then."

"Really, you don't have to, Mom. I can handle this."

Mira sighed. "Cordelia, I know you can handle this. But perhaps you should consider *my* ability to handle it. I don't know what impression I must have given you that you decided to keep your pregnancy from me. No matter what opinion I might have about this siren custom, you have to know I'll always support you, right?"

"I know that, but I didn't want to distract you." Cordelia's excuse sounded thin, even to her.

"How do you think I'd feel if I'd have left you to this all by yourself? If I'd only found out about it next year? Seriously, Cordelia. Have some sense. You could have simply told me. I can balance my priorities just as well as you can."

"Don't start in," Cordelia warned, putting her plate back on the table and refilling her glass with water from the carafe.

Mira returned to pacing around the room. The heavy drapes were still drawn, so she couldn't see the ocean, and the upholstered walls blocked the sound of the waves. The lack of her connection to the sea made her feel even less balanced.

"I was back in Atlantis last week to update Atlantea on Amy's research. You also forgot to tell me about that, by the way. Fortunately, or unfortunately, depending on your perspective, she hasn't made much headway. They've hit a plateau, so to speak. But while I was waiting in Atlantis House, several people approached me with their congratulations. I'm sure you'll be happy to hear that everyone thinks your resignation from Court was the wisest decision you've made to date. Your cachet has grown enormously among the old guard, and several took the time to write to you. I have a stack of letters for you, full of their good wishes, believe it or not. From what I can tell — and take it with a grain of salt, because I doubt anyone who really thought badly of you would tell me about it — but it seems that your Reconcilers are still behind you as well."

"Perhaps Atlantea was right," Cordelia admitted quietly. She'd had some time to think about this, even before her mother's surprise visit.

"Perhaps. But regardless of everyone else's opinions, I hope you know that *I* will always support you."

"Mom, I know I could have called—"

"The point is, Cordelia, you *did* call. We've spoken several times since you arrived in Kasos. This was just something you chose not to mention. Did you think I couldn't handle the information? That I would do something rash, like abandoning my post? Or did you think I'd yell at you? Sometimes, Cordelia, you can really be quite cruel."

When Cordelia had seen her mother that morning, she had felt like a teenager caught breaking curfew. What had started out as simple avoidance of an unpleasant discussion had turned into an almost deliberate snub. Her mother's quiet disappointment was worse than if she had yelled at her, and Cordelia cringed inwardly at the truth of her mother's quiet condemnation. "I'm sorry, Mom."

Mira kept pacing. Finally, she drew open the curtains, and the room was flooded with sunlight. The yellows and golds of the satin upholstery warmed in the brilliant light, which seemed too strong for mid-morning. The room immediately felt less oppressive, and Mira stood for a moment, looking at the variegated blue color of the Mediterranean.

But it wasn't her ocean, and she didn't feel embraced by it. As disconcerting as it was to stare at water that didn't cherish her, how much harder must it be for Cordelia, who was even more used to feeling the ocean's constant appreciation? That she was in this strange place, about to give birth next to an ocean that didn't treasure her as its beloved, horrified Mira. Perhaps she and Thomas could persuade Cordelia to return to Ocracoke, at least for her final month.

"Where's Thomas?" she asked.

"I sent him back to Brazil," Cordelia replied, knowing that her mom would be furious if she knew that Thomas had just up and left. And really, she *had* sent him away — to England — so it wasn't that much of a stretch.

"Brazil? He left you here alone? Did he know you were pregnant?"

"Yeah, Mom. But honestly, being in Kasos wasn't good for him. I could tell he wasn't happy here — it was like before when he was at Jarl Georg's court. He needed to get out. And it isn't like Thomas is going to be in the delivery room with me or anything."

"Why not? Who were you planning to have support you?"

"There's Laila, the midwife," Cordelia responded, but knew that sounded inadequate. Still, she had done this before. She would be fine.

"Cordelia, you should be surrounded by family right now; this is absurd. I was told that Zale is the father?" Mira glanced at Cordelia for confirmation. Cordelia nodded. "Then why would you want to stay here for the birth? Wouldn't it be better to return to the Atlantic?"

"Maybe," Cordelia temporized. She didn't want to leave now that she had finally built up a real rapport with the Indians.

"Where are the parents you've selected?"

"They're in Florida. Similar kind of family as the others," Cordelia responded.

Mira left the window to pace back around the room in a slow circuit. Cordelia watched her, wondering if her explanations would be enough. Her mother's face showed signs of strain, and she was rubbing her chin the way she did when she was thinking hard. Cordelia actually felt relieved that they were finally having this discussion. At some point over the past few months, she realized that she ought to have said something. But each time, she had chickened out; and then it felt like it was too late. With her mother so busy, it had been too easy to keep making excuses. She really hadn't thought things through.

"Cordy, next time something this momentous happens to you, would you please tell me yourself? I had to learn about your incredibly good fortune from Daan, of all people. I detest him under the best of circumstances, and hearing that you were blessed with another pregnancy from that stuck-up weasel was gratuitously unpleasant."

Cordelia had to try to keep the amusement from her face; her mother really was an excellent judge of character.

"And I can't believe Thomas actually let you send him back to Brazil," Mira continued.

"Marisol is here—" Cordelia began, but stopped speaking as Mira threw up her hands in exasperation.

"Marisol is completely inadequate for anything like this!"

"What's going on with Amy?" Cordelia asked, sensing that her mother's tirade had turned into more of her usual patter of complaints.

"I don't think we should discuss all of that here," Mira said. "Suffice to say that I have a very highly-placed informant who is keeping me updated about their research. It's nothing we really need to worry about, though we should keep an eye on things. Devin — you remember, my partner since Thomas wasn't available — has been extremely helpful. Honestly, it was perhaps for the best that you took Thomas here, but I'll tell you more about that later. Anyway, Devin sourced me a bespelled phone that provides end-to-end security. Did you know they made such things?"

Cordelia shook her head.

"Me either," Mira continued. "I'm sure they aren't completely un-hackable, but from what I understand, they provide a secure line, even when the other party isn't using one. Before I leave, I'll program my new number into your phone. And I expect regular updates from you from now on. No more omissions."

"Okay. I'm sorry, Mom. Really."

Mira sat next to Cordelia on the couch and pulled her close. Cordelia rested her head on her mother's shoulder. "I know, Cordy. I know."

While born sirens grow up understanding the societal expectations of the siren communities, it can take time for a transitioned siren to find their place in an unfamiliar culture. Unlike enclave-bound mages, sirens have the option to leave their community entirely. Those who survive their self-imposed exile have typically found another fae or construct community with which to ally themselves.

– Sirens: An Overview for the Newly-Transitioned, 3rd ed. (2015), *by Mira Bant de Atlantic, p. 192.*

Chapter 17

It's good when you can kill two birds with one stone, Mira thought. Since they were in Florida anyway for the birth of Cordelia's baby, Mira and Devin had spent a day with the Florida-based research team the Atlantics funded to follow their known U.S. latent population. The researchers thought they were conducting a longitudinal study on socio-environmental effects on mundane fertility, but their real purpose was to monitor for latent pregnancies and alert the Atlantic transition teams.

It was more difficult to follow children placed in less-developed nations, but Mira had persuaded Shravya, at least, that oversight through this kind of "scientific" study was worth exploring. Of course, Mira had a detective agency following her own latent offspring more closely, but most sirens thought that was too intrusive.

Mira didn't really care that other sirens mocked her as overprotective, and indeed "unnatural" at times. Thomas' transition had been almost as terrible as her own, and she wanted to make sure none of her other offspring experienced that. At the very least, her reputation as an unusually involved parent had been helpful in getting Devin out of her way today.

Cordelia had been so uncharacteristically amenable to Mira's demand that she stay in Florida for a while to recover that Mira had started to wonder if her daughter were suffering from post-partum depression. After all, the fae had healed Cordy's physical pains quickly enough. But eventually she concluded that Cordy's unusual acquiescence stemmed from guilt rather than depression.

Mira ignored the pangs of her own conscience when she used that guilt to manipulate Cordelia into visiting Mary and taking Devin with her. This was a fair penance for her failure to tell Mira about her pregnancy — a lie by omission. And really, she needed to get away from Devin for a while. She didn't want Louisa's warrior-spy (even one she liked as much as Devin) to participate in her upcoming meeting with Jonah. Who knew what her Danjou spy might reveal?

Devin must have done his research on Mira too well, because he accepted her condition without question. She herself thought it a rather thin excuse: after all, Cordy had been traveling alone to the States since Thomas' transition. But Mira's reputation, combined with Cordy's air of martyrdom, must have persuaded Devin that the only way to get Mira back on task was for him to shepherd Cordelia to D.C.

Jonah was flying into Ft. Lauderdale, so Mira had arranged to meet him at Dania Beach, a fairly secluded spot less than two miles from the airport. She emerged on the shore around five o'clock in the afternoon. It was even hotter and more humid than usual, so Mira didn't seek the ocean's help in drying off as she walked along the water's edge, scanning the beach for the mage.

There weren't many people here at this hour: the benefit of selecting a beach that lacked restrooms, restaurants, and clubs was that most of the day-trippers were long gone. She eventually located Jonah sitting on an oversized green-and-white beach towel. He had taken off his button-down shirt and shoes, and was now wearing only a white undershirt and rolled-up khakis. As Mira drew closer, she could see that he had aged since the last time they met. His hair was now close-cropped to disguise the gray, and his face was creased with more wrinkles than she recalled.

Jonah smiled and stood up, flipping the switch on his vape-pipe off and sticking it in his back pocket. Mira wondered when he'd begun vaping ambrosia. She knew he wasn't the strongest mage in the enclave, but he had never relied on ambrosia to boost his power before. She did admire the way he always recognized her. Jonah had told Mira that his sole magical strength lay in his acute perception.

"How are you?" Mira asked, after Jonah had enveloped her in a too-tight hug, with three obligatory cheek kisses. The traditional enclave greeting called for air kisses, but Mira endured Jonah's overly familiar greeting because she felt sorry for him.

"I'm better now that I see you," Jonah replied. His flirting had grown more overt over the years. Mira asked one of her siren mentors whether repeated compulsions had any lasting effect on humans, but he had assured her that any change in personality was temporary; as soon as Jonah left her presence, he would be back to normal.

"Was it hard to get away?" Mira asked.

"Not really, no," Jonah replied. "I was due for some time off, and this is a common weekend jaunt for all of us who are over-worked and underpaid, mages as well as mundanes."

"I appreciate it." Mira was always polite. Despite years of subordinating Jonah's will to her own, she still worried at the morality of it. He wasn't the only person she influenced on a regular basis. Eli, for instance, had been under a much tighter compulsion for more than half a year now. But Jonah was the only person who knew exactly what she was doing. He seemed to enjoy their conversations in a way that made Mira feel wrong for taking advantage of him.

"Maybe we should walk and talk. I've been sitting for way too long," Jonah suggested. "Not that I mind, of course. I needed a break. Your call was a welcome excuse to take the weekend off and drown my worries in an endless array of fruity drinks." Jonah took Mira's duffle from her, setting in on the ground next to his own. He pulled a piece of chalk out of his pocket and marked something over the pile. "No one will touch it while we walk," he declared.

Mira marveled at the fact that Jonah was considered a weak mage. Ambrosia, the refined, consumable version of silica-salt that Jonah had been vaping earlier, was said to enhance a mage's powers, but it nevertheless worried her that the smallest of his abilities seemed so much greater than hers.

"This isn't a strong spell," Jonah said, as if reading her mind. "A truly determined person could break through the barrier."

"So what's going on at the enclave, Jonah?" Mira asked as they walked down to the beach, glad when the dull sound of the distant traffic on the abutting highway was finally drowned out by the sound of the waves.

"Same old, same old," he replied. "Still in the process of building the army and enlisting allies. Preparing; always preparing. But life goes on. Giselle miscarried this year, but is doing better now."

"I'm so sorry to hear about your sister," Mira remarked. Mages struggled to carry their babies to term; too much magick was contained in one body for an uncomplicated pregnancy.

They talked about small changes as they walked. Mira knew others would have just sucked the information out of Jonah and been done with it, but Mira couldn't bring herself to do that. He worked as an assistant to one of the enclave's more powerful elders, so he actually knew a lot about Danjou business. With only a slight amount of encouragement on her part, Jonah's free-flowing gossip often provided better information than she could have obtained through a direct interrogation.

Eli was an enormous asset, but his knowledge only went so far. He had some inkling of the DoD's interest in their project, and of course was quite familiar with all of the successes and stumbles that Amy's team was encountering. But he had absolutely no insight into the Danjou Enclave. At Mira's "suggestion" to gather additional information, Eli had contacted Elder Simon, the Danjou point person, but had not really learned anything about their intentions.

When the via-enchanter staffed on Amy's project had been recalled last month, Mira had called Jonah. Unfortunately, her compulsions weren't nearly as strong as Devin's, so Jonah's claim that he didn't know why they had recalled their delegate could have been a lie. Mira needed to be physically close to a man in order to be sure her compulsions worked, especially on one bound to loyalty through the enclave's blood-geas.

After a few minutes of listening to Jonah talk about his boss' latest setback in developing a long-range death spell, Mira asked about Ted. "Oh, yeah. Poor Ted," Jonah said.

"Why 'poor Ted'?" Mira asked.

"They have him under house arrest. It's totally unfair. Simon Riccie blames him for his son's death, when everyone knows Simon and Rachael pushed the poor kid too hard."

"Barry Riccie is dead?" Mira asked, shocked.

"You know him? Yes, Elder Simon's wayward mundane son." Jonah's voice dropped a little, as if he were sharing some choice gossip. He even glanced around to see if anyone were listening. "Now, the Riccies are one of the strongest Danjou families. But even they have a dud every generation or so. It happens to everyone. But not to the great Simon Riccie. Elder Simon couldn't handle his son's failure. He made that kid's life a living hell. His wife's too. Rumor is, he even got a DNA test to make sure Barry was really his.

"So when they started looking for subjects to undergo an experimental operation that turned mundanes into mages, Elder Simon volunteered his son, and it kind of worked: Barry was able to see magick, and who knows, with a little more time and healing, maybe he'd have been able to use it. I mean, it takes children years to figure out the most basic spells. You'd have thought he'd give Barry at least a year to heal up from brain surgery, let alone start casting. But Rachael was thrilled that her son was finally qualified as a mage — whether or not he could cast. Didn't matter to her. She rushed the binding ritual and invited everyone. Barry held up like a trouper." Jonah sighed.

"What do you mean?" Mira asked. Jonah hesitated for a moment.

"Well, most of us never remember our bindings — they're laid on us as toddlers once it becomes clear we can perceive magick. That's a blessing, really, because if you could have seen Barry endure it …" Jonah shook his head. "But Barry never let out a sound; his mother, at least, was proud.

"Anyway, seeing magick alone wasn't good enough for Simon. He never let up, and rumor has it that Barry threw himself off their roof. In any event, Elder Rachael found him, and hasn't been the same since. Of course, it couldn't be Simon's fault for pushing him too hard, or Rachael's for rushing him into the binding. No, it was Ted who handled the operation, so it must be his fault."

"Wow," Mira said. They walked a while along the water as she processed the information. Perhaps the tide was coming in, because the waves picked up some additional force as Mira thought about Patient B. "I guess it only happened recently. Barry's death?"

"Hmm. Maybe last month? My boss has been having a bunch of meetings about it with the other elders. But he isn't a Riccie, so has limited pull with that family. Each clan tends to self-police, and it takes a little more than just a house arrest to get the elders to interfere in what they view as family disciple.

"Of course, Ted's almost an elder himself, and he's got a rare talent, so he has more support than someone like me could expect. And he *was* working on this whole shit-show at the enclave's direction. So it doesn't sit well with a lot of people how he's getting blamed."

"Ted sounds like a popular guy," Mira remarked.

"He's a decent sort. Doesn't throw his weight around all that much. He helped Giselle out when she was looking for a new tutor in the higher arcane."

"What does house arrest mean?" Mira asked.

"What it sounds like. They don't blind him, but he's confined to his house. No visitors. No contact with the outside world. It's meant to be a temporary thing while the elders sort out a more permanent kind of punishment or 'rehabilitation.'" Jonah made air quotes around the word and Mira shivered despite herself at the thought of what that might mean.

"Do you think they'll let him go?"

"Not sure. Depends, really, on who they need more and when. My boss thinks this operation was the sign we've been waiting on. But the fortune tellers are mixed. Elder Simon is a strong battle mage, but Ted's talent is rarer and more necessary if we really do get dragged into a mage war. So, they'll probably let Ted out at some point — if only when they really need him."

"I still don't understand the pivot or the trigger or whatever else you all are waiting on if what you plan to do is just invade another country and start the next mage war," Mira said provocatively. She layered a compulsion into her voice to encourage Jonah to speculate.

"No one starts a war with the strongest mage on the planet on a whim!" Jonah announced. And Mira knew at that moment that the Danjous were planning to invade Arabia. If even a relatively low-level mage such as Jonah was aware of the elders' plans, this move was imminent.

"Elder Hilda is very close to solving the djinni problem," Jonah continued. "There's just been too much waste by the Dictator. For centuries, he's had the richest silica-salt fields in the world, and what does he have to show for it? A closed country. The Danjou would make better use of it — to help everyone. Plus, everyone knows the Cabal is planning their own invasion. And what a disaster for mundane-mage relations it would be if they imposed apartheid on another country! You think the U.S. has problems with racism? Think about another Australia. Another Australia with the riches of Arabia."

It was clear that Jonah was speaking the party line. "What's your role in all this, Jonah?" Mira asked, trying to sound more sympathetic than she felt at the moment. Taking what wasn't yours was the classic reason people went to war, and Jonah's party-line, the classic justification. Those who have it, waste it. And righting the injustice of life's unfair bestowal of gifts on the unworthy was somehow a noble undertaking, instead of just plain robbery.

"*I* plan to be so useful to Elder Tyrone that I'm *never* dispatched to the front lines. I don't know why we need to do this, but what choice do any of us really have? This isn't a democracy, you know." Jonah was clearly conflicted.

"So what's the plan? The Danjou invade Arabia, oust the Amir, and gain access to the fields? Then what?"

"Then what? I don't know. I don't need all that power; couldn't use it if I had it. I can't even expend all the power in *this* country. And we have an active skimming industry of our own in the Southwest that our mages aren't close to tapping out. It's almost as good as the Sahara's silica-salt."

"Jonah, my offer stands." Mira was worried about him. In some ways, her relationship with Jonah was even deeper than her relationship with Amy and Mary. For more than thirty years, she had met with Jonah at least once a year. Back when Mira had first moved to Brazil, Jonah started having trouble with Elder Tyrone. She had offered him sanctuary in Brazil, surrounded by the were-jaguars and under the umbrella of the Amazonian fae's protection.

"Yeah, well, I'm not that desperate." There was also little possibility that a mage like Jonah could kill an enclave elder. It took no small amount of talent and a great deal of skill to create a lifelong binding like the enclave geases.

"Jonah, what is the Danjou Enclave doing with all these joint research projects? The one that Ted was working on with those Harvard doctors? What do the Danjou want?" Mira paused, looking out at the sea. The waves were now cresting at three feet; she took a deep breath to try to calm herself.

"I don't know exactly what they were doing with all the genetic research they funded before this. Clearly the Arabs are researching mage sight. So if the Dictator can figure out a way to weaponize it, our enclave has to have it too. A lot of our research is focused on long-distance spelling." Mages were keen to overcome their greatest limitation, but Mira counted it a blessing that mages needed to see their targets to cast. Enchantments would work after the mage had left the scene, of course, but such magicks didn't have the same widespread and immediately destructive force as a battle mage's spells; mage specialists could eventually counter the effects of almost all enchantments.

"So the idea is if you can restore sight, or understand how it works physically, you can overcome the line-of-sight limitation?" Mira hazarded.

"Maybe. I don't know. I only overhear things, really. And this isn't Elder Tyrone's project. I only know about it because he's been trying to help Ted."

"Jonah," Mira wove a direct compulsion into her voice for the first time since they'd started talking. "Why do you think the Danjou are sponsoring the mage sight project?"

"Ah, Mira," Jonah sighed, looking longingly at her. "I wish I knew for sure, and I swear I will try to get you better information. But I think ... I think the elders want to control the pivot, to turn the tide of war towards the Danjou. So that we can claim what we should have owned before the sirens refused us passage and the Dictator raised his djinni. No, please ... don't let up."

Jonah shivered under the influence of her compulsion. But Mira did let up, and Jonah's euphoric expression faded into a disappointed pout. She felt mildly disgusted at herself for resorting to such a heavy-handed use of her magick, but was even more disgusted by the Danjou. Before emigrating to the States, the European enclaves had long desired to claim the deserts of Africa and Arabia, but the Mediterraneans prevented them from crossing the seas. Then the Amir had been born, and the miracle of such a powerful mage arising out of the desert had stymied the Europeans' ambitions.

"How will the Danjou get past the djinni?" Mira asked. Air travel may have mooted the sirens' control of the seas, but the Amir's geas-barrier still stood between the Danjou and Arabia's rich silica-salt fields.

"Elder Hilda is perfecting a counter-spell. Or so she tells Elder Tyrone," Jonah replied.

Despite Mira's pressing, Jonah didn't know much more than that. She left him to find his fruity drinks and forget his troubles for the rest of the weekend. As she dove back into the water, Mira wondered if it were now time for them to try to get direct access to one of the Danjou elders. That would be hard though; the elders so rarely left the enclave, and it would be beyond dangerous to interfere with the most powerful of the Danjou. Still, her conversation with Jonah proved Atlantea was right: this war was coming — will she, nil she. Mira looked forward to the swim up to Boston to clear her head; she did *not* look forward to telling Atlantea what she had learned.

Most active sirens dwell exclusively in siren settlements for community and protection. Attempting to continue your mundane life among people who are now instinctually driven to passionate and irrational hatred of you is extremely dangerous. Fertile humans, even latent sirens, have no control over their reactions. The only known means of preventing their response is through biological fertility elimination; mage spells are ineffective. The prevalence of hormonal birth control, combined with the relatively lower levels of aggression and societal power in human females, has made it increasingly possible for female sirens to settle in mundane communities. These factors, however, make it more difficult for a male siren to settle outside a siren community. It is strongly discouraged for any male siren to even make such an attempt.

– Sirens: An Overview for the Newly-Transitioned,
3rd ed. (2015), *by Mira Bant de Atlantic, p. 17.*

Chapter 18

Thomas dragged himself back into the house, waving absently at the gate guards who monitored his front entrance. The women were competent in the extreme, their natural affinity towards him amplifying their professional concern for his well-being into near obsession. He had spent the morning playing soccer with Kadu and the rest of the were team, and felt a pleasant soreness from the activity. Of course, the jaguars treated sports like combat training, so playing soccer with them could be extremely dangerous. Thomas felt a bit of a thrill at having escaped the match without serious injury.

He was also relieved to be back in Brazil. His mother had given him an earful for failing to tell her about Cordy's pregnancy; he was still smarting from her lecture, but at least she had decided to stay with Cordy. And now that her baby was born, Thomas was off the hook to go to back to Kasos ... or Yorkshire. He refused to let himself feel guilty.

But he wondered how Angus was doing ... and all the Aos Sí. He'd even called Marisol to see if she were headed back there anytime soon. Her power was infinitely stronger than his. Unfortunately, she'd gotten the wrong impression, and thought that Thomas wanted to go back to the preserve. He'd had a difficult time explaining to Marisol why he cared. Indeed, he had a difficult time understanding why he cared.

Thomas shrugged the memories aside to focus instead on the ache in his legs. Despite all of his racing with the fae, he was out of shape. The jaguars were the toughest group he'd ever met. He was punching well above his weight with all the company he kept; sometimes Thomas marveled that he was still alive. Maybe he did have a death wish.

All in all, Thomas was having a harder time fitting himself back into his Brazilian life than he had expected. The short break in his routine had thrown him off his game. Or maybe he would have found himself in a rut even had he stayed in Salvador. There was so little for him to do with his business, really. It wasn't a failing enterprise to be rescued anymore; after five years, it was running smoothly.

Even their latest novelty sport that he'd been so excited about before didn't interest him now. Thomas had never been involved in any of the day-to-day operations — it would have been far too dangerous for him to have led any of the tours himself. They had female tour guides to handle all the face-to-face interactions, and his partner, Marcia Santos, piloted all their flights. Thomas simply dreamed up new amusements, then developed the marketing strategy to attract their foreign clientele. He'd originally been annoyed that Cordy's summons had delayed the rollout of their new skydiving offering, but now he didn't even care that the Swedish National Team was coming at the end of the month to try the wingsuits.

Thomas' cellphone rang. It was a blocked number, and he debated answering. But his heart started pounding in the vague hope that it was her, and he picked up. "*Olá.*"

"Thomas? It's Kevin."

"Kevin, how are you?" He felt like he had just seen his biological son, but thinking about it, realized it had been over a year since they last spoke. While it seemed to Thomas that mundane parents typically initiated calls to their children, it was the reverse in siren communities: offspring called their progenitors, hassling them for being out of touch. Or perhaps it was only Thomas who never called anyone; that was one of Mary's common complaints.

As Kevin started filling Thomas in on the latest events in Kōkai-Heika's court, Thomas wondered why they didn't speak Japanese to one another, now that Thomas knew the language. Well, they had always spoken in English before. Given how infrequently they actually talked, it would probably be weird to shift to Japanese.

"I have good news." Kevin was finally getting to the point of the call. While he may have been born in America, his mannerism of polite indirection was completely Japanese. "My second child will be born in December."

"Congratulations!" Thomas said. Kevin already had a son, who would now be about five or six. Mira sent Thomas fairly creepy updates about his offspring's lives every now and again. He supposed he should be grateful for his mother's obsession in ensuring transition survival, but he would rather not know so many details about the life of a near-stranger.

His mother had actually argued with Kevin about the wisdom of placing the child with a Japanese family. Ultimately, her pitch regarding the risk of a culture with a low birthrate won out, and Kevin's son had been adopted by a well-off couple in the Philippines. Mira had wanted the child in the United States, of course, where it would be easier for her to keep track of him, but her winning argument had cut both ways in that regard.

"Thomas, I have given much thought over the years to what Nanna Mira said when Adrian was born. And recently, I have begun to feel more of a — I'm not sure how to phrase it — a *pull* perhaps to the Atlantic."

"A pull?" Thomas asked. Kevin had been raised in the Pacific, home of his biological mother, but Thomas was an Atlantic on both sides.

"Ever since my first trip through the Atlantic for the Festival of Aphrodite."

Thomas murmured his assent, but only vaguely remembered that Kevin had even gone to Kasos.

"I sometimes think I hear the Atlantic in my dreams. I hear ice cracking and it seems to call out to me..." Kevin's voice trailed off.

"You're a cross-Oceanic child, Kevin. It was never certain that you'd feel welcomed by the Pacific instead of the Atlantic. I expected my father's ocean to embrace me, but it didn't work out that way. I'm far more at home here in the Southern Atlantic than I ever was in the North." Thomas wondered how he could have wasted so much time at his progenitor's court. Looking back, he could see how unhappy he had been then; but at the time, he had felt only a grim determination to make it work.

"Liu Yang, my daughter's mother, is also of both oceans. But the Pacific favors her, and she doesn't hear the Atlantic calling. Still, we've been discussing it and think that Panama City would be the right choice."

For a moment, Thomas didn't know what Kevin meant. Then he realized Kevin was talking about finding adoptive parents in Panama. "That could be a good location for a cross-Oceanic child, latent though they will be," Thomas temporized. He had never been to Panama.

"How do you find living among the mundanes, Thomas?" Kevin asked, and Thomas thought this was perhaps the real reason his son was calling him now. Many sirens yearned to be part of the "real world," as they called it, only to be destroyed by mundanes when they attempted it.

"The only way I've made it work is because I live in Bahia, which is controlled by the were-jaguars. My home borders their largest estate. I don't think I could survive as my mother did, truly living among mundanes. I—" Thomas swallowed. "I would not recommend it."

"Are you far from Panama? I mean, if a transition were to occur, would you be close enough to feel it and get there?"

"They say distance doesn't make a difference with respect to feeling a birth in your line. But it certainly matters in terms of saving the transitioned siren … Salvador isn't close to Panama, but it's certainly closer than Ryukyu Arc.

"Kevin, if you don't feel the Pacific, and the Atlantic is perhaps calling to you, don't stay." Thomas didn't want Kevin to waste years like he had, trying to fit himself into a place that wasn't quite right, but also wasn't bad enough to drive him away.

"I was thinking of going to Panama to find suitable parents. Perhaps afterwards, I might visit you? See the Southern Atlantic?"

Thomas struggled for a moment with his deep desire for Kevin to stay far away from him. His mother had barely been able to save Kevin when he was born. If anything were to happen to him here, there would be no doubt that it was Thomas' fault. But he couldn't say any of that. So he simply said, "Of course," and got off the phone as quickly as he could. He'd have to tell Juliane to hire additional guards. Maybe Kadu would be interested in staying with him as well … unless it was a full moon, of course.

His brief call with Kevin had delayed his shower, and the sweat had dried into an itchy mantle around his back. As he went upstairs to finally wash up, his attention was caught by the framed picture on his wall from Christmas 1988: his last year as a human, and their last year together as a family. Of course, Mom had looked so different then. Mary had crimped her hair, and Amy and Cordy both looked impossibly young. And there he was, tall, blond and smirking slightly. While he looked the same then as he did now, his frivolous expression in the photo made him feel like a completely different person.

Thomas shook his head. Not for the first time he wryly imagined that he was perhaps the only person who would be telling the literal truth when he said Bon Jovi had changed his life.

He'd been on Varsity since his freshman year — and had even just set the Loyola record in the 800m butterfly. He might look the same in a photograph, but he was sure he could never carry off that same careless look as he had when he was twenty, when he'd been full of the kind of *joie de vivre* that only people who never faced any real problems had.

It had all started the fall of his sophomore year. Like most college boys, he'd been short on cash. Then one of his buddies told him about a sperm bank paying thirty dollars a pop for college guys to jerk off in a cup. That had been a no-brainer way to get some quick cash. When the New Jersey band Bon Jovi came to Long Beach on their *Slippery When Wet* Tour, he had enough to take his latest girlfriend to see them live.

It had been little over a year after that concert when he woke up unusually early with an overwhelming urge to head down to Playa Del Rey. Thomas wasn't by nature an early riser; his teammates joked that if he didn't have so many girlfriends to get him up for practice, he'd never stay on the team. But that day, he wasn't even groggy. Charlene wasn't sleeping over because she had a test that morning, so no one would be surprised if he missed practice this time. He grabbed his wetsuit, towel, and goggles, and headed off to the beach for a swim.

The moment Thomas waded into the water, he paused uncertainly. He had mindlessly set off to the beach, but now that he was there, he felt somewhat bemused. *Why* was he there? The sun was barely up, and he wasn't planning to compete in the Open Water Swim this year, so why had he felt so compelled? Christ, he was missing swim practice to go swimming in the ocean! That was stupid.

But he was already there, and surprisingly, the water didn't feel cold; it actually felt great. It was around dawn in March, so the beach was completely empty. No one came for sunrises on the Pacific Coast — especially when it was like fifty degrees out. The water was warmer than the air, and Thomas had come all this way for a swim, hadn't he? So he plunged in and started swimming past the point where the waves were breaking. But instead of turning parallel to the beach, he just kept swimming farther out to sea. He wasn't cold and wasn't tired. At some point, his mind caught up with his body, and he turned back towards shore.

By the time he got back to the beach, the sun was midway up and it was almost noon. Thomas felt invigorated and somewhat astonished that he wasn't at all tired. Maybe he should compete in the Semana Nautica this summer! He walked back towards campus, generally oblivious to the people around him. He felt so great. Before getting lunch and heading to class, he headed back to the dorm to shower and change. When he got into his room and tossed his keys on the desk, he noticed the red light blinking on his answering machine and reflexively hit play.

"Thomas, it's your mother. Listen, something terrible has happened. Please, please listen carefully to this message." His mother was not prone to hysterics, and her voice was tight, anxious. Thomas' good mood evaporated and his heart started pounding.

"Do not, whatever you do, do *not* leave your room. Lock the door and don't let anyone in until I get there. Please—" his mother's voice broke in a brief sob, "please lock your door. Don't go outside. I promise I'll explain everything. But you have to stay inside. Alone. It's — it's a medical emergency. I know I'm not explaining very well now. But you have to stay inside. Don't open the door for anyone except me. Best thing is to just pretend you aren't home. Just stay inside. Please. Oh God, I pray you get this message before it's too late. I'm arriving around two o'clock your time and I'll call you when I land. I love you. Please just stay in your room. Lock your door. Okay. Bye."

Thomas didn't know what to think. What was wrong with him? How could his mother know something was wrong with him? Was something wrong with *her*? He played the message again. And a third time. A medical emergency? He had never bothered to set the correct time and date on his answering machine, but after comparing what it believed the current time to be with the actual time, Thomas figured out that his mother had left the message at 6:08 that morning.

What kind of contagious illness could he have? Why didn't she at least tell him what the medical emergency was? Thomas hadn't seen his family since Christmas break, so couldn't think of what kind of illness would be so extreme that he would have to lock his doors. He'd heard of meningitis outbreaks at college campuses; but even if that were the issue, he couldn't fathom why it would be so dangerous his mother would be flying out. Or why she couldn't have simply said so on the phone.

His deliberations had consumed maybe three-quarters of an hour. It was past noon. Two hours to wait. His skin was sticky from the salt water, but Thomas didn't dare leave his room to take a shower in the bathroom down the hall. He had been hungry before, but had now completely lost his appetite. He changed into sweats and wandered aimlessly from his desk to his bed, idly flipping through his books. He couldn't focus.

Thomas remembered those hours as a numb blur. His initial frenetic worrying had subsided into a dull waiting. He even prayed. He remembered feeling somewhat surprised that he knew so many prayers after only going to church when dragged by his mother. *Oh Star of the Sea*, he thought. He fished the Miraculous Medal his mother had given him when he went off to college out of his desk drawer. "For my doubting Thomas," she had said.

Even at Loyola, a Jesuit college, it was fashionable to poke fun at the so-called mysteries of faith. A virgin birth; how silly. All these so-called miracles of the Bible were just the output of unregistered mages. The ancients ascribed the miracles of burning bushes and resurrections to God, but in reality, they were just magical enchantments created by mages who hadn't been well-understood at the time. The modern Science of the Magical Arts could now explain most of the "miracles" that formed the basis of most world religions.

But waiting now, trying to keep from thinking about the unknown risk to him that had his mother's voice quaking, he prayed. He stopped doubting or questioning and simply prayed to the Virgin Mother.

The sound of his phone ringing cut through the daytime silence of the dorm. Thomas' apparent calm was belied by his aggressive pounce to answer it. "Hello," he said. The phone had only rung once when he picked it up.

"Thomas." He could hear the relief in his mother's voice. "Thank God you're there. I'm at the Santa Monica Airport right now."

Thomas broke in, "Mom, what's going on?"

"I'll explain everything when I get there. I'll be at your dorm in about a half-hour. Everything is going to be fine, as long as you just wait inside for me." His mother sounded a lot calmer. Controlled, but more like her usual self.

"Can I just take a shower down the hall?"

"No!" His mother's voice was sharp. "*Don't* leave the room. I swear, Thomas, I'll explain everything when I get there. The important thing right now is that you are okay and that you stay alone—"

"Mom, I mean — Are you bringing an antidote or something? I'm freaking out."

"Listen, it's not exactly … It's not — Please just stay inside, *alone*, for another half-hour until I get there. It will be a lot easier to explain in person. And I'll be a lot more—" she paused, "comfortable when I can see you. Promise me you'll just hang tight."

Thomas sighed. "Okay, Mom. Okay."

"I love you."

"Love you too." His mother hung up. She must have taken a private jet; chartered flights were the only thing flying in and out of Santa Monica. Thomas couldn't imagine the expense. But something about his mother's tone alleviated his frantic fear. Everything would be all right.

And he had survived. Unlike Jarl Georg, who failed his father, his mother had not spared a single moment in rushing to his rescue. Because of his idiotic desire to see Bon Jovi, he'd cost her everything. Well, almost everything. She still had Cordy and him, he supposed; and his sons, Kevin and Jason. And there was Lilly, Jason's mother, who owed her life to his mother, too.

It had been his transition that caused her to become a fanatic. He knew she'd been a writer when they were little — how could he not? But she'd explained she was writing instruction manuals. You know, like for the dishwasher and washer/dryer. Once he transitioned and she gave him her book, he realized what a different kind of manual she'd been writing. And once they had sorted out how he had transitioned, they went back to the sperm bank to start the multi-year paper chase to find all his children. He had created twenty-one children who were scattered across the U.S., including three born sirens. It had been almost impossible to find the boys, and they were too late to save his daughter.

The pain ate at him still, and Thomas shied away from the agony. Her loss was a phantom ache that he had to escape. Still wet from the shower, Thomas pulled on his swimsuit to find his surcease in the Atlantic's embrace. He was about to walk out when his cell rang again. Another blocked number. Thomas sighed. He hadn't spoken to Kevin in almost a year; twice in one day was too much.

"*Olá?*"

"Thomas, do you remember me?" a soft voice asked in English.

"Kyoko," he breathed.

The contribution of fae magick and genetic content makes sirens unique among all mage constructs. While mage magick is predominant, fae magick runs through the siren spell as well. This combination of powers makes the siren spell unique, with sometimes unexpected side effects. For example, the absolute were immunity to mage magick is partially negated by the fae origins of the siren spell. During the Fourth Mage War, it was discovered that sirenic magick could strongly affect weres when either party had contact with the sea.

– Sirens: An Overview for the Newly-Transitioned, 3rd ed. (2015), *by Mira Bant de Atlantic, p. 115.*

Chapter 19

"Thomas, I need your help. I need to get out of Rio."
Kyoko's voice felt like rain running down a window: a
soft patter that thrummed relentlessly on Thomas' skin.

"Now? Where? What do you need?"

"I'm at the Sugar Loaf. But it will be dark soon. I
need to be gone before night falls and she wakes up. I
didn't know who else to call." Kyoko's voice faded, as
if she worried that she had overstepped.

"Of course you called me. I will get you out. Kyoko,
everything will be all right." Thomas thought for a
moment. "There's a helipad on the Sugar Loaf. I know
someone who runs a tourist program. Let me call him
and arrange a flight for you from there to the airport.
Can I call you back? What number do you have?"

"I think this phone will work a little longer," Kyoko
replied. She gave him the number and Thomas hung up.

In a few minutes, Thomas had spoken with his
acquaintance and arranged for Kyoko to be taken to
Vitoria by helicopter. It would cost a fortune in both
money and favors; he was bouncing some German tourists off their "Rio by Night" tour in order to take Kyoko
the two hundred and fifty miles or so to the port city.

Thomas looked at the clock on his phone. It was a
little after four o'clock. The helicopter would be refueled and on the Sugar Loaf by five. He'd meet her in

Vitoria. Thomas was already dialing Marcia to arrange his flight there. He could feel his pulse thrumming. What was it about Kyoko? He felt pulled to her almost as if he were the fertile human, and she the siren. The attraction was instant, visceral. His heart had actually skipped a beat when he had recognized her voice on the phone, and he had grown light-headed. When thinking of her (as he had every day since they had met), his heart beat faster.

There's a reason the heart is the symbol of love. Because even though he didn't know her — not really — not at all even — his body knew that he loved her. Thomas' mind caught up with his body and he stumbled over the truth of it: he loved Kyoko. And he wasn't sure whether he was scared or excited to find out why.

"*Óla*, Marcia," Thomas called out in Portuguese as he approached the Cessna, which was in the process of being refueled. "Thank you so much."

Marcia Santos came out of the plane and down towards the runway to greet him. She was a tall woman with a broad face and dark, deep-set eyes. "It's no problem, Thomas! Of course, we owe a few favors to Joao, who moved us way up in the departure queue, but next month is his wife's birthday and I told him we'd take them out on a private boat tour."

"I owe you," Thomas said, but she just laughed and pulled him into a hug.

"You could never owe me anything. Get on board; I need to complete the preflight checks. Also, you shouldn't be on the runway while we're refueling. Someone might get annoyed." Though Marcia smiled when she said it.

Thomas started dialing the number Kyoko had given him as he climbed up the few stairs to the open hatch. "How long do you think it will be until we arrive?" Thomas asked.

"I'll know better when we take off, but I estimate between a quarter to seven and seven."

"Thanks," Thomas said to Marcia, pulling the phone up to his ear while it rang through. Kyoko picked up on the second ring. "It's me," Thomas said, coughing a little to clear the lump in his throat that had suddenly appeared when the ringing stopped, and he heard her on the line.

"Thomas," Kyoko said. "Thank you." Kyoko spoke in English, even though Thomas had addressed her in Portuguese. He could hear the wind behind her.

"The copter will be there very soon. The pilot's name is Luiz Ferreira. He's going to bring you to Vitoria, and I'm flying out to meet you now. We'll arrive around six forty-five or so. Tell Luiz to bring you to—" Thomas paused and put his hand over the phone. "What gate are we going to arrive at?" He called to Marcia.

"There's only one for private planes. You walk out to the hanger behind the main terminal."

"She's coming in by helicopter," Thomas said, "Is it the same area we'll land at? Is there someplace she can wait?"

"Yeah, have her wait in the hanger. Then you can go get her when we land," Marcia responded.

"Tell Luiz that I'm picking you up by the private plane landing area and ask him to wait with you in the hanger until we arrive," Thomas responded to Kyoko in English. He hesitated. "Are you all right?"

"I'm okay. I'll ... be okay."

Thomas wondered if Kyoko's heart was beating as fast as his. He wondered why she had called him, of all the people she could have called. He wondered if Gerel was going to wake up at sunset and come after them. He wondered how fast a vampire really was. But most of all, Thomas wondered if Kyoko felt anything at all for him, or if he were the one ensnared in a net of unreciprocated adoration this time. Wouldn't that be a horrible kind of justice for a siren?

"I know you have questions." Kyoko sounded fainter than she had before. "I promise to tell you everything. But I'm just so tired."

"Rest. Wait. Luiz will be there soon. Are you at the helipad?"

"Yes." It was almost five o'clock now.

"Do you want me to wait on the line until Luiz arrives?" Thomas hoped she would say yes. She sounded so exhausted. Talking to her now was somehow even more unreal than his dreams had been. Their one actual encounter had only lasted perhaps fifteen minutes, but he had held her hand and she had danced through his mind. He used to think love at first sight was a fae illusion. But this was inexplicably real, like the magick that he couldn't see, yet knew was there.

"Please stay with me," Kyoko asked quietly.

"All right then." Thomas felt that she just wanted to know he was there, and said nothing more until he heard the sound of the helicopter over the line.

"That must be Luiz. Don't hang up until you're in the air."

"I won't." Kyoko's voice was almost unintelligible over the noise of the helicopter.

Thomas heard the whirr of the helicopter, and the line went dead. She was on her way.

Thomas had never watched anyone sleep before. It wasn't boring in the least; he actually found it almost as peaceful and clarifying as swimming. Kyoko lay in his bed, while he sat next to her on his puffy chair. Thomas told himself that putting her in his bed made sense, because the escape tunnel was accessible from his closet. But truthfully, he liked seeing her there.

Kyoko had fallen asleep practically the moment he arrived, and hadn't even woken when he'd carried her into the waiting car and then into his house. It was almost as if she had been waiting for the safety of his presence, and her trust felt like a precious gift.

Dark circles like bruises shone beneath her eyes against the translucence of her skin. Thomas hoped it was only exhaustion. She had been sleeping the entire day, and he was loath to wake her. He watched her chest rise and fall evenly; he studied the light fluttering of her eyelids. He had heard that mages sometimes went into a kind of hibernation after a major working; perhaps this was what that looked like. He decided to let her sleep until at least sundown; surely by then she would need to eat or drink something.

His security team was on high alert; he didn't know whether Gerel would be coming to reclaim her escaped mage, but assumed she would. Still, Thomas didn't feel worried. He just watched Kyoko sleep.

"Kyoko-*sama*," Thomas whispered later, holding Kyoko's hand lightly. She stirred, but did not open her eyes. "Kyoko-*chan*?" he asked again lightly stroking her forehead.

Kyoko's eyes fluttered open. "I am dreaming," she said in Japanese.

"No," Thomas replied.

"It doesn't feel real. I've been dead for so long, but now I feel almost alive. I must be dreaming of a time before. But you are here, so perhaps it is true, and I am finally free," Kyoko slowly shifted her body up to sit on the bed. "I am here," she said, "with you."

"You are here with me. A thousand miles away from Rio. You're safe with me," Thomas promised, sitting next to Kyoko on the bed. He hadn't shifted his eyes from her face. Her gaze flickered down to their linked hands. She closed her eyes.

"I'm here with you. *Free*." Kyoko whispered the last word in English.

"Can I call a doctor? *Should* I call a doctor?" Thomas asked. He pulled the sense of responsibility around him like a winter coat, heavy but warm.

"No. At least, I don't think so. I think I just need to rest a little more. I'm still very tired."

Thomas wanted to ask what had happened; what did she mean that she was free? But he didn't. "Can I get you something to drink or eat? It's been more than twenty-four hours since you called me, and I don't think you've had anything."

"Maybe some fruit juice or water?" Kyoko asked. "Then I think should sleep for another few hours. I don't know. I just need another day. Another day with you."

"Of course." Thomas left and quickly returned with a glass of juice. He marveled at his energy, his new-found clarity. Kyoko said she felt alive, and that was it. Now, he too finally felt alive. Truly, this was love.

Now that he had spoken with Kyoko, Thomas was able to bring himself to leave her side. He put his headset back on and checked in with security; so far, they had seen nothing. He again warned the guards that they could be facing a vampire-led attack. Juliane again assured him that they were prepared. They had called in Maria Eduarda, even though it was her day off. She had grown up in the favelas of São Paolo. Maria Eduarda knew what a vampire was and how they attacked; she had advised all of them. They were all as prepared as they could be. Yes, blessed bullets would be effective. Thomas clicked his mike off and paced for a moment. Then he opened the gun safe next to his closet and selected the M4 carbine.

Neatly labeled boxes were in the lower drawer. Thomas found the one with bullets blessed by the Order of Our Lady of the Good Death and began meticulously reloading several magazines, while reciting the same prayers he had said in his dorm room thirty years before; his faith seemed only to emerge in a time of crisis.

His younger self may have expected safety, but his current self expected attack. Kadu often warned that Thomas' worries would be a self-fulfilling prophesy: if you always expect the worst from people, you will be sure to encounter it. But Thomas' optimism had been burned up after the fourth attempt on his life had sent him scurrying for the safety of Jarl Georg's court.

Thomas adjusted the wooden blinds over the window in his bedroom and sat back in the chair next to his bed to wait. Cordelia used to tell him to relax, mocking his worrying as needless anxiety. When he ignored her, she tried to convince him that there were costs to his endless preparation: missed opportunities, wasted time. But she didn't get it. She hadn't experienced the real world like he had.

If nothing happened, he would feel relieved, as opposed to chagrined at "wasting" his time. Thomas might only be the last line of defense behind his gates and his guards, but even Cordelia would have to concede that in this case, his precautions were justified ... though she'd probably also call him insane for harboring a mage-escapee from the vampire who ruled Rio. Thomas rested the M4 lightly on his knees and adjusted the volume controls on his headset to better hear his guards' vocal traffic.

Kyoko woke to the sound of birds and the ocean. She sat up, but the clarity of the colors in the room were disorienting, and she immediately lay back down and shut her eyes to the dizziness.

"You're awake," Thomas said, coming to Kyoko's side.

"What time is it?" she asked, closing her eyes again.

"It's around noon. Is it too bright?"

"A little," Kyoko said, her eyes still shut. "I think I just need to get accustomed to the brightness a little more slowly."

Thomas closed the interior wooden shutters so that only a dim light prevailed in the room. "Better?"

Kyoko opened her eyes slowly and blinked. Her pupils dilated, then contracted. "Much better." She turned to look at Thomas. "Thank you."

Thomas handed her a glass of water and Kyoko sipped slowly. They just looked at each other for a heartbeat, then Kyoko noticed the M4 carbine on his chair. "Has there been any trouble?" Kyoko spoke hesitantly.

"No," Thomas moved back to pick up the rifle to holster it in his shoulder harness. "I just believe in being prepared." He paused. "I don't want to push you…"

"I'm feeling better. Much better."

"Good. Do you think you can stand up? Get something to eat?" Thomas moved to the side of the bed and offered Kyoko his hand.

"Yes. That would be good." Thomas escorted Kyoko slowly downstairs, settling her at the table before drawing the blinds and laying out a simple meal for them. Cold meats, fruit, bread and cheese.

Kyoko watched him, and he watched her watching him. The silence in the room seemed somehow warm and inviting simply by the feel of her gaze on him. By tacit agreement, neither of them spoke until they had both eaten. Despite her obvious exhaustion, she was beautiful.

"I thought my feeling of lightness was due to the great working, or hunger," Kyoko broke the silence. "But I think this is just the feeling of freedom. It's been so long since I was handcuffed to Gerel that I had forgotten how heavy the chains were."

"The great working?" Thomas asked.

"I broke my indenture," Kyoko said. "I had only one year left. But…" Her voice trailed off. Thomas waited.

"But mages indentured to vampires don't often survive beyond the term of their indentures," she whispered.

"Was it a standard term?" Thomas asked. Mages were ordinarily indentured as apprentices to a more senior mage for seven to ten years, depending on their talent and the anticipated challenge of their initial training. Most mages were bound in their mid-to-late teens. Kyoko looked older than a twenty-something, but Thomas suspected that was due to the draining nature of working for a vampire; literally, perhaps.

"No. My parents bound me for a double term to guarantee our family's safety." She must have seen the expression on Thomas' face, because she added hastily, "I agreed. Insisted even. I was more of a romantic then, and had no idea of what kind of 'heroic' sacrifice I was really making. I don't think they knew either."

Thomas was unconvinced; he would never sacrifice a member of his family like that.

"I'm not mage-born. I know it's rare. But my parents are mundane, and they themselves had been vassals to Gerel for years. They wouldn't have known which mage could be trusted or which had the right skill. Better the evil you know, right?"

Kyoko could defend *them*, Thomas thought. He would defend *her*. "You've been bound as an apprentice for more than a decade?" Thomas asked, a bit surprised. Apprentice indentures were known to be uncomfortable at best, and he could only imagine how hard it must have been for her.

"Almost two." Kyoko closed her eyes and stretched her head back, as if feeling the release afresh. Thomas loved the sound of her voice, and didn't mind that she was telling the story at her own pace.

"Vampires may have lost their mage-sight, but they are like fortune-tellers when it comes to predicting how long a person will live," she said, rolling her shoulders back. "How can they know to only take one day or one month or one year of someone's life if they don't know precisely how long that life will be? The terms of the indenture specified a day for a day. No more, no less.

"And what's twenty years of my life anyway? I knew when I agreed that after Gerel taught me the spells for cellular renewal, I'd outlive my family by at least a hundred years ..." Kyoko's voice trailed off.

Thomas took her hand and gave it a slight squeeze. She smiled at him, shaking off whatever bad memory had momentarily captured her. "Sometime last year, the pain of Gerel's daily takings increased. So slightly, I didn't notice at first. Maybe Gerel began stealing only a few extra minutes or an hour. So gradual. But I started to notice. And I started to believe the rumors."

"The rumors that a mage indentured to a vampire won't survive their term?" Thomas asked, and Kyoko nodded. "That's in all the movies I've seen. But then, in the movies, the vampires drink blood." Thomas kept his voice light. Kyoko was trying hard and he didn't want to push, but he had to know what risks she faced in order to keep her safe. And if Gerel had been the first to break their terms, then whatever killing Kyoko had done to break her binding would be justified even before a mage adjudicator. "Thank God you broke free. Was the binder in service to Gerel too?"

"The binder?" Kyoko seemed confused by the conversation's change in direction. "I don't think he even lives in Rio. Gerel never mentioned him to me, at least. I know he bound me more tightly than most apprentices, because Gerel can't cast anymore; I remember her demanding that. But I haven't seen him since I was fourteen."

Now Thomas was confused. "But how did you kill him if you didn't see him?" Kyoko still looked perplexed and he clarified, "Didn't you battle him? The great working?"

"I broke my indenture. That's all. I didn't kill the mage who worked the binding. At least, I don't think I did. I didn't try to. Gerel didn't trust the mages in her service to work bindings; she always used a contractor."

"You broke your indenture," Thomas repeated. "You broke the magical binding *itself*. But not by killing the mage who forged it? I thought that was impossible."

Kyoko shrugged. "Necessity. Desperation, maybe. I don't know. I was always taught it was impossible. But it isn't. It's just very difficult. Maybe if I had been indentured to a mage, they would have known what I was trying to do and stopped me. But Gerel is blind."

Thomas shunted aside his amazement to concentrate on the main problem. "Can Gerel track you, though? Or the other mages in her service? You were worried on the phone."

"I don't know. Maybe. She's been able to track others whose lives she's eaten. Her connection fades with time. She wouldn't be able to track you now. She only nibbled on your life, after all, and it was so long ago. But she knows where I am."

Thomas stood up. "That's what I was afraid of. This house is secure, but it's not a fortress. I expected her last night, but it's been a day and a half since you came, and we're a thousand miles north. Perhaps she doesn't care enough to fetch you personally."

"Oh, I doubt she would come personally. She can't, really. She can't leave Rio without forfeiting it to the other vampires who itch to unseat her." Kyoko looked worried. "But she can't afford the insult either. She'll have to do something. Send someone."

"Who does she have to send?" Thomas had closed the shutters in the dining room also, out of deference to Kyoko's condition. Now he crossed the room and opened them a bit more to look out.

The dining room led out onto his back patio, and the closed rear gate was visible in the left corner of the wall. The guard was on high alert, behind a barricade two yards in front of the gate, with an automatic M240B machine gun ready. The day was bright and beautiful, with barely a cloud in the sky. "If she isn't coming herself, then a daytime assault is possible. Do you know who or what kind of person might owe her? Mages? Weres? Army?" Thomas continued to look outside.

"All of them. But I don't know. I didn't think." Kyoko sounded worried and Thomas crossed back to take her hands and draw her to her feet.

"It doesn't matter. I don't care. I'm so glad you're here." Kyoko leaned into his chest, and Thomas wrapped his arms around her, barely touching her head with his chin. He almost lost himself in the peace of the moment.

Kyoko broke away first. "I wasn't thinking. Before. I didn't really have a plan. Didn't know that I could unravel the binding. Then I was just so tired." She stopped speaking and pulled away.

Thomas came back into the moment with a decisive clarity that came from having only one priority now: Kyoko's safety. "We have to go. Now." There was only one place that would be safe enough. Only one possible route to travel.

Thomas led the way down the tunnel to the sea. His house was only a few hundred feet from the high-water mark of the beach, and the tunnel itself was typically filled with sea water. But when Thomas opened the hatch, the water receded to let them walk its length. They climbed back out onto a rocky part of the tree-lined beach. Kyoko paused as Thomas stepped into waves gently lapping at the shore.

"Thomas," she said. "I can't swim very well." Kyoko gulped.

"That won't matter. Do you trust me?" He held out his hand and Kyoko nodded. Thomas said, "The ocean loves me, and I love you. All will be well."

Kyoko took his hand, and he drew her slowly into the warm water until it came up to her waist. Her dress billowed up around them as Thomas stepped further into the waves, which seemed to have calmed for them. He pulled her close and turned to look out to the horizon.

"Climb on my back, and I'll take you there. I have a boat waiting about three miles off-shore. It won't be long."

Kyoko reached and wrapped her arms around his neck. Despite the urgency of the moment, Thomas relished the feel of her arms around him, her body dependent on him. He launched them into the water. The sea enveloped them and propelled them forward.

They had only gone maybe half a mile when the sky darkened for a moment, as if with a sudden cloud cover. Thomas had barely registered the change before the world brightened with a sudden halogen intensity that caused him to pause a heartbeat before the deafening sound of an explosion reached them. The water rippled as a wave of force dissipated along its surface.

Thomas looked back. If Kyoko said anything, he couldn't hear her over the ringing in his ears. He stared, confused. His house was gone. He treaded water for a moment in shock as he stared at the red-orange glow where it used to be. Black smoke curled into the sky, and suddenly he could again hear the sound of the water lapping gently at his shoulder.

He couldn't look away from shore though; the gap in the landscape where his house had been was suffused in a hazy glow, and he thought perhaps his house would be there again when the air cleared. But it wasn't. Thomas had built his home to be his fortress, impregnable and secure. But it was as if nothing had ever been there. This kind of absolute destruction could not have come from anything so mundane as a bomb.

"Battle mage," Kyoko breathed in his ear.

"My God," gasped Thomas. The reality of the moment caught up with him, and he swiftly turned away from the scene. The Atlantic redoubled its efforts, pulling them so fast a deep wake of white-churned water trailed behind.

In coastal regions (defined as within fifty kilometers from an ocean) it is estimated that one out of every eight mundanes is a latent siren. While latent sirens can procreate with humans and fae alike, the most common pairing are with other latent partners, changelings, fae, and mundanes, in that order. Latent/mage pairings are rare, and usually do not result in children. There has never been a reported case of a child born of mixed construct heritage (i.e. siren/were).

– Sirens: An Overview for the Newly-Transitioned, 3rd ed. (2015), *by Mira Bant de Atlantic, p. 63.*

Chapter 20

"Mary, let's go out this week. It's been a long time since we went out," Mike said as he headed downstairs.

"Summer auditions are going to start soon," Mary called down. Mike was running late again. This spring, Mary's schedule shifted later, so she was no longer getting up at six a.m. When she didn't prod him, he had trouble getting out of bed.

"I know. That's why I'm saying we should go out now — things have slowed down a bit for me, so we should go on a date night or something again. It's been too long."

Mary caught the gist of what Mike was saying without hearing every word. Their narrow townhouse had too many levels to keep shouting at one another. "Okay," Mary called down. She didn't bother telling Mike she'd make the reservations; he would know that she always handled that.

Mike's phone rang as he was looking for his keys. He hoped it would be Christine, letting him know that his nine a.m. had canceled. But it was an unknown number on the caller ID. No such luck.

"Hello, Michael Arnold?" Mike didn't recognize the man's voice.

"Who is this?" Mike asked, looking through his jacket pockets for his car keys.

"My name is Lieutenant Steve Allen. Your office gave me your cell."

"Okay," Mike said noncommittally. Given his security clearance, the DOJ loaned him out from time to time to other agencies. He never wanted to work with the CIA again, but his engagements with the DoD had generally been good. At least the officers he had worked with seemed to lie a little less often than members of other federal agencies, which made for a much more comfortable working relationship.

"I spoke with Ms. Watkins and she approved a temporary assignment. There is a meeting we need you for at the Pentagon today."

"This is highly unusual, Lieutenant." This was the first time Mike had ever been called in by the DoD on such short notice; it had happened once before with the CIA, and he *never* wanted to listen to anything like that again.

"I realize that, Mr. Arnold, but you are the only truth-teller with sufficient security clearance and skill. It's last minute, but I assure you, I wouldn't be calling you if it weren't extremely important."

While phrased politely, Mike had worked with enough members of the military to hear the request as the order it was. "Lieutenant, I am not part of the armed services. Nor am I part of the Department of Defense or the CIA. There are some matters that I should not know about — regardless of my security clearance."

"Mr. Arnold, I assure you that this is not that kind of meeting."

Mike sighed; he couldn't be sure what kind of meeting it would be, but at least he wouldn't be late for his nine a.m.; he was sure Christine would have already canceled it.

"I appreciate the clarification," Mike said carefully. "Just let me know where and when." He jotted down the information, then called his own boss to find out exactly what the DoD's request had been.

"Do you need to be in the room, or can you just observe from outside the door?" Major General Hayden asked.

Lieutenant Allen had escorted Mike to the enormous but rather empty briefing room, introduced him to the waiting Major General, then quickly left. Mike was nonplussed at meeting such a senior official alone, without any preparation or warning. He was also surprised that the Major General had been waiting for him, instead of the other way around. This whole set-up was at odds with all of his other interactions with the DoD.

"I can't be completely sure of the subject's veracity unless I can hear and watch them without the aid of amplification or video. Even glasses can interfere with my perception. How accurate a report do you need?" Mike hated working on projects with people who failed to give him any context, and this surprise assignment was starting to look like one of those. It was impossible to do your best work when they treated you like a human machine.

"I want to know the truth, which is why I asked for a truth-teller," Major General Hayden said wryly. "All right then. You'll sit with me, but I won't introduce you beyond giving your name. You shouldn't say anything at the meeting. I'll answer for you if it comes to that. How much detail on the subject's veracity can you provide?"

"Sir, it's important that you understand that I can only recognize the truth as the subject believes it to be. Reality can often be quite different. If a witness believes that the sky is brown and says so, I'll hear only truth. But my hearing truth won't change the color of the sky."

"Yes. That was explained to me already. I understand that limitation. Our concern is really about what the subject believes. Whether the subject is *shading* the truth. Misdirection, that kind of thing. Your boss told me that you are quite skilled at identifying nuances."

"I'm not simply a human lie detector, sir," Mike said, nettled, despite his resolution not to let the man get to him. "The reason I'm so valued by the DOJ is because I can recognize any deception, something few truth-tellers are able to do. I can tell when people shade the truth, when they exaggerate or understate. I can tell the difference between an exaggeration or understatement and an absolute mistruth. However, while a subject's intent to deceive will be apparent, I can't discern the truth or falsity in what they do *not* say. Misdirection is still completely possible."

Hayden nodded along with Mike's explanation. "That's sufficient."

"Sir, a little context would help. The more information I have, the easier it will be for me to make nuanced distinctions."

Hayden thought for a moment. "Fine. The subject is Elder Hilda Lefran. At my request, she is coming here today to explain in detail the specifics of a supposed breakthrough she has made. I need to know whether she's exaggerating about what her new spell can do in any way. We also believe the enclave received certain key intelligence reports, which they have told us repeatedly they did not receive.

"I'm not a truth-teller, Mr. Arnold. But I have a pretty good sense of when someone is hiding something. And I have long thought that the Danjou Enclave has been hiding too much from us." Hayden's change in demeanor was refreshing. He was also extremely honest; that was a relief. "I've heard good things about your work, Mr. Arnold. But I wouldn't have pulled all the strings I did to have you here today if it weren't absolutely necessary."

"Sir, I don't know whether you are testing me, but you are exaggerating. You don't believe it is *absolutely* necessary that I am here today and you didn't pull any strings, at least insofar as you think of pulling strings."

Hayden looked taken aback for a moment, then smiled broadly. "My God, that was amazing. If I didn't think I needed you before, that clinches it. Maybe I should keep you on staff permanently. Can you give me any of that insight while the meeting is going on? Like if you sit next to me, tap me on the arm or something? Do you have any codes that you've used before?"

"It's not that easy to learn signals when you haven't practiced," Mike said warily. "But there are some simple codes we use on the rare occasion the attorneys don't want the subject to know they are being monitored." Most of the time, the whole point of Mike being there was to make sure the witnesses knew they had to tell the absolute truth. The only time they ever used signals was when they weren't sure whether or not they wanted to flip a particular witness.

"Good, good. Let's get started. We only have a little while before they get here. Let me get Lieutenant Allen and Colonel Cox in here to help us practice."

By the time the meeting started, Mike was rather impressed with Major General Hayden. He must have played baseball, because he picked up very quickly on how to watch for Mike's slight signals without losing focus on the conversation.

It felt odd to be in such a large briefing room with only four people. The thermostat had clearly been set for the comfort of people in wool uniforms, so the chill made it even more uncomfortable.

The subject was a mage, which Mike had realized as soon as he heard her name. He couldn't recall previously reading a mage; seeing her now, he felt a new sense of trepidation. Elder Hilda Lefran was a tall, heavy-set woman who looked to be in her late thirties. She had a ruddy complexion with close-cropped brown hair. Her eyes were the most striking thing about her: they were such an extremely pale shade of blue, her pupils looked almost lost in their depth. Her white pantsuit was made out of a peculiar material that shimmered when the light struck it in just the right way. Perhaps there were silver or steel threads woven into it. Mike figured a mage would wear a unique kind of armor.

Colonel Cox had escorted Elder Hilda into the room. The colonel was an older woman, with a lean frame and lined face. While Mike wasn't overly familiar with all the decorations on dress uniforms, he at least knew that Colonel Cox was Air Force and Major General Hayden, Army. It was interesting that they weren't in the same branch. The other DoD projects he had worked on had only included people in the same branch.

"At your request, Elder Hilda, we limited this meeting to three people on our side. This is our most secure room at the Pentagon, but if you feel the need, please feel free to inspect it yourself." Hayden swept his hand around the room in an invitation.

Hilda said coolly, "I can see from here, Major General, that all is in order. While it is a large space for such a small group, when I explain where we are on Project Hurricane, I think you will agree that such precautions were worthwhile." *Truth.*

The group moved to sit at the large table, with Colonel Cox seated at one corner between Major General Hayden and Elder Hilda, and Mike seated at the General's right hand. Mike had a clear view of Elder Hilda's face from this vantage, and sat slightly askew so that Hayden could see him out of his peripheral vision.

The codes they had worked out were quite simple, really. Mike would touch his face for an outright lie, write on his pad for an exaggeration and sit back in his chair for an understatement. In his experience, Mike had found exaggerations to be the most common form of lying, and these basic signals were the best way of disguising the information he provided.

Elder Hilda seemed to be a very truthful woman. She was extremely proud of her new spell and seemed to have nothing to hide. She went through a lengthy explanation of its intricacies, with only a few exaggerations and understatements. No outright lies.

"Do you understand what this means, General?" Elder Hilda asked after she completed her explanation.

"It sounds like your spell will funnel the djinn away from the area?" Hayden asked.

"In a nutshell, yes." *Truth.*

"How do you know it will work?" Colonel Cox asked.

"We have tested it extensively," Elder Hilda said. *Truth.*

"How could you test it when no one apart from Amir Khalid is able to create a djinn?" Colonel Cox pressed.

"We created multiple simulations. We are extremely confident that it will be successful." *Truth, but incomplete.*

Mike's mouth watered a little at the missing information, and he swallowed.

"Can you describe these simulations, Elder Hilda?" Cox asked.

"We used lesser versions of a spell, which we believe to be structurally similar to the djinn spell. The counter we created suborns elements of that spell into a new design. The new spell whisks the djinn away." *Truth.*

Hilda appeared very self-satisfied.

"What weaknesses do you see in this design? What are the risks?" Cox wanted to know. Major General Hayden hadn't asked many questions, but he was watching Elder Hilda very closely.

"It's a well-crafted spell. There are few risks." *Lie.*

An acrid taste filled Mike's mouth, and he could smell burning flesh. No mere exaggeration. This was a full-out lie. He rubbed his chin.

"I find that hard to believe, Elder," Hayden said calmly.

"But it is the truth, nevertheless." *Lie.*

Mike rubbed his face and swallowed hard. He had to take a drink of water after that one. Her face was quiet, but her lies were outrageous.

Hilda's eyes narrowed as she looked at him. "There is no risk whatsoever in the djinn dissipation spell." *Lie.*

Mike scratched his nose and coughed. Hilda stood up. "Who is he?" she demanded.

"Michael Arnold," Major General Hayden replied. "As I told you."

"Better stated, *what* is he? You've brought an outsider to this meeting, General. That is a violation of our accord."

"Not true. Michael Arnold is a federal employee and senior civil servant in the Department of Justice. He was seconded to my staff on a temporary assignment today. That is the truth, but what you have been telling me is a bunch of lies. Which *is* a clear violation of our accord."

Hayden did not stand up. Somehow, this made his position seem even stronger. Hayden was even better at this than the senior attorneys Mike worked with at the DOJ.

"Tell me what he is, or this meeting — this alliance — is over." *Lie.*

"You need us more than we need you, Elder Hilda Lefran of the Danjou. So if you wish to terminate this alliance, we are more than happy to indulge you." *Lie.*

Mike hated it when subjects other than the target lied. He took another sip of water. If their outright lying continued, he would need to open the can of soda that sat waiting in front of him, or he wouldn't be able to concentrate on anything except the taste of their deception.

"I see your magick, Mr. Arnold. You sit atop a steel-framed chair at a steel-framed table. You are no faerie, yet you spark faerie magick. You've either been bespelled, or you're a changeling." *Truth.*

"Elder Hilda, please sit down."

"I do not appreciate being ambushed." *Truth.*

"Mr. Arnold is a truth-teller and a valued member of my staff. Would you please sit down so that we can continue this meeting?" *Exaggeration.*

Hilda made a show of sitting down. Some of the drama was likely intended to buy her time to think.

"My intent in having Mr. Arnold at this meeting was simply to obtain better advice than I've received in the past. Given where you stand in your research, we need better information before agreeing to commit any additional resources." *Truth.*

"You brought in a changeling truth-teller." Hilda nodded. "You are a wiser ally than some thought." *Truth.*

"Perhaps now we can be honest with one another, then. Your spell has many risks. We need to understand what those are in order to ascertain whether we can mitigate or accept them."

Elder Hilda sighed. "I don't believe you're capable of understanding all the risks of any magical spell, let alone one as complex as this one. *I* believe these risks are worth taking." *Truth.*

"Have you received any intelligence on the Cabal that you haven't shared with us?" Cox interjected.

"Have you received any intelligence that *you* haven't shared with *us*?" Hilda responded.

"I believe that is an affirmative, Colonel Cox," Hayden said, eyeing Elder Hilda.

"The only thing we have not shared are matters involving mages, which wouldn't concern mundanes." *Lie.*

As if she knew that Mike knew she didn't believe what she was saying, Elder Hilda quickly corrected herself.

"What I mean is that there are some matters that shouldn't be shared with mundanes." *Truth.*

"If you have information that might impact this joint initiative, which you are refusing to provide to us, that would be a breach of our accord." *Truth.*

"I am not authorized to provide such information." *Exaggeration.*

"Elder Hilda, we know you have better sources among the Cabal than we do. You haven't shared any of the information you've gleaned from those sources." Colonel Cox's voice was sharp. She was telegraphing annoyance.

"I think you are authorized to provide more information than you have. You need to disclose what you have learned from your Australian sources to the extent they impact our Arabian initiative," Hayden said.

"I am not sure to what extent they might impact our initiative, Major General." *Truth, but carefully stated.*

"Any information that could impact our accord must be shared," Colonel Cox insisted.

"We have already shared the oracular prophesy we received, as well as our suspicions regarding the identity of that pivot." *Truth.*

"Yes, and the Danjou have benefited greatly from our accord in securing her cooperation through Project Hathor," Hayden replied.

"We have both benefited from our accord." *Truth.*

"As agreed, the enclave has not *interfered* with the pivot, though, correct?" Cox asked.

"We have not bewitched her or cast any spells on her to compel her cooperation, if that is what you are asking." *Truth.*

Elder Hilda managed to sound offended. Mike sensed the possibility of misdirection, but he couldn't be certain, because Colonel Cox failed to ask whether the enclave was bespelling others or using non-magical means to influence the pivot. He made a mental note to mention this after the meeting.

"I hope you appreciate that I am subjecting myself to this ridiculous interrogation so that you can finally get comfortable moving forward." *Truth.*

"We appreciate your candor, Elder Hilda." *Exaggeration.*

There wasn't a hint of irony in General Hayden's tone. Colonel Cox leaned forward in her chair. "What does the Danjou prophesy have to do with the Australians? Have you discovered anything about their prophesy? Have you identified other pivots?" Cox asked.

"We don't *know* anything. We *suspect* much." *Lie.*

Mike swallowed at the taste of Elder Hilda's lie that overpowered her truths, and General Hayden looked at him. Although Mike knew the General had wanted him to remain quiet during this meeting, he doubted that desire stood now that the mage clearly knew him for what he was. "Elder Hilda both knows and suspects things." Mike clarified.

"I could spell you into silence, you know," Hilda said, her tone implying that that was the least of what she might be able to do to him.

Mike swallowed. This interrogation was not as disgusting as the CIA's questioning of the Natural Order terrorists, but it was more dangerous to him personally.

"Elder Hilda, there is no need to threaten Mr. Arnold. In fact, that would be a violation of the accord and our hospitality. We too, can make threats." Hayden's voice was cold. *Truth*. "You were asked a question. If you can't share the information we need, this alliance is over." *Lie*. Major General Hayden stood up as he made his declaration. Colonel Cox rose as well, and Mike followed, a beat behind them.

"I do not appreciate being questioned like this." *Truth*. "But I value our accord. While I doubt the information will be of much use to you—" *Exaggeration*. "I do wish to make sure our alliance remains sound." *Truth*.

Hilda paused, while the three of them sat back down. She poured a glass of water from the carafe in front of her and sipped it before continuing. "We know of a second pivot in the coming conflict. There may be more, but there are at least two individuals whose actions or words will be—" Hilda hesitated, as if searching for the right word. That happened a lot once people realized how sensitive his truth-telling capabilities were. "— *critical* to the outcome of the war. Influencing those people remains a priority for the Danjou." *Truth*.

"We have agreed to disagree on this point, Elder Hilda, and as discussed previously, we advise on significant caution. Influencing, or seeking to control, those 'pivots' as you call them fails more often than it succeeds. We need to avoid the Oedipus example." *Truth.*

"We believe it best to know who the pivots are, and to keep watch over them. The Oracle gave the Cabal a different prophesy, and we thought we had discovered the second pivot, but they disappeared." *Truth.*

"What is the prophesy?"

Hilda hesitated. "I don't know if I should disclose this." *Truth.*

"If you don't disclose it, we are putting this project on indefinite hold." *Exaggeration.*

"What are you worried about?" Cox pressed.

Hilda laughed a little, but looked at the three of them in turn. "Perhaps it makes no difference. According to our source, the Oracle's words to the Cabalist were: 'Under sea, break free.' This was obviously a great warning." *Truth.*

"I don't follow," Hayden said.

"We believe this refers to the recovery of one of the strongest mage powers that ever existed: the power to break spells, to break — well, to break anything, really." *Truth.*

"The Gobi Desert," Cox said softly, considering.

"Yes. There has not been a mage capable of breaking a spell, let alone a desert, since Zulong broke the Asian deserts during the First Mage War." *Understatement.*

"You are not telling the full truth," Mike stated. He could hear the misdirection, taste Elder Hilda's hope that they would not pry.

"The prophesy speaks of a breaker mage, you believe? One that would be the ultimate weapon against the Djinn?" Hayden asked.

"That is our belief." *Truth, but incomplete.*

Mike cleared his throat, and the General looked inquiringly at him.

"That isn't all you believe," Mike stated.

Elder Hilda narrowed her eyes, but clarified: "A breaker mage can break anything: even spells that cannot be countered." *Truth.*

"What kind of spells can't be countered?" Hayden wondered aloud.

"Enclave bindings," Cox replied, and an expression of enlightenment flitted across Hayden's face.

Hilda's voice was cool. "Among other things." *Truth.*

"Does this mage exist?" Cox wanted to know.

"Yes," Hilda said, reluctantly. "But we lost her."

Perhaps in your latent life, you were accused of being unusually fixated on fairness or of cutting off your nose to spite your face. Like the fae, sirens have a greater need for equal exchanges than do mundanes, and will often reject even a better deal than no-deal if they perceive it to be unfair. Since transition, you may have noticed that you have an even greater desire for balance in your bargains than you did before.

– Sirens: An Overview for the Newly-Transitioned, 3rd ed. (2015), *by Mira Bant de Atlantic, p. 122.*

Chapter 21

Cordelia had chosen 2 Amys Pizzeria because of its name and proximity to Mary's work. When she'd called Mary to tell her she was in town, Mary acted like there was no way she could leave for even two seconds. She'd been the director of the National Children's Choir for twenty years, and Cordelia thought she took this job more seriously than she had her own performance career.

She and Devin had cleared out the small restaurant fairly easily, persuading the manager to close early before Mary arrived. Devin now sat in one corner, picking at his pizza and trying to look like a tourist.

Cordelia watched Mary approach through the large plate-glass window. She paused when she saw the closed sign on the door, shading her eyes to peer in. Cordelia stood up and waved at her. Mary hesitantly opened the door. She looked good. The handful of wrinkles adorning her face softened rather than aged it, and whether expertly colored or natural, her hair was still blond and lush. She barely looked forty, let alone in her mid-fifties: the benefit of latent genes, Cordelia supposed.

"Come on in; we're the last customers of the day," Cordelia said, walking towards Mary as the cashier came around the podium with the register.

"Yes," the cashier said to Mary as he locked the door behind her. "We're closing early because we're all going to a baby shower this afternoon." Cordelia hadn't told him to say that, but indirect compulsions could have a strange effect on some people. The other two men making the pizzas behind the counter quickly fell in line with the cashier, agreeing with him that they were celebrating the birth of a new baby.

Cordelia hoped her own daughter would do well with the Goodwins. They seemed like a nice couple, and Cordelia had a good feeling about this placement. She knew her ease with the adoption shocked her mother, but it really hadn't been a hard decision. Maybe one day, she'd raise an active siren child sired by one of her latent offspring, but she certainly wasn't going to do what her mother had done.

Cordelia supposed her mother considered her a traitor. Transitioned sirens had odd notions. Thomas seemed to feel guilty about not taking in his sons — but even by mundane standards, he had signed away parental rights, so it was an odd thing to feel about. Cordelia sighed. Her family wasted too much time and energy reexamining the past. That was going to be her. She was happy to finally be moving

don't we order first, and then you can tell brings you to D.C.," Mary said, walking to her and looking at the menu board above. She wasn't quite as fast as Amy did, but never gave the impression of being in a hurry. Cordelia felt impatient. She couldn't tell Mary, but to D.C. to get away from their mother's hovering. While coming back to the States had been a good call, she'd been ready to leave immediately after the delivery.

But her mother wanted her to "rest," and it had taken almost a week before Cordelia could break free. Fortunately, Devin had also had enough of Florida, and finally told Mira that they'd better get back to Boston. Promising to visit Mary before heading back to Europe had clinched the deal; that had been a hook her mother couldn't resist — though Cordelia had to agree to take Devin with her. A ridiculous precaution, but at least they'd all be getting back on track now.

They ordered their food and sat down at one of the tables close to the back. Devin lingered over his own meal, staring at his phone, but Cordelia suspected he was listening closely to them.

"It's nice to see you again, Cordy. But a little more notice would be better next time."

Now that Mary had finally worked her way around to hinting that she was irritated by Cordelia's sudden appearance, they could have a real conversation. They'd already almost finished their meal, so much of her time and effort in arranging the visit had been wasted on Mary's silent pique.

"I'm sorry, Mary. It's great that you were free for lunch. I just wasn't sure I'd be able to squeeze in this detour; I'm headed back tonight." Her older sister was a passive-aggressive pain in the ass.

"Of course, I had to drop everything to see you!" Mary said. "Since you're so rarely in the area, I could hardly miss the chance! I'm impressed that you're even able to brave a public restaurant."

"Small steps. This is a fairly empty place. But I did take a car. Not quite up to walking around yet."

"Still, that's a huge improvement," Mary continued to praise Cordelia, who grew increasingly uncomfortable. While it was true that she found mundane crowds terrifying, it wasn't due to agoraphobia.

"Didn't your choir just win some big global competition?" Cordelia asked, changing the subject. She liked watching Mary's eyes spark with pride over their latest award.

Cordelia's mind wandered as Mary talked about the choir. Conducting was a better fit for her than performing as an opera diva. There was something about great artists that seemed to require them to be impossibly self-centered; Mary might be a pain, but she wasn't egotistical. Cordelia laughed at Mary's anecdote about another insane parental demand, while noting the clever way she had derailed their objections to smooth things over. Ever the adroit conciliator. Mary was so much like their mother, Cordelia felt the need to escape all over again.

"So, what's going on with Mike?" Cordelia asked instead.

"Well, that case that was driving him crazy ended right after Thanksgiving, so that was good. Now he's been seconded onto some DoD matter. He was worried at first, but now he says it's fine. Nothing like that CIA thing."

"That's great," Cordelia said. "I thought he was going to quit after that."

"It was a near thing. That's the only time he said the truth was worse than the lies. He still sometimes has nightmares, but he says he's glad he stayed in the public sector."

"It's an odd sort of magick," Cordelia observed.

"Truth-tellers are a rarity, that's for sure. Mike says there's a greasy taste to the bespelled liar that he finds hard to take. But really, all lies cause him some sort of discomfort. I'm just glad he's at the DOJ, even if he's doing projects for other agencies. Much, much better than the FBI."

"Is there that much of a difference? I got the sense from what he was telling Amy at Thanksgiving that there are a lot of similarities between the different agencies."

"The people, yes. The type of cases, no. There's a huge difference. But even the FBI is a lot better than CIA."

Cordelia shuddered. "I don't think I could have handled listening to the Naturalists. What we saw on the news was almost too much."

"That kind of work is too much for anyone but a psycho. It doesn't matter how heroic the agents are when they sign up, being surrounded by that kind of evil takes a toll. You know, all the guys who worked with Mike on that left the agency too? I wish he'd go back into private practice. The pay was a lot better, and the topics so much less stressful. But I guess as long as he's happy ..." Mary shrugged and finished her slice.

"And not with the CIA," Cordelia added, and Mary nodded her agreement. "Well, I couldn't do what he does, but then, I think he'd hate your job and you'd hate mine. We'd all hate Amy's."

Mary chuckled. "I have to tell her we had lunch here. She'll get a kick out of it. I should have brought her here last time she visited. Food's good, too. I mean, not bad for D.C. pizza."

"It's so close to the Cathedral, I'm surprised you never came in here."

"I'll probably come back now. I go to the sandwich place around the corner almost every day. I guess I'm a creature of habit."

"Well, I'm glad to shake things up."

"Why do you have to hurry back so fast? At least stay and have dinner with Mike and me."

"I can't. Really. I should have left earlier in the week, but things just took a bit longer than I expected."

"Are you going to publish some more photos?" Mary asked.

"Probably." Cordelia shrugged.

Both her sisters thought she was an underwater photographer. She did take pictures from time to time. Even without using compulsions, it was fairly easy to get them published — the ocean always showed her interesting things. She really ought to take some photos in the Mediterranean. Or the Black Sea; there were some really stunning shipwrecks preserved in its low-oxygen waters.

But what Cordelia really wanted to do was visit Yorkshire on her way back to Queen Sophia's court. Despite numerous phone calls since Thomas' abrupt departure, he had still not been very forthcoming about the situation. Cordelia was now free to see for herself; visiting Mary had been less of a chore than she'd anticipated, but she was glad to finally be back on track.

Well, it had been nice to see Cordelia. She looked different somehow, but Mary couldn't quite put her finger on it.

She seemed to have adjusted to her new project fairly well, though. Cordy had been pretty depressed at Thanksgiving; even Amy had noticed it, and Amy was not exactly observant when it came to people's feelings. While Cordy seemed preoccupied today, she didn't seem nearly as unhappy.

Mary's cellphone rang; it was Mike. She suspected he was calling to tell her he was going to be late. "What's up?" Mary asked.

"I owe you two compliments today. I haven't forgotten." Mary had to smile. When they'd started dating, she'd had the nerve to tell him she expected at least two compliments a day, and that if he couldn't think of at least two *honest* compliments about her on any day, they shouldn't be dating. Twenty-five years had faded her mandate somewhat, and he said that to make her smile. Yup, he was definitely running late.

"I'm going to be late." Mary was right.

"Why don't you just meet me at the restaurant?" Mary suggested. She'd gotten them reservations at one of Mike's favorite restaurants in Penn Quarter.

"I'll still be late," Mike warned.

"Should I change the reservation?" Mary knew better than to ask why he was going to be late again. Never ask a question unless you were prepared for an honest answer, especially with truth-tellers: their inability to gloss over unpleasant truths was the reason most got divorced before their first anniversary.

"If you can push it back maybe a half-hour, that would be better."

"Okay. I'll text you the time."

"Love you," Mike said.

"Love you too," Mary responded, and hung up.

Dating Mike had required some adjustments, but it had helped that even before they met, she'd avoided polite lies. Maybe that had been her mother's influence. Mom would just tell the church ladies that she wasn't going to help with the bake sale, not that she was too busy or that she wished she could. She just said no.

Mary might not get two compliments a day anymore, but she loved that she could rely on Mike's truthfulness. He never pretended to be anything he wasn't; he never told her he loved her performance if he didn't. But he did like most of them, and she never felt insecure about his love for her.

She flipped on the TV for background while she got ready. When Mike was around, they didn't watch TV. While audio-visual recordings didn't have the same effect as in-person lying, any form of pretense grated on him. The evening news was on, and it just kind of flowed over Mary in a vague wave. She was tired of the never-ending cycle of politicians condemning the Djinn Dictator and blaming him for everything — from the same human rights violations they'd been talking about when she was a kid, to his new ban on silica-salt exports.

So some magical products like air conditioners and garbage disintegrators cost a lot more now than they did two years ago. Didn't they skim silica-salt in the Mojave and Chihuahuan deserts? At this point, the embargo seemed like a thin excuse for the enclaves to charge more for their already expensive products. Mary was only half-listening while trying to pick out which dress to wear, but her attention was caught when she heard her sister's name.

"… said Dr. Amy Bant, a neurologist at Harvard University at a press conference this afternoon." Mary turned to look at the TV and saw the camera cut to a shot of her sister sitting behind a table next to Dr. Eisner and two other men in white coats. The Harvard University Hospital banner hung behind them. Dr. Eisner looked a lot older than Mary remembered; but then, he had to be pushing eighty now. Maybe that was why Amy was doing the talking.

"Magical energy exists in the form of white light, which mundanes perceive as brightness. But as we know, the color white is actually a combination of colors, and mages are able to perceive white light in close to its true full-color spectrum. This visual perception is known as mage sight or magical vision."

Amy spoke authoritatively and calmly, despite the flash of numerous cameras in her face. She didn't look particularly pleased at being the center of attention, but also didn't seem unhappy or nervous either. She explained how her team had done the first comparison mapping of mage and mundane brains and had successfully given a mundane mage sight through nerve grafts.

She had already told the family this much at Thanksgiving, and Mary wondered why she was doing a press conference about it now. Perhaps this was some kind of academic one-upmanship. Research into magical capabilities had been going on for years, but mostly in genetics; finding the magick genome had been on the cover of *Time* a year or so ago. Mary had only bought the magazine because she wanted to have something besides the kids to talk to Amy about.

A dark-haired man asked Amy the first question. "Dr. Bant, are you saying that mundanes are disabled because they lack this 'sub-optic' nerve?"

"No. It's simply a biological fact that mages have functioning sub-optic nerves and mundanes do not," her sister replied calmly.

That reporter was a jerk, Mary thought. Amy should have asked him whether he thought men were disabled because they had nipples, but couldn't lactate.

A woman with shellacked blond hair and an emaciated frame stood up next. "Do you think creating more mages is a wise idea? Isn't that dangerous?"

Mary shook her head. So many mundanes fretted over the number of mages around. But everyone knew most mages didn't have all that much power.

Look at how they hid away in their enclaves, terrified of another set of pogroms. Or worse, kidnapping by the Natural Order. Mary doubted there were enough strong mages in the whole world to control the United States. Sure, there was the Djinn Dictator, and the Cabal had run Australia for over a century, but really powerful mages were rare. Every now and again, a mage usurper had overthrown a small country's government. But those were tiny tin pot countries, where the brief rebellions were typically preceded by instability and upheaval. And really, what was the difference between a mage-led coup and an army-led coup anyway?

Mary picked up her phone to send a quick text congratulating Amy. Then she texted Thomas and Cordelia telling them that Amy had just been on TV. She started to remind them to call Amy, but deleted that part of her text; they should know that's what they were supposed to do. Mary put down her phone, then picked it back up. She sent a quick text to Thomas suggesting he call Amy. Better safe than sorry.

Amy had handled the press conference like a pro; Mary knew she didn't do this very often. She didn't lose her temper, even with those ridiculous questions. Still, Amy's project must be a big deal if the networks were covering it this much — and why hadn't Amy told her she was going to be on TV?

She figured she could always ask Amy when they next spoke; she still had to change their reservation.

Aphrodite was allegedly blessed with a form of magical synesthesia, where she both heard and saw magick. Similarly, Morgan le Fay also sensed magick through sound as well as sight. Some speculate that this form of magical perception is related to their ability to draw power from the ocean, as well as through light and silica.

– Sirens: An Overview for the Newly-Transitioned, 3rd ed. (2015), *by Mira Bant de Atlantic, p. 15.*

Chapter 22

"So we shift our focus onto other projects. You've been fairly clear about this for a while. I'm just not comfortable handing over all of our proprietary research to another lab or group of researchers that I don't know. I'm more than happy to authorize a joint project." Eli paused on the phone, listening.

Amy hovered in Eli's waiting room; he hadn't closed his office door all the way, and she'd been about to knock when she noticed he was on the phone. Eli probably didn't realize she was there, and she knew he didn't realize how loudly he was talking. Amy had been trying to get him to see an otologist to get his hearing checked for years now.

"I've told you before that this is not the same as infrared. If you want to explore a type of night-vision-like goggles for magick, we can't follow the same path. I can't imagine any reputable physicist would give you different advice."

Amy listened to the conversation with a knot in her gut. Both before and after yesterday's press conference, Amy had tried to elicit more information from the DoD. But they had been assiduously elusive. While Eli had been a little more forthcoming, she was still in the dark. All she'd been able to get out of Eli was that the Danjou Enclave was considering pulling out of the project. Without Danjou support, they might not be able to proceed.

You think you prepare for the worst, but no amount of preparation can actually alleviate the shock of the moment when the worst happens. Her project was over. This whole week she'd tried to come up with a hook to bring the Danjou back on board, but now she wouldn't even get the chance to try any of her gambits. Amy cursed the mages again. Neither Ted nor anyone at the enclave was picking up the phone. How do you argue with someone who won't even speak to you? She'd refused to believe they could let their hard work go to waste. Not now, when they knew how to correct all the side effects from their first attempt!

Why were the Danjou so quick to give up? It takes at least six weeks to heal from any kind of brain surgery. Any operation involving nerves takes even longer. Total restoration of sight after the Bant Procedure could take more than a year, and that was with vision therapy. They had told Elder Simon that before they even accepted Patient B as their first subject.

If she only had Patient B's one-year scans to review, she'd know for certain that their revised procedure could enable mage sight without compromising mundane vision. But even without the scans, both she and Arnie were confident that their error had been in the positioning of the sub-optic nerve. They should have brought it to the anterior right, instead of posterior right of the optic nerve.

Amy was willing to go to Arabia; she'd reconciled herself to that trip months ago as the bargain she made when she landed this project. But it would be insane to put herself or her team in the Amir's line of sight without testing this operation first! How could the DoD still think they could send a team to Arabia without knowing whether the revised procedure would actually work? Elder Simon certainly hadn't been impressed by their pre-op warnings and consent forms. If Amira Loujain failed to regain her mage sight and lost her mundane sight at the same time, God only knew what the Dictator would do!

"I agree, Commander. Our work will definitely help in the development of magick-vision goggles. But this is a completely new direction, and we'll need to set up a new team."

This was so much worse than Amy had imagined. She had perhaps been *too* adamant in her opposition to trying out the surgery on Loujain, and now the DoD was giving up. After months of searching, no other prospective patient had been found. But she had the answer now! She was sure their revised procedure would work.

"I would be happy to meet Colonel Cox and review the work we've done and what she's been able to do with — um-huh ... Of course. That makes sense. Next week is no good. I'm giving a speech on Monday, and there's a fundraiser Wednesday. How about tomorrow afternoon? Or Thursday?"

Amy left Eli's office. There was nothing else she could overhear that would help at this point. She needed another patient *now*, before Eli came back with whatever spin he planned to put on this disaster. That was the only possible way to get the DoD back on board, or at least give truth to the lies of omission she'd just made on national TV.

They had been foolish to restrict their MRI screening to soldiers. Perhaps the genetics that caused the partial development of a sub-optic nerve in the first place led to flat feet or some other disqualifier for military service. Well, she didn't have flat feet, so that couldn't be it.

Amy abruptly stopped walking; the lab technician she had just passed in the hall almost ran into her. *She* was the prospective patient. The project didn't have to end ... Ever since Ted had insisted the whole team undergo MRIs, they'd known she had a compatible nerve structure for the surgery. That was why she had believed Patient B wasn't a fluke, insisted that if they just kept searching, they'd find another patient.

Graham was a great surgeon. He had done his postdoc with her and she'd watched him operate. By now, he was even faster than she was at most operations. She could still prove the procedure worked. Amy started walking again, but much more slowly than she usually did. By the time she got back to her office, her heart was racing. She was thinking crazy things. The idea was ridiculous and unethical and utterly insane. But she sat down and opened her desk drawer anyway. She looked at the glasses case. When the Danjou had suddenly recalled Ted, he'd asked her to keep the enchanted spectacles for him. They were an interdicted item, he'd said; he couldn't bring them back to the enclave.

Amy tried them on, but couldn't see clearly through them. It was almost like looking through a foggy window. But they had worked for Barry, even though he'd rejected them. Clarity of sight was the most important thing, anyway. A lack of color wouldn't really change her life; black and white movies weren't that bad. In truth, she hadn't sat through a whole movie in years, so what difference did color make?

She took the glasses off and rubbed her chin. Eli would object, Amy knew. But Amy managed the project on a day-to-day basis, and Eli was too preoccupied to focus on the team's activities. In any event, Eli would be out of the lab this week.

She didn't care about Phase Two of Project Hathor. In fact, she'd had nightmares about going to Arabia since the DoD suggested it, but now that it was off the table, she didn't even feel relieved. Now, she just wanted to finish what she had started. To prove it could be done. No, really, she just wanted to finish the work *properly*; they were too close to give up.

Until now, Amy had never allowed herself to actually consider the benefits of the operation. Barry Riccie had been so taciturn, it would be almost impossible to write up a description of his perceptual change. But as a neurologist, her ability to articulate her perception would be so much better than the average patient. And if the operation was a full success, her unique understanding of the differences between mundane and mage sight could advance the field immeasurably.

Amy stood up abruptly and looked out the window, her hands on her hips. This was utter foolishness. She was only parroting back to herself what Ted had argued to her in the months before his recall. It was the obvious solution to their lack of a subject, he'd said. Didn't she have confidence in her surgical team?

They'd been searching for months, and the only person they found with an unattached sub-optic nerve was Amy. She'd even had multiple scans just to be sure. If she were a mage, she'd have had no choice …

Ted had spent hours trying to persuade her that this was the only logical step forward, ethics be dammed. She had slammed the door so harshly on that line of thinking, she thought their working relationship was probably permanently damaged. Especially now that Ted wasn't answering her calls. But now Amy stared out at the skyline and let herself think about what it might be like to see "all colors and none … blended into an overload of purity."

"Ted, it's Amy again." Amy had gone straight into his voicemail. "I could really use your advice. I know we didn't leave on exactly the best of terms, but it would be extremely helpful if you could just give me a call back. Listen, I'm sorry about what I said." Amy hung up and paced around the office. She'd spent most of the day thinking about this, how she could actually push this through. But this was crazy, wasn't it? She needed to talk to someone, if only to get her own thoughts in order. She plopped back into her chair, and almost reflexively dialed Mary.

"Hi Mary, it's Amy."

"Hey! How are you? You were amazing yesterday! I can't believe how you handled those reporters' questions. I mean, what a bunch of jackasses." Mary sounded so upbeat and genuinely happy to hear from her that Amy felt herself relax a little.

"You're being really too kind. I could have been a lot clearer. Listen, I need some advice; do you have a minute?"

"Sure," Mary replied. "I'm actually on my way crosstown and the traffic is worse than ever. What's up?"

"I'm scheduling another operation." Amy paused.

"What operation? You mean another mage sight surgery? That's terrific!"

"Yeah. It *is* terrific. I've gone over all of Patient B's results and reviewed our new plans. And I'm extremely confident that this will work."

"Fantastic," Mary said. "Well, that's good news. Right off the back of your press conference, too. You didn't mention that yesterday."

"Well, it's actually a rare mundane who's even eligible for this kind of surgery. There's someone we've had in mind for a while, but it didn't seem like a risk worth taking until now."

"What risk? Well, I guess any brain surgery has risks."

"There were some complications with the original procedure that we now think we can avoid. We didn't go into all the details in the press conference."

"Oh, well that sounds all right then. What kind of complications?"

"The major side effect was the elimination of mundane perception, but we think we know what caused that now."

"You eliminated his mundane perception? You mean the patient is blind?" Mary sounded confused and somewhat horrified.

"Blind from a *mundane* perspective, but his mage sight is off the charts in terms of clarity." Amy knew she sounded like she was downplaying it.

"I can't believe you didn't mention that yesterday; you went into so much detail about everything else," Mary said.

"I know, but that's one of the reasons I want to do this operation now. We have the solution. We *think* we have the solution," Amy clarified. "I can't leave it like this, especially after making that announcement. After we do the second operation, we'll have proven the success of the procedure."

"And does your next patient understand that you're probably going to blind them in this — I don't know what you'd call it — this elective procedure? Amy, this is nuts."

"The revised procedure won't make the patient mundane-blind. And in any event, I have a pair of enchanted spectacles that our enclave partner gave me before he left. I watched Patient B try them; they work," Amy said.

"Enchanted spectacles?" Mary asked.

"They enable the blind to see. Well not perfectly. They enable mundane visibility in black and white. But I have a back-up plan if the operation isn't a complete success."

"You mean the mages have glasses that let blind people see and are just sitting on it? Holy shit, Amy. That's unbelievable."

"They were made in Arabia, Mary, so they aren't exactly easy to come by. And Ted, you remember, the via-enchanter? He was recalled a few months ago. But he was pretty clear that they weren't readily available. I mean, who knows. I could be holding the equivalent of Durendal or Excalibur or something like that."

Amy twirled the glasses case around in her hand. *What's the worst that could happen?* she pondered.

"Wow. Well, hopefully the operation is a success, and you'll be able to give them back. Hey, why didn't the other patient take them? Are you sure they work?"

"They work. Patient B didn't want them. I asked a lot of questions. You know me." Amy knew she sounded testy.

"Okay. It sounds like you know what you're doing. But you said you wanted advice?" Mary didn't sound impatient, though Amy knew she would have been in Mary's place. She took a deep breath.

"Maybe not advice; more of a favor, really. Can you spare a week or two to come to Boston? I know it's last minute."

"Amy, now is not a good time. I have auditions starting soon. Why do you need me to come to Boston?" Mary asked.

"I think I need someone to stay with me after the surgery. I wouldn't discharge a patient without appropriate home-care."

"What are you talking about, Amy? You operate all the time, and unless you just broke up with some live-in boyfriend you didn't tell me about, this is kind of absurd." Mary liked finding opportunities to remind her sister that there was more to life than her job.

Amy rolled her eyes at her sister's nagging. "I'm going to be the patient, Mary. That's what's different about this operation."

There was a long moment of silence, before Mary asked: "You're going to be the patient? That's ridiculous. How are you going to operate on yourself?" Mary sounded confused, her voice rising in pitch.

"*I'm* not going to do the operation. Graham, my lead surgeon, will. He's even better than I am. He's faster, at least. Graham is more than competent to perform the operation. And this is our last chance, Mary. They're giving up on the project. The DoD pushed us to make the announcement, and now they're ready to drop the entire thing to move in a different direction. I know this will work. Seriously. I'm sure of it. After talking with Ted, it does seem like a unique opportunity to actually experience a new sense. Think of what a gift it would be to have a mundane able to actually describe how mage-sight works, in a way we can understand it! It's an opportunity we can't pass up." Amy had started off speaking slowly, but her voice got faster and more certain as she spoke.

"Amy, I don't understand half of what you just said. It all sounds crazy. I mean, this is your *sight*, for Christ sakes! So you have a pair of enchanted glasses. So what? This is a mistake, and you know it. That's why you called me."

"Mary, I called you because I can't leave the hospital and stay home alone. I need you to come to Boston."

"You're being ridiculous. You're the doctor, not the patient. I can't imagine that any halfway-decent doctor would be willing to perform such an operation! What are you thinking? God, your fear of failure is causing you to go completely off the rails!" Mary sounded shrill, but her intense opposition was actually making Amy feel more confident that she was making the right decision.

"I'm not going to change my mind, Mary. If you won't come, I'll call Thomas or Cordelia. But honestly, I would rather have you."

"Please don't do this," Mary begged.

"I have to, Mary. I'm doing this. I've thought it through." Amy's voice was firm.

"Why are you really calling me?" Mary asked.

"Please come to Boston." Amy knew she sounded like she was begging, but she needed Mary. "I *have* to do this. It's the only way."

Mary was quiet for a moment. "Amy, this is a mistake. A serious mistake. I don't approve."

"I'm not asking for your approval."

"I know," Mary replied unhappily.

Highly-trained, skilled mages can see the siren spell entwined in our genetic structure. However, there are some common physical signifiers of our mixed mage-fae ancestry that can help in identifying latent sirens. For instance, latent siren eye shape and color typically reflect their mage ancestry, and latent sirens rarely appear older than middle-aged due to their fae heritage. Unique siren-like attributes include above-average physical beauty and an attraction to the sea. Latents living outside coastal regions also contract illnesses at a higher rate than non-latent mundanes. But only mage-testing can definitely determine that a mundane is actually a latent siren.

– Sirens: An Overview for the Newly-Transitioned, 3rd ed. (2015), *by Mira Bant de Atlantic, p. 108.*

Chapter 23

"Dr. Bant, if you can hear me, raise your hand." Amy recognized Graham's voice through the foggy state of partial awareness she found herself in. She twitched her right hand, but found the effort required to lift it was too great. She heard his voice speaking, but the twilight haze of anesthesia had muddled her senses. Until she tried to open her eyes, and panic shot through her: she couldn't see.

Amy's heartrate spiked and she heard the monitor beep. Then she remembered that her eyes would have been bandaged shut after the operation. She twitched her left hand.

"That's it. Amy, everything went perfectly." Graham continued to speak, reviewing the surgery he had just performed. A few of his words punctuated Amy's haze, and she vaguely understood that Graham had successfully lifted and reattached her sub-optical nerve. The surgery had taken less than five hours. There had been a small bleed in the anterior choroidal artery, which had been repaired.

"Graham," Amy whispered hoarsely, her throat sore from the ventilator. "Thank you. We should wait another day before removing the blindfold."

"Yes." Graham sounded relieved. Amy smiled a little. She had not been the only one worried about the operation. She had been so certain the day before while they were doing the pre-operative brain scans for comparison. But when the actual pre-op prep had started, Amy had begun to worry and second guess herself. Usually she felt much better after making a decision, but she had never been so impulsive in her entire life. Perhaps this was her mid-life crisis. Some people bought sports cars and had affairs with men half their age. She had brain surgery.

"Amy?" Mary had come into the room. Amy felt her sister take her hand and squeeze it. "They'll only let me stay a minute. But I wanted to let you know that I'm here. I'm staying in your apartment. You need a better cleaning lady, by the way. I'll be here for the next few weeks. It's no problem."

"Thank you," Amy whispered, then drifted off to sleep.

Mary squeezed Amy's hand, then caught the doctor's eye as he gestured for her to precede him out of the room. He pulled the door mostly shut behind them. Mary paused in the corridor. "How is she, really?"

Dr. Graham Litner smiled. "She's doing extremely well. The surgery went exactly as planned. We'll remove the blindfold tomorrow, but because the operation was on her nerves, it is quite possible that her vision will not be clear. Also, we know that it can take the brain a little while to ascertain exactly what it is perceiving through the new linkages. It's possible that she may have false sight or visual hallucinations as she acclimates to her new sense."

"How long will she be in the Neuroscience Critical Care Unit?"

"Because we will be continuing to test her functioning, we'd like her to remain here for a week. But her condition is stable. If this had been any other surgery, we'd be moving her to a nursing unit tomorrow. Go home, Ms. Arnold. Amy is going to be fine. She just needs to rest right now."

"When should I come back?" Mary asked.

"Tomorrow morning. She should be more alert then."

They said their goodbyes, and Mary walked slowly towards the elevator. She had never spent time in a hospital, really. It was a terrifying place when you weren't familiar with it. Both of her parents had died suddenly, sparing her, she supposed, the lengthy hospital visits and frantic calls that many of her friends had faced with their own aging parents. Her only experience in a hospital had been when the kids were born.

She hadn't been prepared to see her sister hooked up to so many machines; so weak, her voice a mere rasp. Amy looked near-death, despite the doctor's blithe assertions. The elevator was taking forever to arrive and she felt her blood pressure rise as she waited. Mary didn't get angry often, and didn't like the feeling. She looked down at her hands and was surprised to see they were trembling. She was so angry, she was actually shaking.

Neither Thomas nor Cordelia had answered their phones. So Mary, of course, was here alone. She had told Mike not to come; it was ridiculous for them both to come to Boston just to wait around. Besides, this was her foolish sister, not his.

Mary shook her head. *Why did Amy have to do this now, just as auditions were about to start?* Of course, she reminded herself, her assistant could handle the preliminary organization, and she could continue to work on this season's repertoire while staying at Amy's apartment, but she couldn't miss the auditions themselves! Amy was so utterly thoughtless.

Why did Amy have to do this at all? She thought in despair. Her hands were firmly balled into fists when the elevator arrived and she stepped in, just as her phone pinged with a text. She fished her phone out of her purse; it was Alicia again, asking about Amy. If John's favorite aunt was Cordelia, Alicia loved Amy.

Amy joked that it was her life's goal be the kind of rich maiden aunt who spoiled her nieces and nephews outrageously. But Amy hadn't only been generous with her money, she'd been generous with her time: Amy had always been there for Alicia and John. Despite her insane work schedule, she had always shown up. Alicia's text helped calm Mary somewhat. Thomas had never been around, so why should she expect him now? Cordy was often unreachable too. Her mother used to say that no matter what happened, they would always be family. For Mary, family meant showing up.

As the elevator door opened to the lobby, Mary took a grim pleasure in the fact that she had shown up; that slight, petty feeling of delight in doing the right thing while her siblings had again failed in their responsibility. *Whatever it takes to get yourself through this*, she told herself.

"I'm ready," Amy announced. It was just after sunset. They had drawn the curtains and replaced the white lights with red and amber safelights, so it must have felt like an old-fashioned dark room used to expose photographs. But instead of watching a picture develop, they would be watching to see if this surgery had succeeded where the first had failed.

"All right, then. Remember, nerves take a long time to heal. So what happens today may not reflect the final outcome." Amy found Graham's tone irritating, but he was speaking more for the benefit of her sister, who hovered anxiously in one corner of the room. Graham slowly cut the bandage that served as her blindfold.

Amy wasn't sure whether the IV drip included a sedative, because she didn't feel worried or anxious at all. She either would or would not see. That's all there was, and the emptiness she felt at the prospect enabled her to focus exclusively on providing the information necessary for their research.

"We should try an EEG and MRI tomorrow, regardless of the outcome tonight," Amy said. She felt a coolness on her eyelids as Graham wiped a wet swab over the area.

"Okay, try to open them." Graham was backing away as he gave Amy the instruction. She hadn't detected a difference in brightness from before he had cut away the blindfold, but the room was so dim, that was as expected. She blinked her eyes slowly open.

Amy saw. The images were grainy and blurry, as if seen through a rain spattered window, but she could see the hospital table across from her, the framed whiteboard on the wall (though she couldn't make out the writing on it), and she could see her sister, standing to the left. She turned to Graham, and could see him in better focus, his glasses reflecting strangely in the red light. The room was awash in a red haze, such that she couldn't tell what colors Mary and the nurse were wearing other than that they were dark and that Graham's lab coat was lighter in hue.

"I can see," she said. Mary let out a deep breath, and Graham stepped closer.

"The room is a little blurry, but I can see you, Mary, over there," Amy gestured towards Mary in the corner, "and you, Graham. Stop. Let's not test the acuity yet," Amy held up her hand to forestall Graham from pulling out the cards. "I can't read the whiteboard, but I can see that it's there. No, wait, I think my eyes are just grainy from being closed for so long. Graham?"

Graham obliged by putting drops in Amy's eyes and gently swabbing her eyelids again. When Amy opened her eyes this time, the room was in sharper focus, but she still couldn't read the whiteboard. That wasn't predictive, though. Barry had seen nothing when he awoke in the darkroom, and it took patients undergoing the Bant Procedure a median of eighteen weeks to achieve 20/20 vision post-surgery.

Graham was clearly excited, but Amy herself felt removed from the moment — like she was hovering on the outside, observing herself answering Mary's questions and listening to herself speak to Graham about the tests they should do tomorrow morning. All the while, she wished Ted were here to perform the mage sight testing; without him, this would perhaps be a literal case of the blind leading the blind.

Magical constructs are not mages. The magick a siren is able to perform is simply part of the multi-level siren spell. Sirens cannot perceive the magick they themselves wield any more than a mundane human can. While mages spend their childhood learning to perceive magick, then decades more learning to cast spells, there is almost no learning curve to working siren magick: it is generally as straightforward as learning how to operate an air conditioner or other magical device. The biggest challenge is in managing your own reactions to the experience of sirenic magick.

– Sirens: An Overview for the Newly-Transitioned, 3rd ed. (2015), *by Mira Bant de Atlantic, p. 16.*

Chapter 24

How had Eli missed this?! Mira was practically speechless in her dismay. Amy had undergone the experimental procedure herself? Devin didn't seem at all surprised, but this was beyond what anyone could have expected.

"*Siren surgeon sight. Siren surgeon sight.*" The Oracle's words throbbed in Mira's mind as her headache tightened around her temples like an elastic band, snapping out an agonizing rhythm.

She and Devin sat in their Boston apartment, after sending Eli back to the hospital. Actually, Mira was lying down on the couch with a wet washcloth folded over her eyes. Meanwhile, Devin used his bespelled phone to call Atlantis. Atlantea had not been pleased to hear about Amy's operation, but unlike Mira, she hadn't cared personally about Amy's well-being. "As we feared, the pivot is pulling us into war," Atlantea said unhappily. Devin had set the phone between them on the coffee table.

"The pivot won't pull us into war if you don't choose to take us there," Mira countered. "The Atlantic barely borders Arabia's frontier in Africa; there are no fae preserves in Arabia. Nothing in that area of the world need involve us. The actions of one latent siren — or even one family of sirens — will not pull the Atlantic into anything."

Atlantea snorted. "Don't be foolish. The Fifth Mage War. A latent *Atlantic* siren whose siblings and mother are *de Atlantic*? Of course we are being drawn in. The fact that you have lost contact with both Thomas and Cordelia at this juncture is also extremely concerning."

"Atlantea, please—"

"How is it possible that you only just discovered this? After it was already done? We should have stopped this project months ago; Amy should have never been allowed to have performed these operations!"

"That's the problem with prophesies. They are unavoidable." Mira didn't mean to sound flip, but the pain in her head was making it hard to think clearly.

"Are you actually trying to make excuses?" Atlantea sounded curious, but Mira knew better than to answer. After a moment, Atlantea continued briskly. "Second-hand information is obviously not good enough. It's indisputable now: Amy Bant is one of the pivots on which this war will turn. Devin will be able to handle her once she is off birth control. What kind of birth control do you have her on?"

"Atlantea, no one will interfere with my daughter in that way."

The silence on the line was deafening. Atlantea had to know that if Mira was forced to choose, she would choose her own children above the sirens. Until now, Atlantea had bent over backwards to avoid forcing Mira to make any choices. For now, at least, Mira still believed their interests were aligned. She sincerely hoped Atlantea did too.

Devin sat so still on the chair, Mira wondered if he was waiting for Atlantea to tell him to kill her now. Kill her and kill Amy too. Mira's headache worsened; if the pain in her skull didn't let up, she thought perhaps that would be a mercy.

"Your daughter is the pivot. Controlling the pivot is imperative."

"Only if you want to win a war." Mira sat up, her head pounding. "I thought you wanted nothing to do with this mage war, Atlantea! If we control the pivot, who fights us for control? You want to fight the Danjou Enclave? Perhaps the Cabal? Or Amir Khalid himself? Do you want to be in the middle of this? Surrounded by mages on all sides?"

"I sent you to Boston to find out what kind of influence the Danjou were attempting to wield. But you said they'd pulled back." Atlantea's voice was tight.

"They *did* pull back. Probably a feint, an effort to force Amy into this impossible situation without *influencing* her magically. But they must be hovering. I told you what I learned from my enclave source. The Danjou look to capture Arabia, to somehow evade the djinn and destroy the Amir. Somehow, they think Amy is key to that."

Atlantea didn't answer.

"Do you want us to interfere?" Devin asked, speaking for the first time. Mira closed her eyes. Atlantea was silent again for a long moment.

"No. If we are to fight in this battle, I want it clear to the world that we are blameless. But I will not be surprised again. All right, Mira Bant *de Atlantic*, do it your way. But I must know when the tide turns. You have failed me once in this already; do not fail me again."

The line clicked off. Atlantea was angry, but Mira was still alive. So that was a start. And her headache was so bad, she didn't think she could handle much more.

According to Eli, the operation was a "success," so at least Amy was as yet unharmed. Amy's precipitous decision was so unlike her that Mira suspected the Danjou had manipulated her. She shuddered; attempting to control a pivot was contrary to all conventional wisdom. But mages always thought they could dabble around the edges without repercussions.

She'd known, of course, that the Danjou were dabbling, but she thought they were using Amy to create a super-soldier or perhaps trying to entice the Amir into dropping his barriers with the lure of a cure for his sister. Manipulating Amy like this was beyond her worst speculations. And now Mary was involved too, after dropping everything to come to Boston. She'd spent her entire life caring for her family when Mira could not. Amy was perhaps beyond either of their abilities now.

Cordelia had slipped off — not unusual for her, but still. Worse yet, Thomas was missing. His partner, Marcia Santos, had called, sobbing, to tell her that Thomas' house had been destroyed. Investigators believed a battle mage was responsible, but Marcia was too bereaved to provide much more information.

Mira knew Thomas was still alive; her powers had not faded in the least over the past week. When Thomas' newborn siren daughter was suffocated, Mira felt the loss keenly. Marcia couldn't understand that Mira would have felt the death of a siren child like an amputation. She hadn't felt anything; ergo, Thomas was alive. That didn't mean he wasn't hurt or injured. But the jaguars were looking for Thomas; Kadu and his

346

mother had both pledged to find him. The weres had been designed as the ultimate weapons against mages. The clan had practically adopted Thomas, and if anyone could protect him, they could.

When Amy woke, the curtains were still drawn, but the red and amber lights were on. She felt much less tired than she had the day before, though her vision was still blurry. She pressed the call button, and the nurse opened the door. This time, the curtain had not been drawn around her bed, and the white light from the hall stretched into the room.

And the light *did* stretch. It turned and glided and spun in an array of millions of hues of blue and green, blending to purple and brown as it confronted the red haze that enveloped her room. Amy gasped.

"Good morning, Dr. Bant," the nurse said, shutting the door, and with it, the dance of light subsided to a small line of rippling green and purple spots in the crack beneath it. Amy stared at the line of light under the door, momentarily speechless. Her non-responsiveness clearly alarmed the nurse, who walked quickly to her bedside.

"Sorry," Amy said, collecting her thoughts and moving her focus to the nurse. "I just wondered what time it was."

"It's almost nine-thirty," the nurse said.

"Ah. Thank you. What's your name?" Amy asked.

"Carol Dorio," she responded, checking the monitor above Amy's head. Despite her blurred vision, Amy could see that the nurse was wearing patterned scrubs and her dark hair haloed her face in a long bob. "We haven't met. I'll be the day nurse today and tomorrow."

"It's Saturday, today, correct?" Amy asked.

"Yes, it is. And a dreary Saturday for sure. The hurricane that was supposed to hit the mid-Atlantic may have veered off and petered out, but now we're in for a rainy weekend. I say better this weekend than next. My niece is getting married next Saturday, and better for all the bad weather to hit now so we can have blue skies then."

Amy murmured her agreement, then asked if the nurse would help her up.

"Hmm. Not sure you're supposed to be getting out of bed as yet. Let me check the chart."

"Carol, it will be fine. If you'll just take my hands, I'd like to just assess my stability. If there's any imbalance, I'll just lay back down."

Amy's tone and conviction were clearly persuasive, and the nurse stood in front of Amy as she swung her legs around to reach toward the floor. She stood up and was gratified by how little weakness she actually felt. It was akin to having had a bad flu, but no dizziness or vertigo. Amy smiled. "I'll actually have to tell myself not to overdo it," she said. "I didn't expect to feel this stable. But I know I need to take it easy. Can we try walking just a little bit?"

"All right. Let me bring the IV around. But if you feel at all dizzy, let me know." Carol's deference was a relief. Amy had worried that being a patient would be more challenging than it was proving to be.

"Of course. I was thinking that I'd just like to see if I could use the toilet, then maybe sit in the chair for a while," Amy said.

"That's a good plan. We held your breakfast; Dr. Litner ordered no unnecessary interruptions until you called. He should be here around ten."

After Carol left, Amy stood up and pulled the curtain back just a little bit. She knew she ought to wait for Graham, but she had to know.

It was amazing. Indescribable. Now she knew why Patient B had such difficulty explaining what he saw. Why Ted read her poems instead of just telling her outright.

White light, even that from the weak sunlight filtering through the dark cloud cover outside, was *alive*. That was the only way Amy could think about it. And she thought she heard something, too. It wasn't the hum of the hospital monitors, though she could hear the whirring of those as well. It was like the sound of a boat floating on the Gulf Stream on a calm day. The sound of fiberglass rolling atop three-foot swells. As she stared out the window at the pulsing colors, Amy thought she heard the sea.

The blurriness she had experienced under the red haze of the safelights was gone. Even though she was staring through a rain-spattered window, she could make out the words on the neon sign on the deli below. She could see the people standing at the cross-walk distinctly. But it was hard for Amy to focus on the individuals, because she was captivated by the multi-hued trails being laid in front of her. It was as if the air itself were visible in colored layers, pulsing red then blue then green in an ever-changing flow. Whoever invented tie-dye must have been a mage, Amy thought. That was as close as she could come to describing what she was seeing. The world was a psychedelic tie-dyed shirt.

Sirens generally do not raise their own children. Transitioned sirens are typically deemed too immature to care for an active infant. While no one will force you to give up your child, you will be strongly encouraged to do so. Most commonly, sirens become parents when one of their latent offspring gives birth to an active siren. In that way, parenthood is delayed until a siren is mature and better acculturated.

– Sirens: An Overview for the Newly-Transitioned, 3rd ed. (2015), *by Mira Bant de Atlantic, p. 52.*

Chapter 25

Mira and Devin had both transformed again, and despite the grateful kobold's healing touch, Mira still didn't feel well. Back in their apartment, she went into her bedroom to hide; she was having a hard time keeping up the pretense of calm. She paced back and forth, staring out the window at the ocean in the distance, but the choppy water didn't provide her any comfort.

Atlantea wanted them closer to Amy, and Devin had figured out a way to make that happen. Unlike Mira, Devin wasn't fazed in the least by the news about Thomas. Instead, it had given him this ludicrous idea to disguise themselves as health aides sent by Thomas while he was detained in Brazil. With Devin's remarkable gift for compulsion, it had been a small matter for him to call Marcia Santos and request her assistance on Thomas' behalf. Marcia trusted Devin implicitly; she was overjoyed to hear that Thomas was alive, and happily agreed to call Mary, for him.

Everything Devin did was done with a calm efficiency of effort that only made Mira more aware of her own inner turmoil. She wasn't so fae-like that this kind of deception was fun for her. "Mira" wasn't a common name. Devin had suggested she use "Kiera," his great-granddaughter's name, and close enough to her own that she would hopefully remember to respond to it. So now Mary was expecting "Kiera" to come and help during Amy's recovery, because Thomas couldn't be there himself.

Mira sat down on the bed and covered her face in her hands. She had never expected to cross paths with Amy or Mary again. Her mundane daughters, at least, should have been safely removed from anything like a mage war! Even as she'd fretted over Amy's work on the project, she had never expected … Mira's train of thought broke off; she didn't really know what she'd expected.

She started pacing again. Now that she was so close to seeing her daughters, *interacting* with her daughters, Mira couldn't think straight. She wished Cordelia were here to help her calm down. But Cordelia had slipped away, and she was stuck here with Devin, who couldn't understand.

She had thought deceiving them would be easier if she took on a completely different look from her original self, but now she only felt more lost. Transformation after transformation, the only constant had been her name. It had taken her years to be able to recognize herself within a new body, and now she had nothing to ground her.

Before visiting the kobold, she had found a mark who seemed less likely to lust after the kind of blond, blue-eyed woman she had been originally. While Devin wore the guise of another tall, tan and chiseled man, with a strong jaw and sparkling eyes, Mira was now a slightly-built woman with dark skin, sharply-arched eyebrows, and a high forehead.

She stared at the stranger in her bedroom mirror. The older gentleman whose fantasy she now embodied probably had a thing for Dorothy Dandridge. Mira reminded herself that she wasn't often this lucky: she should appreciate the proportionality of her top and bottom half, the pleasure of not feeling any strain in her back from the weight of an oversized chest. Her hair fell effortlessly to frame her face in loose curls; a style that would have taken a human woman hours to do, and the hot pink of her lacquered nails contrasted beautifully against the shade of her skin.

Get a grip, Mira told her reflection sternly, taking a deep breath. She only had another couple of hours before her interview, and had to calm down. Marcia's second-hand explanation of Amy's condition differed slightly from Eli's. But from both accounts, it sounded like Amy was a lot better than she would have expected for someone who had undergone brain surgery only a week before.

Apparently, Amy's vision was blurry at times and she was subject to slight auditory hallucinations, but she was walking and able to use the bathroom alone. She was on very few medications and wasn't supposed to drive. The post-discharge instructions seemed rather basic. According to Marcia, Mary's biggest concern was how Amy would wash her hair, given the number of staples holding the incision site closed. Mira hadn't even realized that Amy would still have hair; she had assumed that with brain surgery, it would all be shaved off.

While Marcia had told Mary that Thomas was sending two aides, Mary had firmly declined to see Devin. Mary simply wouldn't be comfortable having a man stay with her sister under the circumstances, even a man vouched for by Thomas. On the one hand, she was glad that Mary was unwilling to leave her sister with a strange man, but it did complicate things.

Mira took one last look in the mirror, breathing in and out slowly, before walking into the living room. Devin was sitting on the couch, the personification of resolute readiness, and Mira felt herself tense up again. Her fleeting sense of calm dissolved in the face of his composure. But when he spoke, he didn't sound very composed; he sounded worried. "It doesn't matter if your daughter does not want me there. You will determine an appropriate time to bring me in directly."

"Devin, I don't know how I am going to do this, let alone how to persuade Amy to let you stay in her apartment," Mira pleaded. She was having a hard time keeping it together, and couldn't seem to grasp a coherent thought. She was flailing.

"Mira, sit down." Devin's voice may have held a compulsion, but of course it slipped right off her. "Just take a deep breath. You can do this." Devin's tone wasn't encouraging: it was as if he were merely stating a fact.

"Do what?" Mira asked, rubbing her temples with both hands. "I can do what, exactly? Lie to my daughters? Pretend to be a stranger? Pretend Amy isn't headed straight into the middle of a war?"

"Mira, you know as well as I: No one can change a prophesy. You can only ride the waves that part around it. I wouldn't want my children anywhere near this either. But you and your daughter are very fortunate that Atlantea had enough of an interest to send me here."

Mira's mouth dropped slightly, and Devin smiled. "Mira, think about it. If Atlantea wanted the pivot dead, she would be dead. Instead, she has sent me to ensure you both survive, at least until the war starts and I am needed elsewhere."

And suddenly, Mira felt better. It wasn't Devin's matter-of-fact tone, or his infernal competence, but suddenly, Mira felt like she would be safe; more importantly, that Amy would be safe. She sat down.

"Atlantea herself told me that my job was to make sure you and your daughter remained alive. But I was not to interfere. *You* were not to interfere." Devin smiled. "And yet, here we are, interfering."

"I thought she was going to order you to kill me when I told her I wouldn't allow Amy to be influenced," Mira admitted, rubbing her chin.

If possible, Devin's smile grew wider, but it wasn't a cruel smile; he actually looked amused. "I'm sure Atlantea was counting on your refusal. Who else but you, Mira *Bant* de Atlantic, would refuse her direct order to influence the pivot? No one has ever successfully changed a prophesy, and only rarely has anyone who tried to manipulate a pivot actually come out on top. But it is *so* tempting. Like the moral dilemma of whether you ought to kill baby Hitler or blind the apprenticed Chía if time-travel were possible."

"Louisa wouldn't hesitate to do either. Does she know that Amy is a pivot?" Mira finally asked the question she had worried about since learning Atlantea was sending Devin with her.

"You know how close Atlantea keeps information, so I doubt it. Louisa doesn't need these kinds of details to ready the armies. She only *seems* to complain about a pending conflict, but her eyes sparkle. She's been preparing for the worst her entire life, and is thrilled to spend her final years burning out in a blaze of glory. The details of any prophesy would be wasted on Louisa."

"It's hard to serve two masters."

"I have only ever served one. Can we be true allies now, Mira? Can you trust me that much?"

"I can't focus on Atlantea's needs or the Atlantic or the fae. I can only deal with my own crisis," Mira cautioned.

"Right now, your crisis *is* the Atlantic's crisis."

"Monitoring Amy this closely is foolish. We'll be too close to the pivot and any warmongering mage is going to make the wrong assumptions if they realize we're sirens," Mira doubted Devin would agree, but she had to try.

"You know Atlantea won't accept anything less," Devin replied gently. "She wants us with the pivot."

"Devin, I have no idea how to get you closer to Amy."

"It would be easier to protect you both if I were in the same room." Devin shook his head. "I would have thought Amy, as a doctor at least, would have known you invented that story about hormonal deficiencies."

"Maybe if Amy had studied endocrinology or something like that, she might have questioned it further. But when Mary went off the pill, she almost killed Cordelia. Amy had to literally pull her off. That incident wiped out whatever doubts the two of them might have had about our 'family secret.' Anyway, I thought you agreed that *influencing* Amy would be a mistake"

Devin sighed. "I also said it was tempting. At least Mary has accepted your presence. That will have to suffice for now. I can wait in the lobby at first; but you'll have to find a way to get me closer soon. Things are moving too quickly."

"Miss Santos, so nice to meet you," Mary said. "Amy is resting. Come on in."

Mary ushered Mira inside, shutting the door behind her. Mary was so much lovelier in person than Mira had imagined. It was the warmth in her expression, the sparkle in her eyes; attributes that simply didn't come across in the photos Thomas had sent from Thanksgiving. Mira struggled to keep her voice even. "Please, call me Kiera," she said. She was wearing a pair of purple scrubs she had bought at a local uniform supply store and thought the color helped age her.

Amy's apartment was decorated in a modern style, but since it was in an older building, the combination of old world with the modern was actually rather appealing. Cordelia had said it seemed cold, and Mira supposed the lack of clutter might make it seem sterile to Cordelia, who favored a more lived-in kind of style.

"I'm Mary. I really appreciate you coming on such short notice. How's Thomas? What a disaster! Do they know what happened yet?"

"I don't know much — just that the investigation is ongoing."

How easily she skirted the truth, Mira thought, disgusted with herself — and at the same time, oddly proud. Proud that she was having a calm conversation with Mary. Proud that she wasn't crying or screaming. She really could do this.

Just before they left for Amy's apartment, one of the guards had called Devin to tell him that Thomas had just arrived in Atlantis by boat, accompanied by a mage! At least Mira no longer had to wonder if he were hurt. But bringing a mage to Atlantis presented a whole different kind of risk. She wondered if she should call in a favor from Isioma or even Zale. Atlantea listened to Zale. Mira shook herself mentally; she needed to focus on Mary right now.

"Your aunt is Thomas' business partner?" Mary asked. She seemed stiff. Mira wasn't sure whether she felt anxious about meeting Kiera, or suspicious of her capabilities. After their lunch in Washington, Cordy had reported that Mary would be holding auditions soon; Mary must be torn between staying with Amy and getting back.

"She called to ask if I could help — and of course I said yes."

"And you're a nurse in New York City?" Mary asked, eying Mira's scrubs.

"I'm a home health aide," Mira said. "Not a nurse. But Devin is. Thomas asked us both to come—"

"No, no." Mary said. "I don't think a nurse is necessary. The written discharge instructions are here. It's more about having someone available in case Amy has a turn for the worse, more than anything else. A nurse would be overkill."

"Can I meet the patient?" Mira asked. "Is there anything else I should know?"

Mary walked her around the apartment, showing her the guest room that she would be staying in, and asking more and more questions about her experience. Either Mary wasn't sure she should leave Amy at all, or else she wasn't convinced Mira would be right for the job. Mira hoped her own awkwardness wasn't causing Mary's hesitation.

"Mrs. Arnold, I swear. I want nothing more than to provide the best care I can for your sister. I've taken care of children; I've cared for the elderly and the sick. I've done housekeeping. Truly, I have the experience you need. Thomas trusts me, and our families have been close for years."

Mira's sincerity must have come through, because Mary finally took her to meet Amy. Amy appeared to have been sleeping, but woke when the door to her room opened. "Amy, this is Kiera Santos, the aide Thomas sent." Mary spoke softly, as Amy sat up in bed.

The room was dimly lit, so it was difficult to see Amy clearly. Nevertheless, she didn't look as ill as Mira had feared.

"Great. Hi Kiera, I'm Amy." Amy stared at Mira as she walked over to her bed to shake her hand.

"Pleased to meet you," Mira said, swallowing.

Amy seemed to shift her focus after blinking several times. "I don't know what Mary told you, but I don't think I need all that much. Just rest, mainly. I'll need you to drive me to the hospital and you'll probably need to make sure I eat, since I tend to forget to do that. But I don't need much. I plan to be back at work next week. But Mary has to head back to D.C. tomorrow, right?"

"Yes," Mary agreed.

"So, she's convinced me that I shouldn't stay alone, despite how well I'm feeling. Relatively speaking, of course," Amy sounded upbeat, but forced. Her gaze kept sliding off Mira to focus on the sheets instead. Mira thought she seemed tired.

"Of course," Mira replied. "I can be here whenever you need me. But right now, I think you need to go back to sleep. We can talk more after you wake up."

Amy addressed Mary. "She'll be fine, Mary. Stop fretting. Kiera, at least, recognizes that I'm exhausted." Amy turned back to Mira. "Thank you for coming."

Mary ushered Mira out and softly shut the door. "Well, that's that," Mary said briskly, the relief evident in her voice. She gave Mira the discharge instructions and they agreed on a time for Mira to return tomorrow.

While sirens form strong friendships, romantic pairings are typically fleeting. You should not expect the same kind of exclusivity or longevity in a siren relationship as you might have had with partners in your mundane life. Contractual arrangements such as marriage are generally formed solely for the purpose of generating offspring, and can be more a form of business arrangement than romantic partnership. While some sirens have formed enduring romantic relationships, those are generally considered somewhat risqué, and are typically conducted by the lovers in secret.

– Sirens: An Overview for the Newly-Transitioned, 3rd ed. (2015), *by Mira Bant de Atlantic, p. 184.*

Chapter 26

A few days of relaxation in the relative safety of the Atlantic seemed to erase Kyoko's exhaustion. When they landed at Atlantis, she fairly bounced with eagerness to get off the boat.

"I'm not that bad a sailor for you to be in such a hurry to disembark," Thomas complained as he looped the lead line around the pier and pulled them close to the dock.

Kyoko threw her arms around him after he had tied off. "I'm not. I just feel so alive! It's amazing. We can set back out, if you like. With you, I don't care about anything else."

Thomas couldn't stop the half smile that lurked on his face. He was happy. Despite everything, despite the destruction of his house, the people he had lost. He couldn't bring himself to feel more than a twinge of sadness at what had happened. They had spent the past week crossing the Atlantic alone. If he had any doubt that what he felt for Kyoko was love, this brief honeymoon had erased them. He couldn't even bring himself to worry about what might happen when they stepped onshore and came back into the real world.

This was the best crossing he had ever made, despite not being immersed in the Atlantic directly. Instead, he had been immersed in Kyoko. She told him about her life before her indenture, but skimmed a lonely picture of her life under its yoke. She'd lectured him for hours about the intricacies of magick, but Thomas wasn't bored, because it was Kyoko talking.

Kyoko worried that her parents would not be safe from Gerel, and Thomas agreed to call Kadu when they reached shore to see if the were-jaguars would extract them from Rio and bring them safely to his mother's house. She asked Thomas about his family, and he described his sisters, which made him smile. He should call them, too. Thomas even told her about the shock of his transition, and about his sons, one of whom lived on Ascension Island, and the other on Ryukyu Arc, the Pacific capital.

"Your sons seem to have done quite well. You must be happy to have learned Japanese, since one lives in the Pacific." Kyoko smiled at him with a mischievous twinkle that made his loins jump. Then a passing pod of dolphins caught her eye, and she continued, almost absently, "Smart decision not to try to take on two babies when you were basically a newborn yourself."

Thomas was struck by her offhand remark. Kyoko's words resonated; it didn't matter that others had said essentially the same thing, or that he shared her view on an objective level. Sometimes you needed to hear it from the only person whose opinion truly mattered. But he still didn't tell her about his daughter's death; some pain was too great to share.

"Our apartment is rather small, but I hope you'll like it," Thomas said in a carefully offhand way as they strolled down the pier. After his transition, Mira had decided that it was time to find a place of their own in Atlantis, and tasked Thomas with decorating it — her way perhaps of trying to make him feel at home. He had selected every piece of furniture, every rug, every knickknack. Everything. That had been thirty years ago, of course, but he'd handled every update as well. He had redesigned himself when he'd designed their home, so was anxious to see Kyoko's reaction to his first sanctuary.

One of Atlantea's guards approached them as they stepped off the pier. "Thomas Bant de Atlantic?"

"Yes," said Thomas. "Is everything all right?" He was not used to any special attention being paid to him in Atlantis, and felt his face tighten as he tried to keep his anxiety from blossoming across his face.

"The Port Master has a message for you from Atlantis House."

"Ah. All right. We'll pick it up on our way out," Thomas' skin itched with the desire to get Kyoko out from under the man's gaze. Kyoko gazed back at the guard, and while she didn't have that lovesick expression on her face that many women had when they encountered a male siren, she wasn't nearly as impassive as Thomas would have liked.

"Thank you." The guard turned and walked back to the covered pavilion where he was stationed. Thomas took Kyoko's arm and escorted her past towards the port offices at the end of the quay.

As his jaw began to ache with the strain of maintaining his insouciant expression, Thomas realized that he was jealous. It had been so long since he had felt that way that it almost didn't register. He paused for a moment, gently turning Kyoko towards him and cupped her face in his hands. "I love you," he said.

Kyoko smiled, bringing her arms up around his back to grip his shoulders. "I love you too."

Thomas caressed her face and released her. "I didn't consider what it would be like to bring a human among all the sirens of Atlantis. This is the safest place for you — at least until we can figure out the scope of our vampire problem — but I hadn't thought about the siren impact on you." Thomas stared into Kyoko's dark eyes.

"But I have," Kyoko said lightly, reaching her hand up to caress Thomas' neck. His pupils dilated with desire. "Don't worry. You have an apartment, and we'll go there. I've spent a lot of time by myself in the past, and don't want any company but yours. Come on. It's a beautiful day, but I've had enough of the sun and salt. I want to take a real shower and eat something that neither of us cooked." Kyoko drew Thomas back towards the harbor entrance.

Thomas ducked into the port master's office and retrieved the letter. He decided not to open it until he got to his apartment, just in case it was an immediate summons. In fact, he decided he wouldn't open it until after Kyoko had her bath and meal, exactly as she requested.

"Thomas, your apartment is lovely," Kyoko said as he ushered her in and went to draw the blinds. Small motes of dust swirled in the air as the sunlight flooded in and Kyoko held out her hand to catch the shadows as she looked around.

Thomas watched her walk slowly around the main room, but couldn't read her expression. He tried to see it through her eyes, wondering if she felt as much at home here as she had when she had danced through his mind. He was reassured when Kyoko smiled at him warmly, and let out a breath he hadn't realized he'd been holding.

"Cordy won't mind if I loan you some of her clothes." Thomas shied away from borrowing clothes from his mother's closet; when he looked at Kyoko, he only wanted to think about her. But his sister had taken most of her favorites with her when she left for Kasos, and only a few of her casual pareos and kimonos were left. "First a shower, then dinner. Have you ever had Senegalese food?" Thomas asked.

"No, I don't think so," Kyoko replied.

"One of my favorite restaurants on the island is Waly-Fay. The chef is from Dakar and I think you might like it."

"Do sirens use money like we mundanes? I know the enclaves use some kind of point system, but they don't allow any mundanes in their territory. The fae don't need restaurants and such." Kyoko sounded fascinated.

"We don't prohibit mundanes like the enclaves," Thomas replied. "And we don't print our own money or anything — our exchanges with other sirens are perhaps more fae-like than human: we trade favors and the like. But with mundanes..." Thomas paused. "I guess it's kind of similar to Australia. Mundanes are only allowed on the island by invitation. And when they leave, their sponsors compel them to remember their time here as if they had been on a fae preserve."

"But they come willingly?" Kyoko asked.

"Oh yeah," Thomas replied hastily. "It's a mark of honor to be a sponsor, and they tend to pay the humans very, very well." He didn't want Kyoko to think they treated mundanes like the Cabal. Mundanes settled in Australia as second-class inhabitants; in Atlantis, they were guest-workers. *Honored* guests. Thomas struggled a bit with the comparison, though: except for the fact they were well-paid, some mundanes were perhaps not much better treated here than in Australia.

"Here, let me show you my room — *our* room — and we can have that shower you asked for." Thomas wanted to distract Kyoko from her questions about siren society almost as much as he wanted to see her in his bed again.

Eventually, a different hunger drove them out of the bedroom, and Thomas grudgingly escorted Kyoko back into the main room to order dinner. She looked absolutely stunning in a gold pareo with an emerald-green design he couldn't recall Cordy ever having worn. The fading light outside glinted off her damp hair. He watched her watching him with equal fascination while he ordered several dishes he knew she wouldn't recognize. Her eyebrows raised, and a slight smile hovered at the edge of her lips as she appreciated his desire to please her.

"How long? Yes, female delivery. Okay, thanks." Thomas hung up, and came around to sit next to Kyoko on the sofa.

"It must be hard to have to pay attention to gender all the time like that," Kyoko said. She noticed everything, was interested in everything.

"You get used to it," Thomas replied, shrugging. "I guess when you look at the constructs — sirens or even the weres — there's a peculiar balance of power with debility. I've always thought that was the mages' way of ensuring their own creations never got the better of them."

"It's possible," Kyoko replied, considering. "Certainly were susceptibility to mage magick during the light of the full moon is a fail-safe Chía designed. But I doubt the same-sex hatred fertile humans feel towards sirens was a deliberate design element in Aphrodite's spell. I can think of a lot of better controls than that."

"You want to build a better mousetrap?" Thomas snorted with amusement combined with pride. "I'm sure you could."

"Maybe not redesign you," Kyoko spoke slowly, stroking a line in the air above his chest. Thomas felt her cool touch within his very core and shivered in pleasure. "But I've been looking at this odd distortion in your pattern. I don't know that you even realize it's there?" She dropped her hand to toy with the sleeve of his shirt.

Thomas shook his head.

"It's a magical chain, a binding. I think it's a very old blood-geas. The kind that's inherited, not cast on you directly." Kyoko's eyes focused and unfocused, and Thomas thought he heard a light arpeggio of bells in the distance as he felt her magick stroke his skin. "I don't see it entwined in the cell structure — though the siren spell gleams in that. This chain is actually layered on top, so I don't think it's part of Aphrodite's original design. But it *is* bound into your very DNA."

Thomas enjoyed Kyoko's fascination with him. For the first time in his life, he was pleased to be a magical construct. "I don't know for sure, because I can't see what you see. But that's probably Morgan le Fay's curse. All sirens have it."

"Hmm. Yes. You were born bound, so you don't even know how it feels to be free."

Thomas was a little flustered by Kyoko's tone. "I know what it is to be free. I wasn't born a siren. I remember my life before and my life now. And one isn't better or worse than the other — it's just different."

"No, no. You misunderstand," Kyoko responded quickly. "I'm sorry; that came out wrong. This isn't a binding connected to your siren existence. It's bound to your DNA, which didn't change, really. Parts were just activated. I can see them."

Kyoko traced a bit of the air around his chest again, and Thomas enjoyed the feel of her light magick around him. "This is different; that's why I said I didn't think it was part of Aphrodite's design. It would make sense if it were layered on later. What does the binding do?"

"Morgan le Fay's curse? You don't know?" Thomas asked and Kyoko shook her head. "Really? Maybe there's still a little mystery around us." Kyoko's focus had Thomas aching to put her in less of a serious mood. He loved her attention, but didn't want her thinking he was somehow damaged or weak.

"Tell me," Kyoko demanded. She didn't seem the least bit distracted by Thomas' teasing tone.

"At the end of the Third Mage War, as the story goes," Thomas kept his tone light. "When Morgan le Fay was about to be overrun, she used her death to fuel a blood-geas on the sirens. Not just those fighting in the war, but all sirens. It's based on a simple fae confoundment spell. The geas binds us to ignorance of sirens when we're mundane, and prevents us from telling our latent relatives about sirens after we transition."

"What would happen if you tried to explain?" Kyoko asked.

"You just can't. If I tried to say, 'I'm a siren' to my mundane sisters, I wouldn't be able to get the words out. My mother wrote a textbook about sirens — but could only do it after writing 'Active Siren Eyes Only' on the flyleaf using bespelled paper. If anyone says anything about sirens to a latent, they either don't understand or they mishear it. A pretty insidious curse, really, given how precarious it is after you transition. A lot of people think Morgan le Fay killed more sirens with that curse than were killed in the war itself."

"I suppose the curse is why most humans think sirens were destroyed in the Atlantic War, same as the sphinxes during the Second Mage War. I can see the geas on you. I can even see its tethers leading off — probably connecting you to your mother and your sons." Kyoko's focus shifted from something only she could see back to Thomas.

"Well, it's not going anywhere. Sadly," Thomas replied, trying to maintain an upbeat tone. He could see that Kyoko was fascinated, but this topic ran too close to more painful reality. He changed the subject. "Have you ever seen a siren work their magic?"

"No, but I want to. I want to see how Aphrodite's spell works," Kyoko replied. But her focus had shifted back to that inchoate space near Thomas, and he knew she was still thinking about the geas.

Although it was a minor breach of etiquette to toy with a sponsored human, Thomas obliged Kyoko when the delivery came. "Put the food on the counter," Thomas commanded, threading a light compulsion into his voice. The woman complied with a sigh, her eyes fluttering as she watched Thomas from beneath them. Her eagerness to obey him made him feel petty.

"I don't like how she looks at you." Kyoko's voice was sharp.

"Don't look at me," Thomas ordered, and the woman looked away with a slight gasp, her lips parted. "Thank you for coming so quickly. Now, turn around and leave." The woman opened her mouth to say something and Thomas forestalled her. "Silently. Shut the door behind you." He had increased the strength of the compulsion laced under each command, as the woman grew increasingly reluctant to leave.

Thomas looked at Kyoko, who glared at the closed door.

"I didn't like her," she said.

"I only wanted to please you," Thomas replied, disappointed. Kyoko's face softened.

"*You* did," she replied, sighing. "I suppose I'm jealous. It is a wonderful spell design. I want to see it again, but I don't want to see *you* work it."

Thomas felt a mild thrill at her possessiveness.

While they ate, Thomas' attention was drawn back to the letter from Atlantis House, which he had tossed on the counter. It remained in his peripheral vision, a reminder that he deliberately ignored while he watched Kyoko try the new spices for the first time.

"These flavors are so rich," Kyoko remarked with true enjoyment.

"Perhaps we'll go to Cape Verde when enough time has passed," Thomas said. "I think you'll like it there. It's not so different climate-wise from Brazil, but I think you'll find it marvelously exotic since you've never been out of the country." Kyoko had barely even left Rio for that matter. They had talked about perhaps going to Japan, where Thomas had never been, and where Kyoko's ancestors had emigrated more than a century ago. Both of them spoke Japanese now, after all.

"Wherever you want to go," Kyoko said.

"I want you to be happy," Thomas replied.

"With you, I *am* happy. Safe. To be with you is all I've wanted since the moment I first touched your thoughts. I loved being in your mind," Kyoko sighed, resting her head on his shoulder.

"You're always welcome," Thomas said rashly, eager to bare himself to her; though at the same time, his heart fluttered with trepidation at the prospect of her dancing through his soul again.

"Maybe we should explore other things first," Kyoko suggested coyly. Thomas raised her hand to his lips, pressing a kiss first upon the back of her hand, then turning it over to graze the inside of her wrist.

"Maybe we should," Thomas agreed.

One of the more difficult aspects of integrating into siren society is understanding the different markers of status and value that exist. Unlike most mundane societies, wealth, beauty, and strength convey little status in siren communities. Instead, siren society more closely resembles that of mages, insofar as magical power provides the primary measure of status. One unique aspect of siren communities, however, is that a demonstrated ability to cultivate valued skills in others is highly prized. Siren sponsors therefore frequently seek opportunities to showcase those they have trained in an effort to win greater acclaim from their community.

– Sirens: An Overview for the Newly-Transitioned, 3rd ed. (2015), *by Mira Bant de Atlantic, p. 120.*

Chapter 27

It was midmorning before Thomas ventured back into the kitchen, where the unopened letter from Atlantis House sat in mute accusation. He had delayed so long, the letter now felt like a toxic threat waiting for him to touch it so it could poison his joy. He sardonically congratulated himself on being courageous enough to sidle up to the counter and actually tear it open.

It could be worse, he thought as he read the elegant calligraphy. Kyoko had followed him in, and Thomas turned to tell her. "I've been summoned to see Atlantea. Not as bad as I'd thought, given our welcome. But it's unusual."

"Your sister was a courtier, and is now Atlantea's personal envoy in Europe. You said your mother is often with the queen. This can't really be that unusual. After all, your house was blown up. I'm sure someone told Mira," Kyoko replied sensibly.

"Yes. That's true. And I've been completely out of touch since we left. But I somehow doubt that Atlantea is summoning me just to tell me to call my mother."

"Stranger things have happened," Kyoko giggled.

"They sure have," Thomas said as he swept Kyoko into an embrace, twirling her around. Kyoko's lightness of spirit raised his, and he felt as though he were looking out on the ocean just after a squall had passed through. The sharp ozone in the air cleared his heart.

He tried calling both his mother and Cordelia, but only got voicemail.

"Are you sure you'll be fine by yourself?" he asked.

"Stop it already and go," Kyoko replied. "I've counter-spelled your mother's textbook so I can read it. So it's a good thing you'll be gone. You're too distracting, and I want to learn more about sirens."

Thomas left her lying on the couch, perusing his mother's textbook. It would be hurry up and wait, he knew. A summons to Atlantis House with no time specified typically meant waiting in the Grand Salon for hours. At least there were always musicians there, so there'd be some entertainment.

He wasn't an expert like Mary, but he had never heard a bad performance in Atlantis. A lot of sirens competed in their cultivation of musicians. Performing at Atlantis House was their sponsors' way of tossing down the gauntlet, so to speak, or picking it up. Even sirens who weren't there to see Atlantea or a courtier would come and linger in the Salon, just to follow the competition. Thomas hoped today's serenade would be more melodic than the last time he had waited interminably. That time the room had been packed with spectators eager to hear a rap battle followed by a drum-off. Thomas didn't care for it, but the crowd had been excited to witness what was apparently the duel of the season.

When he arrived this time though, he was immediately directed into one of the smaller side chambers, as opposed to the Grand Salon. He didn't have much time to wonder about that because shortly after he came in, a different guard entered and asked Thomas to follow her. The guard escorted him into an octagonal room that was far more modern in décor than the rest of Atlantis House. This was Atlantea's famed private meeting room, enclosed in glass on five of eight sides. It was visible from the ocean on the east side of Atlantis House, where it jutted out over the walls.

Atlantea sat in an intricately-carved wooden chair that had been placed on a thick octagonal carpet in the middle of the room; the only other furniture in the room had been arranged against the interior walls. The view of the Atlantic behind the queen was breathtaking, but the light streaming through the windows cast Atlantea into shadow, so it was hard for Thomas to focus on her expression.

Clearly he was intended to stand before her, and he took a deep breath as he approached. "Atlantea, my queen." Thomas opted for deep formality. He bowed, with his right hand closed across his chest.

"Thomas Bant de Atlantic," Atlantea responded in kind, then stopped speaking. She watched him for a moment. Thomas knew better than to say anything. Less was more when facing an uncertain adversary. "Mira asked me to ensure your well-being. Since you survived the attack on your home without the need to change form, I trust you are well."

"Atlantea, I am."

Since he couldn't change form, it was a good thing he hadn't needed to. But she knew that. Thomas supposed there was a buried meaning in her words, but didn't know what it was. He hoped Atlantea was merely hinting at his lack of power or needling him for his relative weakness ... though both his mother and Cordelia insisted Atlantea was not cruel. Perhaps the purpose of her summons had indeed been to tell him to call his mother as if he were a child.

"Your house was destroyed by a battle mage. Why?" Atlantea's voice crackled with a compulsion that slipped off Thomas, but reminded him why Atlantea rarely left Atlantis anymore. Her voice was an uncontrollable weapon that could drive both mundanes and mages insane.

"Atlantea, I believe that Gerel, the vampire ruler of Rio de Janeiro, ordered it." Now that his eyes had adjusted to the light, Thomas could see Atlantea was displeased with his answer. He tried to elaborate. "You may be aware that Mira contracted with Gerel to gain knowledge of Portuguese when she mediated the Were-Jaguar dispute some years back. The mage who performed that work requested my assistance in leaving Rio, which I granted."

Atlantea's face was unreadable. "I see. This mage is the woman you brought to Atlantis and who is currently staying with you at 30 Shearwater Tower."

Atlantea was letting him know how closely he was being observed. Thomas swallowed. "Yes. Her name is Kyoko."

"Did you consider the danger you were bringing to Atlantis when you granted her sanctuary, Thomas?" Atlantea's voice reverberated with barely contained power, and the room shook a little, as if buffeted by a non-existent wind. But her expression had not changed.

"My queen, I did not credit Gerel as a threat to Atlantis. Honestly, it is highly unlikely that she would leave—"

Atlantea raised her hand, and Thomas subsided instantly.

"The danger in bringing Kyoko here," Atlantea clarified, "a mage so skilled she can glean and infuse knowledge of a language without any damage to the subject. A mage so skilled that the vampire ruler of Rio hired the strongest battle mage in South America to destroy her before she decided to take vengeance for years of oppression. There are no mages in Atlantis!" Atlantea's voice rose throughout her tirade until the windows around the room rattled. She took a deep breath.

"I swear she will not harm anyone while she is here—"

"And how can you, Thomas Bant, stop her if she chooses to destroy the city?" Atlantea raised one eyebrow.

"Atlantea, Kyoko will not destroy Atlantis because it is my home and her refuge." Thomas could see Atlantea was unpersuaded. He looked out at the ocean, which was growing increasingly agitated, and spoke more firmly. "Kyoko will not harm us, because she loves me."

Atlantea sat back in her chair. "She loves you."

"Yes," Thomas replied simply. To say anything more would have revealed too much, but Atlantea picked up on his unspoken words nevertheless.

"And you love her," Atlantea surmised. "Mind mages. This is what comes of letting mind mages root around in your head. It's too close. Too close! Mira was a fool to set this up."

Thomas opened his mouth, but Atlantea held up her hand again. "No, don't bother. I will grant that you have perhaps sufficient power to have beguiled even a mage as powerful as that one. And perhaps that will be sufficient. But she has beguiled you just the same, and now you are both a danger. A risk." Atlantea rubbed her index finger along the grooves in the arm of her chair, thinking. The ocean swells remained high.

"Atlantea, we only need to stay long enough for Gerel's tracking ability to diminish. My sister is your envoy; my mother has served you since she transitioned. You can't doubt our loyalty."

"*Their* loyalty, perhaps. Cordelia is mine, though Mira is not such a fanatic that the Atlantic will come first for her. You, though," Atlantea looked more sharply at Thomas' face. "You are more of an unknown. Georg has told me somewhat of you, of course." Thomas' eyes widened slightly, and Atlantea smiled. "Of course my vassal keeps me informed about his court. That's his primary purpose now in any event. So, I know *of* you. But I don't *know* you. And I don't know *her*."

"In my time at Jarl Georg's court, I did nothing that could give you cause to distrust me." Thomas paused for a long moment, and Atlantea inclined her head in what he took as agreement. "Kyoko loves me. As you say, I have beguiled her. So you should trust that she will do no harm. But beyond that, she can be valuable to you, perhaps to all Atlantics," Thomas said desperately. In his haste to escape Brazil and in his lust for Kyoko, he had somehow forgotten Atlantea's renowned hatred of mages.

Atlantea shook her head. "Mages destroy. It is as much in their nature as a siren's love for the sea. They can't help themselves."

"Perhaps; but Aphrodite, after all, was a mage. Jarl Georg has found his mage's work so useful, he's relied upon him for decades. Please, Atlantea. Give us a chance. If not for me, for my mother's sake. For Cordelia. For all their past service. Give me the chance to serve."

Atlantea looked at him and said nothing, but the waves gradually relaxed into the undulating backdrop they had been when he had first entered the room. She raised her hand. "Very well. A chance you have. But this balances the scales, Thomas Bant *de Atlantic*, against all I might owe your mother and sister. Figure out a way to persuade me that you can be trusted. That granting your mage sanctuary is the correct decision."

"Yes, Atlantea." Thomas kept his voice steady, though internally he wondered how he would ever be able to do this, given how much she hated mages. How could he have been so stupid?

She inclined her head, "You may go." Thomas bowed and turned to leave when Atlantea called back to him. "Oh, and Thomas, call your human sisters."

All fertile humans are susceptible to the siren spell, whether mage or mundane. Because the fae are not fertile without siren intervention, siren magick does not affect them, except in that rare window between the gifting of fertility to a faerie and their actual procreation. Weres were designed for immunity to mage magick, but due to the unique combination of fae and mage magick in the siren spell, there are limitations to were immunity which will be covered in chapter nine, infra. It is quite rare, however, for anyone to realize they are under the influence of a siren spell. Generally, only mages with strong visual acuity are able to see the spell working.

– Sirens: An Overview for the Newly-Transitioned,
3rd ed. (2015), *by Mira Bant de Atlantic, p. 105.*

Chapter 28

"Well, I think the first thing to do is for you to call Mary," Kyoko said after Thomas had told her about the meeting.

"Yes. Or Amy," Thomas replied grimly. He was still unsettled by his audience with Atlantea, and her final comment had been deliberately designed to unsettle him further. Thomas was grateful that his mother was old-fashioned enough to keep an address book, since his cell phone had been destroyed along with his house, and he had never memorized any of their phone numbers. He dialed Mary first, but only got her voicemail; Amy, however, answered on the third ring.

"Hello." Amy sounded fine, and Thomas let out the breath he hadn't realized he'd been holding.

"Amy, it's Thomas."

"Thomas, I'm glad to finally hear from you! Are you all right? Marcia told us what happened to your house. I'm so glad you're okay."

"I'm fine. Fine. It's a mess — obviously. But I'm totally fine." He felt a pang of guilt; he'd been so utterly focused on Kyoko, he'd forgotten everyone else. When he hung up with Amy, he resolved to call Marcia. He'd also have to do something for the families of his security team.

"Thank God. Thomas, I was so worried! I mean, you should have called earlier. And don't give me that crap that you didn't want to upset me while I was in the hospital. You know me."

"You're in the hospital?" Thomas couldn't keep the question out of his voice.

"No. I'm at home. I mean, I'm still going back in for the tests, but I was discharged on Monday. And I have to thank you for sending Kiera. She's been extremely helpful."

The name 'Kiera' sounded so like 'Mira' that Thomas wished he had spoken to his mother before calling Amy. Clearly, she'd gotten involved in some way on his behalf. Perhaps this was why he had been unable to reach her or Cordelia on the phone. "How are you feeling? Seriously now? Don't keep up the front," Thomas said.

"Really, I feel fine. I'm still just a little tired. Mary went home yesterday, and Kiera is staying with me now. It's hard to get used to the change, honestly. I sometimes have double-vision, so I wouldn't want to drive or anything. But I can't imagine a better outcome."

After a few minutes of talking with Amy, Thomas gleaned what had happened. It was so unlike her that Thomas could barely bring himself to ask any question other than why she had done it. Of course Amy didn't answer that question, but in her effort to avoid answering, she filled him in on all the information he should have already known.

"I promise," Thomas said, "I'll get to Boston as soon as I can."

"I'm so sorry, Thomas. About your house. You don't need to rush up here. Just take care of what you need to take care of." Amy was probably sincere in her sentiment, but Thomas knew that she wanted to see him. He also had a strong suspicion that their mother was this "Kiera," his business partner's purported niece, who just happened to be a home health aide living in New York City. Amy had been even more talkative than usual.

When he hung up (the phone was still a rotary dial connected to the kitchen wall) he turned to Kyoko, who had heard his half of the conversation.

"I thought your sister was a brain surgeon?" Kyoko asked.

"She is. But now she's apparently also a patient. She says she's fine, but I'll know more when Mary calls back. You know how she was doing research on mage sight? Something about the neural pathways or connections and how to operate on the nerves to link something up in mundanes with mage backgrounds?"

Kyoko nodded.

"So, Amy apparently thought her lab was about to shut down her project or take it in a different direction — I didn't quite follow exactly. She apparently decided to push ahead. And since there were no other suitable subjects, she did the operation on herself. Well, she didn't operate herself — one of her colleagues did. She says it was a success, and now she's trying to figure out how to use her new mage sight."

"That's incredible," Kyoko said.

"I'd call it pretty insane."

"No, really; it's incredible that she's gained a whole new sense — just like that! I've never heard of anything like that being done by magick, and there isn't much that a fae healer can't do."

"Well, I wish she hadn't used herself as a guinea pig, but it sounds like she made it through fine. I'm not so sure how this relates to my meeting with Atlantea, though. Both Cordy and my mom know her well. They never said she liked to play games. So, I don't know why she didn't just tell me what she obviously knew. I mean, I'm sure my mom is in Boston with Amy. I hope she calls back." Thomas walked toward the window to look at the calm sea.

"Atlantea doesn't trust you, maybe? Perhaps she's testing your resolve? Testing us. Pulling about the edges to see if something unravels. I don't know that I'm so powerful that she needs to be this worried." Kyoko shook her head.

"You broke an unbreakable spell, and you don't think you're powerful? Let's just leave false modesty aside, my love." Thomas sat down next to Kyoko and inclined his head to brush hers. "Maybe you're right about this being a test. It's really the first time I've ever spoken to Atlantea. She doesn't know me, and I think she's afraid of you. It *is* odd that we don't have any mages in Atlantis. The Jarl has had a court mage since forever, and I've heard that the Pacific court has a trio."

"Maybe that's what I'll be," Kyoko said.

"No," Thomas straightened. "I won't let you escape one master just to be yoked under another — even if this one won't drain your life force. How long, do you think, till you're untraceable?"

"I don't know, Thomas. I was thinking, perhaps, if staying here is a problem, maybe we could go to Australia?" Kyoko's hesitancy showed. Non-mages were second-class citizens under the Cabal's strictly enforced apartheid regulations.

"Australia?" Thomas was taken aback. "Seriously? You think we should go to Australia?"

"I know it sounds crazy. But any mage is automatically a citizen and can't be extradited. Any assault on a mage outside of a registered duel is investigated and punished. I think it would be the safest place for me. And you would be safe with me," Kyoko said quickly.

Thomas thought for a moment. Kyoko was an incredibly powerful mage, and would be welcomed — even celebrated — in Australia. She would have privileges and protections there that he could never provide for her here. And best of all, there would be no sirens to lure her away from him.

"Not a crazy idea," Thomas said slowly. "Let's think about it. I don't know that we have to rush away now."

"I can think of better ways to spend the afternoon," Kyoko agreed.

Thomas half-woke in the night, reaching for Kyoko. She wasn't beside him in the bed. He sat up, now wide awake.

"Shh," Kyoko whispered. "I didn't mean to wake you." She was standing next to the bed. The blackout curtains were open, and moonlight shafted through the window to draw a rectangular outline across the room.

387

"What are you doing?" Thomas asked. "Come back to bed."

"In a minute. The moonlight is clarifying." Kyoko seemed intent on something. It was a little unsettling to have her full attention on him while he slept.

"What do you mean?" Thomas asked.

"Even though I cast in full sunlight, I design my spells in reflected light. You can see more subtleties and work through the nuances when you're not over-whelmed by the full power of the sun." Kyoko tilted her head to one side as she looked at Thomas. "I can see it so much more clearly now."

"See what?"

"The blood-geas." Kyoko traced her hand slowly in Thomas' direction. "It's so clever. There's such a beauty in its design that it's hard to imagine she cast it in such a moment of stress. Or without any planning." She shook her head, as if bringing herself out of a trance. "Sorry. You can't see it. And I know it's evil, but at the same time, so very elegant in its composition. But I think I see now where the joints are. If I press here and here, it will begin to crack, I think."

Kyoko pointed at a few spots just inches away from Thomas' neck and chest. Thomas shivered; she wasn't touching him, but he could nevertheless feel her fingers gentle on his skin.

"Kyoko, wait," Thomas took Kyoko's hand. "The moon isn't even full tonight. You don't have nearly enough power to do a working, and I don't think you're completely recovered from that last spell you cast."

"I'm not going to cast anything now," Kyoko replied. "I'm just looking. You really can see things by moonlight that aren't visible in the brightness of day. All that color washes out all but the faintest outline of the spell."

"Kyoko, you don't have to do anything. This geas has been around for fifteen hundred years. It isn't necessary to try to change it right now. It doesn't bother me — I've never really noticed it."

"You never noticed it because it's always been there, strangling you. But that doesn't mean you won't feel better once it's gone. Think of a lifetime of being only able to inhale this much," Kyoko placed his hand on her chest and breathed in and out shallowly, then took a deep breath and exhaled slowly. "What a difference to be able to really breathe. What more you could be able to do if you weren't so constricted."

"It's too much," Thomas said. "You risk too much."

"And what about your family, your sisters? It can't be good to have such a separate life from them. You say you love your family — but this geas has forced you to hide most of your life from them. This is the test, Thomas. I know it. This is how we prove to Atlantea that I can be trusted; that *we* can be trusted."

God, she was seductive. Her words and her body silhouetted in the moonlight were a spell that Thomas shook off with a will. "An indenture cast by a regular mage is one thing, Kyoko. But this is a geas cast by one of the greatest mages in history! I know you're talented, but there are risks — you could pour yourself into it and fall into a coma or disappear." Thomas worried at how obsessed Kyoko seemed.

"I won't disappear, Thomas. I can take it slowly. I know I can do this. It won't be as sweeping as her death spell — she enchanted an entire species — but I can break just one link of the chain without fueling it with my own death."

"Kyoko, we'll go to Australia. I was thinking about it before." Thomas had never been as tempted as he was at that moment to compel Kyoko. His voice actually trembled as he suppressed his power.

"You need to trust me a little more," Kyoko said flatly. "I understand more about my own limits than you do."

"I do trust you. Okay, I don't know what your limits are. But can you really stand there and tell me you know them yourself? That you are absolutely certain breaking a blood-geas won't be too much? Let's go to Australia, and you can consult some of the greatest mages in the world about it first. Promise me. I want you to do this, I do. I just think you're pushing too hard, too fast. Slow down."

Kyoko looked down for a moment, then back at Thomas. "I can't. I can't slow down. It's just too alluring. Maybe it's your influence, but that spell is intoxicating. It calls to me in a way that I just can't explain. I swear I won't do anything rash; that I'll be careful. But I can't swear not to touch it."

"I don't understand magick." Thomas said, a note of despair creeping into his voice.

"No," Kyoko agreed.

"But I'm not completely ignorant. You were in a near-coma for almost two days after breaking your indenture!"

"Thomas, this is different. It's so much harder to cast a spell on yourself. You can barely see the bindings, let alone undo them. It's like operating on yourself; you feel at the same time you are trying to cast — and the muddle of experiencing your own touch is almost overwhelming. This, I can do. In some ways it's much easier, even though the spell itself is a higher magick."

Kyoko was persuasive, but Thomas hated his lack of understanding. "But you're not doing anything now. It's too dark. Study it, explore it. But don't *do* anything yet. It could backfire on me, also, right? I mean, you don't want to hurt me."

"I won't hurt you. I can't hurt you. I'm not casting tonight," Kyoko agreed, and Thomas had to content himself with that.

Part Three

Under Sea, Break Free

While sirens enjoy some immunity to passive fae magicks, great caution must be used in approaching them. The fae do not think like humans, and when visiting their preserves, it is critical that you adapt your mindset to their different perspective. It is recommended that an experienced mentor accompany any newly transitioned siren on their first ten to twenty visits into fae territory. Please note that some sirens generally deem it prudent to always *travel in pairs. But do not let this cautionary note dissuade you from your purpose: the fae need sirens. So long as their need for us remains, we enjoy a measure of safety in their presence.*

– Sirens: An Overview for the Newly-Transitioned, 3rd ed. (2015), *by Mira Bant de Atlantic, p. 108.*

Chapter 29

The North York Moors National Park was about five hundred and fifty square miles on the northeast coast of England, and much of it was covered in a purple expanse of heather that waved like a lavender sea in the wind. For all its visual beauty (and certainly September was the time to visit), the whole landscape felt hostile and unwelcoming to Cordelia.

She had not forgotten the feeling of drowning on dry land when that ancient faerie had bespelled her on her first visit. Nor the terrifying emptiness that had followed. While she still wasn't certain the faerie had shown her an absolute truth like an Oracle, she did believe the suffering of the Aos Sí was quite real.

Zale may be right: she was meddling without thinking things through. But the increasing turnover in siren support staff, as well as Thomas' sudden flight from England, meant that she wasn't the only siren disturbed by what was happening here. So what if Zale made her feel like an idealistic teenager, attempting to save the whales with little thought to the collateral damage on the poor fishermen of southeast Asia? Something had to be done.

The fields' beauty was countered by a musty odor that hung in the air. It reminded her of the flooded shed she had cleared out as a teenager: not quite the smell of rot, but certainly of decay. She shivered, despite the humidity, and turned back to Titania, who had accompanied her this far. "The moors are as uninviting as the forest was," Cordelia stated.

"Yes. We feel it too. The hostility grows as more of us fade," Titania didn't look at Cordelia, but also stared out at the undulating hills of heather before her.

When Cordelia had presented herself to Titania four days ago, the Aos Sí queen had worn a crown of blackened silver enhanced with diamond stars. The old-growth forest's dim light was reflected into white streams that pierced the gloom like a halogen flashlight bouncing off a disco ball, alternatively blinding Cordelia while illuminating the woods. The brightness of Titania's crown had been a display of power that made Cordelia wonder whether the fae could be freed without igniting the world.

Today the Aos Sí queen again wore a crown of silver so tarnished it gleamed black in the sunlight. Her glamoured crowns were always in the form of tarnished or blackened silver, the true message of which Cordelia was still trying to interpret. Was Titania trying to remind her of the fae's suffering? Demonstrate the extraordinary length of time they had been imprisoned? Indicate that the Aos Sí had been so weakened, they were no longer a threat? But Cordelia looked at the crown and hoped it signified that once free of this place, the fae could shine again.

She knew that to be around the fae was to be unable to trust the reality you experienced, but she had to try. In her first meeting with Titania, they had probed one another in what felt like a verbal joust. The queen was clearly interested in understanding why Cordelia was there, and Cordelia tried to focus on the extent of rage and hate Titania had hidden beneath her impassive exterior.

Titania, though, had the experience of millennia to hone her speech, and Cordelia felt eminently outclassed in their conversations. She understood why Zale was so ambivalent about whether the Aos Sí would destroy them if they could.

Since their initial meeting, Titania had gradually altered her style from the ornate to the ordinary. Today she looked like a modern mundane, wearing a sensible wool plaid coat over blue jeans and walking shoes. Even the blackened, silver circlet about her head didn't detract from the commonplace appearance the queen was cultivating. But no fae voluntarily appeared without their glamour unless in the company of those they trusted most. Their glamours changed with their moods or whims and seemed designed to intimidate or seduce the mortals they encountered. Cordelia thought that Titania had moved from intimidation to seduction.

She knew only that she shouldn't allow herself to believe anything she experienced here: she could never be sure that she was actually getting to know Titania's true self, as opposed to simply the image of herself she believed Cordelia wanted to see. And despite Titania's agreement that the land felt hostile, it seemed unlikely that Titania experienced the same feeling of unwelcome that Cordelia did.

"I think the land's hostility is directed at me," Cordelia probed. "After all, this is land you have claimed, and we sirens are not completely innocent bystanders to your suffering."

"Bystanders is perhaps the right word," Titania stated. Cordelia noted that Titania chose not to agree or deny the truth of what Cordelia had said. While the fae could not lie, they could avoid the issue.

"Culpable bystanders?" Cordelia asked.

"Do I think you are culpable? No, you are innocent." Titania stated firmly.

"I'm innocent, but the Atlantics perhaps not. And I've certainly been passive."

"You've been more active than most."

"I was warned that if given the opportunity, the fae would rise up against their oppressors. That is, against us." Cordelia said.

"There are some of us who would if they could. But much of that is likely due to despair and the pain of surviving. We aren't long-lived because we nurse grudges, Cordelia. We are a race that lives in the moment, looking neither backwards nor forward."

"That's not exactly true," Cordelia countered. "You remember what happened in the past well enough, and have the strength of focus to plan for your future."

"We fae are a resilient species because we don't dwell on the past or future the way you humans do. We experience the moment for all that it is. Of course, we can also strategize and plan for the future, and we can also look back with regret. We are distractible, but not stupid."

"You may not dwell on the past, but you aren't oblivious to it. I look back at choices my people have made and am so ashamed. This situation is intolerable!"

Cordelia's voice rose. "But what's the alternative? If your magick weren't drained to a barely functional level, would you really go back to your pre-war life of parties and games? There's no going back. And how do we move forward?"

Titania turned to look at Cordelia. Slowly her appearance misted into a much taller woman, with long, bleached white hair, and purple, wide-set eyes. She wore a pale green dress bordered in purple and her feet were bare. Instead of a metal crown, a wreath woven of heather encircled her forehead before trailing down into the field so that Titania appeared anchored to the moor by a wide train of grass.

"I'm appearing to you now in almost my natural form," Titania said, her voice strained. "I hope you appreciate the effort it takes for me to expose myself like this to you." Instead of the impassive expression Titania had been wearing, her face was lined with evidence of the stress she was under.

"Your Majesty, please don't exert yourself like this for me." Cordelia was genuinely surprised.

"I do it to demonstrate my sincerity when I tell you: we are dying. More than two hundred and fifty thousand fae were confined here when we lost the war. Before the mages salted the earth with iron, two hundred thousand of us remained. Now we are fewer than fifty thousand. It used to be that one would fade away each week; now three or more fade in a day." Titania's voice cracked.

"The day before you arrived, Angus mac Og died. His perpetual smiling youth and beauty are gone from the Earth. His grace, his joy and delight are gone. How many more of us will succumb without Angus here to remind us of how wonderful the world can be? Cordelia," Titania closed her eyes, then opened them as she took a deep breath. "I am begging you to help us. I can't swear that there will be no consequences; I can't guarantee that the fae will forget and move forward. But we can't go on like this."

A tear dripped down Titania's face and she looked at her hand, whispering, "I see myself fading. My Oberon died centuries ago and now my last joy has faded with Angus. What is left for me?"

Cordelia looked into Titania's eyes and saw suffering. Maybe it was a manipulation, but the empathic pain Cordelia felt looking at her was true enough. Watching Titania standing naked of illusion before her, dripping tears that formed pearls as they rolled off her cheeks, caused an agony of indecision for Cordelia.

Now that she was finally here, she wished she hadn't come. For years, she had been so stupidly naïve, thinking she could persuade the High Court. Cordelia had sworn to act as Atlantea's hands, but Atlantea refused to give orders. *Atlantea should be here, not me,* Cordelia thought desperately. There was no way the queen could refuse to act if she were here to witness the Aos Sí's suffering herself, instead of learning of it through filtered reports from Vincent and the other courtiers.

While Cordelia's mind swirled with the possibility of disaster, the aphorisms her mother sprinkled throughout her childhood roared back: "It isn't what you do that will haunt you, it's what you don't do;" "Ninety-nine percent of life is just showing up;" "Don't make the perfect the enemy of the good;" "Blessed are the merciful, for they will be shown mercy." She silenced the whirlpool of thoughts and firmly decided not to care if she were being deceived or what the future might hold. The High Court would not act. Zale couldn't make a decision, and Atlantea refused to. There was no one else, and she would not be a bystander anymore.

She took Titania's hands. "*I* will help you." But Titania continued to cry. It was as if once she started, she was unable to stop. Cordelia awkwardly pulled the queen into her arms, embracing her. They stood in the sunlight for several long moments while Titania wept and Cordelia whispered that she would help. And the more they stood there, the more certain Cordelia began to feel. Relieved that she had made her decision, Cordelia reached under the veil of heather to stroke Titania's corn-silk hair.

Slowly Titania's sobs subsided. Perhaps it was a new spirit of hope that lifted some of the oppressive weight from the air, because the wind began to whistle through the heather again, sending it into purple waves as she stepped back and Cordelia let go. Titania's form misted, as if she were again donning her armor. In a moment, Titania's impassive face looked out above her sensible plaid jacket and jeans. Only the trailing heather crown and the gleaming pearls scattered on the crushed field evidenced the moment that had come and gone.

"You can't stay here," Cordelia said.

"We will go back to the forest," Titania replied.

"No, I mean the fae can't stay in England. I can't remove the iron from the ground. And even if I could, we couldn't risk the kind of disturbance that would provoke."

"This ground is killing us," Titania said.

"I know it is." Cordelia bit her lip softly, thinking. "You said there are fifty thousand fae here, right? Are they as healthy as you appear to be?"

"Yes. Most are still fit — until they suddenly aren't."

"But it's the iron that is making you fade?" Cordelia asked.

"That and the despair," Titania replied.

"But most of you can walk?" Cordelia had an idea. When she had originally developed her relocation solution, she had envisioned taking the fae to Africa by boat. The problem with the fae was that their very existence depended on their connection to the Earth. They couldn't survive in an airplane hundreds of miles above, even if a plane weren't composed of poisonous steel.

But the ocean floor was the Earth.

"There are some who are too iron-ill to walk," Titania replied, "but most of us can, yes."

"One of the legends of the Third Mage War holds that Morgan le Fay's army donned seven league boots to cross the Taiga to defeat the Nga's mages at Tallinn. That you covered seven leagues in each step across the boreal forests of Russia and arrived in the nick of time." Cordelia wasn't sure bringing up a memory of the war was the best idea, but if true, the boots would make her nascent plan feasible.

Titania looked sharply at Cordelia. "Parts of the legend are true. Parts are not. History is written by the victors, after all."

"I can't change the landscape of England, and I can't keep an exodus of fifty thousand a complete secret, but if you truly have enough boots or their like for all, I think perhaps I can take you beneath the sea to Africa," Cordelia said quickly.

Titania stared at her for a moment. Then she sighed and extended her arm to Cordelia. "If you are willing to trust me, I shall have to trust you also," Titania said as Cordelia took her arm.

Cordelia reminded herself that with the fae, there was no gratitude and no love, only bargains and obsession. They walked in silence back down the moor as the heather was flattened in broad strokes under the increasing wind. Eventually they arrived in the old-growth forest, where they had met several days before. Instead of the forbidding darkness of that morning, the dim light of the overcast day filtered through the heavy canopy to surround them in a dull twilight.

The heather crown that encircled Titania's head changed into crown of leaves with white flowers and blackish-red berries, which floated up from the forest floor into the trees that formed a circle around them. Cordelia realized that she was standing with Titania in a faerie circle, and her heart skipped a beat. If the Aos Sí queen had played her false, she was done for: not even a siren could survive a casting within a faerie circle formed by ancient trees.

Titania sat onto a high-backed chair of light wood with scalloped edges that rose from the ground to catch her. "Please sit," Titania invited, gesturing to a chair that was similarly rising from the ground. Cordelia sat, and for a moment, they listened to the bird calls. The forest still felt oppressive to her, but not as ominous as it had before. When Cordelia looked back at Titania, she was pouring tea into a delicate cup painted with tiny violet flowers. A small round table, decked with a bright white tablecloth and carrying an old-fashioned tea set, had appeared between them. A tiered serving tray held tiny sandwiches and scones.

"Cream and sugar?" Titania asked.

"Cream, please," Cordelia responded.

This was the first display of the fae's famed magical hospitality that Cordelia had been offered since her arrival. There had been a dinner in Helmsley Castle, but that had felt more like a dinner party at Atlantis House than a fae feast. Cordelia suppressed the urge to giggle. She wasn't sure whether her giddiness arose out of nervous tension or the absurdity of having high tea in the middle of the woods. Perhaps Titania had conjured tea as some kind of binding to seal their compact. Or maybe because she sensed that Cordelia needed something to settle her nerves. Or perhaps Titania had simply wanted tea.

Cordelia resolved not to speak first. When in doubt with the fae, it was better to say nothing. She sipped her tea and attempted to appear nonchalant as she peered into the dim light of the forest, wondering how many fae were concealed within the shadows. So it was Titania who eventually broke the silence.

"There are many legends and myths around the mage wars. I have been alive for two of them now, but there are some of us who fought in all four of them. They have stories that seem fantastical even to me."

Titania put her cup down. "I was no one special during the Atlantic War, Cordelia. I was never the battle leader that the Morrigan was or that Ares is today.

Not many of the fae are really warriors. We are barely adequate soldiers at best. So, while we have been participants in all the mage wars, we have been perhaps a sideshow to the human battles. Sometimes scapegoats."

"I don't know why you are telling me this," Cordelia said, hoping she wouldn't offend Titania, who had been rumored to be extremely proud. So far, Titania had not appeared extraordinarily proud or arrogant, and that made her wonder whether the image Titania was presenting was another illusion or her true self.

"As background perhaps. You asked about artifacts from the war. Enchantments that I had hoped would have faded from mortal memory by now."

"Why would you want the memories to fade?" Cordelia asked.

"Humans take. Fae take. Everyone covets what they do not have, and takes with violence or seduction when it isn't given freely. You sirens are more like the fae; you take by compulsion and the illusion of love and lust. Weres are like humans, taking with violence and aggression. I have lived so long and seen so much. When I see the tree of war in full bloom, I know the roots lie in theft. Do your histories discuss how the war started?" Titania poured herself another cup, adding several spoonsful of sugar before stirring silently.

Cordelia knew she meant the Third Mage War. "I learned that it started in an argument around a chalice, but even our accounts differ as to who owned what and who took what from whom."

"*I* made the chalice as a gift for my changeling daughter so that I would not have to bury another child. A gift to make her fully fae, without sacrificing her inherited humanity. Nga called it my greatest design, dreaming of a changeling army at his back, with human immunity to iron and all the powers of the fae. *He* demanded it as 'rent' owed on lands held by the Aos Sí for millennia.

"Regret is futile, but how I wish I had never made it or given it to her. I know you sirens suffer when your children die, and perhaps our physical pain is less, but how I *suffered* when she died." Titania's voice was raw and broken. The light in the forest dimmed further into a gloom more reminiscent of true twilight than the filtered sunlight of midday.

"I'm sorry," Cordelia knew the words were too little and stupidly banal in the face of Titania's remembered pain, but she didn't know what else to say.

"She lived a remarkable life. But it's a true saying: beware the gifts of the fae. She would have led a greater life without that gift. Certainly, a longer, if less remarkable one. But I gave it to her in good faith, and she drank from it and transformed from Morgan le Malle to Morgan le Fay. Done."

Cordelia wasn't certain why Titania was telling her this either. She had the impression that Titania was perhaps talking to herself, and Cordelia was only an excuse for her saying what she needed to say. Titania's face remained impassive, but her voice was husky and harsh. "And so started the coveting and the taking and the war. So perhaps you'll understand if I'm not so eager to talk about seven league boots."

"I only ask about the boots because we need to get you off this poisoned ground," Cordelia said reasonably, hoping Titania's mood would shift back to the present, instead of the pain of the past.

"And how do you plan to get us past the mages left behind to watch our passing? Or your fellow sirens who are here, barely keeping us alive? What do enchanted boots matter if we can't leave the moors themselves?"

"There are few mages left in England since the Cabal's exodus. If you're powerful enough to manage the illusions you've cast so far, you're strong enough to cast a veil to conceal your exit."

"And what of the sirens?"

"The sirens are triaging the fading fae. They won't doubt that I have authority to speak for Atlantis on the relocation. By the time they contact Vincent, we'll be gone. Some will probably even volunteer to help."

Since the fae maintained the park as a kind of faerie mound, impervious to satellites and radio waves, phones didn't work, and contact with the outside world was highly restricted. But even so, Cordelia thought that if she asked the siren support staff to delay their return to Atlantis to give her more time to navigate the politics, they would.

Before heading deeper into the preserve to meet with Titania, she had first met with the large contingent of sirens stationed here. They had explained how the support staff turnover rate had increased dramatically in the past decade, something Vincent had neglected to inform the High Court about. Except for a handful of utterly-devoted fanatics, most of the sirens had been in Yorkshire for less than a year, and were counting the days before their replacement. Some were terrified of their charges, some horrified by the decline in health they had witnessed. Some had cried when they recounted witnessing an actual fading. A few seemed resolute or indifferent, but they were the minority. Most seemed deeply relieved that Atlantea had supposedly sent Cordelia to investigate. They were waiting for direction, waiting for their time to be up. They would not question her, and she thought they would do what they could to help.

"And how will you explain your part in this once we're safely away?"

Cordelia hesitated. "I don't know. I think if I just disappear for a while and let things settle down, I can decide next steps. My guess is that most of Atlantis will feel relief that this has finally been resolved. Atlantea will claim this as a sanctioned step, or she'll denounce it as a rogue act. Either way, she may decide I'm a liability and take action." Actually, talking through the potential risk was a relief. Sometimes you needed to put your fears into words to puncture the inchoate terror.

"When Morgan le Fay brought us to England, she parted the sea like Moses and we crossed the channel on the bone-dry sea floor. But she was a mage, and we were a lot stronger then."

"There were also a lot more of you and she wasn't trying to be discreet." Cordelia was amused. The Atlantic loved her for sure, but Cordelia was no mage to carve a channel like that. She wasn't even certain the Atlantic loved her enough for *this* request.

"You think you can do this? Regardless of what you've heard, we can't breathe underwater. We are immortal, but not unkillable." A breath of humor infused Titania's tone as well. Perhaps like Cordelia, she was giddy at the thought of attempting this.

"I don't think I could keep you, let alone fifty thousand fae, from drowning if we had to walk at a normal pace beneath the ocean. But if you do have the ability to cross seven leagues in a step, then I think maybe it is possible. Maybe then the ocean will love me enough to let me take you safely beneath the water."

Titania looked at Cordelia for a long moment, then drained her tea and set the cup down on the table. "Linden," Titania said, and one of the trees that formed the faerie circle dissolved into a short man with dark curly hair and a dark complexion.

"My queen?" He asked, inclining his head.

"Ready the people. Our Moses has arrived to bring us to the promised land."

Linden misted into a huge raven and flew off, cawing loudly. Cordelia still wasn't sure what to make of Titania's dramatic statement, when she suddenly felt as if she had been struck. Every nerve in her body was suddenly on fire; her senses darkened. She couldn't hear, see, smell or taste. But as suddenly as the moment came, the moment lifted. Cordelia felt as if all the air had been knocked out of her lungs, and struggled to inhale. She was utterly exhausted; all her energy went into trying to breathe.

As she drew in a shaky breath, she also felt amazingly light, but not dizzy. Had she not been gripping her chair with a cramping hand, she felt as if she might have floated away. Cordelia wondered if this were some kind of fae spell to seal her promise.

"Are you all right?" Titania asked, clearly concerned.

But Cordelia still felt as if she couldn't draw in a breath. Titania raised her hand and a brilliant glass chandelier appeared in the air above them, illuminating the clearing in a blue-white light.

Titania stepped over in front of Cordelia, who was still trying to catch her breath. Her jaw dropped, and she turned Cordelia's head to one side and stroked the air in front of Cordelia's neck and chest.

"Morgan's geas is gone," Titania said. "I don't know how, but I can just make out the remnants of the broken spell."

She waved her hand as if flicking away a cobweb, "But it's dissipating as I speak. Soon, you won't even know it was there. Amazing. I wonder how it was done. All that magick, now released. Where will it go?" Titania's voice trailed off.

But Cordelia's silence must have worried her, because Titania quickly continued, "This is a good thing, I think. Cordelia, I swear no faerie did this. I'd be amazed if Num himself could even crack it. I'd like to meet the mage with the skill to break Morgan's death binding."

Cordelia was starting to feel more centered, though she still felt unbearably light. She cautiously let go of the chair, wondering if she would float to the sky or if Titania would catch her before she went too far. But Cordelia's feet remained on the ground and her sense of being lighter than air faded into a mild euphoria. She opened her mouth, but swallowed before she could speak.

"I feel so ... different," Cordelia said finally, and her voice rang out with a resonance that caused the tea cups to rattle on their saucers. She tried again, more softly. "I *am* different. You say the curse has been lifted? Morgan le Fay's blood-geas?"

"I think so," Titania said. "I could feel it before, a light webbing of sound echoing around you. But it's gone now."

Cordelia laughed. She was overcome with the conviction that she had done the right thing. She didn't know how or why the curse had been lifted, but felt certain the timing was no accident. She felt almost drunk on the sense of euphoria, and she called out in her new voice that hummed with the ocean's vitality: "Titania, First and Last Queen of the Aos Sí, I will bring your people out. This I swear by the grace of God and all the power of the sea. I will bring you out!"

There is no known counter-spell to the siren spell; thus the spell cannot be 'deactivated' once active. Indeed, despite substantial study, counter-mages have not been able to develop a counter-spell for any of the construct spells. Notably, during the early part of the nineteenth century, Chinese mages devoted enormous resources to developing a counter for Chia's were-spell in their effort to restore his vampire victims. They were ultimately unsuccessful, and the current consensus among counter-mages is that all construct spells are invulnerable to counter-spelling. While some experts believe that construct spells might be removed through "breaking" magick, such techniques were lost around the time the Gobi Desert was destroyed.

– Sirens: An Overview for the Newly-Transitioned, 3rd ed. (2015), *by Mira Bant de Atlantic, p. 137.*

Chapter 30

"Are you all right?" Mira asked Amy, her ears ringing. She felt wrecked, forcing the words out while struggling to draw in sufficient air to speak.

"I'm not sure," Amy replied after a long moment. All the air had been knocked out of her. "That was ... intense. Are *you* all right?" Amy looked down at Mira, who was still on the ground.

Now that Mira had caught her breath, she felt nothing but relief — like taking off your high heels at the end of a long day. The ringing became more distant, almost as if there were a brass band playing across town. "My butt feels a little bruised, but otherwise, I actually feel better than I did before." Mira's sudden sense of exhilaration caught her by surprise, and she slowly sat up. She had been standing next to the table, and was glad she hadn't picked up Amy's cup before she'd been struck down.

"I'm relieved that you felt it, too. For a moment, I thought something had gone terribly wrong with the surgery," Amy admitted. "I felt like someone had stomped on my chest and tried to rip it open. Then it was gone."

"Maybe I should turn on the news. Something could be going on. I saw this *Dateline* report once where soldiers set off a sonic bomb. It flattened the camp, and that's how it felt," Mira said.

Mira fumbled with the remote. Eventually she handed it to Amy, who turned on the TV. It was almost 9:30, and most of the morning shows were national programs, with no breaking stories. Amy found one with a local news segment, but nothing was reported. They watched intently, flipping through the channels. The sense of lightness was distracting. After almost an hour, they had seen nothing to explain what they experienced. Mira stood up and started looking for her cell phone. "I need to call Devin," she said belatedly.

Amy looked at her quizzically, but simply went to get her laptop from the bedroom. Perhaps there would be something mentioned online.

"Devin," Mira said when he picked up. "Did you feel something odd a little while ago?"

"No. What's going on?" he replied.

"I don't know, but both Amy and I were flattened by — something. It was only for a minute, but it was extreme. There's nothing being reported on TV."

"Are you all right?" Devin asked.

"We're fine now."

"Better than fine," Amy called out, as she walked back with her computer open. She was clearly listening to the conversation.

"We both feel better than we did," Mira clarified.

"I didn't feel anything," Devin said, his voice tense.

"We're trying to look into it."

"Don't leave the apartment until I get there." Devin hung up before Mira could respond.

"There's nothing on the Internet," Amy reported as she hit the refresh button again.

"I don't get it," Mira finally said. "We both felt something. I still feel different."

"But it's a good different, right?" Amy asked, and Mira nodded her agreement. "I know what I would tell a patient who came in telling me he suddenly felt a lot better than he used to and wanted to get it checked out," Amy snorted. "But given that both of us felt similar things at the same time, I don't think this can be explained by a regular diagnosis."

Mira looked anxious. "I remember reading about a Russian assassin using poison gas to kill a British guy and his daughter."

The doorbell rang, and Mira went to the door. "Yes?"

"It's me, Devin."

Mira opened the door; Devin strode purposefully into the apartment, sweeping his gaze over every inch of the room.

"Amy, this is Devin. He's my—"

"Bodyguard. Thomas wanted to make sure nothing happened to you after the attack on his home. He didn't want to worry you before, but given the fact that unknown perpetrators assaulted him this severely, he wanted to make sure you had protection as well."

Mira was a bit astonished by Devin's explanation. It was so reasonable, she wished they had come up with it before.

Amy stared at Devin. It looked like he was wearing a priest's cassock until she blinked and the entire garment shifted, its black color dissolving into a golden glow. She squinted, and it appeared as though he were wearing a robe made of gold mesh, with tiny red pinpricks of light weaving through it. As he turned, the red lights seemed to swim through the fabric in sinuous, synchronized strokes.

Devin stalked around the room, stopping to look more closely at the HVAC unit under the window. Amy shifted her focus back to the problem at hand with some difficulty. "Do you think this could be some kind of attack on me because of Thomas?" Amy asked.

"I don't know. What happened?" Devin asked.

"We both had the wind knocked out of us. I literally fell flat on the floor. And then, in a moment, it was gone. I feel amazing, now."

"Like when you go to the hair salon, and chop six inches off your hair. Your head suddenly feels too light for your body," Amy added.

"Yes. Like I'm suddenly ten pounds lighter," Mira agreed.

"I don't think this is the same as that poison gas attack," Amy said, responding to Mira's earlier suggestion. "But it could be some form of neurotoxin that's inducing euphoria."

"We need to get you out of here," Devin said swiftly. "Do you have those robes I gave you?" he asked Mira. Mira hurried to her bedroom to get the enchanted cassocks Devin had brought for them both.

"I'm not sure this is a gas, though. It doesn't have the same—" Amy's cellphone on the table buzzed and she answered it reflexively. "Hello?"

"Amy, it's Thomas."

"Hey, Thomas, it's actually not a great time—" Amy began.

"I know what happened to you. I just hung up with Mary. Um, are you sitting down?"

Amy's phone started buzzing with a second call from Mary. She sent it to voicemail. "Yes. What's going on?"

"Amy, a friend of mine was just able to lift a — a curse that was on our family line for generations. I know this sounds crazy, but it's true. Our ancestors were put under a blood-geas at the end of the Third Mage War, and until now, it bound all of us."

Thomas spoke rapidly, and Amy, disconcerted by Devin's looming presence right behind her, wasn't sure she understood. Amy turned to look at Devin, while she repeated back Thomas' explanation in an effort to make sense of it. "You're saying that a mage you know just removed some spell that's been on me and you and anyone related to whichever of our ancestors fought in the Third Mage War."

"More or less. Yes."

Devin's mouth gaped open in surprise.

"So, the reason I now feel so much lighter is because a restriction that's been on me my entire life, but which I somehow wasn't aware of, has been removed." Amy had always been good in a crisis, but it was Thomas' obvious understanding of what had happened that enabled her to focus so keenly on the essential facts.

"Yes. At least, I feel almost drunk," Thomas replied. "That one moment was pretty rough — but I don't think there will be any other effects."

"How do you know?" Amy asked.

"I trust her," Thomas said, taken aback by the challenge in Amy's voice. "Anyway, you can see magick now, right? Look at yourself in the mirror and see if you notice anything different. My mage friend said she could see the binding before, but I couldn't. Maybe you'll see a change. There are other people I had better call. I've got to go."

Amy started walking towards her bedroom, where she had a full-length mirror on the back of her closet door. "But Thomas, Kiera had the same reaction I did. Does that mean she's related to us? Did you know that before you sent her?"

"Amy, there's a lot you don't know — mainly because of the geas. I'm not really sure how to explain it. I tried to tell Mary, but honestly, it didn't go very well."

"Why didn't it go well with Mary?" Amy asked. Perhaps she should have picked up Mary's call and asked her to hold on.

"I'm not sure Mary believed me," Thomas admitted. "Listen, there are a lot of people I have to call, and I don't know everyone's number by heart. I couldn't even reach Mo — hey, actually, is Kiera still there? Can you put her on the line for a second?"

Amy turned back to Devin. "Can you hand this to Kiera? Thomas wants to talk to her." She wanted to look at herself in the mirror to see if she noticed a difference.

Devin took the phone as Amy opened her bedroom door, pulling it partially shut behind her. She turned on the overheads along with the closet light so she could see better. Her mundane sight was still somewhat blurry when it was too bright, but given that she wanted to see through mage sight, more light would probably help. Amy really wished Ted or another mage were around to help her interpret what she was seeing. Now that their initial bout of scans and tests were done, finding a mage was the most important next step. At least Elder Simon had begun returning Eli's calls.

She couldn't see much of a difference in herself from what she remembered before. Since the surgery, she had learned that auras were real — or at least everyone seemed to have a glow around them, an odd kind of shifting mirage that looked like colored steam, or perhaps more like multi-colored heat waves rising off hot pavement.

Some people's auras (at least, that's what she decided to term the ambient glow) looked like a kaleidoscope turning, with colors and patterns writhing in a seamless flow, while others stayed fairly consistent in their pattern and only changed color. Hers had been a pale pink with streaks of green that reminded her of a cathedral in Florence she had visited once. She had thought her aura's pattern looked a little like the headband she wore every day when she struggled to fit in at St. Paul's and started using the *Preppy Handbook* as a guide.

Now, her aura was no longer plaid or striped. The shades of green and pink were undulating in waves of color that alternated in an almost hypnotic flow. Perhaps this new, relaxed pattern was why she felt so free. Amy stared at herself in her mirror for a moment. Was this an acid trip gone wrong? Maybe all she had accomplished with her surgery was to recreate the same psychedelic visions researchers had caused with their LSD experiments in the 1970s.

"Amy?" Devin's knock startled her; she wasn't used to hearing a man's voice in her apartment, especially one so deep and gravelly.

"Coming," Amy replied, hurrying out of the bedroom. Devin held out her cellphone. "It's Thomas, still."

Amy took the phone. "What has Mary so upset?"

"Let me try to explain this better. I couldn't tell you or Mary this before because of the curse. Please don't hang up on me."

Amy was impatient with Thomas' warning. Of course, she wasn't going to hang up; she wanted answers and didn't share Mary's inability to handle conflict.

"Cordelia and I are something called sirens. You probably never have heard the word — I know I almost flunked World Lit because I couldn't actually understand the essay question on the *Odyssey*. But sirens do still exist, and it's a weird process to become one. But we are."

"You're what? A siren? What is that?"

"Sirens are mage constructs like the weres. Except created by Aphrodite, not Chía. We've got some magical powers. We're part fae, like Mike, but our ancestry is from the sea nymphs so it's different—"

Amy interrupted. "Okay, so what does that have to do with the geas that just broke? You were what, bound to secrecy?" Amy didn't understand exactly why this kind of revelation would be so upsetting or shocking to Mary. Thomas and Cordelia had always been a little more free-spirited than she and Mary were, so the fact that they had biological differences as well wasn't too much of a stretch. It wasn't like Thomas was telling Mary *she* was a mage construct.

"Yeah, kind of. Listen, it's a shock to be having this conversation. I mean, I've tried before. But I just couldn't. I physically couldn't get the words out. Couldn't explain anything to anyone who was descended from a siren. And its effect on you meant that you couldn't actually hear or understand any discussion of sirens."

Thomas' voice had a new resonance that came through despite the static on the sea-to-land long-distance call. It was causing Amy to see flashes of color as his voice echoed through the line. She had to close her eyes. Devin took her arm just as her legs started to wobble, and he helped her to the couch.

Amy tried to focus on Thomas. She put him on speakerphone so Devin could hear in case she missed something. "All right. So, I understand that you've been hiding this fact — through no fault of your own. But why is Mary having difficulty? Did this change hit her harder?"

Amy wanted to call Mary, but figured it would be best to know what she was getting into. Mary could get so set in her views that it was hard to talk her around. So far, this was odd, but it didn't seem odd enough to have Mary angry.

"I don't quite know how to say it. I said it all wrong with Mary."

"Thomas, just spit it out." Amy's head had begun to ache a little listening to him, but she needed to get more information.

"Mom's alive."

"Thomas, you aren't making sense. No wonder Mary's annoyed with you." Amy felt her heart start to pound. This was an off-limit kind of discussion. They didn't talk about Mom and Dad, except when alcohol was involved. There were charlatans out there — or maybe real mages, though the enclaves swore it couldn't be done — who promised to hold séances and contact your loved ones from beyond the grave. Mary had insisted on trying it, but Mike had met the various mediums and said they were lying.

"Mom isn't dead."

Amy didn't say anything. She couldn't. It was fairly unbelievable, like the dreams where your deepest wish was somehow fulfilled, but then you woke up with tears leaking into your pillow because it was just a dream. "Thomas, stop messing with me. This isn't fair." Amy could feel the pounding in her chest like a hammer and was glad she was sitting down.

"I'm not messing with you. Mom's alive, and not in the guardian angel sense. I mean, she never died, she just … changed." Thomas must have realized how weak he sounded, because he started talking fast again.

"Amy, I transitioned into a siren just before I dropped out of college. I mean, that's why I dropped out. Because of all the changes. But the main thing is that when I became a siren, it really affected Mom. I mean, changed her. She was, like, out of control. Or really, overpowered is maybe the better word for it. Oh my God, it's too much to try to explain all of this. There's a book I could send you—"

"Mom's alive? Is she in some kind of trouble?"

"No, nothing like that. It's just that when the boys were born and I changed, her power increased exponentially. She couldn't handle the changes, couldn't maintain her appearance anymore. And then we had to find the children and we couldn't tell you anything about any of it because of the Goddamn geas. You wouldn't have recognized her, believed she was Mom—"

"What are you saying? That Mom's been around all this time and I just didn't know it?" Amy knew she sounded rough. Sharp maybe.

"Yes."

"So, where is she?" Amy demanded.

"Here." Mira walked back into the room.

"Kiera?" Amy looked at Mira.

"Yes," Thomas answered. "I know she doesn't look like Mom, but she is. Amy, I—" Amy hit end on her phone, and looked at Mira. "I don't believe you," Amy said flatly.

"Devin, can you call Thomas back and give him these numbers? It's a list of everyone he needs to call. Could you call Atlantea and Marisol? Maybe use the bespelled phones."

"Fine. But we need to talk more about this; I want to know what else Thomas told you."

"Of course," Mira replied, trying to maintain her outward semblance of calm.

Amy handed Devin her phone, and he went into the kitchen. For a long time, Mira just looked at Amy, her heart pounding. She had never in her wildest dreams imagined a moment like this. Mira now wished now she had chosen a different man to drain, someone whose fantasy might have been closer to the woman she used to be. Not that it would have mattered; she could never reclaim her original self. Mira thought for a moment.

Amy had closed her eyes; this was too stressful. Too much.

Mira rubbed her chin, then spoke softly, her voice just audible over the whir of the air conditioner. "Do you remember back in first grade, when you told me that you'd been the one taking the plastic counting bears from school? I told you that it was all right. The important thing was that you told the truth and that we give them all back. So, you took me into your room, and pulled out this shoebox full of tiny bears that Mrs. Ruane had used to teach counting. There must have been a hundred of those things. You had apparently just slipped one or two into your pocket every day and didn't bring them back. At some point, the teacher noticed that there were a lot missing and sent a note home to all the parents asking us to talk to you kids and look for the bears.

"The next day, I had the janitor let me into the school, and I put the box on her chair with an unsigned note saying that you hadn't meant to bring them home; and then, once you had them, you didn't know what to do with them all. But we had discussed it, and you wouldn't take anything ever again.

"You were so worried that you had been stealing and now you were going to Hell. You were so sweetly earnest. But you cried as if the world had ended, and when I told you everything could be fixed and for-given, you practically leapt into my arms with relief. I guess I hadn't been paying enough attention, and you had been moping around for weeks under the weight of this awful burden."

Tears started to trickle down Amy's face as Mira told the story. This woman didn't look anything like her mother. She was at least thirty years younger than Amy. Short and black, with brown eyes. She sounded nothing like her mother. But *no one* knew that story. Amy had almost forgotten it herself, it had happened so long ago. She felt almost as if she were outside of her body watching the scene unfold. Sometimes a feeling is so strong you don't even know what it is.

Mira was still talking, but Amy wasn't listening. *This is my mother*, she thought. *My mother is here.*

Most permanent geases are either inherited (such as Morgan le Fay's curse) or imposed on the very young (such as enclave bindings). Temporary geases can be laid on children, though are more commonly imposed on apprentice mages (teenagers) and questors (adults). While those bound by temporary geases often report feeling confined by their bindings, those permanently bound generally do not report any discomfort. However, Australian scholars opine that those bound by permanent geases do not recognize their discomfort only because they are unaware of life without bindings, and are therefore better adapted to their yoke.

– Sirens: An Overview for the Newly-Transitioned, 3rd ed. (2015), *by Mira Bant de Atlantic, p. 96.*

Chapter 31

Mary was stuck in Beltway traffic when she felt as if a tornado lifted her out of her seat, cast her two stories into the air, then slammed her back down until suddenly the law of gravity no longer applied. After the breath was knocked out of her, she suddenly felt weightless, as if floating in the eye of the storm. The only thing that saved her from a major accident was the fact that she had just put her car into park to get her phone out of her purse in the backseat.

Once she was able to breathe again, she heard the honking of the cars behind her and pulled over to the side of the road, putting her flashers on. Mary just sat for a moment, wondering if she'd had a heart attack or stroke. But since that sudden storm of pain had passed, she felt drunk. The kind of sloppy, happy, party-drunk where everyone is your best friend and the world melts into an effervescent joyous hum. Mary felt so good, the memory of that excruciating pain seemed remote.

Then Mary's phone began to ring in her purse, which was still in the backseat. It was Thomas, of all people! As she spoke with him, all of the joy she had felt dissolved again into a kind of vague anger. She just sat in her car, feeling empty and rather afraid.

This wasn't the first time her understanding of the world had crumbled. Her father's death when she was eight, then her mother's when she was twenty-three. Now her mother's what — resurrection? Reemergence? She pulled back onto the highway and drove to work in a kind of daze.

"Why didn't you call me?" Mike demanded when Mary had told him what had happened earlier in the day. "Did you talk to Jack and Alicia?" he added, without giving her time to answer.

"And tell them what? That they've been under a spell that was just broken or that their aunt and uncle have been lying to them their entire life?"

"So your mother is still alive, and has apparently been masquerading as different people since 1988 to keep an eye on you?" Mike asked.

"That's about it. Sirens. What a load of crap," Mary said.

Mike was having a hard time understanding how he had failed to detect the amount of lies and deception that had gone into this preposterous charade. "I don't understand how this could be. I mean, I would have sensed it if your family had been lying about this."

"How often though did we talk about any of this? I can't remember Cordy or Thomas really saying something like, 'since Mom passed away,' or anything like that. And no one has really told me what a siren is, anyway." Mary was almost slurring her words at this point.

She had gone into work on autopilot and spent most of the day just staring at her computer screen. Her accompanist actually had to come get her for rehearsal, when normally she got set up in the hall well before he did. Mary knew that they had rehearsed one of the new pieces, but for the life of her, she couldn't remember which one it had been.

And then she had driven home in a fog. When she got there, she walked straight to the liquor cabinet, and decided to drink until Mike got home. It was as if she couldn't think properly without him to bring her back to Earth. She still felt as if she were lighter than air.

"I never liked Thomas," Mike said, pouring himself a second drink. When he walked in and saw Mary, drink in hand, he knew something must be wrong. But this was far stranger than he could have ever expected.

"I know. But you loooove Cordelia," Mary said, flopping back on the sofa.

"Have you spoken to Amy?" Mike asked.

"I called her and it went into voicemail. Then she called me back and I didn't want to talk anymore." Mary felt her lip curl into a pout. It was nice to be this drunk, she thought. She never drank. Well, not much, anyway.

"I'm going to call the kids, then let's talk."

Mary half-listened to Mike talking with Jack and Alicia. She really should have thought to call them. She had almost gotten into a car accident, after all. They could have been hurt. But she could hear Mike talking to them, and knew they were okay. She didn't really feel worried; one of the benefits of heavy drinking, she supposed.

Mike came back to the couch.

"Thomas called them," he said. "Alicia was studying for a test and thought it was a migraine, so she was a little surprised to hear a few hours later that she was actually a 'latent' form of a mage construct. Thomas promised to send her a book about it. Jack was in a car on his way back from a client meeting when it happened, and his reaction freaked the driver out. He was at the ER waiting to get checked out when he got Thomas' call. What is this book Thomas is talking about, anyway?"

"Thomas said something about that to me, too. Mom was always writing when we were kids. She said she had a job writing appliance manuals. Ha. I guess that's what we are, a kind of appliance. Look at me; I'm a vacuum cleaner, Mike!"

Mike ignored Mary's off-balanced portrayal and started to pace. "So, let me talk this through. Sirens are constructs and have been around since the age of Aphrodite. They were cursed during the Atlantic War with some geas that prevented them from telling their children about sirens and their children from understanding anyone who told them about sirens. Okay so far?"

"You betcha," Mary closed her eyes, but felt like she was spinning, instead of that nice floaty feeling she'd had since the morning. She quickly opened them again. Perhaps she'd drunk too much on an empty stomach.

"Your mother is a siren, but she hadn't always been a siren. Something about Cordelia's birth 'activated' her and your father."

"Presto!" Mary announced, "Sirens."

"Right. So sirens have some weird effect on humans, where the opposite sex loves them and the same sex hates them. That's how your dad died. Because he didn't know he'd been changed or whatever and the men who beat him to death were somehow compelled to do it because he was a male siren."

"Yup. Like phero... phero..." Mary couldn't get the word out.

"Pheromones," Mike finished for her, and Mary tried touching her nose, but missed and nodded instead. "And your mother and Cordelia would have the same effect on you, except you and Amy have been on the pill since puberty, which counteracted the effect."

Mary nodded again.

"But then, your brother turns into a siren — not sure how that happened," Mike looked at Mary, who shrugged.

"And after he changes, your mother's appearance starts changing frequently. So, because she can't explain herself to you, she fakes her death at sea. And since then, she's shown up from time to time to watch over you from afar."

"That's what Thomas said." Mary swallowed more of her drink, knowing even as she did it that she had taken one sip too much. She bolted to the bathroom and threw up.

When she staggered back into the room some time later, Mike was on his laptop. He pointed to a glass of water and Mary sat down and started drinking it slowly. "So, there are a lot of myths or legends about sirens that I found online. Some of the articles detail what you describe, others are a bit different. All of them describe sirens as having incredible power in their voices. Power to compel members of the opposite sex into doing things.

"Some talk about siren power over fertility — describing an ability to take fertility from one person and somehow bestow it on another. Some others talk about sirens as having the ability to change into fish, or half fish, like mermaids or mermen. And others talk about the sirens as a kind of gift to the fae to help protect them from iron poisoning. There's a lot out there, but none of it from any reputable source. I don't know what's real or not. I can't discern truth from lies without the person in front of me. Some of these sites talk about sirens as having a shape-shifting capability, but they are kind of sparse on the details."

Mike turned away from the computer and looked at her. "They never recovered your mother's body. I've tried to think about all the different interactions I've had with Cordelia and Thomas. I can't say they've been lying to me and I just didn't notice. But maybe. When you lie to me, it doesn't feel the same way as when other people lie. Maybe that's a siren thing."

Mike looked troubled. "Should we go to Boston?"

Mary finished her water. She was wrung out, and the room was still spinning. "I think I need to go to bed," she said.

*Sirens are sometimes called "children of Aphrodite,"
because Aphrodite used her own genes as a key
element of the siren spell. This almost poetic term
is most commonly used in admonitions to remind
sirens of their primary purpose of fae preservation.
However, it also speaks to the fact that all sirens
are descended from one of the greatest mages who
ever lived. While a siren's magical powers are far
narrower in scope than those of a typical mage,
they are nevertheless formidable.*

– Sirens: An Overview for the Newly-Transitioned,
3rd ed. (2015), *by Mira Bant de Atlantic, p. 13.*

Chapter 32

Mira started a full pot of coffee, then sat down at the kitchen table to finish watching the sun rise over the harbor. They had talked late into the night. Devin was sleeping on the sofa in the living room now, but Mira felt wired. She didn't know whether the unholy optimism coursing through her stemmed from the geas being lifted, but she was almost giddy in her joy. She had her family back. Mary was taking it hard, but that was only to be expected. She would come around. Mary had never been comfortable with change or uncertainty, and hid her anxiety in a flurry of anger. She just needed a little time. Mike would help her. He was a good man.

And Amy was already coming around, though it seemed like she had suddenly switched off her emotions when she started peppering Mira with questions. Amy had been almost like a robot. Jack used to do that, too: separate himself from a conflict to lay out the issues logically. There were times she thought him cold and unfeeling, but mostly she had been grateful for his calm under pressure. He was always reliable in any sort of crisis, and Amy seemed to take after him.

Last night, while Amy flexed her researcher muscles, Mira tried to tamp down her bubbling joy to respond in kind. Amy wasn't ready for a hug, or any emotional contact; she wanted answers. So Mira had slipped into her earnest professor persona to try to accommodate.

Amy had quizzed Devin as well, watching as he sweated trying to even say the word "siren." The geas still held him tight, and Amy seemed fascinated by its effect. She remarked that she could see something constricting or twisting around Devin as he tried to answer her questions or talk about sirens in her presence. Mira finally had to tell Amy to stop; it was like watching torture. Amy's inquisition was probably why Devin hadn't woken up yet, despite being a light sleeper. Mira knew how exhausting fighting the geas could be.

Atlantea had definitely felt the breaking, and Devin's explanation had not helped. She called Mira directly several times — and she rarely contacted Mira at all, except to "request" her attendance in Atlantis. Atlantea hated any form of communication other than face-to-face conversation.

While the breaking of the geas caused Amy to become almost single-mindedly focused, it had pushed Atlantea into a maelstrom of contradiction. Atlantea was simultaneously terrified that the mage Thomas harbored could break such a powerful spell, while seeming to rejoice at the same sensation of lightness they now all felt. In their final discussion, Atlantea had raged that Thomas had brought his mage "paramour" to Atlantis, only to whisk her away after performing the impossible.

"If you want the mage back, have the Atlantic bring her back," Mira finally said in exasperation. "They left by boat, right?"

"Yes, but they boarded a plane on Ascension Island, and I don't know where they are now," Atlantea complained.

Mira wasn't sure whether Atlantea truly wanted them back. It was far easier for her to rage now that they were gone, than to have acted to keep them close while they were still within her reach. "You waited too long to pull them back," Mira said sharply. Perhaps not the wisest thing to say when Atlantea was this emotional. Today would not be a good day for anyone to venture out in the water.

Devin didn't hide his shock at Mira's tart tone. Maybe she was being overly familiar with Atlantea. But there was something about feeling so utterly lightened that made her want to be as reckless as Thomas. And maybe her bluntness had helped Atlantea achieve some semblance of calm, because they had ended the call on a more familiar note: with Atlantea cautioning Mira to remember the reason she was in Boston. She was not, under any circumstances, to leave Amy's side until she had ascertained the full scope of Amy's enhanced sight, and discovered what the mages wanted with her.

Mira heard Devin stirring on the couch before he sat up, twisting his neck from side to side. The cracking seemed louder than normal in the silence of the morning. Devin padded into the kitchen as the coffee pot beeped. "Coffee's done," Mira said to Devin unnecessarily, but she enjoyed hearing her voice over the soft gurgle of the machine. It seemed somehow richer than before.

Devin poured a cup of coffee for Mira, adding a generous amount of milk and sugar. One benefit of their spending so much time together was that he knew how she took her coffee. But it wasn't the broken geas or the easy familiarity that came from being together for so long that had changed her mind about Devin.

She knew she trusted people too easily and had steeled herself against Devin out of fear that he was another of Louisa's pawns, set to eliminate any risk to Atlantis. But after months of working together, culminated by his willingness to help Amy last night, Mira finally allowed herself to believe that Devin was exactly what he appeared to be: an honorable man. His mission was to keep both her and Amy alive, and she was infinitely grateful for Atlantea's foresight in pairing him with her.

"Who is this mage Thomas is with?" Devin asked, as he poured himself a cup of coffee. The few hours of sleep seemed to have only paused their conversation.

"She's the via-enchanter who was indentured to Gerel, the vampire ruler of Rio. I'm not sure how they got together. Honestly, I didn't think she and Thomas had been in contact since we bargained for languages more than five years ago. But Thomas seemed beside himself with pride that he had been able to extricate her."

"It seems odd that she would go to Thomas, or that Thomas would take her in, from what I know of him."

"Everyone deserves to be a hero sometimes," Mira remarked sharply. Thomas was still a child by siren standards, and it was unfair for anyone to judge him as they would a siren in his prime just because he had sired two active children.

Devin shook his head. "Gerel is a dangerous enemy to have. She was one of the first to survive Chía's working and kept more of her past-self than those who were sacrificed later on."

"The were-jaguar clan found the battle mage who destroyed Thomas' house. Kadu shipped his remains to Gerel directly." Mira said a silent prayer of thanks for the protection of the weres. They could be so utterly charming, she often forgot how dangerous they were. But they had been designed to destroy mages, and vampires had once been mages.

"You're popular with the clan for them to challenge a vampire ruler for you," Devin remarked, raising his eyebrows.

"*Thomas* is popular with them," she corrected. "I'm simply tolerated."

"Perhaps Thomas is taking his mage back to Brazil," Devin speculated.

Amy's bedroom door opened and she walked through the living room into the kitchen, where they were seated. Devin poured Amy a cup of coffee, raising the milk and sugar in a silent question. Amy shook her head, sitting across from Mira at the table.

"I'm not going to call you Mom," Amy announced.

"I wouldn't expect you to," Mira responded briskly, matching Amy's tone and demeanor. "Can you call me Mira?"

"I don't know. Maybe I'll avoid calling you anything, like when I was a teenager and barely spoke to you." A wisp of a sad smile hovered around Amy's lips. Clearly their fraught relationship before Mira's "death" had caused Amy some regret over her natural teenage rebelliousness.

"I think we should show you something," Mira said. She had spent the hour before sunrise considering how to move them into a sense of normalcy, now that the possibility existed to have a true relationship.

"What?" Amy asked.

"I thought that I might show you how my appearance shifts, and then I thought we might take you to see some of the fae. I promised Cordelia I would help a group on a nearby preserve while I was in Boston." After Amy's scientific interrogation of siren nature last night, Mira thought a demonstration might appeal to Amy; she also hoped to bargain with the local fae in a way that could benefit her.

Amy liked the idea of trying out her mage sight to observe a magical working. She was feeling increasingly handicapped by her inability to make sense of what she was now perceiving. Until last night when she watched Devin struggle against the geas, she couldn't discern any logic to her mage sight.

Watching him fight it, Amy could almost find a commonality in how the colors lashed around him. While the patterns and colors continued to change almost randomly, their *movement* had been similar. And when she had concentrated, she could hear the same sound each time he tried to respond to her questions: it was like a dentist's drill grinding against her molars and reverberating in her jaw.

It could only help to observe another kind of magical working — especially one that didn't cause someone the kind of pain Devin experienced last night. But visiting a fae preserve to observe magic would be even more foolhardy than flying to Arabia. "I would like to see a transformation, but I think I'll have to pass on the fae preserve," Amy responded after mulling it over for a moment.

"There are only a few dozen fae in the Blue Hills Preserve. Honestly, it's probably more accurate to call this a werewolf preserve than a fae preserve at this point. Just a small community of forest folk and a leshy couple that Cordelia had been helping. I'm sure she didn't tell you that she made a point of checking in on them when she visited you. I told Cordy that I'd visit when I came back to Boston."

Mira's explanation didn't help Amy understand why she needed to go. "I have nothing against the fae, but I have no particular need or, honestly, any desire to meet them now. You sirens seem to take a lot of risks. I mean, Thomas goes skydiving, you and Cordelia visit the fae... While you all may think nothing of hanging out with them, to me, visiting a fae preserve seems like an unnecessary risk."

Despite herself, Mira was nettled by Amy's sanctimonious tone: she was one to talk about unnecessary risks, after undergoing experimental brain surgery!

Amy reached for her cup, but missed the handle by an inch: she was seeing double again. The morning sun was particularly tricky for her enhanced vision. "Your eyes are bothering you," Mira said, standing up to close the blinds. The sunlight in the kitchen was reduced to a cheery glow instead of the intense brilliance of white countertops and cabinets on this cloudless day.

"You're wise to be cautious around the fae," Devin said. "They see the world differently, and their customs can make interactions more dangerous than most would believe."

"I sense a *but*," Amy said, with a smile of relief. Dimming the room had helped, and now she was able to re-focus to see only one image.

"But they will owe me and I would ask a favor of the forest folk," Mira said.

"A favor?"

"An exchange of favors, really. The fae view gratitude and obligation as one and the same," Mira replied.
"So, while you share some of our genetic resistance to
fae magick, their stronger, active spells will affect you.
And I know you're healing rapidly, but I wonder if you
would consider speed healing."

Amy was taken aback. "Ask a faerie to cast a spell
on me?"

"The forest folk have a very natural kind of magick," Devin explained. "It's really just a boost to your
own natural healing process. It doesn't do anything
different from what your own body would already do,
given time. But forest folk, and in particular the moss
folk, can heal in a moment something that would take
your body significantly longer on its own. I understand
that nerves take a long time to heal."

"I am not going to walk into a fae preserve and put
myself at their mercy," Amy said in a tone that brooked
no argument. This was beyond ridiculous.

"Amy, it really is safe. You've done this before and
healed beautifully. The faerie healed in moments what
would have taken weeks," Mira said.

"What are you talking about? I've never been magicked," Amy said, worried even as she said it that she
was about to be proven wrong.

"It was our first summer in Ocracoke. You fell off
the swing set at the park and broke your arm. Right at
the beginning of the summer."

"Of course I remember that. But there were no fae
involved in my treatment: Dr. Mervine set my arm. I

remember because that was what first made me want to be a doctor when I grew up."

"Yes, Dr. Mervine was a great doctor. But after you saw him, I decided I didn't want you to spend your first summer in a new town in a cast, unable to swim and play with the rest of the kids. So I exchanged favors with the will 'o the wisps and moss folk of Alligator River. That's why it healed so quickly."

Amy sat in silence and thought back. She clearly remembered Dr. Mervine wrapping her arm in plaster, and the funny star tattoo on his hand that he said he'd gotten while in the navy. He'd distracted her with stories of his buddy who'd had his ex-girlfriend's name tattooed on his arm and another one with a mermaid tattoo that covered his whole back.

Be careful not to make decisions when you're twenty that you'll regret when you're forty, Dr. Mervine had warned. Amy remembered nodding solemnly. He had made an impression on her. But her recollection of getting her cast off was foggy. Too many things were turning out to be different than what she remembered. "I remember walking on a muddy road," Amy said hesitantly.

"Yes. We couldn't drive or bring any metal. So we took the boat — it was fiberglass, of course. And then we had to walk into the marsh."

Amy recalled how hard it had been to walk. She'd been off-balance with her arm in a cast, and had worried she was going to fall into the mud. "There was a lady." Amy tried to remember, but it was hazy. She concentrated on remembering the feel of her shoes being sucked into the mud. At the end of the path, there had been a lady dressed in a cloud. She had gotten totally wet when the lady approached, and had worried because she wasn't supposed to get her cast wet.

Then an image of bulging yellow eyes flashed through Amy's mind, and her heart started to race. That had been her recurring nightmare: Round, yellow eyes, piercing through a fine mist, staring at her without blinking. Amy shuddered as the strength of the image drove away the fog that clouded her memory of that night.

She remembered her awe of the lady, enveloped in mist, with sparkles in her hair as droplets condensed on the dark strands, but didn't drip away. It had been so still, with no wind or rustling of leaves to break the quiet. Then the lady's hand slicing through her cast with a purple shell that was somehow sharp enough to cut through plaster, but didn't touch her skin. The arid heat like a hair dryer blowing, but the mist didn't dry up. And then she remembered seeing those eyes bulge through the cloud — and screaming.

"God, I still have nightmares about those eyes! Now I remember! How could you have taken me to that place?"

"I'm sorry, Amy. I thought it would be a grand adventure; you used to love hearing fairy tales, and I'd visited Danica before. She was delighted to create a fairy tale experience for you. It didn't occur to me that you would be able to see through fae glamours. You were only a little girl, not even an active siren.

"And then you were so scared when the frog prince peeked out from behind her, you didn't stop screaming until he left. I'm so sorry, Amy. Danica said she would soften your memories and make them less … real. Or perhaps more remote. I didn't want you to have night-mares." Mira said sadly.

Amy couldn't even look at her mother. How could she have put her in such danger? The idea that fae illusions made a faerie somehow safe was absurd.

"We can only do our best." Mira wished Amy understood. She had no idea Amy had been so affected by that one night. "I only wanted you to be happy. To settle into the new town. And you *did* have a great summer. You made so many friends before school started."

"I can't believe you thought it would be a good idea to take your five-year-old to visit a fae preserve! Seriously? And then you hid it from me? Had a faerie glamour me to make me forget the truth? I mean, I understand how the geas restricted you from telling me you were a siren. But this?" Amy shook her head. "I don't like finding out now that I've had *magick* worked on me.

"You know, every time you fill out a questionnaire, you get asked about magick use? I've certified maybe fifty times that I've never been magicked. I would have thought you'd have mentioned it sometime. Maybe not when I was five, but when I was older? I mean, what else don't I know about myself?" For the first time, Amy realized that even though the woman sitting across from her didn't look at all like her mother, she had started thinking of her as *Mom*. That was perhaps more disconcerting than anything else.

Mira sighed. "I don't know. It didn't come up. Maybe I should have found a way to tell you. But I didn't think of it as a big deal. Back then, we didn't fill out all the forms you have nowadays. It was a disappointment for me, really. I had wanted it to be a special experience for us. After that night, you never wanted to hear another fairy tale again. But Amy, you're older now. Can we try a do-over?"

They sat in silence for a moment, and a cloud must have passed over the sun, because the room dimmed further.

"I left my girls, you know." Devin said. "It was safer that way, and I suppose my sister raised them well. But I missed them all the same. You make your choices and you move on from there. Like the fae say, 'if you get bogged down in the past, you forget the present and lose your future.'"

"You told me you're finished with all the necessary scans at the hospital. You've gotten the results, and you know that the grafts have taken hold, but it will take more time for them to heal completely. If all you really need is time for your body to finish healing, I know that the fae can speed that up." Mira looked pointedly at Amy.

"It's true." Devin added his support for this idea. "And it would be even more risky to do nothing. Too much is happening, too quickly. It isn't safe for you to remain at less than full health."

Mira worried that she was springing too much on Amy too fast, but she wasn't sure trickling the information out would be received any better. She needed to know about the prophesy. Mira took a deep breath and hoped Amy could handle one more disclosure.

"Amy, the reason we're worried — why we're even here with you now — is because we think you need to be protected. The Danjou have an Oracular prophesy regarding another mage war, and believe you're pivotal to winning it."

Amy was startled. "A mage war?"

After Mira finished explaining everything she knew about the prophesy, the numbness that had cocooned Amy since yesterday's revelations dissolved.

"How dare you keep this from me! You've been here for a week, 'monitoring the situation' and didn't see fit to tell me that we are *on the brink of Armageddon* and that my operation was somehow pivotal? You lie and lie and lie. And for what? The geas had *nothing* to do with this prophesy. You weren't somehow prevented from telling me about the Oracle, were you? How could you lie like that!" Hot tears of anger rolled down Amy's cheeks, and her hands shook.

"Amy, it's not like that! I didn't lie—"

"A lie of omission is the same as a lie!" Amy tossed one of her mother's oft-used expressions back at her. "You should have said something the moment you arrived!"

"Like you would have believed me? Mary wouldn't have even opened the door if I had started spouting gibberish about prophesies and oracles. She was suspicious enough that if she hadn't been so worried about her auditions, I don't think she'd ever have believed Thomas sent me."

Amy shook her head, and wiped her eyes with a quick flick of her hand. The room had taken on a reddish haze, and her vision blurred with tears. A plume of yellow flame suddenly extended from the table in a wide arc, searing a hole in both the floor below and ceiling above. Startled, the three of them jumped out of their chairs and backed away from the table. The flames went out, leaving the dull smell of burnt plastic lingering behind.

"Ah … did I just do that?" Amy asked in a hushed voice, still husky with emotional residue.

"I think so," Devin replied cautiously.

"I don't know how I did it," Amy whispered.

Mira swallowed. "I think your operation may have been more of a complete success than you expected."

They stood for a moment as the smoke faded. It was as if none of them knew what to say next.

"Maybe we *should* visit the fae," Devin said at last. "Your enclave mage isn't here and the fae may have some advice. They use magick too."

"And if they can't help, I know a mage — one who actually knows Ted — Jonah, the guy I mentioned to you before—"

"Your spy," Amy interrupted flatly.

"Yes," Mira kept her voice expressionless. "Jonah may be able to help. But he'd have to fly out here, and he's usually in the Danjou Enclave in California. The fae are closer."

Amy knew she had rushed this operation, and this wasn't the first time she'd experienced second thoughts since waking up. But now she was starting to wonder. The *Danjou* had received a prophesy about her before she'd even started high school, let alone graduated from medical school or developed the Bant Procedure. The *Danjou* had approached Eli about a joint vision restoration project. The *Danjou* had kept the DoD interested after every setback.

Ted had been so persuasive about her trying the surgery. Amy started to wonder whether he'd been sent to join Project Hathor just to orchestrate her operation. Perhaps he had manipulated her in some way?

She had brushed aside Mary's objections so easily. And at the time, Amy thought Graham's eagerness to perform the operation had been due to his desire for professional recognition ... but perhaps it had really been Ted's influence that prevented Graham from putting forth any real objections.

Looking back, Amy wondered at how uncharacteristically impulsive she had been to rush the operation, somehow burying her qualms under articulate and intricate arguments. Impulsivity was Cordelia's weakness, not hers. But here she was. And instead of feeling thrilled at this new display of success, Amy felt the hard ache of fear in her stomach. She had been manipulated into making a terrible mistake.

She no longer cared about the success or failure of the project, her reputation, or anything else. She had practiced medicine for twenty-five years, and was now one of the most experienced, most skilled neurosurgeons in the entire country. Amy understood the risks of surgery and could recommend which were worth taking. But she utterly lacked any experience, training or guidance whatsoever with respect to magick. Now Amy wasn't only worried that she might kill someone with her new sight; now she wondered if she'd been tricked into starting a Mage War.

The sirenic power of transformative fertility includes both (i) the ability to harvest sex drive as well as basic fertility from fertile donors, and (ii) the physical transformation of the siren into their donor's fantasy partner. Sirens generally do not achieve the power of transformative fertility until they have at least three active siren descendants. While the power of transformative fertility requires more practice to control than basic fertility transfer, it is still more of an instinctual than a learned skill.

– Sirens: An Overview for the Newly-Transitioned, 3rd ed. (2015), *by Mira Bant de Atlantic, p. 21.*

Chapter 33

"Stay here for a moment," Mira said when they walked into the church.

"This is a gift I can give them," Mira had explained to Amy on the way there. "They struggle with lust like everyone else. I can remove that struggle and, in the process, use their lust to help another have a child. Before Thomas transitioned, it was harder to justify. I can't quite say it's God's work. But now, it's a lot easier to believe that I'm doing the right thing."

Amy had thought Mira's explanation of why she chose priests made a lot of sense. She had not pried too much into the mechanics of how sirens took and gave fertility. While both she and Mira had taken on a clinical, detached approach to their discussion yesterday, Mira stammered as she tried to explain the nuances. Devin had watched their discussion with a vague smirk on his face. He seemed to find Mira's practically incoherent explanation of the quasi-sexual element in siren magick ridiculous and somewhat entertaining. At least his presence had helped Amy find the humor in the situation.

Both Devin and Mira had insisted she wear a white overrobe that looked a lot like pictures of what the sheiks in Arabia wore. Mira wore one too, but hers fit a bit looser than Amy's. Devin explained that these acted in the same way as bullet-proof vests, except that there was no metal in them. In the dim light of her apartment, the robes seemed to be awash in a glow of colors: almost like a watercolor Monet with rainbow dots. But when they walked into the bright light, the psychedelic intensity increased again; the polarized sunglasses she put on dampened the saturation somewhat, but didn't soften the edges of the color.

There weren't many people in the sanctuary. Devin went in first, choosing an aisle seat in a middle pew, where he would have easy access to the front or back of the church. Mira gestured for Amy to follow her, but Amy caught her arm first. "Could you take off that robe? I want to see clearly, and I think it may interfere with my sight," Amy whispered.

Mira glanced into the church and scanned the empty rows. "Okay. Hold it for me?" She unbuttoned it, and beneath was wearing a rather ugly, paisley-printed wrap dress.

Amy smirked a little and Mira shook her head. At least she knew it was an ugly dress, Amy thought. Mira handed the robe to Amy and walked to the front right of the church, Amy trailing behind. There were two elderly women and one man sitting in kind of a scattered row in the first few pews. A small room with frosted glass walls was situated to the right of the pews, and seemed oddly modern and out of place amidst the older architecture and age-darkened wood of the sanctuary.

In the wake of the abuse scandals that erupted out of Europe, traditional confessionals had been replaced with these glass boxes. They provided additional transparency and the pretense of privacy. But Amy missed the old ones. This new way of reconciliation, with the light of the confessional illuminating your silhouette to all those in the dark church around you, felt more like a public performance of penitence than true confession.

Mira and Amy sat silently a few rows behind the others waiting their turn for the priest. Amy wondered if she should say a prayer. She could certainly use the help. But the words didn't come to her, and she simply sat while a numbness from the chill of the surrounding stonework and the hard wood of the pew beneath her seeped into her body. Numbness was the kind of relief she would have perhaps prayed for, if she could have formed the words.

In turn, each of the elderly parishioners made their way into the glass room, then gradually departed in a slow escape from the claustrophobic enclosure. When the last woman came out, blinking as she emerged into the dimmer light of the sanctuary, Amy and Mira rose and walked to the door. The level of light in the sanctuary had been easier for Amy's still-blurred vision to handle, but the white light of the confessional gleamed in a shifting haze of brown, green and yellow that made it hard for her to see inside the room. The priest rose as they walked in. He was a young, Hispanic man, who seemed quite nonplussed by their entrance.

"I'm here to support my daughter," Mira said. "She's recovering from surgery and has blurred vision from time to time." Mira handed Amy her open water bottle and moved closer to the priest. The priest fixated on Mira's face, barely looking at Amy. Mira could see him struggle to tamp down his feelings. By now, she was used to it. She was glad that he didn't curse her, as some did, thinking that she was an agent of Satan.

"Father, I have a gift for you," Mira continued, her voice husky and compelling. "You look at me, and perhaps other women, and are torn apart by forbidden lust. I can see it on your face right now. But I can help eliminate that temptation from you. I can free you from all sexual desire so you can serve God without distraction, as Paul did. Will you let me help you?"

The priest opened his mouth to speak, but closed it again, as if he couldn't bring himself to say anything. Mira watched his hands tremble a little and saw that he was sweating.

"Father, I swear I mean you no harm. I only want to help you. And I can help you if you'll let me." Mira wondered if any consent he might give while under her influence could be accepted as real.

She'd struggled with the morality of her justifications in the past. Ultimately, though, she decided that this was a gift, and gifts should be given. The priest had taken a vow of celibacy, and she had the unique ability to help him keep that vow. When Mira targeted a priest, she planned to drain him completely, taking not just his fertility, but also his ability to feel desire. And it was true that draining someone this completely was a much stronger form of magick. When transferred, the fertility combined with desire was far more likely to help the receiving faerie regain sufficient strength to procreate.

Mira crossed more closely to the priest and took his trembling hands. Amy tried opening and closing her eyes to try to make the double images collide into one. She wasn't sure why Mira had chosen such a semi-public place to do this. The room was translucent to prevent the kind of untoward behavior that could happen in a private room — and this definitely felt like untoward behavior to Amy.

"Shh," Mira whispered and the priest closed his eyes. "Just a chaste kiss and you will be free."

Amy was very uncomfortable watching this moment. It felt way too intimate, and altogether wrong. She hadn't attended church regularly since college, but it still felt almost sacrilegious to coopt a sacrament for this other purpose. But Amy forgot her discomfort quickly in her awe at seeing Mira's magick unfold. The room's brown and green haze was swallowed into their bodies as Mira leaned in and kissed the priest full on the mouth, her hands running beneath his loose sleeves to grasp his forearms. The colorful glow pulsed and intensified as if concentrated inside them.

In a second, the glow left the priest completely, pouring into Mira in a metallic copper-colored eruption of brilliance. Amy heard the sound of waves crashing so loudly, it was as if she were standing on the shore in a storm. Then the sound was gone, as if it had never been there, and the light that had enveloped Mira tamped down like the glow of a coal after the fire was banked. The room grew dry; Amy instinctively lifted the water bottle to drink, but saw that it was empty. Mira wobbled, then sat on the floor, obscured by a fine mist that slowly dissolved. After a moment, she stood up and turned back to face Amy. Amy gasped; she had become a completely different woman.

Mira moved away from the priest, who stayed frozen in place. It was almost as if he were in shock. Then his face slowly relaxed from the rictus of passion bordering on pain. Mira, too, grimaced with pain, then leaned down to pull off her shoes. Amy's jaw hung open and Mira shut it gently as she walked past Amy to open the door.

"We have to go," she whispered, and Amy noticed that it wasn't only Mira's face and body that had changed, but her voice as well. Mira was now taller than Amy, with dark tousled hair and café au lait skin. Thick eyebrows crowned large brown eyes in a heart-shaped face. But it was hard to focus on Mira's face because her chest had grown into two almost perfectly round orbs, which strained against the fabric of the thin wrap dress. The dress' ugly pattern now framed her substantial cleavage like curtains on a window, which seemed oddly appropriate to this new form.

When Amy didn't move, Mira reached over and took the white robe from her, pulling it on. Then she took Amy's hand and led her out the door. The metalic glow that roiled underneath Mira's skin pulsed when she touched Amy, and that small sting helped jolt Amy back into the present moment and she began moving again.

Devin was standing right outside the door when they emerged. Mira let go of Amy's hand and started buttoning the robe. "Ready?" he asked Mira quietly, and Mira nodded. Devin marked a swift pace as he led them down the side aisle.

"Are you just going to walk out barefoot?" Amy whispered, quickly catching up. She noticed that Mira's toes were now manicured in the same shade of red as her suddenly-painted fingernails.

"I forgot to bring my bag into the church. I have a bigger pair of shoes in the car." As she crossed the threshold, Mira instinctively dipped her index finger into the font by the front of the church and crossed herself with the holy water as she walked outside.

The Taiga in northern Europe and North America is considered the cradle of fae civilization. Ruled by Nga and Num since before the First Mage War, roughly half of the world's fae population remains there. Other large fae settlements exist in the rainforests of South America, the dense forests of India, and scattered forests within North America. The mage wars impacted fae migration even more so than they did human migration, with attempted fae migration into China and Africa halted by the First and Second Mage Wars, respectively. As detailed in Chapter 21, infra, the Third Mage War resulted in the resettlement of a sizable fae population in England. Since 1910, disaffected Taiga fae have been negotiating with the Cabal for dominion over the Daintree forest in Australia, but as of this publication date, have not yet reached an agreement.

> *– Sirens: An Overview for the Newly-Transitioned, 3rd Ed. (2015), by Mira Bant de Atlantic, p. 84.*

Chapter 34

They were headed towards the Blue Hills Preserve, about an hour's drive outside of Boston. It was one of the largest preserves in Massachusetts, with most of its 7,000 acres off limits to the general public and reserved for the fae. The Ponkapoag Pond was a popular campsite for kids in scouting programs, where human-fae contact was encouraged as a kind of cultural exchange. Otherwise, almost all of the old-growth forest was cordoned off.

The day was practically cloudless, and the brilliance of the sunlight caused Amy to wish she had brought a blindfold; even polarized sunglasses weren't enough. She closed her eyes in the back of the limo and tried to clear her mind. The last time she had been in a limousine had been at Mary's wedding. Even with Mary in her huge dress sitting on one seat, and Thomas and Cordelia sitting with her across, the limo hadn't felt as cramped as it did today. Somehow, Devin and Mira seemed to take up more intangible space, even if they didn't consume the same physical volume.

That said, Devin's new form was significantly taller and more muscular than his last one. He looked like a cross between a model and a body-builder, with a deep tan and blond, shoulder-length hair, parted in the center. Amy thought perhaps he resembled the kind of man she'd seen on the covers of historical romance novels.

Devin had also obliged her with a demonstration before they left Boston. While Amy was about to get out of the car at the second church, a middle-aged woman passing by struck up a conversation with Devin, who was standing with Mira on the sidewalk. Devin had exchanged a quick glance with Mira, who had simply shrugged and handed him a gallon sized jug of water from her tote bag. Devin gestured for Amy to stay in the limo, then invited the woman to join them.

That transfer had been faster than Mira's, and the colors Amy saw were different. Devin's taking had been infused with orange and violet, with licks of canary yellow flickering in and out. She was closer to Devin during this transfer. So perhaps it was her proximity or maybe only because of the slightly dimmer light in the limo, but this time Amy was just able to make out a shining silver line, almost as thin and translucent as fishing line, that connected the siren to his mark. When Devin finished transforming, the line dissolved with the mist that had enveloped him.

Mira had visited one last priest before declaring they were ready. While sounds and the intensity of the participants' reactions were similar, there hadn't been any consistency to what Amy saw with her mage-sight when Mira worked her magick. The copper glow of the first church switched to purple and red flames in the second. But by watching for it, Amy could just make out the same fine line connecting Mira to the priest that time. Somehow, seeing that familiar sight gave Amy hope that she might actually be able to figure this out.

But it was hard. The patterns each of the three times had been different, and even the speed with which the colors had coalesced and brightened in the two sirens varied. The only thing that had remained the same in each of the three workings had been the sound of the ocean in the distance.

While Amy didn't enjoy playing the voyeur, the melting of the sirens' bodies into their new forms had been an extraordinary sight. Amy stared at Mira after each change, absorbing the totality of her transformation, and no longer had any doubt that the woman sitting across from her was her mother. Watching Mira change forms had perhaps been the tangible evidence Amy needed to accept that she wasn't an orphan anymore.

As they drove deeper into the forest, the canopy provided enough shade so that Amy could open her eyes without feeling the nausea induced by her double vision. The road turned from pavement into gravel then dirt, a huge sign warned that they were approaching the Blue Hills Preserve. More hazard signs lined the road, each with a different symbol and all of which made Amy's heart pound with fear. It was like they were driving into a war zone.

Even those fools who thought the fae were somehow benign should have been dissuaded from proceeding further when they saw the notices that this preserve was guarded by werewolves. Yet every year, a few teenagers chose to test the limits, resulting in at least one missing person and regular hyperbolic news reports regarding how the government turns a blind eye to the "danger among us."

By now, everyone should know that venturing uninvited onto a fae preserve was foolhardy. Even if you didn't pay attention to the news, the warning signs posted along the road were sufficiently disturbing that only the most desperate should be willing to risk traveling further in. While Amy knew the teenage brains were still developing the capacity for accurate risk assessments, she nevertheless had a hard time understanding how anyone would venture into the forbidden woods.

The driver pulled to a halt when they reached the plastic turnstile that blocked the final road into the fae area. Devin got out of the car to raise the barrier, and a camera mounted on a nearby pole swiveled to get a clearer view of them. Amy suspected a police chief somewhere was getting a team ready to collect their car if they didn't return before dark.

As they slowly crept along the dirt road, Amy closed her eyes for a moment and tried to calm herself. She pictured her father as a guardian angel, hovering over the car, and tried to feel safe. For the first time in a long while, she didn't conjure the image of Mom beside him. When Dad had died, she promised Amy that he would always watch over her, and even now, she held onto that promise. When she was eighteen, her vivid image of angelic protectors had expanded to include Mom. But now she didn't need to imagine her mother as an angel.

"You told me you'd been watching over me," Amy said.

"Not all the time, of course. But from time-to-time, yes."

"Like when?" Amy asked, guardedly eager to hear more about how her mother had watched over her.

"Well, when you cured amblyopia, I spoke to Dr. Eisner to make sure he gave you the credit you deserved. I didn't compel him to do more. You earned your success, and I only wanted to make sure it wasn't taken from you, like it is with so many young doctors. And I worried about you and Mary being young professionals; I know how hard it is for women. I wanted to make sure you were respected and not harassed, so I made sure you were treated with respect. Things like that."

Amy sat there reconsidering her relationships with her professors and mentors over the years. It was so odd. So hard to imagine. She'd written a letter in support of Dr. Olivan when he'd been accused by the Board of sexual misconduct. How much of her good relationship with him and all the others had been because of her mother's intervention, and how much had been because they were really just good men and good friends? She thought about Eli. He had been such a supporter for so long; she had revered him. But what was real about that?

"You can compel any fertile man to do anything?" Amy asked.

"More or less. Siren powers of compulsion fade with time, of course. And the strength of the siren varies. Some sirens can't compel a fertile man to act against his values or instincts, but others could compel him to kill himself and his entire family if they wanted to," Mira answered, sounding much like a professor.

"And you're resistant to fae magick," Amy said. It made sense in a way. Sirens had been created to aid the fae, and so were supposedly resistant to their illusions and bindings.

"To some degree. I don't really know to what extent; I avoid testing it," Mira replied. Most of what they knew about siren immunity was based on legends from the Third Mage War, so Mira tried not to rely on that talent too much.

They parked at the edge of a dirt trail that led into a very dark wood. It was like something out of a fairy tale, with overgrown ferns trailing down a rocky out-cropping and tall trees with thick, mossy trunks. Amy got out of the limo, and squinted to make out the words on the yellow caution sign. The light was even dimmer in the preserve and she was happy to finally see only one unified image again.

"No Entry," Amy read the sign aloud. There was a depiction of a snarling wolf below the letters. She shuddered.

"We have an open invitation," Mira said as she came around the front of the car. "Take my hand as we cross the threshold and you shouldn't trigger anything."

"I'm going to take point," Devin said as Mira let the way into the heart of the preserve.

They walked onto the trail and climbed up the incline through the darkness stretching between the trees. The trees lining the path were so close that the branches on either side formed an overlapping can-opy that hid the sky. Devin had explained in the car that the Blue Hills Preserve was a larger preservation than most. This meant that there would be a significant number of fae illusions and protections, especially over the points of entry.

Sure enough, after only a few yards, Amy started to feel like she was walking through cobwebs. She ran her hand over her face, but nothing was there. "Do you feel that?" she asked.

"No," Mira replied, as she huffed a little on the path. The trail was steep, though fortunately free of roots and other obstacles. She was hampered a little by her firm grip on Amy's hand. Mira didn't know if her invitation extended to guests, and didn't want to risk letting go of Amy. Their first trip into a preserve when Amy was a girl had not ended the way Mira had imagined it would, and she wanted to make sure this trip left a better impression on her.

"It's like there's a barrier of sorts," Amy said. She could just make out faint glimmers of silver floating in the air in front of them. It looked like they were climbing through cobwebs, though the pattern was more of a haphazard zigzag than a natural web.

"I don't sense it. But I'm sure the fae know we're coming. Cordelia mentioned the fae always greeted her by the time she got to the top of this hill."

The path widened into a small clearing at the top of the incline, with an entrance to a bluestone cave flanked by ferns on the left. Mira could hear the soft rushing of a river or stream in the distance. She'd heard that there was a dwarf settlement in this preserve as well, and wondered if the cave were the entrance to their home. The fae liked dwarves because they pulled the iron out of the soil for them, but Cordelia hadn't mentioned meeting dwarves on her various visits here. However, true to Cordelia's experience, they were greeted just as they stepped into the clearing.

"Hail, sirens and siren-daughter!" Mira couldn't see the speaker, but the thin, reedy voice seemed to come from the right side of the clearing. Mira turned towards it.

"Hail, wood wife. My name is Mira, mother of Cordelia, who visited you often."

A small round figure emerged from behind a tree to the right. She had a tan wrinkled face, prominent nose, and blue-streaked, curly green hair that seemed to merge with the ivy and moss growing on the surrounding trees. The light around her pulsed with a neon green glow, flecks of black and red sparking about her bare feet. "Yes, Cordelia promised you would come to give the leshiye a child."

"This is Devin, and this is my daughter." Mira chose not to give the fae Amy's name. You could never be too careful.

The wood wife smiled, and the flecks of black and red surrounding her flickered for a moment. Amy saw her transform into a tall, thin, young woman, with light gray straight hair, black eyes, and a luminous white face. Amy blinked and the flecks of black and red intensified, then vanished, leaving the small round figure Amy had seen before.

"You see truly now, siren daughter," smiled the wood wife. "But you could use a touch of the forest to speed you through."

"Yes," Mira replied. "My daughter could benefit from your touch."

Amy opened her mouth to object, then closed it. She didn't want the woman to touch her, even if she didn't have bulging yellow eyes.

"She's been fae-touched before. But I think she needs more healing now than I can offer. One of my cousins could help," offered the wood wife.

"Did Cordelia help them?" Mira asked.

"Oh yes!" exclaimed the wood wife. "You must tell her that Elia is pregnant! Between the dwarves who have cleared this land of poison, and Cordelia's gift to Elia and Grûen, we will have a moss baby before midwinter." The wood wife was clearly happy.

"I'm so glad!" Mira was delighted. The moss folk were typically a gentle group akin to the dryads, but not bound to their trees. It was easy to mistake them for gnomes with their gray skin, but where the gnomes were stern and serious, the moss folk tended to be earnest, but playful. Cordelia's notes indicated that she had visited Elia and Grûen at least a dozen times in the past three years to gift them with her stored fertility. Mira was glad her efforts had paid off.

"Let me fetch the leshiye and the moss folk." The wood wife disappeared swiftly into the forest, but so quietly Amy didn't hear anything other than the wind rustling the treetops and the sound of running water in the distance.

"This is a beautiful forest," Mira remarked, turning around to get a better look down the hill. She had let go of Amy's hand while they had been speaking with the faerie.

"Do you think the dwarves are in there?" Amy asked, gesturing to the cave.

"Most likely, though Cordelia didn't mention them. Probably didn't consider it an important detail to mention." Cordelia was far too blasé about her encounters with non-humans. Thomas too, for that matter. Mira would have thought it was a youngest child problem, somehow too innocent and coddled to imagine the danger that exists, but for the fact that Thomas shared Cordelia's naïveté. Somehow neither of them saw the danger in playing soccer with were-jaguars or venturing into a dwarf mine. Or a fae preserve, for that matter.

Perhaps the apple didn't fall too far from the tree. But then, with the fae, Mira knew she held a key bargaining chip. She would have come to help the leshy couple regardless of Amy's surgery; Mira couldn't ignore their need. But beyond healing, she hoped the moss folk would perhaps help Amy understand her new vision. Since Cordelia had already enabled one of the moss folk to conceive, Mira expected her family already had a lot of credit to burn with the fae of the Blue Hills Preserve.

They heard the leshiye before they saw them. A bright whistle pierced through the dull gurgle of the water, and birds flew off in a cloud as the trees shook. Emerging from the gloom of the deep forest beyond the clearing came four large feet, on which several moss folk perched, clinging to the pant legs of the enormous fae who parted the trees and crouched down to peer at Devin, Mira and Amy. The moss folk jumped off the leshiye's feet, and the two giants shrank down to a mere seven or eight feet tall.

As they changed size, the air around them hummed, almost as if a bow had been plucked and an arrow loosened. The glow of their magick appeared like a translucent jellyfish, pulsing around them in almost a thick glow with pink froths trailing up into the trees.

Sirens Unbound

The leshiye themselves had gray complexions, similar to the moss folk they towered over. But where the moss folk had curly green hair, the male leshy was blond, with hair like hay sticking out in stalks about his head and the female's hair was a strawberry blond whose hair hung around her head as if it had been set with curlers, then brushed out into loose waves. Both had dark green eyes that glowed with an inner light. Without eyebrows or eyelashes framing their large eyes, the green orbs dominated their faces.

"Hello. My name is Mira, this is my colleague Devin, and this is my second daughter. We are very pleased to meet you."

"The pleasure is ours, Mira and Devin and Second-Daughter," the strawberry blond woman replied, in a surprisingly light voice for such a large woman. "I am Ludmilla and this is my man, Olvin."

Olvin grunted, his voice so deep and ominous it felt like the beginnings of an avalanche in winter. Amy shuddered, despite herself. Olvin saw it and smiled an unpleasant smile. Mira didn't like the way he looked at them, either. But she focused on Ludmilla.

"My daughter, Cordelia, has visited you many times. While she regrets not being able to help you today, she sends her greetings. She asked that I come to see you." Mira's voice was even and while she faced Ludmilla, she observed Olvin out of the corner of her eye.

Amy was glad to see that both Mira and Devin seemed to be at full alert. She concentrated on appearing calm, though she was sure the fae could sense her terror.

469

"Cordelia already promised us your aid," Olvin stated bluntly, his voice deep and pitched to woo or perhaps intimidate. It was hard to tell the difference with leshiye.

"Cordelia gave freely to the moss folk, asking nothing in return. She gave you her strength and magick, asking nothing in return. You have no cause to treat with us as supplicants or enemies."

Mira's voice was sharp. Unlike the moss folk and wood wives, leshiye were not reputed to be a kindly group of fae, and these two were not oath-bound to the seelie, who enjoyed human diversions and company. They lived in the deep woods and were fairly reclusive, typically only tolerating the moss folk and wood wives in their immediate surroundings. Given this couple's claim on the preserve, Mira was a little surprised the dwarves had been allowed to settle here; though perhaps their tolerance of the dwarves signaled a greater need on their part.

"You are neither supplicant nor enemy, Mira de Atlantic. You are our promised savior. We miss our children who remained behind in the Taiga. Bless us, and we will bless you." Ludmilla spoke again, tapping her mate on the shoulder, and he slipped back a step or two behind her.

"My daughter sees with a new mage sight, but the operation was recent and she suffers from blurred vision. She needs to understand this new sight and the odd magick that came with it." Mira spoke firmly.

She wanted to make sure they understood what boon she sought. Leshiye might not be the most easy-going of the fae, but they were no slouches in the magick department. They could change size and shape at will, and their strength was so great they could shake the earth with their footsteps.

Ludmilla's forehead furrowed. "We do not understand the magick wielded by mages. But you have a touch of the fae about you also."

Ludmilla extended her index finger close to Amy's face, but didn't touch her. Amy couldn't help but recoil, and Ludmilla's eyes widened at her reaction. But the leshy's desire for a child must have been greater than her desire to torment Amy, because she merely cupped her hand a few inches away from Amy's face before withdrawing it abruptly. Ludmilla turned back to Olvin, speaking in a Slavic-sounding language.

"Psst." A hand pulled on Mira's robe and she looked down. One of the moss men stood next to Mira, and she bent down to hear his whisper.

"The leshiye won't be able to help with mage sight. It's too strange to them. They are mages like you sirens are mages. They perform magick, but see it not. They will argue and want to lie and mislead you because they so badly want a child." The man shook his head. "The fae can't much help with your child's magick. Her fae element is much too buried beneath the mage. But *we* can speed her healing. Not them, us."

Amy didn't want Ludmilla to come anywhere near her again; not even her newfound desperation to avoid another magical accident could get her to stand still if the leshy tried to touch her. The leshiye argued, growing taller until their torsos disappeared into the trees.

The moss man smiled at Mira, and she smiled back reflexively. "Cordelia has made me a father for the first time!" he confided. His joy was infectious and Mira's smile widened. Even with the sirens' help, it was rare for the fae to conceive. His happiness made Mira happy. Amy smiled too. The small, gray man with his wrinkled face seemed impossibly young, and the air about him glowed with an iridescent sheen like sunlight on dragonfly wings. She tried to tell herself that the fae were just like humans: some nasty and others nice.

"How do such different groups of fae share this preserve? I imagine it must be difficult," Amy asked, as the booming voices of the leshiye echoed like thunder above them.

"It is not too hard," answered one of the moss women, whose face was almost charcoal gray and her hair such a pale shade of green it was almost white. "They are less tolerant of other leshiye than of us. But they are jealous that my niece is pregnant. Jealousy makes them uglier than they usually are."

"You're just an uncommonly easy-going faerie, Belutha," Devin said with a smile.

"Ah, Devin, so you do remember me!" The moss woman replied.

"I'm glad you have established your home here. Are you happy?" Devin asked, but before Belutha could answer, he turned to Mira and added, "I ferried Belutha and some of the other forest folk across the sea when they decided to seek out a territory free of Taiga politics."

"This is a much friendlier place. Especially now that we have made our bargains with the dwarves,"

Belutha said with a smile. But Amy noted that she didn't answer Devin's question.

"Would you want to return to the Taiga?" Devin asked seriously. Amy suspected that he would drop everything and take her back if she but asked.

"No, no. Here is much better. Happiness is but a fleeting sensation. We are content with this land and our joy strengthens the trees, which strengthens us, so all is well with the world." The pale-haired moss woman smiled a full smile and it seemed as if the air around her shimmered with a silver light.

Perhaps it was because Devin knew Belutha, but Amy thought this faerie at least seemed less intimidating than she had before. "Can you help me understand what I am seeing?" Amy asked.

Belutha shook her head. "Sadly, no. I don't think so. I don't think any faerie could. We feel the currents, but we don't see as finely as you humans. You mine sunlight and sprinkle silica-salt to work your magick, but we pull the heat of the Earth through the trees and grasses. I think we are too different, although you do have a touch of the fae about you."

The moss woman cocked her head to one side, considering Amy for a heartbeat, then straightened. "But even that is too different, I think: more sea nymph than forest folk, and I never understood the sea."

Amy was honestly more relieved than disappointed that a fae tutor was out of the question.

"Still, I think I can help the leshiye, and I promised Cordelia that I would try," Mira looked at Devin, who nodded in agreement. Mira cupped her hands and shouted up to the couple. "Ludmilla! Olvin!" She had to repeat herself several times while two of the moss folk jumped on the leshiye's feet to get their attention. The leshiye shrank down.

"An even exchange may not need to take place now," Mira said when she had their attention. "The moss folk will heal my daughter; I will gift you the virility of three humans. You will both owe me a future favor when Ludmilla conceives."

"This is fair," Ludmilla said, and turned to the light-haired moss woman. "Belutha, this will cancel our debt, do you heal her now."

Her imperious tone filled Amy with even more dislike. She had almost felt sympathy for the leshiye, who seemed brittle, with an air of desperation underpinning their loud posturing. But she only had a vague sense that she *ought* to pity them, as opposed to actually feeling any true compassion.

Belutha approached Amy and gestured for her to kneel down. She only stood four feet high, if that. Amy took a breath, then steeled herself and knelt. "This won't hurt," Belutha said gently, and placed her hands on either side of Amy's head, her breath grazing Amy's face. Amy felt like she had dipped her feet in an ice bath, after standing on them for hours. It was an instant relief that rolled up her body in waves. She didn't quite know what she'd been expecting, but it wasn't this shocking coolness. Beads of sweat formed on her forehead and trickled down her jaw.

Amy closed her eyes as the intensity of the relief poured through her. Until the pain was whisked away, she hadn't realized that she'd had a faint headache since the operation. Or that the throbbing in the back of her neck was perhaps related to the surgery; all of her aches seemed to dissolve simultaneously.

Eventually, Belutha pulled her hands from Amy's face and patted her gently on the shoulder. Amy stood up. "I think you will feel better now," the moss woman said. "The trees say you have more healing to do, but they have helped speed it up. Perhaps another few hours, and you should be as good as new."

Amy smiled her gratitude, but carefully didn't say more than, "I feel much better already." While her vision did seem crisper, that might have been simply due to the dim light of the forest; she hoped that her double-vision wouldn't come back when they emerged into the brighter light of the clearing.

Mira nodded at Amy, then walked over to leshiye. "Who will be first?" she asked.

"Olvin," said Ludmilla. Amy wondered if Olvin tasted Ludmilla's food first to make sure it wasn't poisoned before she ate it.

Mira grasped both of Olvin's hands and pulled him down to kneel in front of her so they were facing each other eye-to-eye. As she leaned in and kissed him, full on the mouth, the light that had swirled inside and around Mira ballooned up like a cloud of pink gas to envelop them both. The colors were so much richer and stronger than they had been before.

Amy wasn't sure whether that was due to the healing Belutha had just performed, or the different nature of the magick Mira was working. Amy again felt like a voyeur, but couldn't pull her eyes away from the scene. Red sparks like fireworks crackled through the pink fog;

and watching the kiss, Amy felt a heated pulse in her belly. The sound of waves broke the moment, and Mira pulled back. Olvin's iridescent glow was now broken by red sparks. He stood up, and Ludmilla pulled him into a fierce embrace, broken only when Mira called out, "Ludmilla, if you would please come closer."

Mira repeated her kiss with Ludmilla, but this time as the fog extended, it dissipated around Ludmilla and vanished. The red sparks had a golden tinge and swirled around the two women in an ever-faster maelstrom to ultimately plunge through Ludmilla's abdomen and soften into a red sunrise poking through the horizon. The sound of lapping water filled the clearing until it faded into the ever-present burble of the stream in the distance. As Ludmilla pulled back, her face had softened.

"Even do I not conceive this time, siren, you will have your future boon. Such a passion deserves it!" Ludmilla's voice was husky and she turned to Olvin, who took her hand as they stretched tall up through the forest's canopy. The couple strode soundlessly away through the trees.

Mira and Devin politely declined the forest folk's invitation to dine. Although by now she was broadly familiar with their customs, Mira's past visits to the fae were so frequently accompanied by cultural misunderstandings that she didn't want to keep Amy here longer than necessary.

Amy was grateful they weren't staying longer. She felt extraordinarily invigorated by Belutha's touch, and was impatient to see if the improvement in her vision would last even in full sunlight. The strands of silver on the pathway back still shone, but even the sensation of heavy stickiness didn't cause Amy to pause as she rapidly strode down the path.

When they emerged, Amy was mildly disappointed at the continued cloud cover: while her mundane vision seemed normal, a brighter light would be a true test. Still, she blinked several times, and her vision oscillated between mundane and mage in an odd kind of overlay. Even when she saw without the pull of color and pattern, the air itself looked alive in a way. It was so hard to explain, even to herself, that Amy wondered if she would have to write poetry to describe it in a medical journal.

Mira followed more slowly behind Amy and they both paused a few yards away from the car. Devin walked carefully around it, motioning for the driver to remain inside. Mira trusted that he knew what he was doing. "How do you feel?" Mira asked as they waited.

"Honestly, I think they helped a lot." It was as close as Amy could come to admitting her mother had been right to bring her here.

Mira sighed, releasing the tension she hadn't realized she'd been carrying. Thank God for the fae. But Amy still needed help understanding her new sense; if the fae couldn't do more, there was only one other person she could think of. "I'm going to call Jonah."

"You don't have to do that," Amy began to say, as the clouds parted and the sun started peeking through to illuminate the dirt of the parking area in a dappled pattern. Amy blinked, distracted; despite the strength of the light, she only saw one image with her mundane sight. She blinked again, and the air hummed in a sliding kaleidoscope of blue, silver, and orange, the car still visible beneath it. She smiled; perhaps this time, the risk had been worth it.

Devin motioned them closer, and the driver jumped out to open the door for them.

Mira got in first and took her unhackable cell phone from her bag. "You need a mage to help you understand how to deal with your new sight, and since Ted's unavailable, Jonah will be able to help."

Devin and Amy climbed into the limo. "You seem to have known the moss woman for a long time," Amy noted.

"Belutha? Yes. I met her when I was quite young, actually," Devin replied, but whatever he might have said next was interrupted by Mira's telephone call.

"Hello, Jonah. It's Mira," Mira said.

"Mira, thank God it's you!" Jonah's voice sounded strained, and he spoke rapidly.

"What's wrong?" Mira asked.

"Things are *nuts* around here. Ted and I are about to head to Boston to meet up with your daughter. I've been trying to reach you, but I think I had your old number."

"Why are you coming out here to meet Amy?"

Devin and Amy both looked at Mira sharply. Mira made sure the partition was closed, then put her phone on speaker. Her days of secrecy with her daughters were over, and if she didn't trust Devin, there wasn't any way to keep Amy safe.

"The enclave knows that I've been feeding you information." Jonah sounded harried. "But Tyrone said that it was as it should be — my bindings led me to you or made sure you knew what you needed to know for the benefit of the Danjou. I don't know. But anyway, they've released Ted from house arrest and are sending him to Amy."

"What? Why now?" Mira asked. "Is this some kind of revenge? Is he coming to hurt her?"

"No, no, no!" Jonah spoke quickly, and Mira wished she had Mike here to discern any lie in his swift denial. "The enclave needs Amy. Or at least they think they do. They're sending Ted because she knows him. God, everything is happening so fast." Mira could hear someone else, and there was a rustling on the line.

"Mira Bant de Atlantic, I'll be honest with you. But I have to speak quickly." The voice was deeper than Jonah's, and more composed.

"Who is this?" Mira demanded, while Amy whispered, "It's Ted."

"I'm Theodore Riccie of the Danjou. I worked with your daughter on the recent vision restoration project. While Jonah seems intent on making everyone as paranoid as he is, please believe me: there is nothing that you need to worry about. We are merely coming to join Dr. Bant on her humanitarian mission to Arabia."

"Her *what*?" Mira was perplexed. Amy shook her head and mouthed, "Later."

Ted huffed, "We don't have a lot of time right now. Jonah and I need to be at the airport in a few minutes. Ask Amy about it; the DoD has been working with Eli on the arrangements ever since that press conference she gave last month."

The line went dead. Mira and Devin both looked at Amy. "When were you going to tell us about that?" Devin asked.

Alliances are the ties that bind the different sentient species together. While such ties have been generally beneficial, they have also been the primary means by which isolated territorial conflicts have erupted into global wars.

– Sirens: An Overview for the Newly-Transitioned, 3rd ed. (2015), *by Mira Bant de Atlantic, p. 217.*

Chapter 35

"Did you know the word 'honeymoon' came from southern Europe before the Atlantic War? Back then, the newlywed couple would be sequestered in their new home for the first month after their wedding. To encourage them to provide him with grandchildren, the groom's father would deliver mead to their house every day." Kyoko trailed her finger down Thomas' chest as he stroked her hair and stared at the ceiling fan that whirled above them in a soft, slow rhythm. "The groom's father made sure that no one bothered them. And they would just stay inside and make love for a whole month."

"We need less interruptions and more honeyed wine," Thomas murmured. "Traditions must be upheld."

They had arrived in Brisbane a few days ago, only to be greeted with what they both considered an alarming amount of attention. Thomas had chosen Brisbane because it was reported to be a mundane city; most mages stayed close to the inland deserts and the major cities in the southeast.

According to the gossip on Kasos, if you stuck to the coasts, it was supposed to be pretty easy to come into Australia without attracting unwanted attention from the apartheid state. As mage constructs, sirens had a kind of in-between status in Australia: they weren't required to register with a specific mage patron, but were expected to have an invited purpose to be there. They had planned to spend a little time getting oriented before Kyoko approached anyone official to apply for sanctuary.

But when they arrived, a mage delegation was waiting for them. Apparently, Kyoko's sundering of Morgan le Fay's geas had caused ripples (that was how the mages explained it) that echoed across the world. The Australian mages had triangulated their location, then tracked their flight from Africa.

So instead of staying in Brisbane, they were now in Canberra. Instead of relaxing anonymously on Australia's famed beaches, they were about to attend a state dinner as the Cabal's "honored guests." Despite the Cabal's relentless hovering, Thomas nevertheless felt infinitely freer than he ever had before. Only his concern for Kyoko's safety kept him from recklessly telling their mage companions to get lost. Kyoko had been right about the geas. Thomas had never realized how unbearably heavy that binding had been. He was amazed that Kyoko had survived twenty years under her indenture, when she had known life without it.

"You get used to it," Kyoko said, and shrugged. "But I'll die before being bound again. Now that we are in Australia, I want to speak with their professors of vampirism."

"After nineteen years of daily takings, Kyoko, I doubt Gerel's tracking capabilities will fade anytime soon," Thomas cautioned. "But I hope so."

"I don't care if I have to wait twenty years. Gerel's time will come." Kyoko smiled, and he thought she looked almost fae-like in her passion.

"I'm going to destroy her, Thomas. I should have realized much sooner that she would never let me live past my term: she taught me too much. It would have been too risky to let me go free. But she was stupid, and I want the Cabal's professors to teach me all the counter-spells the Asian clans tried in their attempts to undo Chía's masterwork. Then I'll unravel the spell and break her apart *slowly*."

Kyoko's eyes glowed with an intensity that scared Thomas, but excited him too. That old rebel cry, "Give me liberty or give me death," made a lot more sense to him now. Of course, Patrick Henry had been rebelling against the imposition of the enclave bindings on independent American mages, and not indentures or geases, but Thomas now understood that drive for freedom in a visceral way. Kyoko should have her revenge.

The Australians were bending over backward to give Kyoko whatever she wanted; if she asked to meet their foremost expert on vampirism, they would arrange it. "How long do you think they'll keep us in Canberra?" Thomas asked.

"Maybe we can get them to agree we ought to go on a tour or something. I don't think they'll let us out all on our own, but at least we'd be able to get away from this city and all these events," Kyoko replied.

It became crystal clear to Thomas within the first day of their arrival how much Kyoko hated the attention the Australian mages were paying to her. She had spent so many years hiding in Gerel's shadow, he wasn't surprised that Kyoko wanted to avoid notice. However, Thomas didn't think she would ever come to enjoy being the center of attention; Kyoko wanted to be left alone to cast. Except for him, she didn't seem to care for other people.

It was also clear when they arrived that some of the male mages could barely restrain themselves from assaulting him. Their hatred was just barely held in check by their fixation on Kyoko, and Kyoko's clear demand that they treat him with respect. He needed a break from attending all the events the Cabal had invited Kyoko to, but Kyoko wanted — needed — him at her side. And Thomas would never abandon her.

Kyoko seemed to be gaining in magical strength at least. Her stamina was impressive. It had taken her days to recover from breaking her indenture, and he would have thought that breaking a blood geas laid by one of the greatest mages who ever lived would have laid her out for at least as long. But she had bounced back within hours.

"I'm sick of this," Kyoko said. "I don't want to be involved in more politics."

"We can't insult them, my love," Thomas said, kissing her gently. While he could understand why the Cabal was interested in winning her over, the more they fawned, the more Kyoko retreated. "One more night, Kyoko. I promise. Just one more." He would have to try something different at tonight's dinner. He hated these affairs almost as much as she did.

"Fine. One more. But let them wait for us," Kyoko said, kissing his stomach. Thomas gasped, inhaling sharply at her gentle touch, then stroking his hand down her shoulder and back to delight in her softness.

Their handler, as Thomas called the mage assigned as their liaison, met them in the lobby of the hotel, where they waited for the carpet. Wilhelmina was a tall, thin, stately mage, with deeply-lined black skin and an afro that haloed her head in a white puff.

Wilhelmina had brought them a variety of Australian fashions for their stay, and Thomas admired the way the silk dress clung to Kyoko, emphasizing her beauty without overpowering it. The clothes she brought for him were less inspiring, but he didn't really care much about his appearance. Kyoko, on the other hand, had been outraged at the first set of clothing and insisted Wilhelmina bring something more suitable.

She'd initially refused to explain her reaction, then admitted that the garments included sigils only visible to mage sight. The apartheid regime required patronage of non-mages, but there were apparently degrees of patronage that ranged from near-slavery to a consort-spouse kind of class. By ensuring that Thomas fell within the latter status, Kyoko was affording Thomas protections under Australian law that he would not otherwise have had — mage construct or no. As an extension of Kyoko's own self, he was essentially untouchable by other mages except through formal application to Kyoko.

Why any non-mage willingly traveled to Australia was beyond Thomas' understanding; except that was exactly what he'd done. Perhaps there were other desperate souls here seeking safety from their own enemies at home. In any event, Thomas consoled himself, this would only be a temporary visit.

The carpet arrived in a smooth arc, and the driver somersaulted off with an acrobatic skill that Kadu would have been hard-pressed to emulate. Thomas was impressed, but Wilhelmina looked as impassive as ever. He wondered if she had just seen everything there was to see before, or whether she was simply highly skilled at hiding her reactions.

"You will be joining the four members of the Cabal who are in residence now, along with their partners, a few select ministers, and the Pacific delegate," Wilhelmina explained as she gracefully swept her skirt aside to sit mermaid-style on the carpet, and beckoned them to follow.

Neither Kyoko nor Thomas had traveled by carpet before coming to Australia. The U.S. had prohibited them outright well before Thomas was born. While the Brazilian elite used them to avoid city traffic, Thomas preferred cars, where you were more hidden from view. But throughout Australia, Asia and Africa, flying carpets were the primary means of transportation.

This carpet was clearly a luxury vehicle, boasting spells that ensured a smooth, climate-controlled ride, and even an adjustable wind-shield. Their carpet rides had been the best part of their visit so far. Carpets were as exhilarating a means of travel as motorcycles, but much faster and more comfortable. Perhaps he would learn to operate one while they were in Australia.

When they first arrived, a Cabalist had met them, but had quickly handed them over to Wilhelmina. Both Kyoko and Thomas had been relieved. Kyoko said that the Cabalist looked at her the way Gerel did after a draining: satiated in an ugly way. And Thomas had kept a close eye on the Cabalist's tightly clenched fists; he was holding back from killing Thomas — but just barely. So Wilhelmina was a relief, even if she were a bit reserved.

"Another siren will be attending the dinner? From the Pacific?" Thomas asked.

"Yes, Bo-Long has been an ambassador here for the past century. He is well-regarded by the Cabal."

Thomas and Kyoko looked at each other. Wilhelmina was clearly trying to tell them something with that, but neither understood the import. The name sounded familiar, but Thomas had avoided politics as much as Cordelia had immersed herself in them. He couldn't remember who Bo-Long was, and felt a wash of impotent anger at the prospect of another siren being in the same room as they were. No one would interfere with Kyoko's love for him. If he were honest with himself, keeping Kyoko from other sirens had been one of the main reasons he'd agreed to come to Australia in the first place.

"Bo-Long has been here for a long time. I don't know much about the sirens, especially those in the Pacific. It seems like a special favor to include us and him in such an intimate gathering." Kyoko framed the question carefully, and Thomas thought he saw a glimmer of approval in Wilhelmina's otherwise inscrutable expression.

"It is a high honor to attend one of the private dinners. There will be no more than twenty guests. The Pacifics are our closest allies; the Cabal has always had good relations with the sirens." Wilhelmina actually smiled at Thomas; and while he smiled back, he felt his stomach contract in terror.

What had started as an intra-fae war had erupted into the Third Mage War after the losers of the territorial struggle over the Taiga sought new lands. The European mages and Atlantics became allies to withstand their invasion. While were-mage alliances were common — after all, Chía had constructed the weres for that very purpose — sirens had been constructed to aid the fae, and siren-mage alliances felt unnatural. Unholy even.

"I'm looking forward to meeting Bo-Long. He's been here for most of Australia's existence, and must have unique insights into your culture," Thomas remarked, glad that Wilhelmina wasn't a truth-teller like Mike to feel his lie.

"Yes, we thought you would enjoy meeting with him," Wilhelmina replied, and Thomas again got the sense that everything about their trip to Australia was being staged and carefully curated.

They arrived at the main upper entrance of Parliament House, which had been built in the 1980s in an architectural style that was more appealing to Thomas than the ornate, castle-like Atlantic House. Thomas smiled to himself at the irony of naming these state buildings "houses," as if that appellation would somehow grant a sense of modesty to their massive grandeur.

Inside, the marble floor was inlayed in a black-and-white mage-pattern, the meaning of which Thomas couldn't discern. He made a mental note to ask Kyoko about it later. He hopped off the carpet gracefully, swinging Kyoko down beside him. A servant extended his hand to Wilhelmina, who carefully slid off.

As the mage, Kyoko took precedence and Thomas continued to be impressed with her seamless imitation of the Australian style. Although she had never been out of Brazil, almost never out of Gerel's presence even, she had carefully observed others at the endless stream of events they had attended, and keenly put her observations into practice. She placed her hand on his forearm, Thomas covered it reassuringly with his other hand, and they swept forward. So far the Australians had been stultifyingly formal, and Thomas felt himself wishing they had never left Atlantis.

Several soldiers stood guard around the large receiving area, perhaps a third of whom wore the black-on-black jacquard uniform that designated mages. The majority wore royal blue, signifying mundanes. All of the soldiers' sleeves were embossed with the distinctive seven-pointed white stars of Australia, and all carried assault rifles. Thomas fixed an easy smile on his face, while praying silently that none of the guards would shoot him. But as they drew closer and he studied their faces out of the corner of his eyes, he noticed that there didn't seem to be a single man present; all the soldiers were female. That was an interesting courtesy.

An older couple stood at the foot of a massive white marble stairwell ahead of them, each wearing an elaborate crystal seven-pointed star pin on white sashes: Cabalists.

"Your Honors, may I introduce Kyoko de Brazil, via-enchanter, and her consort, Thomas Bant de Atlantic," Wilhelmina stated, and both Kyoko and Thomas inclined their heads. Kyoko squeezed Thomas' forearm slightly, and he hoped no one was expecting them to bow and curtsy as if to royalty. Or worse, to shake hands as if they were Americans. Thomas had no desire to touch any of the Cabalists.

"Kyoko, I am Cabalist Eloise ric Western, and this is Cabalist George ric New South Wales. We have been so eager to meet you." Eloise was a plump woman, with dirty blond hair swept into an elaborate up-do. She was wearing what appeared to Thomas to be a pure white dress, studded with clear crystals in a swirling pattern that seemed to shift in the light. From what Kyoko had explained, he was sure that to mage-sight, the dress would have a very different appearance.

George, in contrast, was rather thin, with steel-gray, close-cut hair and a deep tan broken by a thick white scar that extended from the corner of his forehead down to the edge of his mouth. He too wore white: a white jacket and pants, with a royal blue shirt beneath. Thomas suspected that George was probably the weaker of the pair. Western Australia was Australia's richest state, with most of the continent's deserts contained within its borders. To hold onto such a territory, Eloise had to be one of the strongest in the Cabal.

Eloise and George led them up the sweeping staircase. Halfway up, Thomas realized that Wilhelmina had stayed in the receiving area below. He wasn't sure whether this was a sign that the Cabal was unhappy with the job their handler was doing, or whether she simply didn't rate an invitation to what was probably a highly elite event. Meeting one member of the ruling Cabal was probably a high honor; Kyoko must be very important to them if they were to introduce her to four in such a manner.

The two Cabalists kept up an innocuous chatter on their way to the dining room. What did they think of Australia so far, the weather, what a shame it was that only four of the Cabal were in residence at the moment... Thomas thought it was interesting that so far, no one had asked them how long they intended to stay in Australia or why they were there.

"Kyoko," Thomas began, "You were telling me that you wanted to see more of Australia."

Kyoko picked up on the hint. "Eloise, please tell us more about your state. We'd like to tour the continent, and know very little about Western Australia."

"I would love to show you my state!" Eloise gushed. "The Great Sandy Desert is spectacular. Our most productive silica-salt fields are located there, and the patterns and colors are unmatched across the continent." Eloise continued to regale them with descriptions of the landscape and architecture in Western Australia until they arrived at what was probably one of the smaller dining rooms in Parliament House. Butlers opened the heavy, inlaid doors and Eloise swept inside, pausing her description of the latest museum opening in Perth.

A large rectangular table was centered in the room, decked with a royal blue tablecloth. Where white tablecloths seemed to be the norm everywhere else, in

Australia, all the tables were covered in blue. Kyoko had speculated that it might be because the color white was rather distracting when seen through mage-sight. Since Australia had been founded as a sanctuary for mages, it made sense that everyday items would cater to mage comforts instead of mundane traditions.

Perhaps a dozen people were clustered by the floor-to-ceiling windows opposite the main entrance. "George," called a woman in a red dress holding a vape pipe, "Come here! You have to see this."

They walked in a group towards the others looking out the windows. Across the tree-line in the distance, a jagged fork of green lightning flashed across the early evening sky. It was quickly followed by a purple flash, then yellow. Thomas didn't hear any thunder, and the sky was otherwise clear.

"Dahlia is playing again," the woman in red stated, shaking her head and exhaling a jasmine-scented vapor from her pipe.

"Who is Dahlia?" asked Kyoko.

A thin man standing next to the vaping woman responded. "Dahlia ric Northern is showing off for her latest fling instead of coming to visit our honored guests. I'm Trevor ric Victoria, and am most happy to welcome you to Australia," he smiled, and his teeth shone white against his ebony face. Thomas marveled that someone in a powder blue tuxedo could actually look stylish. Like Eloise and George, Trevor also wore a white sash with a crystal star.

The woman in red turned to them. "I doubted Dahlia would come tonight, despite Eloise's pressuring. She is consumed by interests other than the Cabal at the moment. Nevertheless, we are grateful to finally make your acquaintance. I am Juliana de Northern, Minister of Defense."

Juliana's red dress was cut low in almost a Renaissance style, emphasizing her large chest. Thomas thought her debutante drawl, vape-pipe, and dress were a careful form of distraction from the keen focus she was paying to them, and to the entire room for that matter. Minister of Defense was the title used in polite company; others would know her as the Minister of War or Minister of Death.

A waitress offered them drinks, and Thomas was grateful for something to hold in his hand. He was very eager to avoid shaking hands with any of the mages if they chose to adopt an American-style of greeting. Kyoko also took a glass, but she drank it quickly, and her grip on Thomas' arm remained tight. The Australians might prefer that they separate to mingle, but Kyoko was having none of that.

A wave of people introduced themselves. There were few spouses or consorts in the room. None appeared affected by Thomas, and he thought this might be the first time since his transition that he had been around so many humans without needing to prepare for an immediate assault. Still, he was unable to relax, though he tried to counter Kyoko's taciturn demeanor with a more affable air.

Most of those present were ministers, and except for Bo-Long, the envoy from the Pacific Court, all were mages. Bo-Long only spent a brief moment with them before gliding away so that another Australian could make her introduction. Because of his accent, Thomas thought the envoy had probably been born Chinese, though his current appearance vaguely resembled a 1970s-era American football player: shaggy blond hair, chiseled jaw, and a chin divided by a deep cleft.

Thomas was so pleased that Kyoko didn't act the least bit drawn to the other siren, he didn't bother to analyze the oddity of her indifference. He did feel uncomfortable under the barely hidden interest shown by Bo-Long and all the other guests. They were the center of attention, even when they merely stood and smiled. Kyoko hid the strain well, and Thomas was proud of her.

Members of the dinner party gave every appearance of joviality and openness. They chattered about local gossip. Trevor even lamented about the recent lag in silica-salt production due to worker unrest at the refinement facilities. Nothing, Thomas supposed, that wasn't already in the local papers, but it gave a feeling of openness to the evening.

After Wilhelmina's careful management over the past few days, Thomas found the ambiance refreshing. But he didn't doubt that this conversation was any less carefully selected. Thomas knew he needed to find a way to get the Australians to disclose their purpose so he could strike a bargain and get them to back off. As safe as Australia seemed for Kyoko, the Cabal's incessant attention was making him think that returning to Bahia and Kadu's clan might be a better choice.

The lights in the room went out, and a silent firecracker illuminated the room with white sparks that hovered above the table like twinkling stars. That was a rather extravagant way to ring the dinner bell, Thomas thought. Eloise approached, beckoning them to the table.

Kyoko murmured responses to Eloise's remarks on the pending meal with a small smile, but did not relinquish her grip on Thomas' arm as he gracefully escorted her to her seat. Eloise took her place at the head of the table, and Kyoko was seated to her right, clearly intended as the seat of honor. The seating arrangements made it obvious that they would have to separate, at least for the duration of the dinner. Thomas pulled out her chair, then leaned down to kiss her on her cheek.

"Will you be all right, or should I make a fuss?" Thomas whispered. Kyoko pressed against him for a moment before brushing her hand against his cheek. A tingle ran through his body at her touch. As much as he wanted to protect her, he felt her sigil upon him, and knew that she was trying to protect him as well.

She turned to look at him. "This is the last dinner," she whispered, then sat down. Thomas pushed her in and looked over at the others, who were taking their seats. At least Juliana, the Minister of Defense, was at the opposite end of the table. Trevor, the Cabalist in the powder blue suit, was seated across from Kyoko. Unlike Eloise, he seemed to sense that Kyoko did not enjoy idle banter, and had focused his previous conversation with them on enchantment methodologies.

Thomas walked down to his own seat of honor, at George's right hand, and across from Juliana. It could be worse; he could have been seated *next to* Juliana, like Bo-Long. After all the women had been seated, the men sat down. Australian formality, probably a holdover from past centuries.

"How are you enjoying Australia?" George asked. A question that almost everyone had asked Thomas since they'd arrived, and one that he'd already answered five times that evening. Instead of the pat response he'd given before, Thomas tried a different tact.

"Honestly, we're tired of being under the microscope. We came here to get away. Australia is reputed to be a sanctuary for mages. I brought Kyoko here for sanctuary, to have a quiet honeymoon of sorts, and you're suffocating her with your constant attention. I promised Kyoko a quiet break on the beach. Instead, I've somehow thrust her into the kind of political intrigue my sister enjoys, but which I've avoided for thirty years."

Thomas' honesty was met with silence, and he wondered if he'd gone too far in his blunt attempt to start the negotiations and elicit a different kind of reaction than what they'd encountered thus far.

Juliana looked at Thomas and nodded her head slowly. "We've been so focused on our own relief at her arrival, we didn't consider how she might perceive our attention." She sipped her wine. "Wilhelmina told me that you were not happy, and I thought perhaps we had failed to show you sufficient honor."

"You mentioned sanctuary," George said. "Why does Kyoko need sanctuary?"

"I met Kyoko in Rio years ago, while she was still indentured to the vampire ruler of the city. When she broke her indenture, I got her safely out of the city. But her escape didn't go unnoticed, and a battle mage destroyed my home only minutes after we left. Atlantis is no place for her; she can't walk freely among all the sirens without being bespelled. I brought her to Australia for her first breath of freedom since she was indentured. I thought we could fly under the radar here. Explore the Great Barrier Reef, walk on the beach. I brought her here to rest and recover. I didn't bring her here to be monitored and corralled, as kind as you've been."

George's wife patted Thomas' hand. He barely kept from recoiling. "We've been anticipating the Breaker's arrival for decades. I'm a prognosticator, you know. When the ocean roiled, and I felt the backlash from a great working, I knew she was close. I spent days casting to follow you on your journey here." Her voice was gentle, but the feel of her touch simultaneously froze and burned. The only mage Thomas ever wanted to touch him was Kyoko.

"The Breaker? You mean Kyoko?" Thomas asked.

"Whether you or your mage want the attention or not, she has a powerful and unique skill. The fulfillment of a prophesy." George's previously bland demeanor seemed harder, but Thomas felt that his new pragmatic tone was less threatening than his empty small talk had been. At least now, they were beginning to negotiate.

Thomas knew objectively that Kyoko's power was incredible and unique. But until that moment, he had also never questioned the common wisdom that the members of the Australian Cabal were the most powerful mages on Earth — aside from Amir Khalid, of course. Listening to them, Thomas realized that perhaps his beautiful Kyoko was in fact *more* powerful.

It was obvious that the Cabal was courting them, as off-putting as it had been. But Thomas had assumed it was simply how the Cabal behaved when any strong mage arrived — kind of like a college recruiting visit for a great high school player. The stakes were a lot higher if her power were infinitely greater than everyone else's at the table. Thomas was glad he'd pointed out how heavy-handed their recruiting tactics had been. It bought them time before the Cabal might perceive Kyoko's reluctance as a threat, and deal with them accordingly.

"I fell in love with Kyoko from the moment I saw her," Thomas said. "She has always been unique and special to me, so I suppose I never considered what she might mean to others."

Bo-Long spoke, his mild Chinese accent contrasting with his beach boy appearance. "Kōkai-Heika has been waiting for the breaking of the Atlantic Curse predicted long ago; the fulfillment of the prophesy given to the Cabal decades before."

The Pacific sirens still viewed the Atlantic sirens' role in the Third Mage War as immoral. They called Morgan le Fay's curse, "the Atlantic Curse," the war, the "Atlantic War," lest anyone forget the guilt of the Atlantic sirens. Thomas ignored his irritation at Bo-Long's semantics. "Kyoko said the geas was almost irresistible. She found it hard *not* to break it."

"Kyoko may enjoy meeting with some of our binders. We battle mages are often able to joust with one another, but practitioners of other disciplines don't often have the chance to play like that." Juliana smiled.

"Practicing magick is what Kyoko loves to do," Thomas replied politely. This was so true, Thomas worried for a split-second that he might be setting her up for the ultimate seduction. He stifled his jealousy and turned to George's wife. "You're a prognosticator?" Thomas asked, his inflection rising in a question.

"That's right. A fortune teller, really. I read crystal," George's wife responded as the waiters served what looked like a miso soup for the first course.

"Now, don't be modest!" George exclaimed. "Ava is the most accurate prognosticator in Australia."

"I simply have the best tools," Ava demurred. "The best crystal balls are made from silica-salt skimmed from the Sahara and smelted with Arabian sand. Mine are practically irreplaceable."

"You can have the best equipment in the world, but without the proper skill, they just won't matter," Juliana said.

"So you saw our arrival?" Thomas asked.

"My visions were constantly changing, which makes sense because of how much was — and still is — in flux. But just before your arrival, I had a very clear image of the two of you, and knew that the Breaker was coming to our country." Ava seemed rather excited by that. While it was odd to think of Kyoko as a celebrity, Thomas was used to thinking of himself as a hanger-on.

"I have to apologize for our delay in meeting with you, but it does take at least three days for the impotence injections to work," George explained.

"Impotence injections?" Thomas asked.

"Once Ava saw that you, a male siren, were accompanying the Breaker, we needed to prepare for your arrival. Sterility spells are unfortunately ineffective against sirens, as we have learned." George smiled ruefully, and Bo-Long laughed.

"Yes, indeed! That is why my visits are short and infrequent. But I am delighted to be able to meet you, Thomas Bant de Atlantic, and extend my King's greetings to you and the esteemed Kyoko. We would be honored if you would visit us in the Ryukyu Arc."

Bo-Long smiled and Thomas smiled back, rather surprised at the invitation. This was the first invitation the Pacifics had made to anyone from the Atlantic that Thomas could recall. Even his mother met with them in Kasos. "That is most generous," Thomas replied.

"We will soon have a binding tie linking us through my offspring, Liu Yang, who is pregnant with your son's child."

That was why his name sounded familiar! Kevin had mentioned Bo-Long. Thomas made a mental note to call Cordelia. After spending most of the past year in Kasos, she'd likely have some idea what kind of player Bo-Long was in the Pacific court.

"I am extremely happy for Kevin. We discussed placing the child with adoptive parents in Panama City."

"Yes, Liu Yang has convinced me that this would be an appropriate location." Bo-Long said, and his tone made Thomas wonder if he truly approved of the placement.

"I would love to see Amami," Thomas said. "I have never been to the Pacific court."

"But first, you should see more of Australia," Juliana interjected. "I understand you would like to visit some of the sites outside Canberra. Perhaps, George, they could stay in Townsville? See the Great Barrier Reef? Bo-Long, you should take them to your villa tomorrow. That way, you'd be able to have that long-delayed honeymoon." Juliana winked at Thomas. Thomas merely smiled.

"Yes, that would be perfect," George replied. "Maybe Kyoko would like me to arrange a meeting with Professor Wanda de Victoria? She teaches binding at the University of Queensland. She's the foremost expert in Australia."

George's tone remained light; despite the seriousness of their negotiation, the Australians wanted to pretend they were all simply friends. For once, Thomas thought, his carefree demeanor made it easier for him to navigate politics. The Cabal's indirect proposal felt like a fair bargain: they wanted Kyoko to break another spell, and Bo-Long wanted the geas on him broken. The Australians had arranged to have an expert available to see how it was done. This request was something Kyoko would enjoy anyway, and then they could have a measure of their freedom back.

Active sirens are also susceptible to certain fae illnesses, including the common heat. While only rarely contracted by sirens, the heat typically only afflicts older, more powerful sirens. The common heat is non-contagious, and sirens typically recover within 3 to 10 days, although the fae can suffer for more than a month. Symptoms include fever (37°-39°C), sweating and a fixation on a particular person, animal, or thing. Afflicted fae are at risk of fading if the object of their adoration is taken from them before they recover. Although sirens cannot fade like the fae, their obsession while in the grip of the heat can cause them to attempt suicide or take other actions that are not only self-destructive, but harmful to those around them.

– Sirens: An Overview for the Newly-Transitioned, 3rd ed. (2015), *by Mira Bant de Atlantic, p. 76.*

Chapter 36

Ted and Jonah had been at Amy's apartment for more than an hour. Their arrival had broken the détente that she and her mother had fallen into regarding the next phase of Project Hathor. Mira was astonished that Amy was still planning to go to Arabia, even after learning about the prophesy. Amy honestly wasn't sure what she was going to do, but there was something about her mother's stark opposition that made her want to argue.

From the start, Amy had known Project Hathor came with political strings attached, and she had accepted that bargain. She had made the discovery of a lifetime, and even gained the ability to see magick herself. Despite all the revelations of the last few days, she felt strangely uncomfortable shirking her commitment.

Mira wanted the three of them to leave for Brazil, but was at least willing to wait for Jonah to arrive. If Amy wanted to go to Arabia just for help understanding her new sight, Jonah would be far better teacher. It was nonsensical for her to even consider remaining part of the surgical team! Mira grew increasingly irate as Amy's stubbornness continued.

As their argument grew more heated, Devin stared out the window of Amy's apartment. He abruptly interrupted her mother mid-tirade, telling Amy that they needed to take a walk. He took Mira by the shoulders and physically walked her out of the apartment, speaking to her in a hushed voice. After they left, Amy looked outside with her improved vision to see what had prompted Devin. The water in the harbor was rolling as if in the midst of a terrible nor'easter. Amy felt guilty that she had pushed her mother so far. When the sirens returned a few hours later, Mira seemed somewhat calmer, but the swells in the harbor were still high enough that the Mayor had issued a flood warning. Nothing more was said about Arabia that night.

The Danjou mages' arrival this morning had been a welcome reprieve from the silent argument still swirling around the apartment. Ted was excited to hear about Amy's operation, and Amy was glad to finally be able to talk to someone who understood it. They'd spent the better part of the hour discussing the kind of magical testing they should do next.

Jonah had not engaged in their discussion or allowed himself to be drawn out by Mira's gentle conversational gambits. Devin had positioned himself on the periphery of their discussion, an assault rifle resting lightly and openly on his knees. He didn't seem bothered by the disdain both mages showed for him, but perhaps that was because he was used to that response from human males.

Devin watched Ted with a focus that seemed to indicate that he saw him as the greater threat. But despite the fact she knew she couldn't trust him, Amy was relieved to have him there. His explanations and insight were so incredibly helpful, she hoped somehow that he had not truly betrayed her, as unlikely as that was. Jonah, in contrast, was worse than useless. His endless pacing around the small apartment, along with the cloying scent of his vape-pipe, was getting on her nerves.

He must have been bothering her mother also, because Mira suddenly spoke out in a voice that filled the room. "Sit down!" she commanded, her voice resonating dully. Waves of color shimmered as if a gong had been struck and the sound painted the room in a purple-red wash. At the sound of Mira's voice, Amy and Ted stopped talking. Jonah visibly startled at Mira's barked command, and immediately sat on the couch. Amy watched as the colored air settled on him like an aura.

"Jonah, why are you so afraid?" Mira's voice resonated even more deeply than before, and Amy thought she heard waves lapping at the shore as her mother spoke.

"Jonah isn't afraid," Ted said, and Mira turned to face him.

"Shh," Mira whispered with more menace than Amy remembered hearing from her before. "Be still."

The air around Ted pulsed with a reddish haze that flared an angry purple. Ted gasped, and that slight noise disguised the faint sound that seemed to accompany her mother's use of magick. "I don't like lies," Mira remarked in an aside to Amy, without appearing to appreciate the irony in that statement. "Jonah, why are you afraid?" she repeated. Amy focused, and the colored auras around Jonah and Ted sharpened into a kind of brilliant line encircling them and extending back to Mira.

"The elders won't tolerate failure," Jonah said.

"What do they want you to do?" Mira asked, rubbing her chin.

"I'm supposed to help Dr. Bant. You don't need to compel me, Mira. I'm happy to tell you everything." Jonah sounded resigned. But the colors around him didn't change.

Mira shook her head in disbelief. "What kind of 'help' do the elders want you to give Amy?"

"Anything she wants. They don't want her to hate the Danjou," Jonah replied. "Ted completely screwed this up." There was a sharp edge to Jonah's voice.

"What did you 'screw up?'" Mira asked, focusing now on Ted.

"I didn't 'screw up.'" Ted sounded indignant.

"Why would they think you did, Ted?" Amy clarified.

"It's ridiculous. This whole interrogation is ridiculous," Ted said. "I always knew Elder Simon was teetering on the edge of dementia, but for Elders Tyrone and Hilda to back him like this... And for you, Jonah Eris, to insult me—"

Mira interrupted, "Answer her question."

Despite the harshness of Mira's command, Ted's face relaxed at the sound of her voice. Amy could see the air around him swirl faster, and Ted's eyes fluttered open and shut for a moment before he spoke. "I feel your compulsion, siren. But it truly isn't necessary. I only desire to answer your questions," Ted responded, his voice husky.

Mira shivered a little as Ted's tone caused frissons of desire to erupt on her skin. Despite her existence as a force of seduction, she rarely felt anything herself. But there was something about the resonance in Ted's voice that stirred her. If nothing else, she welcomed the distraction from the white-hot anger she felt thinking about her stubborn, foolish daughter.

"Mira told you about the prophesy?" Ted asked Amy.

"Finally," she replied. Mira ignored Amy's tart tone as Ted answered the unspoken question.

"I couldn't tell you before, Amy. And honestly, advance knowledge of a prophesy has *never* benefitted a pivot. That's what you are, you know."

"You should have told me," Amy insisted.

"So you could have avoided this project like the plague? You can't escape fate, Amy. Even if you hadn't made the greatest neuro-magical breakthrough in history, you'd still have been thrust into the coming mage war — only without the ability to see the magick that swirls around you. Jonah sees it. Tell her."

"Of course I see it. It would be hard to miss," Jonah replied sullenly.

"See what?" Amy asked, somewhat desperately.

"Ambient magick finds you; the currents alter with your every movement. They have ever since I first met you. You should be able to see it now, although I know you don't understand what you see," Ted explained.

"Even if your sight tests as clear as Ted says it will, you need to be taught a schema," Jonah agreed, but Amy was still confused.

"You said the images you see through your mage sight are a jumble, without any logic," Ted began, and Amy nodded. "Like I told you, that's completely normal. Typically, though, children are taught sight interpretation in the primary grades. Jonah is indeed an expert at training those gifted in mage-sight." Something about Ted's tone made Amy think he didn't much like Jonah.

"What's the matter, Jonah?" Mira asked. She strove to keep her temper on a leash as she crossed the room to sit next to him. If she kept her focus on Jonah's odd behavior, she thought she might be able to get control of her own odd reaction to the via-enchanter. Mira gently reached out and took Jonah's vape-pipe, flexing her compulsion lightly.

Jonah's face relaxed somewhat, and the lines on his forehead smoothed out, until she repeated her question: "Jonah, why are you so afraid?"

Compelled, Jonah answered, his hands shaking. "Mira, Elder Simon shot Rachel. Right in front of me. In front of Elders Hilda and Tyrone and the rest. No one even tried to stop him. I knew the elders could be ruthless, but this — this is beyond anything I'd ever expected."

Jonah looked down. "He shot her and told me to get Ted and head out. One chance, and we had better not fail like her. Like she was nothing. Like murdering the woman who had been his wife for more than a century was nothing." His voice shook, and Mira took his hand and squeezed it.

"Jonah, enough already," Ted said impatiently.

Amy and Mira both glared at Ted.

"Siren, it isn't like your people are a gentle folk," Ted declared and then directed his attention on Devin, his tone changing into something just short of disrespectful. "Tell her what Atlantea did to those who failed her in the War of Succession. Rachael's failure was far worse."

Devin ignored Ted's challenge. "What was Rachael's failure?"

"Rachael was sent to Brazil to retrieve and bind a mage. She failed. And now Giselle could be next," Jonah said.

"Your sister is free, Jonah. Stop worrying about her," Ted huffed.

"Explain," Mira looked directly at Ted, and Amy saw the purple band widen and contract at her word. Amy doubted Mira consciously knew her compulsion was an exercise of magick. Ted gasped again, and Amy was embarrassed to see the obvious sign of his growing lust in his straining pants.

"Arabia won't let a bound mage cross its borders. The djinni tear apart anyone subject to a geas — whether by apprentice indenture or enclave pledge. It doesn't matter. Not even a siren bound by Morgan le Fay's blood geas could pass. Once you were unbound, they needed *us* unbound.

"The geas trigger is why I thought this whole Project Hathor trip to Arabia was either a pretext for something else, or a long-shot attempt to get the Dictator to remove the barricade. Amy couldn't pass unless he did. But then the siren geas cracked. Perhaps that was the sign the elders were waiting for.

"Tyrone had Jonah pull the files on who did my binding. That Jonah had also been bound by Rachael was merely an added bonus." Ted sighed and leaned back on the couch, closing his eyes. While Amy might have been embarrassed for him, Ted didn't seem to care.

"You didn't see them! They're monsters." Jonah took his pipe back from Mira and inhaled deeply, speaking as he exhaled the scented vapor. "You know, maybe Arabia will be safer than home."

"Stop acting the fool, Tutor," Ted said, without opening his eyes.

"Amy isn't going to Arabia," Mira snapped.

"If Simon is willing to kill his own wife, what chance do we have, Ted?" Jonah asked.

Ted sat up. "We are *free*, Jonah, so for God's sake, stop whining. I've never felt this light before. And *I* don't feel guilty. Enjoy the moment and stop your harping. You're ruining this glorious relief with all your fretting over someone else's actions, especially those that freed you from that weight."

Ted looked at Mira, and the room felt even hotter. "Would that enclave bindings were as sweet as yours, siren. No one would ever seek to be unbound. You lash me tightly, so wet and hot, I only want more. The enclave bindings … I never really understood how heavy or abrasive a weight this pledge was until it was lifted."

Mira stared back at Ted, as if transfixed.

"You said Rachael went to Brazil?" Devin asked in a cool voice. It seemed like Devin was the only one of them able to think clearly.

Jonah looked at Mira. "I probably should have called you. There had been a breaking. But I didn't know there was a second prophesy until just before Rachael was killed. I swear!"

"A second prophesy? The one the Oracle gave the Cabal?" Mira asked sharply.

"Rachael was a binder. They sent her to Rio to retrieve the Breaker: the first mage to break a spell since the First Mage War. Tyrone felt the breaking of her indenture, and they triangulated her location. But

Rachael failed to track her down and now they think she is with the Cabal. So Rachael failed. If we fail—"

"Fail in what?" Ted interrupted Jonah. "I wonder what fortunes they read to allow us to leave. Why would they feel so certain of *my* loyalty? I don't care what the enclave wants. I'm free now."

"Tell the truth," Mira commanded, her voice churning the room like the ocean tide flipping a rocky shore.

"I am my own man. Beholden to none, but you." Ted's voice was compelling in its own way.

"But Ted, Giselle—" Jonah began.

"But Giselle what?" Ted mocked mercilessly. "You told me you pulled her file out from the geas pack before you gave it to Tyrone. So they may never see that she's unbound — at least for a while. You called her and told her to get out of town; to take a vacation. They have nothing on you."

"They're a lot more ruthless than I am. Than I could ever be," Jonah admitted.

"Of *course* the elders are ruthless. You've worked for Elder Tyrone for more than fifty years; you've been filing away all the evidence of their ruthlessness every day for half a century. What, they didn't do it in front of you? You didn't *know*?" Ted scoffed loudly, but there was a fragility in his bluster that came through. "Now you have a choice. For the first time since you were three years old, you actually have a choice about what you want to do for yourself." Amy wasn't sure whether Ted was talking to himself or to Jonah.

"I'm not ready for this," Jonah whispered.

"Why did you pull Giselle's file?" Mira asked. The coils of compulsion that laced around Jonah and Ted had faded, but Amy could see them still, lightly trailing in a glittering line from the mages to Mira. A faint sheen of sweat shone on her mother's forehead and Amy wondered if maintaining compulsions was a difficult form of magick.

"I don't know," Jonah lied, gasping as the Mira's compulsion flared.

"Maybe you anticipated this outcome," Ted suggested. "When was the last time Tyrone had you pull files on a binder's bindings? After Alodeous died? You knew. Or suspected."

Ted's accusation swallowed the room. No one said anything for a few beats. Amy wondered what Jonah could have possibly done to change Rachael's fate. These were Danjou *elders* and Jonah was, well, not.

"I'm glad I'm free. I'm sorry Rachael's dead. But at least I'm honest enough to admit that even if I knew it was going to happen, I wouldn't have tried to stop it. Not now that I know what it's like to be free. Being bound like that; it's criminal." Ted's voice cracked a little.

Having experienced her own exquisite release when the blood-geas lifted, Mira knew exactly what he meant. Ted looked at her. "Your compulsions don't feel anything like that, even though they're more intrusive."

Mira swiftly quashed the surge of guilt at Ted's statement. She had years of experience stifling her qualms around compulsions. She used them, even while fearing that doing so might be a mortal sin. It was thin comfort that the Catechism made no mention of compulsions, since the church didn't seem to be aware that sirens existed. But Ted was so *aware* of her. Aware in a way that made Mira's skin contract and her stomach jump.

There was something compelling about him. For the first time since Jack died, Mira felt something around him. She struggled to maintain focus: her daughter was in danger. The Danjou mages were untrustworthy at best. She needed to strategize how best to keep Amy safe, but now all she could think about was how she wanted to feel Ted's voice stroke her skin again. She suddenly realized that she was very wet.

"What bothers me is that they think they have my absolute loyalty, even unbound. What do they know that I don't?" Ted paused in contemplation before standing up and looking away. "You know what? I don't care. I'm *free*." Ted gestured to Jonah. "And I'm glad that you're free, and that Giselle is and whoever else Rachael bound is, too. We can do anything. Go anywhere. You want to escape Elder Simon's reach? Go to Arabia, then. Or Australia — beg the Cabal for asylum. Or run and hide; he won't bother to search for you in Patagonia, though that drained desert won't have enough silica-salt to refine for your pipe."

Ted's voice dropped; he was scorching in his scorn. "But whatever you do, stop your whining. Enough worrying! You're free for the first time in your life, and none of us cares what you choose to do with that freedom."

No one spoke for a moment until Devin broke the silence. "Why was Ted confined, Jonah? What mistake did he make?"

Ted startled at the sound of Devin's voice, and his eyes narrowed. While Ted might have forgotten he was there, Amy hadn't. She found his silent intensity and calm focus reassuring.

"Answer," Mira said calmly, though the leads around Jonah pulsed in a purple flare, and he panted slightly. Despite Mira's compulsion, Jonah struggled to speak civilly.

"He failed to secure the pivot."

"Elder Simon forced me back to Hesperia under house arrest for *months*. The failure was his!" Ted hissed.

Amy looked at Ted, her eyes narrowing. "So the whole reason you were here for the past year was to get me to undergo the surgery, Ted? What did you do? Did you *influence* me?"

"Answer her!" Mira glared at Ted, her voice cracking like a whip. Amy could see violet lines from the leash connecting Ted to Mira explode and wrap around his torso in a gleaming corset.

"Ah, siren," Ted whispered hoarsely. "Your binding is so sweet."

Amy was almost embarrassed to see the way Ted stared at Mira. He was transfixed; Jonah didn't seem anywhere near as affected as Ted by her mother's spell, and even her mother seemed nonplussed by the intensity of Ted's reaction.

"I didn't use magick on you, Amy," Ted replied and gasped. The purple flared tightly around his waist. "No magick, but I did try to persuade you. To show you there was a way."

"You insisted Amy get scanned," Mira accused, glaring at Ted.

"Yes. I couldn't be sure, of course, that she would have a sub-optic nerve, but given her heritage, I knew it was a possibility." Ted's eyes smoldered as he looked at Mira.

"Lighten up, Mira. You're holding him too hard," Devin called out. Mira's face reddened, and she broke eye contact. Amy could see the pulse leaping in her throat as she turned away. Who was doing the seducing here? It was more than a little disconcerting to be in the same room with her mother while she worked her magick. Amy focused instead on Devin. His cold stillness centered her on the issue at hand.

"The MRIs, the poetry, the enchanted glasses? Really, Ted? How can you say you never influenced me?" Amy asked.

"I didn't make you have the surgery, Amy. I wasn't even in town when you decided to do it. You can't blame me for that. Blame the Oracle. I didn't even really try to seduce you. I'm not a whore." Ted replied with a hint of his former arrogance.

"Why do the Danjou want Amy to go to Arabia?" Devin asked, his clear focus a balm for everyone in the room.

"They don't—" Ted began, but Jonah interrupted with a weary fatalism.

"The elders wanted Amy's sight restored so she would willingly bind herself to the Danjou. After the press conference, the Djinn Dictator personally requested Dr. Bant's attendance. Which is maybe the real reason we were unbound," Jonah said, inhaling deeply on his pipe. "In case Dr. Bant decides to go."

"Well, she isn't going," Mira declared. The water in the harbor coursed high, and Amy decided not to argue the point. Her mother was right anyway. The Danjou had broken their side of the bargain with their deception.

Mira was no truth-teller, but she knew Ted wasn't telling the full truth about his manipulation of Amy. She looked into his navy-blue eyes that shone with compelled passion. "And you? If you're such a failure, why would the enclave send you back?"

"I'm not a failure, siren," Ted said without a hint of his past arrogance. His voice caressed her, and Mira shivered in response. "I'm a Class Five via-enchanter who's developed more counter-spells than even the elders know. I worked with your daughter in good faith, as best as I was able. Amy left dozens of voicemails which the elders would not let me answer, but which proved I had not completely alienated the pivot, despite our many arguments.

"Most likely they've let me return because the Danjou prognosticators have seen a greater chance for success if I'm here than if I'm not. Whether that's because a counter-spell will be needed, or because they think I can woo her for them, I don't know."

Ted's full attention centered on Mira, as if none of the rest of them were present. Amy felt like an intruder in her own home, and she was grateful when Devin broke in with his calm observation.

"If the Danjou wanted Amy dead, they would have sent battle mages or even mundane assassins. I've worried about this possibility since Atlantea sent me here. Your daughter is the pivot, the axis on which the world will turn. But instead of combat mages, they've sent these two. And unbound at that."

Mira looked at Devin, and he nodded. If he thought he could handle the mages, that was sufficient. Amy needed help, and going to Arabia was out of the question.

In any event, it was perhaps better to know where the Danjou agents were, than to worry who the elders might send if Amy refused the assistance of these two.

"The enclave wants Amy casting spells on the side of the Danjou," Ted finished, as if Devin hadn't spoken.

"I'm not on anybody's side," Amy insisted.

"Why would you support the Danjou after all they've done to you? I'm doomed. Would that I were re-bound and safe home in the enclave than free and at the fulcrum of this war!" Jonah covered his face in his hands.

"Shut up," Ted snapped, wrenching Jonah's hands down with a shake. "Enough of your drama. No one is *doomed*. If the pivot turns, we'll turn with her. You're not bound to the Danjou! If she chooses the Dictator, you can become *his* man and hide behind his djinni. No one is safe. Rachael wasn't safe. But you're not going to die today. So get a hold of yourself for once and shut the fuck up!"

After a moment, Mira looked at her former spy with compassion. "Jonah, I promised you sanctuary once, and I remain true to my promise," she said in a soft voice before narrowing her eyes to take Ted's measure. Despite his harsh words to Jonah, there was a brittle fragility about him that called to her.

Mira spoke formally as she offered him a bargain: "And you, via-enchanter. To you I'll give that same pledge. Renounce the Danjou. Help Amy gain control over her magick and you can join my house. In Brazil, the were-jaguars defend my household, and the fae extend their mantle over me and mine."

Morgan le Fay was part mage, part fae. Scholars believe that her mixed heritage is one reason why her binding was so spectacularly effective on the sirens, who are also a mixed breed of fae and mage. In addition to causing confoundment, Morgan le Fay's spell diverts a portion of the sirens' intrinsic magical power into linkages that fuel the geas. Some speculate that modern sirens are generally less powerful than those of prior generations due to her last spell.

– Sirens: An Overview for the Newly-Transitioned, 3rd ed. (2015), *by Mira Bant de Atlantic, p. 36.*

Chapter 37

After days of preparation, they were finally ready to leave the island. The fae assembled on the shore, as a pale orange glow burgeoned on the horizon. Cordelia knelt down in the surf, as she had every day since she had vowed to bring the Aos Sí out.

No one had ever asked so much of the sea before. The ocean loved her, but did it love her enough? Could it truly understand what she needed? What they all needed? The water swept around her, encapsulating her in a translucent veil before bursting into a trillion droplets that caught the dawn light in what she hoped was a promise. The cresting waves in the distance reflected the sun in a reddish-orange warmth that Cordelia could feel baking into her very soul. That glimmer of light on the ocean was pure love, and Cordelia knew it was time. She strode quickly from the water to find Titania.

The remnants of Morgan le Fay's army were a mixed group: from the aristocratic seelie to tiny will o' the wisps, whose firefly-like incandescence could erupt in flame at the least provocation. The vila, who called the winds and walked on currents of air turned solid as the ground itself, pulled themselves out of the treetops to wait on the rocky shore. The wood wives and dryads tried to stay off the beach and remain in the heather, but were pushed forward by the jostling of the fae behind them. Surprisingly, Cordelia saw moss folk and bolotniks waiting next to each other; given the enmity of the forest folk with the swamp dwellers, she counted this as a victory for peace.

Finally, Cordelia spotted Titania among the mass of red-booted Aos Sí, many of whom carried others on their backs.

"Are we ready?" Cordelia asked. Dawn was an auspicious time to set off, and she needed to get started before she became too terrified to try. Even with the baked heat of the morning sun on the waves still stored in her heart, and even with the hope of seven-league boots to speed their way, Cordelia feared she wouldn't be able to hold the sea for the length of time it would take to walk to Africa. Perhaps Titania heard the doubt in Cordelia's voice, because her response was certain.

"We are ready, siren. No matter what comes next, we are all prepared. Not a faerie has chosen to stay, despite the risk. None of us has chosen to endure a moment longer of torture in this iron-soaked land. Even the dryads have left their trees, mourning their loss, while praying for their own salvation." Titania's voice was firm and carried over the assembled masses.

Cordelia admired Titania's sense of drama, while continuing to worry. A moment ago, she had felt so certain. Now, she felt the weight of all the lives depending on her to take them safely beneath the sea. "You've tested all the boots?" she asked. She'd asked this question before, but needed to hear the response again.

"Yes. There were a few whose magick had failed, which we discarded. We can all keep up." If Titania was impatient with the question that had been asked and answered before, she showed no sign.

"The rain forests are sparsely populated, and the people of the Congo have already been devastated by numerous wars," Cordelia cautioned.

"We will remember our promises to abide in peace." Titania raised an eyebrow mischievously. "But we will see if the humans there want to play."

Cordelia wondered if it was fatalism that had Titania so unworried about this journey, because it was clear that the Aos Sí had truly reached their limit. She remembered the vila's spell from more than thirty years ago: that feeling of not caring was the scariest thing she had ever experienced. Perhaps for Titania, even the slightest breath of hope was better than that emptiness, even if they ultimately failed to escape. But Cordelia couldn't drown in the sea, so even if the Aos Sí perished, she would remain. She couldn't bear the thought of that kind of failure, so began to drown in worry.

She worried about holding the sea around them while they marched. She worried about keeping an air flow so deep to the ocean floor. She worried about their journey, and she worried about what would happen after they arrived. She worried about worrying too much. Cordelia had to mentally jerk herself out of the whirlpool of useless worry before she got trapped again. She went back to her mental checklist of preparations, but had a hard time remaining on task.

Cordelia wished again that she'd had the time to speak with some of the Congolese in preparation, but of course she didn't speak French. Thinking about French reminded her of Thomas, and she wondered for a moment if she should see if she couldn't pry him away from his hideout in Brazil to come help her integrate the fae if they arrived. At the very least, he could mail her some books of fairy tales in French to distribute among the people living near the rainforests.

"The illusions are set? I can't see them," Cordelia said. Fae illusions often did not work on sirens, so Cordelia couldn't be sure the fae had properly disguised their presence from human observers.

"We're ready," Titania said simply. She looked closely at Cordelia's pale face and added: "We know the risk. Do your best. That's all we ask."

Cordelia nodded. "I'll have to lead, so you should probably be last off the island. Seven abreast, as we discussed." Titania nodded and strode off to the back of the gathering. Cordelia looked at the seelie, the strongest of the Aos Sí. "Perhaps you could scatter among the crowd? Everyone needs to stick together and pace themselves."

She walked to the front of the massed fae, where the ocean lapped invitingly at the shore. Cordelia supposed she ought to say something. Make some grand statement or speech. But she didn't know what to say. So she simply turned and looked at the sea and said a Hail Mary. Then she watched the sun on the horizon glowing ever-brighter and murmured, "'The Lord is my light and my salvation; whom shall I fear? The Lord is the stronghold of my life; of whom shall I be afraid?'"

Whispering her prayers, Cordelia knelt into the water, which lapped joyfully around her. A wave reached out and embraced her, stroking her face with its misty spray. Kneeling in the ocean's love and feeling the sunlight filtering through, Cordelia thought she felt a blessing, a blessing on this endeavor of restitution, and she cast her doubts aside.

Standing up, the ocean parted around her, hovering above like a tunnel. She had never understood how the Atlantic knew what she needed, but counted it as a kind of miracle. A miracle that the Aos Sí needed today.

Cordelia beckoned to the first group, who strode into the tunnel with less trepidation than she would have felt in their place. She backed into the parted sea, and as the first group descended into the tunnel, Cordelia felt the ocean tug her backwards. Cordelia relinquished herself into the Atlantic's care, and watched as the fae mob began its swift march to the bottom of the sea.

"I prefer to cast in the open," Kyoko said, demurring Professor Wanda's invitation to use her lab. They had spent the morning touring the university with the professor, and Kyoko was tired of the woman's fawning over Thomas. Fortunately, Bo-Long was with them, and Thomas was able to side-step her attention by ensuring Bo-Long remained in her view instead of him.

Professor Wanda was an older woman with short gray hair and a sturdy figure, wearing comfortable clothes and sensible shoes. She exuded competence. She'd clearly not reached menopause, though, because the impact the two sirens had on her was obvious. "For all that she's an expert, she doesn't seem smart enough to recognize she's under a spell," Kyoko whispered nastily to Thomas as they followed Bo-Long and Professor Wanda towards one of the open casting centers. He loved her jealousy, and squeezed her hand with a smile.

Thomas was glad Kyoko had agreed with his suggestion that she attempt to break the geas on Bo-Long while the Australian expert observed. Given how shy Kyoko could be, he had worried that she wouldn't want an audience.

Unlike the professor, Kyoko still seemed far less interested in Bo-Long. Bo-Long could compel her interest, Thomas supposed, but he was too smart to do something that would arouse Thomas' immediate wrath. While Kyoko's love for him might be grounded in his nature as a siren, she must feel something special for him to not be flitting from one of them to the other, as a flower follows the sun (quite unlike the professor, who fixated on whichever one of the two male sirens caught her eye).

Thomas noted the vape-pipe Kyoko was inhaling with displeasure. George had presented it to her at the conclusion of their state dinner, along with a box of what he claimed was the most refined, highest-quality ambrosia available in Australia. Juliana had whispered that if it was the highest quality, then it didn't come from the Great Sandy Desert.

Eloise had picked up on the mild dig without more than a raised eyebrow. "Of course it is from the Arabian Desert, Julianna. Everyone knows the best ambrosia is from Arabia." Thomas didn't know enough about mages or ambrosia to know whether it was addictive or not. But it was common knowledge that ambrosia amplified the power of a mage.

"Do you think Aphrodite could have constructed you sirens without ambrosia?" George had mocked when Thomas raised an objection. Thomas hated being mocked. But Kyoko had told him not to worry; one use wouldn't be enough to make her an addict — if indeed vaping were addictive. And she also seemed intrigued by the possibility it would enhance her casting strength, so Thomas let his objections go.

The outdoor casting field reminded Thomas of a small stadium. It was an oval sand-covered expanse, perhaps three hundred feet long by one hundred wide, surrounded by tall white-washed concrete walls. He wondered what the walls would look like to mages, and supposed a little wistfully that it must be much more beautiful than the barren barricade he saw. He could have sat on one of the sets of bleachers that were scattered around the field for spectators, but Thomas had no interest in being that far away from Kyoko.

Kyoko sat down, and gestured for Bo-Long to lie on the sand in front of her. Not quite in the middle of the field, but far enough away from the walls that there was no risk of shadow, even if Kyoko's casting took several hours. It was early afternoon, so the sun was just past its zenith in the sky. The thin layer of white clouds wasn't enough to shade them from its intensity, and the white walls and sand floor seemed to magnify its strength. Kyoko had pronounced the day perfect for spelling, and Thomas could see she was genuinely happy with the location.

Professor Wanda sat a bit further away from their small group. Thomas stood behind Kyoko, and she leaned her back against his legs for support. The last time she had done this spell, the experience had been too intense for him to observe, so he was curious how it would be to watch Kyoko do what she loved best. She looked lovely, as always, and Thomas felt a twinge of jealousy as Bo-Long scooted up to place his head in her lap, her hands resting gently on his shoulders.

Kyoko inhaled her pipe once more, then handed it back to Thomas. Bo-Long's eyes were closed and Thomas didn't need to see Professor Wanda's reaction to know Kyoko had begun to cast. He might not see what the mages saw, but he smelled the sea; he felt the water coalesce out of the dry air around them.

People think that the ocean doesn't have a sound of its own, without the wind and moon to pull waves out to crash on the shore, but Thomas knew it had its own music. The small, brassy sound of bells, overlaid with the soft whisper of a flute and linked together by the sweetness of the strings. The ocean was an orchestra, and it was playing to Kyoko's conducting.

The music tickled the back of his memory, and as Thomas kept trying to recall where he had heard the song before, time passed almost without him noticing. Watching a mage cast was incredibly boring for mundanes, who couldn't see or understand what was going on. For mages, of course, it was almost like watching a sporting event; so it was no accident that the outdoor casting grounds resembled a small stadium.

Perhaps Thomas had gotten lost in the music, because it ended with an abrupt crack — not quite a cymbal ringing or a discordant note, but more like the snapping of a string. The music stopped, and somehow the sky seemed brighter, if that were possible. Bo-Long hadn't opened his eyes, but Kyoko had collapsed against Thomas' legs, her arms slack. Thomas heard the sound of the ocean swell again, and looked up just in time to see a wave of water cresting over the wall, reaching for them.

Thomas gasped.

He extended his hand, but the ocean had never loved him as much as it did his sister, and he worried that he wouldn't be enough. Professor Wanda gaped open-mouthed as the water started to crash down on top of them. But at the last minute, the sea condensed into a rope of water to reach down and envelop Bo-Long. Thomas wanted to pull Kyoko away, but instead knelt down to embrace her, to make sure the Pacific didn't take her with Bo-Long, if that was what it was going to do.

But the ocean didn't sweep Bo-Long away; it held him for a moment, then flicked around Thomas' arms in a cool, wet blanket that inexplicably soothed his anxiety, before retreating back the way it had come. Wanda hadn't moved, except to close her mouth. Thomas wasn't sure whether she was overwhelmed by the experience of having a near-tsunami envelop her, or by the power of Kyoko's magick, but he was grateful for her silence.

And Thomas didn't know whether it was the ambrosia, the casting field or perhaps a combination of both that accounted for the stronger backlash. Regardless, Thomas was sure that this breaking had been even more comprehensive and complete than the one that had freed him.

Cordelia and the fae sped swiftly along the ocean floor, much faster than Cordelia remembered traversing the sea in the past. The fae marched seven abreast, traveling seven leagues with each step. They had estimated it would take around one hundred and forty-nine steps to reach Mangroves National Park.

After only about fifty steps, the ocean suddenly rocked around them with a tremendous force. Cordelia held their tunnel, begging the Atlantic to continue to protect them in their path. The tsunami-like force rocketed past them, and Cordelia wondered what could have triggered the sudden storm. Then the currents steadied and they continued their shockingly rapid pace towards Africa.

Finally, Cordelia slowed as she entered the mouth of the Congo River. The water raised her up onto land, and she felt a little light-headed at the change from motion to stillness. She tried to steady herself as she watched the fae emerge from behind her, fanning onto the sandy shore until at last Titania stood in front of her.

They had arrived, and the fae seemed to have felt no ill-effects from their swift and silent journey. A group of bolotniks writhed up the river bank on their backs before catapulting themselves into the waxy treetops above. The wind started to whistle as the vila stepped from the water onto the solid air in a prancing gait. One stumbled as a will o' the wisp lit a blue flame below her foot, and a red-booted seelie laughed at the sight.

There was a sense of joy in the air that had been missing when they last stood on the Yorkshire coast, and Cordelia smiled as she watched the fae disperse into the mangrove forest. Titania waited until the last faerie had disappeared from view, then focused on Cordelia.

"Gratitude is a human emotion. One of the differences between our species," Titania began. "But arriving here, feeling the clean earth beneath my feet … I perhaps begin to understand it."

Cordelia thought that was as close to a thank you as any faerie could give. She looked up the river, where the thick forest ran down to its wide banks in a lush, green, near-impenetrable mass. She felt suddenly adrift and uncertain, as the adrenaline rush that had spiked during the trip faded and a mild throbbing set in the base of her spine. The trip from England to the Congo had been amazingly quick; less than an hour had passed from when they had first stepped off the shore.

"Did you feel the disturbance in the ocean early on during the trip? Was that something you did?" Cordelia asked.

"You protected us admirably. We felt your touch sheltering us from the release," Titania said.

"The release?" Cordelia repeated.

"We didn't do it; couldn't have done it if we had wanted to. I can't be certain of what it was. I know that we didn't cause it."

"But you called it a release," Cordelia insisted.

"I don't want to misspeak," Titania said impatiently. "It *felt* like a release, but maybe I'm just projecting onto the sea my immense relief at being free of that poison. I don't know."

"It *did* feel like a release," Cordelia mused. "Like the ocean was feeling what I felt a few days ago when the geas was broken. Perhaps freeing you from England lifted Morgan le Fay's spell more widely?"

"I don't know," Titania replied, looking at Cordelia with a glow in her purple eyes. "But even were that the case, you have given more than you have received. We did not bargain a price for our deliverance."

"I didn't ask for anything," Cordelia replied, somewhat alarmed.

"Those are the best bargains one can make," Titania said with a faint smile, "and sometimes the worst." She reached out her hand into the air between them as if pulling open a door, though nothing was there. Nonetheless, she plucked a cylinder from the nothingness and looked at it. "After the war was lost, many thought I ought to have simply given it to those who'd demanded it. Claimed it as their right."

The cup looked as if it had been made out of wood, with the grain running in rings around its circumference as if a stump had been somehow turned inside out. But as the light caught it, Cordelia could see that it was made of metal: gold, silver and copper. *Mokume-gane*. This was Morgan le Fay's chalice: the cup that had driven the Aos Sí from the Taiga fifteen hundred years before. As the light hit it, the hint of a rolling E-flat trill sounded in the distance, like a far-away orchestra imitating the river's swaying currents.

"Take this — not as payment for services rendered, for the gifting of our freedom is a debt that can never fully be repaid. Take it instead so that the Aos Sí might truly have a fresh start. Let us keep this new land clean of the memories of that cup."

Titania reached out with her other hand and pulled Cordelia's rubber bag from the air; Cordelia knew she had left it on the Yorkshire shore in her sudden need to feel unencumbered on this journey. Titania opened the flaps, placing the chalice inside, then secured it and extended it to Cordelia.

"Titania, I'm not sure—" Cordelia didn't reach out to take it, but wasn't entirely sure how to decline.

"Keep it, use it, melt it down, or bargain it away. I care not anymore." Titania smiled a full smile, then moved closer to Cordelia, slinging the rubber bag over her head and shoulder as if dressing her for battle. She kissed Cordelia on each cheek, then took her hands and squeezed them gently. "You will always be welcome here. I pledge you and yours safety and succor for so long as we hold the land."

Titania's formality was a dismissal, and Cordelia found that she was relieved to be dismissed. She inclined her head in acknowledgment, then squeezed Titania's hands and dropped them, turning to walk slowly back into the sea.

Let the fae have their forests, she thought, longing for the comfort of the water. She couldn't bring herself to care what would happen next; she felt completely drained. Let the Atlantic take her where it wanted her to go, she just didn't care. Whatever would be, would be. But she had done the right thing. As the Atlantic swept around her, pulling her into its depths, she looked back to glimpse Titania slipping into the mangroves after her people, a brilliant rainbow trailing down to the river in her wake.

Cordelia was content.

So ends Book One of the Fifth Mage War.